INTO THE PATH OF GODS

INTO THE PATH OF GODS

KATHLEEN CUNNINGHAM GULER

BARDSONG PRESS
STEAMBOAT SPRINGS, COLORADO

Copyright 1998 by Kathleen Cunningham Guler

All rights reserved. No part of this book may be reproduced or utilized in any form or by any means, electronic or mechanical, including photocopying, recording or by any information storage and retrieval system, without permission in writing from the publisher. Inquiries should be addressed to Permissions Department, Bardsong Press, P.O. Box 775396, Steamboat Springs, CO 80477.

ISBN: 0-9660371-0-3

Library of Congress Catalog Number: 97-94387

Printed in the United States of America

First Edition

DEDICATION

*To the ancestors that haunt my memories
You are with me, and I with you,
for all time.*

Guide to Welsh Names and Words

Afon Dyfrdwy (River Dee):   AH-von Duh-ver-DOO-ee
Caernarfon: Car-NAR-von
Ceredig: Ker-EH-dig
Cunedda: Cuh-NEH-tha
Cynnwyd: Cuh-NOO-ihd
Dinas Beris: DEE-nas BER-is
Dinas Brenin: DEE-nas BRAY-nin
Eryri: Eh-RUR-ee
Gerallt: GHER-alht
Gwynedd: GWIN-eth
Hafod (summer dwelling): HAH-vod
Ifan: EE-van
Iorwerth: YOR-werth
Lleu Llaw Gyffes: Hlew Hlau GUFF-ess
Myrddin: MUR-then
Saeson (Saxon): SI-son
Wledig (chief landholder): Oo-LED-ig
Y Gwalch Haearn: Uh Gwalk Hahern
Ynys Môn: UH-nus Moan
Ynys Witrin: UH-nus WIT-rin

Notes:

These pronunciations are approximations. Some of the following are some of the most noteworthy differences between Welsh and English.

The Welsh DD is like English TH, as in *them*; W is either a consonant or a vowel, as a vowel is has as an *oo* sound; CH is hard as in the Scottish *loch*; LL is not found in English but can be approximated as a very rough combination of HL.

The word *ap* means "son of" in Welsh names; Marcus ap Iorwerth means Marcus, son of Iorwerth.

Celtic is correctly pronounced with a hard C, *Keltic*.

MACSEN'S TREASURE

Torque of gold, born of earth
Turned by strong and calloused hands
Heavy grace on necks of kings
Returned by blood, torque of earth.

Spear of wind, born of air
Chased with lines of twining life
Swallow-swift in soaring flight
Removed by stealth, spear of air.

Sword of light, born of fire
Forged with strength of ancient magic
Cries both with life and with death
Cast to stone, sword of fire.

Grail of life, born of water
Deep and wide to hold the source
Empty but for time and memory
Forever lost, grail of water.

Crown of kings, born of gods
Bind torque and spear, sword and grail
So walk in honor, before the shadow
And journey into the path of gods.

—Myrddin Emrys

CHAPTER 1

**Territory of the Welsh Cynnwyd,
Summer, 459 A.D.**

The dream was ending.

The words of the old song scattered away, sorrowful upon the wind, ancient as the story they had just told. The man's voice had carried them sure and strong, his young daughter's harmony intertwining with his, ethereal as water gliding over pebbles. The music had carried their imaginations away with the skill of the storyteller who had composed it, soothing endless hours of working with their hands and backs and strong wills. Now their minds reluctantly eased back into the present.

The dream was just ending. Like a lifetime that had run its course, a soul passing through its next turning point and the only thing left behind was the sadness hanging thickly in the air...

The girl reacted instinctively, coming abruptly alert, jerking aside as the arrow spit past her ear. She whirled to see it thump into the earth a short distance behind her. Frozen in astonishment, she heard her father scream the alarm and scrape his sword from its scabbard.

Attackers rushed out of the trees lining the river, the Afon

Dyfrdwy, full-lunged yells in their throats, weapons in their hands. They crashed out of their hiding places, racing up from the riverbank, screaming in a strange language. Unprepared, the clansmen of Cynnwyd rallied, but they were already too late to reach the weapons that would have saved them. The invaders gored and hacked them down without mercy or conscience.

The girl was stunned, never having seen warriors so close. "Get back, get down, down! Hide yourself!" her father yelled. He swept his arm back, knocking her hard. Not expecting his sudden roughness, she lost her balance and fell, rolling down a marshy embankment to land in a small streambed. But she quickly regained her senses; and, lifting her head, she peered through the reeds and marsh grass at enormous warriors strewing carnage across the turf of her home. Though only twelve summers of age, she felt her blood begin to surge with the same rage of her clansmen, a rage and fear every generation of her people, for time out of mind, had felt as they watched their own die.

The girl scrambled out of the streambed, her fists balled, ready to pummel the nearest of the strangers. Tawny-brown hair streaming behind her, she sailed across the grass, heading straight for her father as he slashed desperately at a huge man with a heavier sword and thick, metal-studded leather armor.

Before she reached him, the eyes of another invader followed her and grinned, amused by the delicate wraith with the face full of wrath. The soldier sheathed his sword and raced into the girl's path. He halted, expecting her to pull up in terror, but she rammed into him instead, the full force of her stride knocking him two paces backward. Regaining his balance, he scooped her up in his arms, laughing at her attempts to claw and kick him. What a prize, he thought, chuckling, and carried her towards the woods.

"No, lass! No!"

The shout came from the girl's uncle. Big and burly, he had just freed the soul from a fourth invader, and now he saw his young niece in the arms of one of the barbarians.

"You're not going to have her, you filthy *Saeson*!" He

charged up the incline, a dagger in his hand. With sheer brute force, the girl's uncle drove the dagger into the soldier's back, thudding to its hilt between the man's shoulder blades. The man dropped the girl, bellowing with rage.

Turning, the man suddenly had his own dagger. Blood was already dribbling out of the corner of his mouth, but the sneer on his face showed his revenge would not be deterred by his failing life. His free hand drew aside, then whipped out, striking the girl, pounding her back against a tree. She slid down, stunned, but remained alert enough to witness how his dagger struck home in her uncle's belly, twisting, the sound of tearing flesh sickening her.

Too horrified to scream, she watched them fall, at first into each other's arms, almost like lovers, then slip past one another into a heap. Mercifully, she fainted.

When she opened her eyes again, voices muttered somewhere in the dark distance. Other than the strange tongue of the invaders, only an owl's occasional hooting broke the night's silence. Remaining absolutely still, the girl waited, watching, listening. Gradually, the voices drew closer. She deduced that orders were being given, reports made, the leaders directing the search for survivors, the ransacking of the buildings.

Two men spoke in Welsh. One voice was heavily accented, a cold, irritating voice that crept like slug slime across a stone. It became clear that he was the foremost leader and the other man a betrayer. They discussed their purpose for several minutes, their words often in vehement anger. Then when every house and barn, rock and reed had been examined, the ugly voice gave the order to burn everything. Absolutely everything.

As the fires grew and consumed the buildings of her home, the girl crawled further into the woods. She watched with widening eyes as the depth of the loss became visible. In clumps and by individual, her people had fallen. As the men had died, their women had fought on, then fell alongside their men. She saw her father, uncle, an older brother, a younger sister, every member of the clan. They had all fought valiantly, with makeshift weapons and their bare hands, trying to deter the brutality. Now the soldiers heaved their mutilated bodies into the flames. In a few hours, only their charred bones and ashes would remain to show for the lives they had sacrificed. To blow away with the wind.

After the last body had been given to the fire, the soldiers gathered and milled for several more minutes. As suddenly as they came, now they departed.

The owl flew across the river, seeking prey elsewhere, his wings beating softly, steadily in the cold night air. Silence descended on the land again, the fires slowly subsiding, the acrid smell of burnt wood and flesh stifling the air. A slow chill seeped into the girl's bones, crawling relentlessly into her soul, giving fear that utterly claimed her mind.

More voices came with the morning. A grey-haired woman called the names of the dead. A girl of nine summers' age wept.

The girl in the woods lifted her eyes, but she did not see her mother's face. Instead, she expected the voice to belong to a soul of one of the dead, the figure of a ghost moving among the smoldering ashes. So many would be passing to the Otherworld. At least they could all go together.

Then the younger girl saw her. Weeping turned to a sudden shriek of joy.

"Cousin! You're alive! You're alive! Aunt Linor! Come!"

Linor rushed to find her daughter stumbling out of the woods. Halting, Linor watched her walk past, towards the ruins, her expression blank with shock and the words of one of the ancient songs on her lips.

"Claerwen?" Linor called softly, unsure what to do. She reached out and clamped a hand on the girl's shoulder. Claerwen stopped, but did not otherwise react. She continued to mouth the words of the song.

"By the gods, Grania, she is the only one left," Linor mumbled to her niece, her skin crawling as she smelled the fear in her daughter's soul. To Claerwen, she said, "We came as soon as we heard, daughter, we came—"

Claerwen remained unresponsive, still watching the smoldering ashes as she mumbled. Grania tugged at her aunt's sleeve. "What do we do now?" she asked.

Linor was silent several minutes, her brows knotted together in frustration and grief. She had no understanding of how to help Claerwen. Finally, she coaxed, "Come, daughter, there is nothing we can do for them now. We must go, in case the soldiers should come back."

Instinctively, Grania came forward. She saw words would not help Claerwen. She gently folded her arms around her cousin and drew her into a hug.

Gradually, Claerwen lifted her face. Her eyes shone with iridescence, tears soaking her long lashes. Her expression frightened Linor, her face utterly drained of color, pale with shock and horror, her mouth and eyes moving too slowly.

"Where will we go?" Grania asked, sniffling, starting to cry again as she clung to Claerwen.

Linor choked back her own tears and stared at the ruins of her home. Swallowing hard, she answered, "We must go north, to the people of Cynnwyd in Strathclyde who migrated from here many generations ago. We will go to Dun Breatann and my kinsman, Lord Ceredig."

"The king of Strathclyde?"

"Aye, he will help us." Linor explained, "Though his people and ours are now only distantly related, we are still of the same tribe."

She gazed again into the terror-dazed face of her daughter and repeated her hope, "By the gods, he must help us."

CHAPTER 2

**Dun Breatann, Kingdom of Strathclyde
Autumn, 463 A.D.**

Smoke curled up from the great hall's central fire pit to its blackened beams, adding more soot and smoke scent to them and the thatch they supported. A slave poked at the smoldering fire, raising new flames amid sparks and ashes, then added more dried peat. The fire perked cheerfully against the chilly autumn air. The slave gazed up at the smoke hole, wishing the wind would draw the smoke better, then shrugged. He knew that soon the hall would be filled with noise and drunken men, laughing and squealing women. No one would care about the smoke in the rafters, or what he thought about all those people.

Voices drifted in from the yard outside. The chieftains, the slave thought, cynicism on his face. He had heard it was to be a small gathering of local lords mostly; a meeting to betroth one of them to a lady from a nearby homestead. The daughter of one of the high chieftain's distant kinswomen. Poor lady, he mused. He shuffled off to the rear door of the hall, headed for the cook house.

Dun Breatann, perched on a double-humped rock on the River Clyde's shore, was the capital of the northern British kingdom of Strathclyde. That autumn was strikingly beautiful, the scrub oak, larch and chestnut trees shined brilliantly in the afternoon sun. No snow had fallen yet, but the land lay quietly in wait, as if anticipating the coming winter. A slight breeze riffled across the forests and meadows, gently fluttering and swaying leaves and grasses. Though very cold, the glens glowed radiantly golden in the setting sunlight.

The slave returned to the hall, going to a rough plank table at the back wall to set an enormous clay jug of mead amongst more jugs, platters of food, and drinking horns. He puttered around softly, straightening things here and there, and watched as three women entered the hall, walking directly to the fire pit to warm themselves. They spoke tersely among themselves, eyes serious under frowning brows. It was a private debate they strove to keep private, yet it had a subtle volatility that threatened to explode very publicly, very quickly.

The oldest woman was frail and wrung her hands nervously as she drew great breaths of air, clinging to the meager strength she had left. From a distance she looked elegant, with an almost regal posture, but her face showed the harshness life had brought her.

The woman was insisting on a point to one of the others, obviously her daughter by their similar features. In spite of her stress, she spoke softly and steadily, her voice low and firm, the words clear and orderly. There would be no shaking her from her convictions.

The younger woman's anger was turning to frustration and she looked very close to giving in to tears. She did not want to cry; she wanted to make her own points as strongly as her mother had, but she was unable to control her emotion and speak rationally. She sniffed back the tears that had started to trickle and held her head stiffly, staring fiercely into the fire pit.

The young woman's lips pressed themselves into a stubborn line when she noticed the slave hovering nearby. She was determined not to be embarrassed by anyone, even if he was just a slave.

"Water, my ladies?" the man prompted, offering a

drinking horn first to the mother.

"No. Thank you," she replied tersely.

He bowed obediently, then offered water to the others.

"Aye, thank you," answered the third and youngest of them.

He bowed again, glancing at their faces. He observed that the mother was still attractive in spite of her advanced years. The one who had accepted the water was very young, perhaps only twelve or thirteen years, and had a sweet, pale face surrounded by scads of long, wavy reddish hair. The angry lady, probably two or three years older than the girl, still had her head turned away to the fire and did not answer him. No matter, he had seen before her large, astonishingly clear, pale green-blue eyes. They matched her gown and the sheer matching veil draped loosely over her flowing tawny-brown hair. He tilted his head, wanting to again see her face, but their silence let him know he was not welcome. They waited for him to retreat.

"I can't let you ruin this for yourself, Claerwen," the older woman began again as she wiped her brow with a kerchief. She perspired in spite of the cold. "Even Grania has more sense than you do! I must sit down."

Claerwen snapped out of her anger and helped her mother to a bench nearby. Grania made her drink from the water horn.

"I am sorry, Mama. I don't want to upset you. But I wish you would have let us meet Lord Drakar before you seal my betrothal to him. How can I marry a man if I don't even like him?"

"He has a reputation for being loyal and courageous among the Strathclyde men and I am told he has some royal blood in him. With so little for us to offer any possible husband for either of you, that will just have to be good enough, whether you like him or not. Few women are given a choice, you won't be any different."

"But, Mama—"

"That is enough now, Claerwen. Wait to meet the man before you condemn him further."

Grania tried to sound enthusiastic: "Maybe it won't be so bad. If he's away on duty much of the time, maybe we will be left to ourselves."

The conversation was interrupted as a handful of men arrived, talking loudly. They had seen the bottoms of several drinking horns, and it had not been water they were drinking. Leading the men was Lord Ceredig himself, king of Strathclyde, a large, red-haired man, full of life, appreciative of a good joke and fierce on the battlefield. He was well-respected and well-followed due to his shrewd judgement when it came to both politics and men.

"Lady Linor, 'tis good to see you again," Ceredig greeted the woman. She looked up at him and smiled tiredly as he took her hands, relieved when she saw he understood it was hard for her to stand very much. He took no offense at her remaining seated.

"This must be Lady Claerwen. Aye, she is a beauty as you said she'd become." He grinned at Claerwen.

"Thank you, my Lord." Claerwen curtseyed politely. Her anger boiled down, but continued to simmer like a geyser ready to explode. She knew she would have to give in to her mother's wishes. As she rose, she eyed the chieftain and decided at least he seemed reasonable enough. Hopefully Drakar would be similar. "This is my cousin, Lady Grania," Claerwen introduced. Grania curtseyed as well, and smiled at Ceredig.

He chuckled, full of his own sense of fun at his part in the betrothal mediation. "And this is Lord Drakar."

The chieftain flourished a hand in the air towards the other men who had arrived with him. The women scanned through the collection of male faces that smiled in various degrees of cheer and drink, and they anticipated which one would answer the introduction. But the reply came from behind the group, as another man strode up. He was even bigger than Ceredig, though more out of gluttony than muscle. He, too, had red hair, a tangled mass of flaming curls mashed into a cap, and a scraggly beard several shades darker. In one hand he held a greasy, half-eaten turkey leg, and he wiped the other unceremoniously off on his tunic before he clapped his lord's shoulder. He then grabbed a drinking horn from one of the other men and swallowed two long gulps of mead to wash down the meat.

Drakar glared at the women with close-set, nearly colorless blue eyes. "Which one?" he demanded.

Ceredig took Claerwen's hand and pulled her a step forward. She stared aghast at Drakar. He looked her up and down, grunting that she was rather thin. Then he glanced at Grania and commented that she must be "the servant." He turned to Ceredig and said, "Aye, close the deal." He strode back to the plank table, straight for the mead. The other men followed.

The king of Strathclyde led Linor to a leather-draped cubicle that he used as an office at one end of the hall, and signaled a scribe to accompany them. They would make the betrothal official and set a wedding date. Claerwen and Grania watched them go, then turned and stared back at Drakar as he stood among the men with both hands full of food.

"Royal blood? Royal worm! I cannot marry that...creature!" Claerwen hissed under her breath. "He is so filthy, so...so disgusting! It is worse than I ever imagined. How can she do this to us? Doesn't she see?"

"Being captured by the Irish for slavery would be better," Grania muttered, astonished nearly to tears. She knew there was no reply to comfort Claerwen this time.

"Dear Lleu, what will happen to us?" Claerwen clung to Grania's arm till it hurt.

"I wish I knew, Cousin. I am so sorry. They won't listen to us."

"I feel sick." They looked again at the men, who were obviously talking about the two young women. Led by Drakar, they winked and gestured shamelessly.

"Look, Mama is done. Grania, can you take her back to the guest house? I cannot face her yet."

"Are you all right? You're so pale. You should come back, too, and lie down."

"Not yet. I want to be alone. I will come in a while, but I cannot face Mama just now. Or anyone else. Please, Grania."

"Be careful."

The hall was stifling. It was not so warm in reality, but Claerwen's upset nerves made her feel as if she could not draw a breath. Smoke from the fire scratched her eyes and she felt dizzy and nauseous. She rubbed her forehead, trying to ease a headache forming there. Standing alone in the hall with all those ugly men, she felt naked and ill. Ceredig had gone with Linor and Grania, and the scribe had disappeared along with the serving slave. She had to go before they noticed her.

Claerwen slipped out of the hall's rear door into the darkness and groped along the wall. The stone felt wonderfully cool under her hands. She came to a small iron gate that opened into a garden and let herself in. Light drifted down from a small window above, enough to keep her from tripping, and she found a bench directly below.

Claerwen sat, leaning back against the wall and closed her eyes, feeling the stone's coolness through her gown. Her reeling head steadied and her stomach settled. She only wanted to go to sleep and forget, to wake up somewhere else...

The sound of leather on packed earth scraped next to her. Claerwen's eyes sprang open and fastened on a dim figure hovering near. She recoiled involuntarily, and stood, then started to back away, into what she hoped was a shadowy corner where she would be hidden. But the figure had already seen her and turned.

Deep, black eyes held her gaze. They were so black the iris and pupil could not be distinguished. As they stared back into her own, she had the impression they were keeping her from falling, or that if she would turn away, she would be forever lost.

"Excuse me, my Lady," said a quiet, young voice that was deep and promised a rich resonance with a few more years. It was wrapped in a soft north Welsh accent. The man moved back slightly as if to turn to go and the light from the window crossed his face. Then Claerwen recognized him as the slave from inside.

"Wait," she stammered out.

The man stopped, his face in the dim light. The black eyes were set in a rugged face, framed by black hair. He looked about eighteen years, yet he seemed much older. The look in his eyes was somber, yet curious.

She did not know why she said for him to wait. She did not know what she would even say to him.

"Forgive me for intruding," he apologized when she did not speak.

She struggled in her mind for something to say, but found nothing worthwhile. Why should she speak to a slave anyway, if only to give orders?

"Are you not well, Lady?" he asked. He brushed back a stray hair from his face. Gold reflections shined dimly from the hand that crossed in front of him.

Claerwen's eyes followed the sparkle, but he dropped the arm too quickly for her to see it. A gold ring? This is no slave, she realized. She had felt it before, though not consciously; his manners were too good, too polite, too smooth. A slave would wear no gold, even if he had stolen it.

The man smiled. He started to speak when a voice came from the window above. A shadow passed across the light and Drakar's voice carried out into the night air. Claerwen's eyes stared up at the window in astonishment and anger.

"Come! Before they see you," the man whispered sharply and yanked her, roughly pressing her against the wall below the window and wedging her between it and himself. He could feel her shaking against him. Above, they could hear Drakar talking with at least two other men, sequestered in one of the hall's draped-off cubicles.

Claerwen and the man stood still and breathless in the dark, listening intently. The conversation above was tersely spoken, involving locations of war bands throughout Britain. At times it was hard to hear the words clearly, but many place names in Gwynedd, the kingdom that spread across North Wales, were mentioned. Strathclyde was strongly tied to Gwynedd by kinship and alliance, as well as to most other Welsh kingdoms and Cornwall in the south. These areas had remained steadfast British strongholds throughout the centuries; not even four hundred years of Roman occupation had been able to change their basic culture.

Claerwen wriggled her head until she was more comfortable, resting it in the angle of the man's shoulder as he hid her. She studied his eyes, intent on the light from the window above, almost as if he was reading. She concentrated on him, feeling his warm breath on her face. He smelled of leather and horses. Slowly, she stopped shaking as she realized his dark clothing and hair hid him easily in the shadows, unlike her light-colored gown.

As she listen to the conversation, Claerwen understood they were hearing a secret plan to infiltrate outsiders into solid British territory. It was well known that Drakar headed Lord Ceredig's war band and was an excellent general when it came to laying out military maneuvers. But clearly none of these men were on Strathclyde's side. They did not mention who the invaders would be or when they would come, but the landings and paths were clear.

The voices faded away as their footsteps led them back into the great hall.

"I must go," the black-haired man said, pulling away.

"Wait," Claerwen blurted and clung to his sleeve.

"I'm sorry. I must know who Drakar spoke with," he insisted, but she refused to let go. Her face registered shock and she stared into the darkness past the man as if she was still listening to the voices.

"I know one of them," she whispered.

The man stood dumbfounded and stared at her. "Are you sure?" He grabbed her arms, his fingers pressing deeply into them.

She was alarmed by the intensity of his eyes as they drilled into her face. "A...aye," she stammered, her innate shyness collapsing her confidence. "I mean...I know of one of them."

The man watched horror claim her face, her eyes clearly in pain from a memory. Anxious to know what she could tell him, he forced himself to be patient.

Finally, Claerwen spoke, "I recognize the voice of a man called Ifan."

"Ifan," the man repeated. He watched Claerwen struggle with the memory, fighting to find the words. Gently, he prompted her, "Please, what can you tell me?"

Claerwen lifted her face and gazed into his eyes. He was a stranger to her, but he radiated a comfortable sense of honesty. Trusting her instincts, she drew a great breath and told him of the attack that had butchered her family and clan, leaving her the sole survivor for her mother and cousin to find. She explained how it was thought the soldiers were Saxon, but later learned they were Irish who had been told hostages of theirs had been hidden in Welsh Cynnwyd lands.

"It was a lie," Claerwen continued. "We had no hostages of theirs. I never met Ifan directly, but I remember his voice. It is the kind you can never forget."

The man studied Claerwen's face, still digging his fingers into her arms. He could feel her shaking again. He pressed his lips together in thought, then speculated, "Ifan would have masterminded the lies, he is a broker of mercenaries and power. For a price he will ruin any life. The other man must be Gerallt, his partner. He and Ifan are very rarely seen together. That means this meeting is yet another brokered deal to bring mercenaries into Britain, probably Saxons. They will have separated and gone by now, leaving Drakar here to do their filthy work." He saw her wince and realized he was hurting her. "I am sorry." He backed away. "I must go."

"Was Drakar behind the Irish raid as well?" Claerwen asked and touched his arm. Her eyes mirrored the harsh ache of rage in her voice and it disturbed him.

"I don't know." Suspicion crossed his thoughts. Perhaps he had said too much. He had not questioned whose side this young woman was on. Perhaps she was a trap to keep him from following Ifan and Gerallt. But the pain in her eyes told him otherwise.

"Have you ever spoken to anyone about this?" he asked.

She shook her head slowly, then answered, "No. I couldn't. Not to anyone. Not even my cousin. The memory of it was too great."

Then it struck him who she and the other women were and why they were there that night. "You are the one Drakar is supposed to marry? You are Lady Claerwen?"

She made a fist as if to punch something, anything. Instead she dropped her hand, sighed heavily and nodded, "Aye, but if Drakar is involved in this..." She looked at the man and suddenly lost her shyness, deciding she could fully trust him. "He is a traitor. And if he was involved with the Irish attack as well...I cannot honor that contract! Will he kill the rest of us, too, and finish the job? And why marriage? The land we have now is small and remote, given to my mother only because she is distantly related to Lord Ceredig. I have nothing to give him. I cannot even bear to look at the filthy man!"

"Your land could have strategic value for the plans we have just heard, I believe. Size and current usage are not so important as control. The marriage would legitimize its theft. From what I know of him, once he has the land, you will be in danger, whether or not you marry him."

She groaned, "What should I do?" Then her eyes brightened. "We must go to Lord Ceredig immediately! He must know this!"

"Wait! We cannot yet." He gripped her hand as she tried to dart toward the hall.

"Why? If we wait, it could be too late! It could be anytime that they come. It's not just for me; we can't risk letting more—"

"Shhhh!" He put a finger against her lips as her voice rose. "I know, I understand what you've been through, and more of that is exactly what I'm trying to prevent. But if Drakar finds out that we know what he is doing, he would kill you and me and the rest of your family right now, easily, and without any conscience. I will let Ceredig know, but it has to be done in a way that Drakar does not know who or where the information came from. I can do that."

Claerwen thought about this for a moment and understood his reasoning. She nodded, then looked up again and studied his face, suddenly fascinated by its strength. His features were even, the nose slightly curved down. His black eyes were deep-set and tended to squint. He had high, proud cheekbones, a square jaw, and thick, black brows that jagged down when he frowned. His black hair was swept back, thick and cut bluntly to chin-length. He had a tough face, one that could stare down an armed highwayman, but could also generate a feeling of trust and safeness.

"Who are you?" she asked, her voice soft and throaty. He was still holding her hand, his thumb absently stroking the softness of her skin.

He smiled slightly, enjoying her face as well, heart-shaped and delicate, surrounded by more than waist-length hair that gently flowed in the night breeze. He was struck again by the clear beauty of her green-blue eyes. He grunted, wondering at himself for being so distracted. His eyes dropped in thought and he frowned, then rose again as he touched her cheek with his right index finger. "You are so very beautiful and deserve much more than life has offered you so far." He leaned back against the wall, his arms crossed over his chest.

She was embarrassed by the compliment and let it pass, then asked him, "What can I do to help you?"

He was surprised by her offer and reached out to lightly touch her shoulder, drawing her closer to him. Then he whispered, "Nothing, Claerwen. I'm a dangerous man to be associated with, so for your own safety and your family's, don't get involved in my troubles. And I will not tell you who I am, for the same reasons. If Drakar, or Ifan, or Gerallt should ever find the least link between you and me, no matter how brief it has been, you would all be in terrible danger. The less you know, the safer you will be. You cannot even tell your mother and cousin. I'm sorry."

"But I'm already in danger if I stay here; what difference would it make now if I do something to help you?"

"No, Claerwen. Believe me, you don't want to get involved. You will be safer here; soon you will know what will happen."

"What are you going to do?"

His brow rumpled slightly at her persistence. "Just believe, and stay here in Dun Breatann."

Her eyes widened and she started, "You're going to—"

"Leave alone what you don't know." He spoke with finality.

She could not see his face clearly in the darkness, but she strongly sensed a deep compassion behind his sternness.

"I understand." She paused. "But, can I at least know your name? I think you are Welsh, too, because of your accent."

He hesitated, then smiled again. He leaned to her left ear and said softly, "I am called Marcus." His breath stirred her hair and she shivered, thinking how the name seemed to suit him. He continued, "You should go. It is late, and they will be worried about you. And I should have long been on my way by now."

But he hesitated, drawn to her by a binding empathy. He could smell the refreshing scent of lavender drifting on the warmth from her hair.

The light went out above, putting the garden in near total darkness. There was no moon, and the mist was rising, quickly obscuring the starlight.

"Marcus," Claerwen started to speak, when he suddenly leaned to her again. This time he kissed her.

It surprised both of them. His face lingered just in front of hers and she sensed his compelling attraction to her. In return, she felt herself being drawn uncontrollably to the mysterious man, unafraid.

Marcus slipped his hands around Claerwen's waist and leaned on the wall again, pulling her with him. She pressed herself to his chest, trying to see his face in the dark. She pushed her arms up around his neck and his lips came down on hers, sealing them in another kiss, searching, craving with increasing strength as she responded with a sumptuous passion. As his hands caressed her back, he felt her body curve into his and relax, a movement so natural that he crossed his arms behind her and hugged, lifting her from the ground.

Their lips finally parted, and Marcus rubbed his face on Claerwen's cheek, amazed at the way he wanted to touch her skin. As they leaned together, Marcus muttered, "I could not seem to help myself. It is as if...as if..."

"...we have known each other for all time." She finished his thought. Her voice almost seemed to echo.

Marcus' hands came up to hold her face. In the darkness, he could not see more than the outlines of her features and what appeared to be a soft glow from her eyes. He fought an involuntary shiver at the eeriness that her words were exactly what he had been thinking. Finally, he forced himself to say, "We must go, Claerwen, before someone discovers us here. Can you find your way back to the guest house?"

"Aye, 'tis not far." Again, they squeezed each other tightly, trying to keep the spell from breaking. Claerwen desperately wanted to ask if she would ever see him again, but decided it just would sound too obviously improbable. They released each other, but their fingertips lingered, tangled together.

"Farewell, Lady Claerwen. The gods be with you always," he whispered.

"The gods be with you as well, Marcus. May good luck carry you on your journey, wherever it may take you."

Reluctantly, he pulled away. Vaulting over the fence, Marcus disappeared into the mist.

CHAPTER 3

**Strathclyde
Autumn, 463 A.D.**

Dun Breatann's guest house was small but comfortable. It was round in the traditional Celtic style, built of heavy timbers, daub and wattle, and a neatly thatched roof. Inside was a ring of curtained-off rooms along the outer wall. In the middle was a common room surrounding the central fire pit. A short passageway ran from the entrance door to the common room and another led between two private rooms to a back door. It was snug with simple furniture and decorations native to the area. The floor was flagged and swept clean.

Claerwen stepped out of the rear door of the house into the dark of the night. She had tried to sleep for several hours, but could not stop herself from thinking about the mysterious man she knew only as Marcus and the common turmoil that had inadvertently engulfed them. Frustrated, she had dressed and decided to go for a walk to ease her tension.

The hill fort was incredibly still, blanketed in deep mist, not a hint of breeze to stir the damp air. Claerwen strode silently around the perimeter of the courtyard, staying hidden in the shadows of the buildings. She dragged in deep, long breaths, trying to clear her mind and resolve whether she should wait to hear if Marcus could accomplish his task to foil Drakar's plans, or if she should go herself to Lord Ceredig with the news, in spite of Marcus' warning.

Hoofbeats pattered from an alley between the building where Claerwen walked and the next one. She halted, and an instant later, a husky black horse emerged carrying a darkly-cloaked man. Claerwen stared, startled at first that someone would be riding out in the middle of the night. Then she realized she was watching Marcus cross the courtyard towards the south gates. He held an object in one hand as he slowed the horse, flashing it momentarily at the guard, then spurred into a charging gallop out of the gates.

She exhaled sharply, feeling as if she had lost the only friend she had ever made in her life. Her hand rose involuntarily to her mouth, touching her lips as if they could still feel the warm taste of his searching mouth. Her hand lingered, then she suddenly shook her head, telling herself she would never see him again; it was just a passing desire. She sighed heavily and retreated toward the guest house.

Claerwen slipped inside and settled in a chair by the fire pit, leaning forward to stoke the low flames until they rose. Then she held her chin in her hands and stared into the fire, the only light in the house.

Claerwen let her mind wander. She had been thinking intently all night, trying to determine how to avoid the marriage to Drakar, and wondering why she had suddenly confided to someone about the Irish attack, a memory she had never intended to resurrect.

Now she finally let go of that pattern of thoughts, letting herself flow with the flames and smoke. In her mind, she could see the hill fort compound, with its yard and many small round buildings. Lord Ceredig's spacious, many-roomed house sat next to the main hall on the highest part of the rocky knoll. In the entryway was a waiting area with tables and chairs. On one table was an intricately woven willow basket. She could see the pattern as clearly as if it were in her own hands. Inside was a bunch of folded papers, letters perhaps, she was not sure. They were tied with a thin leather thong. A hand appeared, long fingered and tanned deeply, with just a few dark hairs growing on the fingers. It was a man's hand, toughened from working, but still young, very strong. It held another package of papers and moved towards the basket, deftly dropping its package and picking up the original in a smooth, unhurried motion.

Claerwen glared into the fire intently, but the vision faded and all she could see were the flames. As her mind struggled to hold the memory of what she had seen, she vaguely realized she had never been inside the king's house. But she was too tired to stay awake longer, to think any more. Her head drifted forward. Moments later, she was asleep.

The sun was an hour away from rising when Grania wakened. The house was very still, but she could hear the fire crackling in its pit. Slowly she rose, washed, and dressed, still sleepy. She thought about the night before, and depression grew in her. Claerwen's intuition about Drakar had been more than accurate; the arrangement was going to be a disaster.

But Linor was right as well. Without a more valuable bride-gift than their homestead, there was little hope to marry into any family or clan except the poorest. The only skills they had were to keep a simple household and basic farming. The alternative was to go to a town, but most towns had disintegrated since the Roman occupation ended more than fifty years before, leaving few or no opportunities.

Grania braided her long reddish hair and wound it around the crown of her head. She looked in the tiny brass mirror she had carefully packed for the journey to Dun Breatann. She pinched her cheeks for color, then sighed, feeling wasted on someone like Drakar, even if she was not the one forced to marry him. She shivered and went to the fire pit to stir up the coals, and was shocked to discover Claerwen sitting there.

"Claerwen? Haven't you gone to bed? It's almost

morning!"

Grania's voice jarred Claerwen awake. She blinked a few times, her heart racing from the disturbance.

"I was dreaming," she whispered hoarsely in the darkness. Her face was lit eerily by the fire. Her head hurt fiercely all of a sudden, and she rubbed her eyes roughly.

"Go to bed, cousin, you must be exhausted. I am so worried about you. You're so quiet. Too quiet."

"Grania, come here. We must talk."

"But you're exhausted. We'll talk later. You know they set the wedding date for tonight. You will have to be ready."

"Tonight!" Claerwen hissed, suddenly resolving to take control of her life. "No, we have to talk now. I have a plan."

Grania frowned heavily at Claerwen, alarmed by the urgent distress in her hushed voice. "A plan? For what?"

"I have been thinking and thinking, all night. I will not marry that man. I can't. We will have to leave Dun Breatann. We can't go home, either. We are not safe from Drakar in either place. He wants our land, not us, and he is cruel enough to kill us for it. I will refuse to marry him."

Grania's eyes widened. "You think he is so dangerous? Why would he want to marry you if he's going to just steal our land?"

"I don't know. But you saw how he was at the meeting. Cold, nasty. He does not want me as a wife like a normal man, arranged marriage or not. If he wants our homestead, he can have it. It's not worth much to us anyway. But he cannot have us."

"If he is so dangerous, wouldn't breaking the contract make Drakar so furious that he would kill us anyway?"

"I don't intend to wait long enough to find out." Claerwen thought of Marcus riding out of the fort. Since then, she had begun to doubt he had halted Drakar's scheme of theft and invasion. She reasoned that if he was not in Dun Breatann, it would be impossible. And she had heard no uproar concerning Drakar, a certainty upon the discovery of his treachery. She resolved that she would have to decide what to do for herself.

"Our home is in Gwynedd, where we were born. I think we should go there. It's far enough away that perhaps Drakar cannot find us."

"But how? We have no gold or silver to buy horses, not even an old donkey. And what will we do once we are there? How will we survive? We have no skills to earn a living."

"I don't know yet. I don't know exactly where the Afon Dyfrdwy is from here either, or if that is where we should end up anyway. Gwynedd is big. All I know is that we must leave here. Lord Ceredig cannot protect us, even in his own kingdom; we will have to flee."

"How do you know this?" Grania asked sharply.

Claerwen opened her mouth to reply but stopped, interrupted by heavy footsteps outside and voices in an argument. She dashed into her room, Grania following, and pressed her ear to the shuttered window as the steps approached.

They heard Drakar arguing with another man, attempting to keep his voice down, but it carried easily in the silence of the fort. "Get yourself to the woman's homestead and tell the others that damned spy is on his way there. Take the short road. And make sure they take him alive. I want the pleasure of killing him myself. And no more blunders this time. I can't believe so many of you didn't see he was here, right in the middle of us. How can so many of you be so stupid?"

The other man took off running, his steps carrying him toward the stables. Drakar paused a moment, then headed back the way he had come.

Claerwen whirled around to Grania and gripped her cousin's arms. "We have to leave now. We have to go back to the homestead."

"But you just said we can't go there. Are you mad? If Drakar's as dangerous as you say, he'll kill us. Why would you want to go there?"

"I have to warn someone."

"The spy he spoke of? You know him? Claerwen, what are you involved in?"

"I can't tell you now. We have to go immediately. Get what you need. Hurry!"

"What about your mother?"

"Lord Ceredig will take care of her."

"That makes no sense. If we aren't safe here, she won't be either."

"She wouldn't come and she wouldn't understand."

"I don't understand, either. Explain it to me or I won't go."

"Don't argue, Grania. Come with me now!"

Claerwen flung a cloak at the girl and dragged her own back on, then roughly pulled Grania with her out of the door. Claerwen scanned the area immediately around the guest house and spotted a strong-looking mare tethered by the great hall. Still dragging Grania by the arm, she dashed along between the buildings. Clucking softly at the horse, she slipped the rein from its post and turned the animal until she could haul herself onto it, then pulled Grania up behind her.

Claerwen was relieved to see that the gates were opening for the day as she maneuvered the horse towards the courtyard, squeezing through the same alley she had seen Marcus emerge from in the night. She halted, watching the courtyard, still empty of people, and swallowed hard, praying to the gods that she could reach Marcus in time to warn him of the trap.

They circled around the yard, and approached the gates from the guard's blind side. The instant they emerged into his line of sight, Claerwen kicked the mare, shooting through the gates before the guard was aware of their approach. He shouted, then saw it was two of the women who were guests of the chieftain. He watched them disappear, heading for the southbound road, then shrugged, guessing they were going out for some morning air.

The road from the hill fort was mostly just a dusty, narrow track, barely visible through the overgrowth in some places, but Claerwen found it easy enough to follow. The homestead was not more than a half-day's ride, the last section leading through a thick forest that covered a long, fairly steep slope. Below, in a large clearing, lay the farm. It consisted of a cottage, a barn, and two small sheds. There was a small corral for animals, though there were no occupants any longer. A garden lay neglected between the cottage and the barn, and a small field leading down to a tiny stream lay fallow beyond the buildings.

Claerwen and Grania led the horse down the last steep part of the trail. Claerwen moved slowly, trying not to disturb the quiet of the forest. She constantly scanned back and forth in search of Marcus, but the silence indicated no one else was there. Grania anxiously loped a few yards ahead. Then Claerwen saw her abruptly stop, whirl, and dash back up the slope.

"Claerwen!" Grania whispered hoarsely. "Look!" She pointed.

Claerwen dropped the mare's rein and her eyes followed the line of Grania's arm. Through the trees, they could just make out the homestead in its clearing. There were at least a dozen men roaming around, heavily armed, all wearing cloaks in the distinctive brown and black tartan of Drakar's clansmen.

"Oh, Lleu, there are so many." Claerwen leaned heavily on a tree.

"What are they doing? Look at them! They're tearing everything apart. It looks as if they are searching for something."

Claerwen strained to see. She frowned, not understanding. Most of the men were dismantling the buildings and digging holes throughout the area surrounding the house and barn.

"They are supposed to be lying in wait to capture someone. Why? It makes no sense." She scanned again, across the clearing, trying to see up into the edge of the forest, if she could spot Marcus. She gritted her teeth in frustration. They had not come across him on the road and it did not appear that Drakar's men had captured him.

"Where is he?" Claerwen muttered and took Grania's elbow. "I want to circle around to the other side, as softly as we can. We must not let them know we've seen them or they'll come after us. We'll leave the mare here and come back for her later when we leave. Maybe we can sell her for some silver armlets to trade."

"I want to leave now, Claerwen," Grania blurted, fear in her face. "I don't know what kind of trouble you're involved in, and I don't think I want to know anymore. I'm leaving."

"No, Grania. Don't be foolish."

"Who's being foolish?"

Grania turned to reach for the horse's reins and abruptly became aware of another presence in the trees up the slope above them. She whispered to Claerwen, "Someone is up there!"

Claerwen spun around, expecting to see Marcus.

Instead, a figure swooped down and landed lightly a few feet in front of them. He was dressed differently, and stood tall and powerful, clad all in black leather gear, a chain link hood and a strangely visored helmet that hid most of his face. The two women had never seen such a warrior before. Soldiers usually dressed in the bright colors of their clan's tartans and were bare-headed. They carried spears, daggers, and sometimes, if they could afford it, a short sword. But this man carried a long, heavy sword at his left hip. And something about the helmet gave him an enormously fierce and cruel facade.

The warrior stood as if ready to pounce. Grania's eyes flew open wide as he reached out gauntleted hands. Before he could touch them, she fainted, falling like so many wet rags into the strewn leaves of the forest floor. Claerwen stared at the man, then at her cousin, stunned at first, then felt her will resolve to fight. She backed up a step and curled her fingers, ready to lash out like a cat. It occurred to her then that her tiny fingers were no offense or defense against thick leather or chain links, and she whirled away from him, leaping for a rock she had seen a few feet away. She grabbed it and swung, flinging the heavy stone directly at his head.

But the man was incredibly quick. He ducked, then lunged, grabbing her around the waist and clamping a gloved hand over her mouth. Her arms were pinned down between her body and his, useless. Panic rose in her heart and she flailed her legs, trying to loosen herself by using her weight to hurl herself away or twist free. She flung her head back and tried to bite the hand over her mouth, but the gauntlet was too thick and her teeth made little impression on it. He hugged her to him, pulling her tighter until her face was shoved into his chest; she could smell the heavy scent of the black leather. Then he pulled on her long skirt until he had it wrapped around her legs and she could no longer kick.

She struggled hard, too busy to scream. Who would help anyway, if she did scream? She grunted and pushed, tiring fast. He dropped her to the ground like a package, and he came down over her, still gripping her arms and bracing her hobbled legs with his knee. She twisted and wriggled, sure that he was going to rape her, then kill her. Her terrified eyes ran with tears as one of his gloved hands reached again to her. She expected him to start ripping at her clothes.

A sudden pain gripped her, under her chin. Her head strained back and she closed her eyes as she felt dizzy. Claerwen fought to stay alert, but felt her body go limp as black and white dots flooded her vision. She fell unconscious.

CHAPTER 4

Kingdom of Gwynedd, North Wales
Autumn, 463 A.D.

Claerwen's eyes refused to open. She felt her mind suddenly waken, but her eyes, indeed, her whole body, were immovable. It occurred to her to just go back to sleep, or to wherever it was she had just been. But her mind would not stop turning, thinking. She knew she had been asleep, but she did not know why or for how long. Had it been nighttime and exhaustion taking over? Or...?

Then she remembered the warrior in the visored helmet that had masked his face and the insistent strength in his arms when he held her captive. She shivered involuntarily and struggled to get her stubborn eyes open, needing to know if he was still there. She dragged a hand up to her face; it was heavy and sluggish, wrapped deeply under a blanket.

She felt wind ruffle her hair, and she guessed she was still in the woods. Rustling steps rushed around her. By Lleu, he must be still here, she thought, and dreaded his presence. Panicking, she twisted around in her blanket, desperately trying to get her eyes to focus and her mind to clear.

Grania! Where was Grania? Claerwen tried to call out, but her throat was so parched that speech was non-existent.

A soothing voice called out to her. A hand touched her forehead, gently stroking hair out of her face, calming her. She stopped squirming and concentrated on focusing her eyes. A dark figure above slowly cleared from the fog of her mind.

"Don't fret, now. Just stay calm." He was wringing out a wet cloth and dabbing her face with it. The voice was clear and pleasant, like soft wool, a singer's voice, or one cultured to speak before people. He sounded assured and comfortable, easing Claerwen's panic. "What is your name?" he asked.

Claerwen started to answer, but the dryness of her throat stopped her. Then she thought, who is this man? I should not tell him who I am or he will return me to Dun Breatann and on to Drakar.

He did not press for an answer. She studied his face. He was simply dressed but clean, had wavy dark hair, dark brown eyes, and a plain, clean-shaven face. She could not guess his age, but he exuded an indefinable maturity, probably a result of the same training that had cultivated his soothing voice. He gave her the impression of an old man of wisdom hiding in a younger man's body.

"My name is Emrys. I think someone tried to poison you and your friend here," he said. He rose to fetch a water skin and returned to help Claerwen drink from it. "You will be all right, but I think you may feel ill for a day or two. Do you know who would do this to you?"

Claerwen stared at the man, stunned at the word "poison." Slowly, she shook her head in answer to his question. It must have been the black warrior, she thought. She realized then she had not been raped as she had expected.

Emrys deduced her pattern of thoughts and queried, "Do you?"

Claerwen turned her head to see Grania and reached a hand toward the girl. She looked pale and limp. Claerwen looked back at the man, questions on her face.

"She will be fine. She is coming around now."

"Who are you?" Claerwen whispered hoarsely. She pulled

at Emrys' hand to give her more water.

He smiled a little as he helped her to drink, but he did not answer at first. Finally he said, "I am a courier, on my way to Caernarfon." He paused, watching her expression.

She looked at him with somber eyes, wondering if he was telling her the truth. Though a bit aloof, he had an easy manner and an infectious likeableness.

"I am telling you the truth." He smiled again, broader this time.

Claerwen frowned, startled by his choice of words. He knew exactly what she had thought. He grinned warmly at her reaction, and she caught his charisma and had to smile back. Her anxiety eased.

"I will make something for you to eat now." He winked and rose to tend a campfire.

Claerwen sat up and shook Grania awake. Her cousin groaned and opened her eyes.

"Grania, wake up!"

"Stop it, stop it." Grania pulled a hand up to her mouth. "I feel sick." She took deep breaths that slowly eased her nausea. Then she realized they were still alive and together, but somewhere different than she last remembered. And there was a stranger with them. She looked at Claerwen, her brows crunched together in consternation.

"Where are we?" she whispered, eyeing Emrys. "And who is that?"

"He said his name is Emrys. He seems to be nice enough. He said it looked like someone had poisoned us."

"Poisoned? Oh, Lleu! Why? Who?"

Claerwen pulled a wry face. "Who else?" she snapped, meaning Drakar and his warriors.

"But the—"

"Shh!" Claerwen nodded in Emrys' direction. "We do not know anything about him. Maybe he is a trap."

"Where is this place?" Grania changed the subject.

Claerwen glanced around and answered, "I don't know.

It's completely unfamiliar. How do you feel now?"

"Still queasy."

"So am I."

They paused their conversation and watched Emrys. He was busy at the fire, preparing a simple meal for all of them. He had boiling water in a pot hung from a tripod of branches over the heat and was measuring herbs from a collection of pouches into it. He stirred it briefly, then poured two cups full of the steaming liquid.

"This will ease your upset stomach and headache," he said, bringing the cups to the women. They looked up at him with uncertainty in their eyes. If he could be another trap, then this drink could be poison as well. He saw their hesitation and grinned, then took a sip from each cup. "I know something of healing herbs. You do not need to be afraid of me."

They took the cups and drank, and found the brew refreshing.

"The food is ready," Emrys announced.

"Where is this place?" Claerwen asked as she accepted a plate of bannocks and broth.

Emrys raised an eyebrow. "There is a road yonder that traverses the north of the kingdom of Gwynedd. It ends in Caernarfon. Where do you remember being last?"

The women looked at each other in amazement. Claerwen turned back to Emrys. "This is Wales?"

"Aye."

She turned back to Grania. "How? I do not understand."

"We must have been unconscious longer than just the night," Grania said.

"But how...how did we get here?" They turned back to Emrys.

He shrugged. "I found you here, in this clearing at dusk yesterday. You were unconscious then and only awoke this morning. I have seen no one else and there are no tracks that I can find. Indeed, it is a mystery."

"I'm scared," Grania whispered, looking all around, afraid

of evil spirits that might come out of the woods.

"What day is it?" Claerwen asked Emrys.

"The eve of Samhuinn."

Both gasped. Samhuinn, the festival of departed spirits, had been days away when they left Dun Breatann. Apparently the warrior had poisoned them and carried them so far away to keep their deaths undiscovered.

Claerwen thought hard a moment, then looked up at Emrys. "You are going to Caernarfon?" she asked him.

"Aye."

"May we please accompany you?"

"Claerwen!" Grania did not want to be near the man. Her skin prickled each time he spoke.

Claerwen clucked at her cousin to be quiet. "I don't mean to impose ourselves on you, and if you prefer, we shall not do so."

"I will be glad for the company." Emrys smiled and sat down to eat his own meal. Contrary to Grania's consternation, Claerwen instinctively felt a safety in Emrys' manners. She did feel better since taking the special drink and ate her bannocks with more interest.

"How far is it to Caernarfon?" Grania asked.

"About two days' walk from here."

"Walk?" Grania looked distressed.

"I am afraid so. I have no horse or mule. And I found none when I discovered you."

Grania's eyes teared up. She hated walking.

"It is good Roman road, paved and clear."

Grania poked at her bannocks and sulked.

Emrys looked at Claerwen and raised his eyebrows. She answered with a shrug. They finished their meal in silence, then began their trek immediately.

Claerwen walked beside Emrys, while Grania trailed a few feet behind, concentrating on how tired and sore her feet were getting.

"What will you do when you arrive in Caernarfon?"

Emrys asked Claerwen.

"We have never been in a town before. I'm not sure what we can do."

"Will you find a way back to where it is you came from?"

"No." The silence following her answer keyed Emrys to press no further.

He suggested, "I don't know if she needs any help, but I know a woman who runs an inn. She lost her husband last year and has a hard time running the place alone. Perhaps she would trade you a place to stay for helping her. There is cooking and cleaning, serving the customers."

"When we set out, we had not thought about what we were going to do or where we were going. Perhaps, if she doesn't need help, there will be another innkeeper who does."

"Just be careful where you go. It's not safe in towns, although Caernarfon isn't much of a town since the Romans left. It's mostly a fortified settlement now. But you can still be easily taken as a slave and sold, sent off to drudge for some chieftain. I can help you for a while, but I will not be staying long and have a lot of business to complete."

"I understand." Claerwen found it easy to listen to Emrys. He had a way of saying a lot with just a few words. As they walked, he spoke of a broad variety of things, ranging from the combination of herbs he had used in the drink to the geography of Gwynedd. She found him to be well-educated, although he gave no clue as to where he had been taught. She was fascinated by the depth of his knowledge and found herself inspired to learn as much as she could in the short time she would spend in his company.

By mid-afternoon, the wind had picked up and brought a gnawing chill with it. Noticing Claerwen's discomfort, Emrys interrupted his impromptu lessons and suggested they stop early for the night under a protective rock ledge. Grania's feet were becoming badly blistered as well, and she complained so much that Emrys and Claerwen felt it would be better to rest and continue in the morning rather than listen more to her whining.

But when they began to set up a camp, Grania was shocked to learn that they were not going to seek out an inn. She fussed, not wanting to sleep out in the open. Emrys pointed out that there were no inns between there and Caernarfon, unless she wanted to walk all night to reach one.

Grania grumbled and sat down hard on a fallen tree. Claerwen went to her and tried to reason with her.

"How can you tolerate him? Why did we have to get into this...this mess?" Grania squalled at Claerwen.

"You don't remember that we had no choice? We are just lucky this man found us or we could be dead."

"Choice? You're the one chasing after spies and such! We may as well be dead."

"Hush! You have to stop this nonsense, Grania."

"Why did it have to be this way?"

Claerwen sighed. "I don't know. We cannot change it now. It's only one more night and then we'll be in Caernarfon. Besides, we have nothing to exchange for a night's hospitality at an inn."

"Aye. I'm sorry Claerwen. It's just that he is so strange." She glared at Emrys as he prepared a fire.

Claerwen frowned and clucked her tongue. She was too tired to argue with her cousin. Emrys had only been kind to them. She hoped she could return that kindness someday.

The night wind drove in hard off the sea to the north, bringing a stinging cold and the smell of sea salt. Claerwen and Grania huddled in their blankets under the rock shelf. Emrys built a second fire for warmth. They tried to sleep, but the cold bothered them, trickling its way in under the blankets.

By first light, the wind had died down, and the sky was heavily overcast, the cold still clinging in the air.

Claerwen woke. She was facing towards Emrys when her eyes opened, and curiosity prompted her to watch him for what seemed a long time. He sat still before the fire nearest his sleeping place, legs crossed, back straight, hands down in his lap. His head was tilted back slightly and his eyes were closed. He faced the east, where the sun would rise, and his silence mirrored the cold air as he meditated.

The fire in front of Emrys burned evenly, oddly never going down or changing as it consumed the wood that fed it. Curiosity chewed at Claerwen as she watched. The serenity on Emrys' face seemed out of place in the harsh cold. She shivered.

Grania slept on; exhaustion had made her finally stop fidgeting. Claerwen slipped out from the blanket they shared and went to sit near Emrys. Inexplicably, she felt drawn to watch him more closely. She picked a spot a few feet behind him, off to one side, and eased herself onto the damp turf.

"It will snow today," Emrys said, more to himself than to Claerwen. His eyes were still closed. Then he said, "Look into the fire."

She stared at him.

"The fire, not me." Reluctantly, she forced herself to obey. How did he know? His eyes were still shut. She turned to the fire.

The flames jigged in a steady pattern. Claerwen watched, and she wondered why, but she did as she was bade without further question. There was something magnetic about the fire, its warmth, its glow.

The light expanded, spreading in all directions. There was nothing else to see than the light, it was all around. Deep in the flames she saw a building appear. Then two buildings. One small, the other large. A house and a barn. An old fence ran between them. It was burning. The house turned black and collapsed, choking smoke plumed out as the roof and walls fell in on themselves. Then the barn did the same. Ashes floated everywhere. It was time to back away, to run. Then the wind came, blowing away the smoke and the flames. Only smoldering, charred wood remained in scattered piles in a clearing. No creature stirred, no bird sang. It was silent, dead, gone.

Then suddenly, beyond the clearing, a lone figure appeared from the edge of a wood. A man in a long, elegant black cloak that streamed out behind him in the breeze. He wore a black, visored helmet that kept his face hidden. He stood still, a terrible sadness in his posture. Only his mouth could be seen below the visor, his lips pressed in a solemn line. He watched a while at the smoldering remains, then finally looked up and whistled. An enormous grey stallion stepped out of the trees behind the man and waited patiently. Then, after a final scan of the clearing, the man mounted and rode back into the woods and disappeared.

"Claerwen." A voice called her from afar. A hand pressed her shoulder. "Claerwen?"

The dream scattered. She felt as if her eyes had just opened from a sound sleep even though they had not closed since she looked into the flames of the campfire. She looked up to see Emrys standing over her, his hand shaking her shoulder. Her head ached terribly.

"How do you feel?" he asked.

"*Gwalch Haearn*..." she whispered involuntarily.

Emrys sat down in front of her and said, "I thought it was true."

She frowned at him, and for a moment, thought she saw a dim glowing in his dark eyes, making their brownness almost amber. Not understanding, her face filled with questions.

"You have 'fire in the head.' I could feel it in you since I found you two yesterday."

"Fire in the head?" She frowned again, confused. "What is that?"

"You just had a vision in the fire."

"A vision?" Then she realized he meant the dream she thought she had just had. The memory came flooding back. The name "Iron Hawk" strung across her thoughts like the steady wind from the night before. She could not stop herself from thinking the name over and over.

She looked hard into Emrys' eyes. "Who is *Y Gwalch Haearn*, the Iron Hawk?"

"He is the man you saw in the vision."

"He burned my home to the ground." Sorrow gripped her, even though the farm had never felt like a real home, only a place to seek refuge. She stared down at the turf around her feet. Then her pale green-blue eyes came up again, showing Emrys that she wanted to confide in him. "He is a warrior who attacked us in the woods when we tried to go home. He must be the one who poisoned us and left us for dead! Who is he?" She gripped Emrys' arm.

"I don't know. But he will become a legend in Britain. He is an avenger. He strikes quickly, out of the darkness without warning. He will kill without hesitation if the mission warrants it. He never speaks and he is always alone."

"But he must be allied with Drakar of Strathclyde! We saw Drakar's men ransacking the farm before the Iron Hawk found us. They seemed to be searching for something. But what? He must have...but what happened to..."

Claerwen's eyes filled with tears. She stopped short of telling Emrys about the Irish attack and her belief that Drakar was connected to that as well. Nor could she speak of Marcus; she was certain he was dead now, at the hands of either Drakar or the Iron Hawk.

Feeling utterly alone, Claerwen wished Emrys had not shown her the vision and she felt their rapport was slipping away.

"He must have had a different reason that you haven't seen," Emrys suggested.

"How can you defend him?" Claerwen snapped in return.

"Have you had visions before, Claerwen?" Emrys countered, not wanting to argue.

She stopped, confused by the swift change in direction and answered, "I don't know. I've had strange dreams before, similar to this one, but none I could remember so clearly. You have this 'fire in the head,' as well, don't you? That is how you know I have it! Is that how you found us? Who are you?" She glared steadily at him but shivered, unnerved by his calm gaze.

Emrys only smiled mysteriously and rose to break camp. She watched him, angry and frightened at the same time, then decided not to pursue her questions further, more afraid to learn who he was than not to know. They packed and started on their way in silence.

Claerwen walked with Grania this time, but spoke little. They followed Emrys, who strode serenely in front. Claerwen thought about the vision and the way Emrys seemed to present it to her. Had he guided her through the vision? And if he had, had he shown all of it to her, or only parts he wanted her to see? And if so, why?

Then her thoughts turned to the Iron Hawk. She vaguely remembered having heard the name before, but from where? Another dream? Or a vision? What he and Drakar's men had done to the farmstead was eerily similar to Ifan's Irish, except for the use of poison instead of a sword. Why poison, unless they were trying make their murders less obvious this time...

It began to snow lightly.

Claerwen was still deep in thought as they approached the gates of Caernarfon. She had not realized they had come so far.

"I will take you directly to the inn I told you of yesterday. I plan to stay there anyway while I complete my business," Emrys told the two women, stopping before the gates to let them catch up to him.

The guard at the gates waved them through. He seemed to recognize Emrys and did not bother to question him or his companions.

Claerwen and Grania had never seen a town before, nor any Romanized settlement. The only settlement they had been inside was Dun Breatann. There had not even been villages along the river of their homeland.

So many buildings, so many people, all in one place! It was frightening and fascinating. The smells, mostly bad, rose from sewers and garbage heaps. Grania and Claerwen gaped at it all as they followed Emrys through the streets. They kept closer to him now, not wanting to be separated from their guide, no matter how he unnerved them.

As he promised, he took them to an old inn on the far side of the town. Built by Romans, the inn was tucked in a corner against the protective town wall. It was styled like one of their villas, rooms all around a central courtyard. Tessellated floors decorated the main hall, which served as lobby and dining room. The courtyard had an ancient stone fountain that held only rust stains instead of water.

Emrys was greeted warmly by a middle-aged woman, giving the impression that he had stayed there many times. He asked her for two rooms, one for himself and one for the women, and he paid for both without hesitation. Claerwen and Grania glanced at each other, surprised, and worried that now they were obligated to him for money they did not have. He had already helped them far more than any other stranger would have. And in addition, he was going to ask the proprietress to give them work.

When they were alone in their room, Claerwen nervously paced the floor, and said, "I just don't understand. Why would he do all this for us?"

"Maybe he felt sorry for us, for the way he found us?"

"I don't know. Maybe he wants something. But what? We don't have anything. Even if the woman gives us work, we still won't have anything, just a place to stay and food."

A knock at the door interrupted them.

Claerwen opened the door and the innkeeper stood there. She was wiry-thin and grey-haired, but had huge, kind, deep, blue eyes.

"Good evening, my lady," Claerwen greeted her, with a slight curtsey.

"By the light, such kind manners, child! If only the young people of this town knew how to be so polite." She smiled a motherly smile. "Please, sit." She took a chair herself.

"Lord Emrys has told me something of your plight and he says he has told you something of mine. I am not really in a position to be of too much help to you, but perhaps we can work something out." She paused and they waited patiently for her to continue.

"My husband died in an accident last year. We ran this place ourselves and had no children or other kin to help us. It's just too much for me to do alone. The building is in good enough shape— except for that blasted fountain and its plumbing out there— to last a long time without much trouble. But I can't keep up with all the cooking, cleaning and trying to make the building look nice all by myself. This place does not make enough to hire someone to do repairs. So when Lord Emrys told me about you two, I agreed with him that perhaps you could do some of the work in return for a room and meals. And if business improves because we can keep the place in better shape, then maybe I could even do better than that someday." She waited, watching their faces.

They looked at each other, communicating silently. Finally, Claerwen spoke up, "We have never worked before, except at our home. I'm not sure we have the knowledge required to run an inn."

The woman smiled again and asked, "You ran a household, no?"

They nodded.

"Then you probably can cook some?"

"Aye," Claerwen said.

"And you cleaned and aired bedding and swept floors and such?"

"Aye," answered Grania.

"That is enough to start. I can teach you some other things. Lord Emrys told me you were quiet and polite young women and would be a big help to me. I have known him a long time and have found his judgement to be excellent."

"Lady?" Grania asked. "Who is Lord Emrys?"

"Grania!" Claerwen elbowed her cousin. "Hush!"

The woman laughed, not offended by the question. "He comes here often on business at the court, when it's held here instead of in Conwy; but to be honest, I really don't know much else about him personally. He has always been very kind." She thought a moment and continued, "He is very simple, you know. He doesn't stay at the court like the other men who go there. I figure he prefers his privacy." She shrugged.

"At the court? The king?" Grania asked.

"Aye, Cunedda himself, King of Gwynedd." She saw awe in Grania's eyes and a brooding silence in Claerwen's.

"I am called Alis. So, what do you say? Will you stay and help?"

Claerwen and Grania looked at each other again, and Grania nodded.

"Aye, we would like to," Claerwen consented. In her mind she was thinking that there was no other choice anyway. She was grateful for the luck they'd had, meeting Emrys and finding work quickly, but she disliked the town and its noise and stink. But until she could think of what they should do next, it was better than traipsing across the countryside with nowhere to go.

CHAPTER 5

Caernarfon, Gwynedd, North Wales
Autumn, 463 A.D.

"I hope this works out," Claerwen said quietly in the dark as she lay in her bed. Uncertainty laced her words. She and Grania had talked with Alis until late, finding a clear and deep rapport with the woman. After Alis had guided the young women through a routine evening of work, Claerwen decided to confide in her, telling Alis that she had run out of a marriage contract to an extremely cruel man. She told the woman no more, not willing to go into further details. Alis suggested that they use different names, citing that Caernarfon was full of people running away from their problems, changing their lives and using false names. She also suggested using Roman names, which were common due to the prolific intermarriage of the Romans and British in the town. After considering many samples, Claerwen picked the name "Olivia," and Grania decided on "Julia."

Grania answered Claerwen's concern, asking, "Why are you worried? Why wouldn't it work out? It's nice here. There is so much more going on here than out in the wilds where we lived before."

"That may just be the problem. What if Drakar, or someone else who can identify us, comes through this town and recognizes us? Or that awful black warrior again? Then we would have to find another place to hide."

Noise stirred in the night. Grania listened a while, then muttered, "I never thought of that. Do you think Drakar would stay at a place like this?"

"I wish I knew. But one of us could be out in the streets somewhere for any reason and be seen. Changing our names wouldn't help then."

"What can we do?"

"I think we should try to change our appearance somehow. Change our hair, or wear caps that cover as much of our hair and faces as possible."

"Aye, we can do that." Grania paused, then said, "I hope we haven't brought trouble to Alis. She's been so kind to us."

"Aye, she has. She's been lonely, since her husband died. We've only been here a few hours and already she treats us like we were her own children. I wish my mother had been like her."

"Claerwen...I mean, Olivia! What a thing to say."

"'Tis true! My mother was so cold sometimes. She could be kind and funny, but she could be so awfully cold. I wonder how she is."

"You're worried about her anyway, aren't you?"

Claerwen was silent for a time, then finally she said, "Aye. I wish I knew what is happening in Dun Breatann."

She was thinking about Marcus more than her mother.

She stared at the ceiling in the darkness until she heard Grania drift off to sleep. Then she turned over, hugged her pillow, and let herself dream of the mysterious spy with the intense black eyes, hoping he was still alive.

Spring, 467 A.D.

Claerwen grew to dislike town-life with a deepening heaviness. In the first weeks, she plotted to leave again, contriving to learn the Iron Hawk's identity and discover what had happened to Marcus. But she hesitated out of consideration for Grania's and Alis' safety. While she had doubted Marcus' ability to stop Drakar's activities, she never doubted the danger he had warned about. She gradually forced herself to accept her plight, allowing caution to overrule her courage. But she was not content, constantly fretting that if she had done more, perhaps the pall of danger, personal and beyond, would have been assuaged. Claerwen disguised her pain with a steadfast silence, sometimes crying from sheer loneliness in the night.

Grania grew from a girl into young womanhood, but always retained a certain childishness. She loved the town and the constant movement of people, and her personality reflected that movement. She chattered cheerfully and incessantly about anything to everyone, which made her a natural hostess for the inn. The women worked hard to make the inn grow into an attractive stopping place for local people to eat and travelers to rest.

News came, most often from traveling merchants. Claerwen listened as she worked the dining hall's tables, her interest piqued because it reminded her of the intrigue Marcus had been ensnared in years before. She learned of the turmoil involving the chieftain called Vortigern, and that he had finally wrested control of Britain's high kingship in the aftermath of the assassination of the former king, Constantine.

Constantine's three sons were too young to wield the necessary power to take the kingship. The oldest lost his life to another assassin; the younger two, Ambrosius and Uther, found refuge in Brittany, in their cousin King Budec's court.

News of Vortigern's victory did not sit well with the Welsh and other Celtic British, from clan chieftains down to thralls. Vortigern hired dreaded Saxon mercenaries to swell his war bands, paying them with land in exchange for their services. Soon after he became High King, this habit increased dramatically because he needed enormous help to keep himself on the throne. The Saxons threatened to spread out across Britain, forcing their cruel barbarism onto the ancient Celtic society.

In the fourth spring after Claerwen and Grania arrived in Caernarfon, Vortigern married Rowena, a Saxon princess. The Celtic Welsh made a collective gasp at that news. That he would set aside his British wife for a Saxon woman was more than they could understand. The marriage had been arranged to further strengthen Vortigern's position by appeasing the restless Saxons and other migrants from the Continent, who continuously threatened full-scale invasions. Vortigern had sought to control the British by using the Saxons; now he had to find ways to control the Saxons. And he was beginning to lose on both sides...

"I wish it would rain. This air feels like wet wool stuffed inside my head," Claerwen observed one evening as she washed the last of the day's pewter plates and cups, tired of listening to the constant talk of politics among their guests.

Alis grinned at Claerwen as she took the dishes to dry. "Aye, a good wash down would be fine. Go to bed early tonight," she told her. "There won't be any more people coming now; the storm coming in will keep anyone else away."

Claerwen sighed and rubbed her temple. "Even a good clap of thunder would almost be fun."

"What's wrong, dear?" Alis asked.

"Nothing...only tired."

Alis' brows lifted, sensing Claerwen's usual somber quietness was deeper than ever.

"Something *is* wrong," she said as she slipped an arm around Claerwen. "I have seen it in your eyes for weeks now, always so distant and sad. Talk to me, Olivia. Aren't you happy here?"

"I don't want to trouble you. I'm sorry." Bitter loneliness filled her eyes.

"Trouble me, she says!" Alis clicked her tongue and tucked the younger woman into her arms, rocking her as she would a young child. "What is so sad that you don't want to tell me?"

Claerwen hugged Alis, accepting the woman's comfort.

"It feels like an uneasiness."

"Are you scared of something, my dear?" Alis asked, holding Claerwen's hand.

"I'm not sure. I feel as if something is going to happen."

"Something bad?"

"I don't know."

Alis thought on this. "You don't like Caernarfon, do you?"

Claerwen shook her head.

"Do you want to go somewhere else?"

Claerwen's head came up sharply and she grabbed both of Alis' hands. "Oh, no! I could never leave you. You have been so good to us. You have been more of a mother to us than my own mother was. You're always so calm and full of good sense. I feel guilty that I have not been able to return your kindness."

"Nonsense, child. Just having your company has made my life worth living again. You and Julia are such a joy to me. Don't you know that by now?" Alis stroked Claerwen's hair back. Compassion stirred inside when she saw the ache of loneliness in her face.

Claerwen sniffled and they clung together silently for a time. Finally, Alis spoke again, "Are you afraid that Drakar might be looking for you?"

Claerwen shrugged, "I couldn't be worth so much time and effort to him, could I?"

"I don't know. I suppose it could be possible. If he is the type to carry a grudge, he might still be searching for you, just to appease himself because you didn't honor the contract. But I seriously doubt he could find you here."

"It seems like such a long time ago." Claerwen sounded far away. Thunder rumbled again, on the sea to the north. "I guess I had best go to bed now."

Claerwen paced slowly out of the kitchen, but instead of going to her room, she decided a walk might ease her edginess. She went through the courtyard and out the front, taking her cloak. The street was dark, most of the torchlight having gone out with the strong wind. Rain began to fall, but Claerwen welcomed it and bundled tightly into her cloak, pulling up the hood. She walked slowly up the street, heading for a grassy knoll that lay a short distance away. Several springs dotted the knoll, and she felt drawn to them, needing to sense the spirit within them.

Caernarfon was quiet, only the hiss of rain and rumble of thunder disturbing the town as it slept. Claerwen walked steadily toward the knoll. A stand of trees covered one side of the top, and the branches creaked and groaned in the wind.

A horse whinnied suddenly, the sound coming from the trees. Claerwen halted, surprised that anyone else would be out in the storm. A second horse nickered, and she frowned, staring up into the trees.

Then a lightning bolt struck somewhere over the sea, strong enough to light the knoll. The trees were so thick that Claerwen could not see who was amid them, only that a group of horse's legs showed through the trunks. She turned around, intending to retreat to the inn, when another flash lit the entire area.

The Iron Hawk loomed directly in front of her.

Claerwen's mouth dropped open to scream her surprise, but the warrior caught her roughly around her waist, clamping a strong hand over her face to keep her quiet. He dragged her into a willow thicket, shoving her down to the ground.

Claerwen struggled, kicking and scratching, trying to scream. The harder the Iron Hawk held her down, the wilder she fought back. He wedged a leg across her knees and gripped both her wrists in one hand. As he glanced up the knoll towards the trees, and Claerwen jerked a hand free and reached for the warrior's helmet. But he was quicker, batting her hand away.

Then he pulled a dagger from the back of his belt.

He held the knife in front of her face, twisting it slightly to make sure she saw how it gleamed. She wriggled again and he flicked it, not menacingly, but to hold her attention. She held still, waiting to see what he was going to do, her eyes staring up at him without blinking.

The helmet created a blank face, and the only detail she could distinguish was rain dripping from it as he hovered over her. She could smell the wet leather of his armor, the same smell from the last time she encountered him. He watched again toward the trees, and she tried to twist out of his grip once more, hoping his distraction would give her the chance to escape. But the Iron Hawk's hand was tight like a steel clamp and she could not dislodge herself. He looked down and gritted his teeth, then pressed the cold knife to her throat.

She froze, her skin tingling where the blade touched her. She was sure he would not hesitate to cut her. An instant later, she could hear the horses begin to move from the trees, the striking of their hooves vibrating the ground underneath her. The Iron Hawk watched them move out, continuing to hold the dagger at her throat until the hoofbeats faded away.

The sky released its tension in a sudden show of grand lightning. A moment later, the Iron Hawk's knife and hands withdrew and disappeared. Claerwen bolted upright, ready to lash out again. Thunder crashed, and another lightning strike flashed, more thunder following. She bounded up, astonished that the warrior was gone, leaving no trace that he had ever been there. Rain poured down, soaking her, and she slowly started back towards the inn. Turning in all directions, she wondered if he was still out there, watching. She choked in her fear, then ran down the hill. Flinging herself into her room, she locked the door behind her and dove into the comforting warmth of her bed.

The morning dawned warm and bright, as if the thunderstorm had completely engulfed the Iron Hawk's presence and dragged it away when the clouds raced out during the night. Claerwen stared at the blue sky, almost believing she had dreamt the encounter. Resolving to keep it to herself, she let Grania persuade her to go to the marketplace.

The market was held in the open space at the bottom of the same knoll where Claerwen had skirmished with the Iron Hawk. She wondered if his appearance was the source of her previous uneasiness, if the fire in her head was warning that she would cross paths with the warrior again. Gradually, she forced herself to relax, letting the peaceful day and Grania's companionship calm her nerves.

"What do you think, Olivia?" Grania asked Claerwen. She was fascinated by a roll of fabric. She had unwound enough to hold up in front of her.

"'Tis beautiful." Claerwen went over to admire it. "But it's not something we need."

"Oh, I know. But I just wanted to look at it one more time."

Claerwen smiled at her cousin. She could be flighty and frivolous, but Claerwen adored her. No one was as much fun to be around as Grania.

"I want to look at the herbs and medicinals, if there are any," Claerwen said. "We can't afford them either, but I want to see if I can learn something from the merchant. Maybe we can make the meals at the inn better. I'll be over there when you're finished." Claerwen walked away from Grania, heading for the opposite side of the market.

She wove slowly, enjoying the spring sun as it glowed on her face and warmed her hair. Clouds were beginning to return from the sea, and would soon threaten rain again. People hurried, finishing their marketing before the weather changed. Claerwen was not exactly sure where the herb seller was; she had seen his booth before in the row with salt and medicine vendors.

She turned another corner and was confronted by a line of horsemen. She stopped, annoyed at their rudeness for not dismounting before entering the market area. They seemed to mill, and suddenly were everywhere around her. She kept her eyes down, trying to avoid them, but finally looked up into their faces when they did not pass.

There were nearly a dozen, all dressed in filthy clothes. Then she saw they were warriors, probably a detachment from some chieftain's war band. She started to back away, ready to retreat into the main market area when she halted, stunned by a particular face.

Cold blue eyes stared out from a dirty, seemingly endless, scraggly red beard and moustache. They glared down at her with an anger and contempt she had never seen before. Her lips parted; her mouth dried like a desert.

Drakar was astride the horse in front of her.

Instantly, she sprang backwards. In the same moment, Drakar grunted an order and each man clanged out his sword, the group surrounded Claerwen. She froze, staring wildly at the circle of sword tips inching closer to her. They glinted in the sun, hurting her eyes. She looked up, searching beyond the soldiers, hoping to see someone who could help, but the marketplace hushed suddenly; people were running from the trouble, only a few staying to gawk.

Drakar dismounted, his frantic hair trailing in the breeze like a nest of scattering red ants. He came forward, his own sword naked and shimmering at Claerwen, his cold, pale eyes raking over her with sardonic arrogance.

"So, I have finally caught up with you, you dirty little slut!" He flicked the sword at Claerwen, making her jump back and nearly pushing her into the swordtips.

"You won't get away this time!" Drakar sneered, and poked the sword again.

Claerwen did not move back this time. She knew he was the kind of man who thrived on intimidating other people; there had been many like that at the inn. And they were most annoyed when they were unable to bring fear to their victim. Claerwen stood still, planting her feet firmly, and crossed her arms in front of herself. She held her head proudly and glared back at Drakar. She was shaking, but she forced herself not to show it.

"What do you want, trader of Saxons?" she called out, loud enough for the few people still watching. Behind Drakar, she noted a man with brown hair running towards the circle of warriors. He halted and stared at her.

"You know what I want, woman. Hand it over. Now!" Drakar shouted back.

"Hand over what?" she shot back, anger rising as she

watched Drakar's face go red. Four years had added several more layers of ugliness to him.

"Don't play games with me! I want it now!"

"Or else what? You'll kill me? You might as well do it now. I don't have it anymore," she bluffed.

"I don't believe you!" Drakar stalked forward again, standing over her, screaming in her face.

His breath made her stomach turn. She saw his teeth were mostly brown stumps and they reminded her of the burnt debris of both her homes. "I don't care what you believe, traitor!" Claerwen's voice was husky with rage.

Drakar drew his hand back and smacked Claerwen across the face, the slap echoing across the marketplace. She crumpled and dropped, sprawling unconscious on the dusty ground.

"We'll take her to the farm," he muttered to one of the soldiers. "Damn, useless slut."

Two men dragged Claerwen's limp body to one of their horses and lifted her, flinging her over the animal's rump. Drakar watched his soldiers mount and ride out, then hauled himself onto his own horse. He spat on the ground where she had fallen.

Claerwen slowly became aware of pain in her face, then more in her arms. She could smell stale straw and dung. Her head was hanging down, making her neck ache badly, but to raise it seemed to take too much effort. As her eyes struggled open, she realized she was sitting on the ground and her wrists were bound to posts to either side.

Gradually, she raised her face, only to see Drakar standing over her again, several of his men behind him.

"Well, have you decided to talk now?" he demanded.

Claerwen slowly looked around and guessed they were in a barn somewhere outside Caernarfon. It looked old and abandoned. Drakar's voice echoed painfully in her head, and she had missed what he had said in her grogginess.

Hands came at her, forcing her head up. They yanked her

hair, banging her head on the wall behind her. Then Drakar came forward and leaned over, his hands gripping the neck of her dress and wrenching apart, tearing it and her undershift. She could feel her clothes slip off her shoulders and her breasts come free, cold in the stale, dark air of the barn.

"Talk, woman! Talk, or I'll take you apart, piece by piece."

Claerwen's mind slowly cleared enough to realize what was going to happen. Her eyes came up and locked with Drakar's, and she sat up straighter, her breasts rising full like two defiant soldiers of her own. She glared hard at Drakar, then spat in his face.

Not expecting such bold obstinance, Drakar struck Claerwen once more, using his full fist. Her head cracked hard against the wall, then hung down, unconscious.

Before he could call an order to his men, a shout roared from outside. An instant later, a dagger sliced wildly across the barn, narrowly missing Drakar and thumping into one of his soldiers. The man dropped, only the hilt showing in the middle of his chest.

Another soldier dashed into the barn screaming, "The spy! He's running up into the hills!"

Drakar shrieked, "Damn him! Go after him! You two, stay here and watch her. We'll catch that bloody spy and roast both of them!"

"What are you doing here?" A harsh, deep voice shouted suddenly.

Claerwen heard it, startling her. She was cold and ached. Then she remembered: Drakar. She tried to raise her head enough to see whose voice it was, but her eyes would not focus.

"What are you doing in my barn?" The voice yelled again, harsher. "Get out, you filthy vermin! I'll have none of this here!"

Claerwen thought the man was utterly foolish, that they would kill him. Just as she knew she would be dead within a short time as well. She leaned her head back on the wall and concentrated. Gradually, she focused on the source of the voice, which continued to rant. By Lleu, he is loud!

She saw a man dressed in a farmer's simple wool tunic and breeches, worn leather shoes, and a wool cap. He had straggly light brown hair and a long, drooping moustache a few shades darker than his hair. His face was dusty, probably from working in his fields.

Claerwen was amazed at the bold ferocity the farmer showed against the two armed guards. His courage stunned the guards as well; they stared blankly at the man as he raged at them. Finally, they glanced at each other, silently communicating that it was time to stop the tirade.

One soldier pulled out his sword, hoping to scare away the farmer. But the man did not budge. The soldier lunged forward, threatening with his weapon. Instead of leaping away, the brown-haired man dropped and rolled, somersaulting backwards toward the barn's door. As he turned, he pulled an object out of the straw scattered over the ground. When he stood again, he held a long sword of his own.

Without hesitation, the man swung, cutting down the soldier who had threatened him. The other soldier panicked, yanking out his own weapon. The farmer dashed at him and caught the soldier's blade edge with his own. He rotated his sword once and flipped the warrior's weapon out of his hands, sending it flying into a beam across the barn. Then the man lunged, running the soldier through.

The brown-haired man cleaned his blade on the straw, then ran back to find his sword's scabbard, hidden near the door. He sheathed it, and strapped it across his back. Then he slipped a small dagger from beneath his left sleeve.

"Who are you?" Claerwen asked as he cut her bonds. He helped her pull up her clothing, but it was ripped so badly, it would not stay in place very well.

"I'm going to get you out of here. Can you walk?" he asked, gripping under her arms and pulling her up.

She took a pair of steps with him, but stumbled, falling against him. He saw her eyes glaze over and he supported her as she slumped in his arms. He walked her out of the barn, straight to a waiting horse.

"We must hurry, before the others come back." He lifted her onto the horse, then wrapped a blanket around her. He vaulted up, settling in front. He instructed, "Clasp your hands around me, like this, then hook them under my belt, so you won't fall." He knotted the corners of the blanket around his belt as well, securing Claerwen tightly against his back. He could feel her slumping against him; he guessed she had passed out again.

The man slapped the reins, urging the horse into a fast run. Seconds later, they disappeared into the edge of the forest.

CHAPTER 6

Gwynedd, North Wales
Spring, 467 A.D.

The man kept the horse moving at a steady pace, constantly going higher into the forest-covered hills. He followed no roads or tracks, but he seemed to know exactly where he was going.

Claerwen clung to him, her face wedged to his back, resting her cheek along the scabbard of his sword. She wandered in and out of the haze of her mind, unable to stay fully conscious. She fought the dizziness, and she knew she was slipping, too exhausted to hold on any longer. She let her hands relax a moment, trying to ease their stiffness. She had no sense for how long they had been riding, and she was too tired to complain, grateful that the stranger had rescued her. Finally, she let go, slipping sideways, and fell to the ground.

Claerwen was not quite unconscious. She heard the horse stop and the man come to her. She felt him run his strong arms under her back and legs, lifting her. Her face rubbed against his rough tunic as he carried her somewhere up the hill into a dark, shadowy place. He clucked at the horse and it followed patiently. Then she was lying down in soft, sweet-smelling leaves, cool against the skin of one of her shoulders where her dress would not stay to cover it. He lifted her head slightly and pressed the neck of a waterskin to her lips, his deep voice telling her to drink. The water was cool and refreshing, flooding her dry mouth and trickling down her chin to fall on her right breast where it showed through the torn dress.

Gradually, Claerwen's senses re-awakened, though she felt weak and exhausted. She became aware it was dusk, the light fading quickly.

"I have only one blanket, and it will be cold tonight," the man said quietly. He spread the blanket over her.

Claerwen grabbed his wrist and hung onto it. She stared up at him, trying to memorize his features in the dim light. "Who are you?" she asked again. "You were there in the market; you saw what happened."

The man smiled slightly, but did not answer. Instead, he poured some water in his hands and roughly rubbed it on his face. As Claerwen watched, she was astonished that the color of his moustache darkened, a brownish film coming off onto his hands. He dug out a kerchief and wiped his face, taking off the dirt, then rinsed his hands clean. He watched her with amusement as he worked, then reached up to remove his cap. She nearly choked when she saw the straggly brown hair come off with the cap.

"Do you remember me?" he asked, raking his fingers through his own hair, thick, long and black.

Claerwen stared at him, and slowly sat up to face him. Her mouth opened and closed, disbelieving, then she recognized his intense, deep-set black eyes.

"Oh, Marcus," she breathed wearily.

She buried her face in his shoulder, gripping his tunic with both hands, utterly relieved.

Claerwen did not remember falling asleep, but she knew she must have let herself go, trusting she was safe with Marcus, or else she fainted. She stirred once in the night, finding him sprawled half-way across her, his head resting on her bare shoulder. If he had opened his eyes, he would have looked across her breasts if the blanket had not covered them. His moustache tickled her, his breath warming the breast just in front of his face. At first she was stunned by his audacity to sleep so familiarly to her, but then she sighed, the pain and dizziness in her head pounding. She knew he meant to keep her warm. She wriggled slightly, trying to ease her discomfort, then drifted back to sleep.

First light came, obscured by a heavy mist. Marcus broke camp. He had the horse packed and a cold meal waiting when he woke Claerwen.

"How do you feel? Do you remember what happened?" he asked, helping her to sit up. He examined her face, testing the bruises Drakar had left. "Are any of your teeth loose?"

Claerwen ran her tongue along them, then shook her head. "How badly do I look?"

He grinned and handed her oatcakes to eat. "You will be fine in a few days. How do you feel about a long ride across the mountains?"

"Where are you taking me?"

He helped her to stand. "I know a safe place you can stay for a while, at least until I can take care of Drakar."

Claerwen froze, suddenly remembering he had killed three men. "Why didn't you kill Drakar instead?" she blurted.

"I would have killed him long ago, except he is a source of information I need. Over the years, I have tried to trap him as many times as he's tried to trap me; each of us always stays one step ahead of the other. Now I want to find out what it is he thinks you're hiding."

"You knew I was bluffing him?"

Marcus grinned broadly. "Aye. Damn, you were brave, Claerwen."

She frowned and replied, "No, I wasn't. I baited him so he would kill me quickly. I'd lost my fear of dying." Suddenly dizzy again, she walked to the horse and leaned heavily on the saddle.

Marcus clamped his mouth shut, stung by her response.

He pulled her around to face him, arranging the blanket more comfortably around her shoulders. "I'm sorry, Claerwen. I'm sorry that I somehow got you involved in this."

"It's not your fault. Drakar's misinformed. The same way the Irish were misinformed when they raided the valley where I was born. Ifan and Gerallt are probably using him as they did the Irish, using him to get whatever it is they want. There's nothing you can do about that now. All we can do is find out what this valuable thing is and why they want it."

Marcus studied her, awed that her logic had followed his own exactly, then softly said, "Aye." He lifted her onto the horse and hauled himself up in front of her again.

Claerwen could not identify where they were. She watched from behind Marcus' back as he doggedly followed an invisible track that she could not ascertain. She determined they were heading east and slightly south, judging by how the trees always leaned toward the east, pushed by the steady winds out of the west.

The area was covered in heavy brush and ancient oak trees, and she could see their journey would be difficult as she scanned the rising slopes of the mountains, snow lingering on their peaks. She knew two main roads ran southeast out of Caernarfon, one of which ran close to the stronghold called Dinas Brenin, an ancient hill fort that Vortigern was rumored to be rebuilding. The other, further east, crossed higher ground and sheer rocky crags. She thought that was the one Drakar had taken the day before. But Marcus had completely left behind any roads or tracks, staying deep in the forest and heading further east.

Movement was slow, Marcus pushing the horse through overgrown brush and fallen limbs. He concentrated deeply, silently keeping a steady pace, careful not to exhaust the horse. They moved in a fairly straight line until they reached a high ridge, then veered to a more southerly route.

The terrain gradually grew rougher and steeper, tiring the horse. Rocks appeared in the brush and the trees thinned out. By midday, the mist had lifted enough for the sun to warm the air. In spite of her constant headache and dizziness, Claerwen marveled at the beautiful wildness of the mountains, the clear, sparkling rivers, lush deep green foliage, and clumps of cheerful flowers. She felt it was a haven after the crowded and dirty town. Then she wondered how much of a haven it truly was if Drakar was following them. Would he find them? And could they fight off him and his soldiers?

Claerwen dashed the thoughts from her mind, telling herself to concentrate on staying upright on the horse. She was tiring again, getting groggier. She hung on to Marcus, leaning on him, tangling her arms in his belt.

Night came again, the rough peaks obscuring the light. The travelers stopped when Marcus found a rocky outcrop with an overhanging ledge they could crawl under for shelter. The mist had come up again, heavier than before, chilling them. Marcus made another cold meal, not daring to light a fire for warmth or cooking. He explained he would not risk that Drakar would find them because of a campfire. She shivered from the cold and dampness as she ate her food, too tired and ill to even taste it.

Claerwen curled herself into the shelter and fell instantly asleep, her back to the rocky wall. Marcus wedged himself in front, sharing an edge of the blanket. He faced outward, his sword unsheathed, its hilt in his fist.

He was awake, watching, at first light.

Claerwen wakened, surprised to discover that her arm was draped around Marcus, and he had tucked her hand up inside his tunic to keep it warm. For a few moments, she felt the rhythm of his breathing, her fingertips resting in a soft line of hair down the center of his belly. Then she rose up on her elbow to see over the bulk of his shoulders and saw the long sword lying in wait on the ground.

"You've seen them, haven't you?" she whispered.

"They are not following us, but going where they think we are headed."

"Can we trap them?"

Marcus rolled over. "After you are in a safe place. Then

I will trap them. I left them a false trail that should keep them busy for another day." She started to speak again, but he cut her off, "No, Claerwen. Let me finish this my way."

She sighed heavily. Marcus stroked her arm and asked, "Are you feeling any better? You don't look well." He made her lean towards him and he probed the bump on the back of her head. "This must still hurt you a lot. I've had some of those myself and sometimes it takes a few days for the headaches to go away. It feels like your eyes won't focus right. By tonight, there will be people who are able to help you."

"Where are you taking me?"

"Over that ridge," he pointed to the south, "is a small convent. They don't often take in visitors, but they will help someone in trouble. They call it 'sanctuary.' Drakar will not think to look for you there."

"Christian nuns?" she grimaced.

"Aye. It's only until I can get Drakar out of the way. I think you should give them a false name, when you enter."

Claerwen smiled ironically, telling him she had used a false name since she arrived in Caernarfon.

They trudged up the ridge, a steep, jagged rock-covered slope too difficult for the horse to climb with riders. Marcus strode, his arms hugging Claerwen to him, half-carrying her along. She panted hoarsely, her unclear vision making her stumble, but she never complained to him about the dreadful aching in her head or the sick feeling in her stomach. She kept one hand on his shoulder, rumpling his tunic where she grabbed it, her other hand hooked in his belt.

At mid-day, they topped the ridge. Far down the slope, on a small shelf of land formed by the confluence of two rivers, was a timber enclosure. Claerwen watched for a while and saw figures move among buildings and a courtyard within the walls. White-robed figures.

"By the light," she said to herself, sinking to her knees.

A moment later, a distant horn called, carried tentatively on the wind. Marcus' head shot up, listening intently.

"What is it?" Claerwen asked, alarmed by his reaction.
The horn called again.
"Damn," he swore. "Soldiers."
"Drakar?"
"Perhaps. I have to find out." He gazed at her, worry marking his brow. "Come with me so I can hide you."

He swung her up onto the horse, then began the descent of the slope, running with the lead rein down an obscure, narrow track. After a short way, he turned off to the left, hurling over scrub oak and gorse for several hundred yards. He came to a thick copse of hawthorn and ivy and halted, tethering the horse.

"Come," he called, reaching to Claerwen. She slipped down to him and he led her through the copse, into what appeared at first glance to be a cave.

"Stay here, until I come back." He gave her his pack of food and the waterskin.

"Marcus?" She followed him to the cave's entrance as he trotted back outside to the horse. He leapt onto the animal and wheeled around, spurring into a fast gallop across the mountainside, dust flying after him. "Be careful." she whispered.

Rain began to fall.

It was after midnight when he returned.

Claerwen had made a bed for herself on the floor and was rolled into the blanket. She was dreaming fitfully, not deeply asleep. Footsteps disturbed her, and her mind associated them with the dream. But then she realized she was awake and still hearing footsteps. They scraped louder, coming towards her. The cave was pitch dark; no starlight or moonglow could penetrate the heavy overhang of vines that covered its entrance. She held her breath, expecting Drakar's hard hand to strike her once more.

"Claerwen?" Marcus' voice called softly.

"Marcus!" she answered, relieved. She scrambled out of the blanket and, following the sound of his voice, found him.

"Wait, I will light a torch."

In the blackness, she saw sparks clicking from an iron and flint set. A tiny curl of smoke, then a flame, shot up from kindling. He dipped the end of a pine tar torch to the kindling and it ignited instantly, sputtering at first, then settling into a calm glow. He placed the torch in an iron bracket on the wall.

"You are feeling better," he said, watching her come towards him. She was clutching her torn dress.

"You came back! You're not hurt!" She saw he had changed his clothes and was wearing a dark brown leather tunic and breeches, tall boots, and a dark shirt. The sword was again strapped across his back.

She realized then she had not truly seen him through the daze of her semi-conscious state over the last two days. He had matured a lot since she had first met him in Dun Breatann. He had filled out into a compact, muscular, heavy-boned frame, trim but tough. He had not grown more, now at twenty-two years, but the poise and confidence that radiated from his rugged face made him seem taller and older than he truly was. The eyes were the same, guileless yet pervasive. His long, drooping moustache, thick and black like his hair, gave him the wildness of his mountain surroundings, and thin lines etched his bronzed skin in a pattern radiating from the corners of his deep-set eyes, tracing the time he had spent gazing into distance and glaring light.

"What happened?" she asked.

"Drakar is going back towards Caernarfon. He's still following my false trail. I will leave at daybreak, to go back and spring my trap."

"Then we'll know what he is looking for?"

"Hopefully. He certainly is insistent. It must be something of tremendous value." He sighed tiredly and sat on a stone bench in a corner, stretching his legs out.

Claerwen settled on another bench, and pondered, "I thought at first he was still angry that I did not fulfill the marriage contract."

Marcus shook his head. "I discredited him four years ago. Ceredig broke the contract for you and exiled him. By the time I knew my plan had worked, you were gone."

She was amazed at his words. "You mean I didn't need to go into hiding? He had no claim on me?"

"Not for a marriage. He turned into a rebel mercenary, working for Vortigern. Banishment infuriated him."

"I hope my cousin is all right. And the woman we lived with in Caernarfon. I wish I could let them know where I am going without endangering them."

"That would be impossible, at least for now."

She leaned back against the wall and sighed again, "I know. What is this place?" Claerwen asked, studying the cave.

"This is a temple built by the Romans hundreds of years ago to worship the god Mithras, the Roman soldiers' god. I found it when I was a boy and have never seen anyone else come here. I think I am the only one who knows it exists. Until now, that is," Marcus explained. He pointed out the remains of the altar stone and benches, and explained it was originally a depression in the rocky hillside that had been carved out into a temple. The entrance was supported by a dressed stone archway, and the hawthorns were planted to keep it secret. "It has not been used since sometime before the Romans left."

Marcus pulled a chunk of bread and some dried meat from a bundle he had brought, offering it to Claerwen.

"You saved my life," she said hoarsely.

He grunted in reply, "Drink some of this water. It's from a sweet spring just above the temple."

She sipped some, and chewed slowly on the bread, watching him. He was just as she remembered him from before, yet different. His intense black eyes still burned with profound purpose, matching her memory. But a rougher wildness, audacious, yet oddly gallant, now radiated from him, appealing strongly to Claerwen's spirit. She wondered why they had crossed again in another desperate race away from Drakar.

"You're a hunter now," Claerwen declared.

Marcus raised an eyebrow.

"Another disguise, for when you go back?"

"Aye." Marcus offered her more of the fresh, sweet water. She drank, and spilled the remaining few drops for the god of the spring.

"You are no Christian." He smiled at the politeness she had shown the god. He had done the same at the spring in thanks for letting him take the water.

"Will the nuns accept me?"

"They will help you, when they see your bruises and the torn dress. They may try to convince you of their faith; just don't let them persuade you to do something you don't want to do. Hopefully this will be over soon, and we can find a better place for you."

He studied her face. Even with the bruises, he could see the astonishing beauty was still there, only more evident with the fine etching her features had been given by the last four years. His eyes wandered down, admiring the womanliness of her figure that he glimpsed from the torn dress. He silently swore again at Drakar.

"Claerwen," he began as he came to sit next to her. "What happened after you left Dun Breatann?" He leaned his elbows on his knees, thoughtfully tapping his fingertips together.

Bitterness brought a stony look to her face. "One of Drakar's men burned our farm in Strathclyde to the ground, after he tried to poison my cousin and me."

Marcus stared at her as if he had not heard her right.

"How—" He could not finish his question. She watched a dozen questions form on his lips but he never spoke. He looked away from her, hurt in his eyes, then looked back again, still unable to ask.

She stopped him with a strange stare. Her pale green-blue eyes seemed to shine from within for a brief moment. "We survived the poison. A man helped us. Then I...he," she hesitated. She could not explain a vision. "The man told me what happened." It was not quite a lie; she believed Emrys had guided her through the vision.

She rested her face in her hands, her breath coming out in

a long, low moan. Her head pounded. "I saw you leave Dun Breatann. Then I overheard Drakar telling one of his men they had discovered you were there and where you were going. I stole a horse and rode with my cousin for home, hoping to warn you, but I couldn't find you."

Marcus' expression was a stony hardness that gradually softened as he studied Claerwen's face. His eyes went sad and he told her, "I was setting a trap for Drakar. I deliberately let him know I was in Dun Breatann. You should have stayed there, Claerwen. I would have come back for you."

She stared at him a long while, then her eyes closed, squeezing shut in knowing her own foolishness. "I spoiled it for you, didn't I?"

"No. I knew he had a trap for me and I tried to reverse it, to trap him instead, but it didn't work. Drakar escaped anyway." He suddenly changed directions in the conversation and asked, "Claerwen, do you have any idea what were they are looking for? Any guesses?"

"I just don't know. I have nothing. We never had anything since Irish the came. What could they be looking for?"

Marcus shrugged, then asked her to continue.

"My cousin and I were turning around to escape back through the woods when a warrior came upon us. A huge, horrible man, all in black leather. It must have been he who poisoned us because he was the last person we saw until we woke up. I thought he might have poisoned you as well, when I couldn't find you. Then we woke up somewhere along the road heading into Caernarfon. Probably left us for dead, and would be, if another man had not found us. He was a strange man himself, but he helped us. He made a potion that cleaned out the poison, then he took us to Caernarfon."

She sipped a little water and continued, "He told us the house and barn and everything were burned to the ground. Just like before." She looked up at Marcus, trying to read his thoughts. Then an idea came to her and she asked, "Do you know who he is? The one they call the Iron Hawk?"

He looked long into her eyes, his own blank. "I have not come across him."

She frowned hard at him and said, "But you must have heard of him in all of your...your spying?"

Marcus rose and paced across the temple, his arms crossed over his chest. "I have heard of him, but that is all, so far."

Claerwen studied her memory of the Iron Hawk in her mind and said with a throaty whisper, "I hope you never have to face him in a fight. In Caernarfon, I have heard it said he appears in all corners of Britain, picking the worst of fights, then disappears without a trace. It was said he fights like no other warrior born of mortals." Then she frowned again, looking from Marcus' face to his sword and back again. "Who are you? Truly?" she asked, realizing she knew absolutely nothing about him other than that he was kind, though sometimes stern, and he was always in a disguise.

Marcus brooded, leaning his upraised hands on the archway and staring grimly through the vines. He did not answer.

Claerwen rose slowly and crossed the temple. "Your name sounds Roman, but you look Celtic." As he turned to face her, she noticed the pattern of the heavy gold ring on his hand matched the design of his sword's pommel. She touched the ring, then pointed to the sword. "Hunters carry bows, not swords."

He was silent a few moments, deciding what to say. If he told her nothing, she would never trust him. Finally he began, "My family has defended land which Drakar wants as much as whatever he was looking for in yours. We are old Celtic from the times before the Romans ever heard of Britain. My grandmother was half-Roman, that is why the name, she insisted. We have been there since before Brutus was High King and have always defended it successfully." He pulled the sword from its scabbard and examined it. It was long and brilliantly sharp, with a simple gold hilt that curled down into rounded tips, the pommel's design a stylized pattern of birds enameled into it. Beautiful and magnificent, it could end a life with no effort.

"Of late, I am a soldier mostly," he concluded as he

slipped the sword back in its sheath. "And now we are back in the same mess we were four years ago, except Drakar is openly allied with Vortigern instead of hiding among our people."

Claerwen sensed she had intruded into his privacy and declined to inquire any further. Instead, she briefly touched her slender hand to his face, finding no words to say how pleased she was that he had found her. She did not realize it, but the look on her face told him all she wanted him to know.

A touch of embarrassment crossed Marcus' brow, but he did not show it. He found his attraction to Claerwen was as strong as it had been before, and he forced himself to keep a level head. He wondered if she would respond to him again, the same way she had before, and if he would give in to that attraction. He hesitated to become involved with her, to keep her from being forced to endure his problems and make her easier prey to Drakar. He was torn as he studied her face, craving to give in to his attraction, his steady good sense holding him back, knowing he could easily get her hurt again, or killed.

A sudden thought struck him and he reached for Claerwen's hand. "You don't know, do you?"

"Know what?" she asked, alarmed by the way he looked at her.

"I heard your mother died. About a year ago, I think. She was still in Dun Breatann."

Claerwen's mouth opened in astonishment, then slowly closed into a shaking line of grief. She turned away, moving back towards the stone seat and eased herself onto it. Marcus followed, and watched patiently as she licked her lips and drew a ragged breath.

"It took a long time for me to forgive her for the cold way she gave away our lives to that horrible man," Claerwen said softly. "She thought Drakar must be a good man, just because he was a high-ranking leader under Lord Ceredig. But she was so naive, so wrong. She never saw life beyond her own little circle, that sometimes things are not what they seem."

Marcus' brows furrowed. He muttered, mostly to himself,

"Aye, most of the time, that is true."

Claerwen missed his comment and continued, "I'm sorry she's gone. I'm sorry she died alone, none of us there with her."

Marcus reached to brush a tear from her cheek. "There was nothing you could do, Claerwen. In the end, we all die alone, anyway."

Her eyes came up and leveled with his, seeing the same depth of sadness in them as was in his voice. "You have seen a lot of death, haven't you?"

Marcus nodded slightly. "Aye. Too much."

Claerwen slid her arms around him and leaned her face into his chest, resting her brow there. He pressed his face into her hair, and he turned, embracing her deeply in his arms, accepting the compassion she offered.

The night paled toward first light. Softly he said, "It is time to go. I can't say when, but I hope soon I can resolve this fight with Drakar. Then you can be free to decide what you want to do." Marcus smiled his guileless smile. "I feel like we have known each other a long time."

"For all time." The thought came flying through Claerwen, her eyes glowing with the odd lightness. She shivered again. Marcus smiled, thinking she was being sweet.

Claerwen stood stiffly, and picked up the blanket, handing it to Marcus. He refused it, replacing it around her. She swayed slightly, exhaustion overwhelming her for a moment. He pressed his hands on her shoulders to steady her, becoming aware of her frailness. Then she looked up into his face, and her breath caught in her throat as she felt herself intensely drawn to him.

He folded her in his arms again, as if to give her a force of protection to take with her. He rubbed his face on hers, groping with his mouth until he found her lips and clung there, searching, yearning, craving the feel of her softness and warmth. As he pressed against her, he was reminded of fragile, ancient crystal. He drew back a moment, watching her eyes, and knew he could not stay away long. He ran his hands over her arms and down her back, stroking long and firm until she relaxed, comforted, and leaned into him like she was a kitten luxuriating on a warm hearthstone. She stopped clutching her dress and reached to run her arms around his neck, the blanket falling to the ground. She saw him glance down as her dress reopened, her breasts pushing up against his rough tunic. She opened her lips and met his, kissing him with a profound energy from far down within her soul.

Releasing her, Marcus grunted again, amazed at the depth of her response and at the way she compelled his thoughts. He took one of her hands and pressed a kiss into its palm, his moustache tickling her skin. Her eyes came up and she smiled, suddenly feeling a moment of freedom from the oppression of hiding all the years in Caernarfon. But the moment passed and she descended once more with the knowledge that the convent was only another place to hide.

Marcus scooped together the leftover food and the water skin, then brought his horse around to the temple archway. He lifted Claerwen into the saddle and leapt up behind her, pulling her back to lean on him as they rode down the slope. They stopped just beyond sight of the convent's oak gates.

Marcus vaulted off the horse and reached for Claerwen to slide down into his arms. Wordlessly, she searched his face. She understood that he wanted to remain anonymous, and she knew that one day he would tell her, that the time was not yet right. She smiled slightly and reached on tiptoes to brush his cheek with a kiss of gratitude. She turned to dash away to the gates, but Marcus held onto her, pulling her back to embrace her once more.

"I will come as soon as I can," he whispered, then finally let her go.

She sprinted to the gates, afraid she would not be able to break away if she lingered. When she glanced back after ringing the bell, she saw he was already on his way, galloping swiftly across the slope, back into the craggy mountains.

CHAPTER 7

Caernarfon
Spring, 467 A.D.

Alis heard the inn's front door open and close, footsteps moving across to the dining hall. She dragged herself from the kitchen; it was nearly midnight and she was weary from worrying, waiting for Claerwen and Grania to come home. In the hall she found a lone man who asked for supper and a few nights' hospitality.

When Alis returned to the kitchen, the back door slapped open, startling her. Grania stood there, momentarily staring at her, too choked up to speak at first. Then she stumbled in, gripping Alis' arms and sputtering.

"What is it? Where have you been? Where's Olivia?" Alis pulled her inside to the warmth of the hearth. Grania struggled to speak, tears filling her eyes. Finally she blurted, soft but frantic, "Olivia's not here?"

"No. I've been worried to distraction about you two. Where have you been?"

"I can't find her, Alis. She's disappeared! I looked everywhere, but there's not a trace of her. I was hoping she'd come home."

"What are you talking about? She can't just disappear!"

Alis shook Grania's shoulders slightly. She gazed into Grania's panic-struck face, then slowly sank down on the hearthstones, remembering what Claerwen had said about a scared feeling.

"Oh, by the light!" Alis cried and her blue eyes filled with dread.

"What? What do you know? Did she tell you something?"

"Oh, Julia." Alis picked up one of Grania's hands in her own, wringing it. She told Grania of Claerwen's uneasiness. "I don't know what to do."

"Do you really think it was Drakar?" Grania whispered.

"By the gods, I hope not." Alis stopped abruptly, remembering their guest. She and Grania rushed him through his supper and saw him to his room.

The night passed and Claerwen did not come home. Alis and Grania trudged through their routines, grateful they were not busy. Their only guest was the lone man. They sat silently in the kitchen until late, waiting and hoping between chores.

Two more days and nights passed, with no news. Their hope was fading, although they had heard nothing of Drakar being in the town.

Next morning, Grania served their guest breakfast, then retreated to stoke the fire pit. As she set her tray down, she burst into tears.

The man rose and strode slowly to Grania, then pressed a gentle hand to her shoulder. When she looked up, he asked, "Can I help, Mistress?"

Grania was startled that the man would ask, and even more startled by his sparkling blue eyes. Somehow, they looked out of place in his somber, drab face. She calmed quickly, and apologized for having disturbed him.

"Something bothers you terribly, Mistress. Please don't apologize. What is wrong?"

Grania hesitated, then confided, "My cousin hasn't come home for three nights and we're so afraid of what's happened to her. Someone must have taken her away." Grania sniffled, tears running down her cheeks.

"I'm sorry, Mistress. You don't know who would do such a thing?"

Grania shook her head. "There's only one man who would. An awful, terrible man called Drakar. But we haven't seen or heard that he's in Caernarfon."

"He is."

"What?!" Grania nearly backed away from the blue-eyed man. "How do you know?"

"I heard it in the marketplace yesterday. People were talking about him. He came with a small band of soldiers and took away a woman. But somehow she escaped."

"Are you sure?"

"Aye, that's what they said. She must have had help, though, to escape so many warriors."

Grania's eyes widened and she shrugged, "Why hasn't she come back here?"

"Perhaps the one who helped her is hiding her somewhere."

"But who? And where would they go? We don't know anyone." Grania chewed on a fingernail, trying to think of anyone Claerwen might have mentioned. Then her eyes sprang up to lock with the man's blue eyes. She said, "That means Drakar may come here to look for her, if she escaped and if he knows she was living here." She briefly thanked the man for his information and dashed back to the kitchen, to tell Alis what she had learned.

Drakar was camped outside the town walls with the surviving men from his group of soldiers. He was stretched out on a cot in his large tent, his head propped on a wadded cloak. He chewed on the tip of a leather thong that laced the front of his tunic. A tin cup of wine sat with a large wineskin next to him on the ground. His eyes were slightly out of focus from the drink.

A knock rapped at the tent pole framing the entrance.

"Come," Drakar said flatly.

A man wearing traveling clothes entered.

"Well?" Drakar frowned at the man.

"Nothing much, yet. They talk about the woman you look for, but she has not come back to the inn."

"Do they suspect you?"

"No. I'm sure of it."

"They don't mention anyone else, no man?"

"No one, Lord Drakar."

Drakar grunted and belched. "Any man at all? Remember, he can look like anybody. He is a master of disguise."

"No one at all. I got the younger woman to talk a little, but she could not think of anyone who would help her cousin."

"Damn that spy!" Drakar roared, getting up. "He must have brought her back here. He's got her hidden somewhere, and I wouldn't be surprised if he's got them just saying they don't know where she is." Drakar pounded a meaty fist on the man's chest. "Go back and keep listening! If you don't find out anything more by tonight and if she doesn't turn up somewhere, then I will go in myself. I'm not going to wait much longer." Drakar waved the man out and poured a great gulp of wine from the skin into his mouth.

The midnight bell had rung across Caernarfon. The town was quiet except for a dog barking somewhere. The air was still and heavy; starlight only hinted at the shadows. Alis was still up, wandering aimlessly around her kitchen, even though Grania had gone to her room.

A clattering skittered across the tiled roof and made Alis jump. She went to the rear door and made sure the lock was secured. It was. Another sound came from the front of the inn. Footsteps.

Must be their guest returning to his room, Alis thought. She turned to go look in the entrance hall. Then she halted.

Drakar stood in the middle of the room, sword drawn.

Alis screamed before she realized an instant later that she should have stayed quiet. Now Grania would hear her and come back from her room. The tension of the last days had broken her usual steadfast calm.

Drakar lunged forward and pushed Alis back into the kitchen. He told her to be quiet, circling the point of his sword in her face.

"Sit! There!" He poked a finger towards a stool. Alis sat and watched the sharp tip hover again in front of her face. "What do you know about the woman called Claerwen?" he demanded.

Alis shivered with fear and stammered out a soft, "I do not know anyone called Claerwen."

The sword jabbed closer. "You're lying. I know she calls herself Olivia. Where is she now? And don't lie."

Before she could answer, Grania skidded into the kitchen.

Drakar whirled on her, his blade flashing in the lantern light. She backed away, eyes terrified. She sidled toward Alis.

"Good! Now I don't have to look for you, too." He turned back to Alis. "Talk!" he ordered.

Alis, on the verge of hysteria, fumbled for words, and every time Drakar threatened her with the sword, she panicked more.

"I d-don't know. We haven't seen her. We don't know where she is."

"Don't lie to me! I know she's hidden here somewhere! She's got something I want, and you're going to tell me where she is!"

"Stop it! Stop it!" Grania screamed at Drakar.

"Get out of the way!" He yelled back and smacked Grania across the face with the back of his hand. She fell against a table, knocking over an oil lantern. She plopped onto the floor in front of the table, her eyes out of focus from the stunning blow.

Drakar's anger rose uncontrollably. He screamed at Alis to tell him where Claerwen was hidden. She whimpered, telling him over and over that she did not know where the woman was. He slid the sword back in its scabbard and pulled a dagger from his belt. Then he bent over Alis, the blade at her throat, and sneered into her face. His stale breath sickened her until she thought she would vomit on him.

Alis watched his face change suddenly. His angry, bulging blue eyes clouded over in a deeper frown and his mouth froze in mid-scream. He backed away slowly.

Behind him, out of the shadows, a black figure emerged, a big, heavy sword pricked Drakar through his leather tunic. Slowly Drakar turned around to face the man. The sword waved at the dagger and Drakar's hands rose up in supplication.

"You!" Drakar spat. He moved suddenly, faster than his bulk would indicate he could move, and flipped the knife around, hurling it at the shadowy man.

The man dodged with a controlled, easy agility. The dagger stuck and hummed in an oak beam behind him. Drakar backed up and drew his own sword.

"Guards!" Drakar bawled for his men. He and the warrior circled, each waiting for the other to begin the fight. "Guards!" he screamed again. No one came.

"You killed them, didn't you? Like you always do. Iron Hawk!" Drakar spat in contempt and anger that betrayed the fear in his voice.

The Iron Hawk did not answer.

Grania was rousing out of her grogginess and jolted awake when she heard the dark warrior's title. She looked up and recognized the strange visored helmet. She was too stunned to scream.

The two men lunged and feinted several times, as if warming to the fight, then began in earnest. Drakar swung hard, using more brawn than thought, sweat pouring off his face and body, making the stench that filled the room heavier than ever. The Iron Hawk easily parried and ducked Drakar's advances, his enormous sword clanging hard and powerful as it hit Drakar's weapon. They circled again, each one's eyes concentrated on the other's moves.

Grania crawled to Alis and whispered in her ear, "We must try to get out while they fight." Alis nodded slightly and tried to stand. Her legs were so weakened from her fear, she sat down hard on the stool, too paralyzed to try again.

The warriors' fight began to take on a wildness of desperation. The swords rang constantly, boots scuffling across the tessellated floor. Firelight flashed from the blades as they flew faster and harder. The Iron Hawk appeared to have the advantage over Drakar with his superior concentration, but he could not advance against the mercenary's furious strength. Both men had cuts, all minor, their blood dripped in spatters across the floor. Furniture in the way was tossed aside like children's toys. Drakar, backed up against the table where he had knocked Grania, was fighting hard. The Iron Hawk heaved his sword, slashing down, but Drakar slipped aside, barely getting grazed. The sword crashed through the table, splitting it in half. The spilt lamp oil splashed across the floor towards the fire pit. It ignited.

Tiredness slowed the warriors, and they grunted with each blow. They circled each other again, taking advantage of the rest it gave them. Then the Iron Hawk suddenly began working his sword with incredible speed, whipping it in a flashing pattern of whirls and spins in front of him that mesmerized Drakar. Then he lunged and dove, sure he had Drakar cornered.

But Drakar still had enough strength to whirl away, his sword slashing back. He had been close to the cowering women, huddled in a corner. His blade, arcing towards the Iron Hawk, caught Alis and sank into her neck before he pulled it forward to plunge. Grania screamed as Alis died in her arms.

Drakar missed the dark warrior, who booted him and sent him sprawling face-down across the room. He rolled and crouched, then leapt. The Iron Hawk crashed his sword again on Drakar's, driving it down. But Drakar rushed forward, smashing his shoulder into the man's stomach, and knocked him against a support beam. The Iron Hawk went down hard, stunned.

By now the lamp oil fire was leaping from broken table and stool, to dry leather curtains, to anything that would burn. Smoke choked the kitchen. Drakar coughed hard and felt the smoke burn his throat. He could barely see the Iron Hawk lying still at his feet, flames creeping towards him. Drakar backed away, sheathing his sword as he moved. He paused at the doorway leading outside, hauling in great gulps of fresh air, then grinned slyly as he realized his work was done. They would all die in the fire. Drakar fled into the darkness.

The Iron Hawk lay flat on his back, his sword still in his grip. Dizziness rolled across his senses as he tried shaking his head to clear away the stunning blow. Pain shot through his neck and upper back when he moved, but he forced himself to roll to one side. When his eyes focused, he saw flames coming straight toward him.

With a grunt, he heaved himself onto his hands and knees, sheathed his sword, and crawled around the flames toward the corner where Alis and Grania had been. He found Alis dead, her blood draining across the floor. Next to her, Grania had fainted. Swiftly, he picked her up and carried her out of the building through the back door. In the rear garden, a grey stallion waited, nervously watching the smoke and flame through a window. The Iron Hawk laid the unconscious woman across the horse's withers and he leapt up behind her. In a flurry of tossed mud, they disappeared into the black shadows of the night.

CHAPTER 8

**The mountains of Eryri, Gwynedd
Spring, 467 A.D.**

"Lady Olivia?"

The soft voice drifted out of the dreamy mists.

"Please wake now, Lady Olivia."

Claerwen lay curled on one side, resting quietly after two nights with a slight fever. Her headaches were slowly subsiding and her eyes were able to fully focus. Sun streamed through a window cut in the timber wall, rinsing the whitewashed walls of the spare cell and warming her pale face.

"There is someone here you need to see. Are you able to come?"

Claerwen stirred, her eyes struggling open. "Someone for me?"

"Aye, please come quickly."

Claerwen finally woke enough to recognize the abbess of the convent leaning over her. Ashamed at her lethargy in the presence of the abbess, she quickly sat up and dragged at the bed covers.

"I am sorry I am so slow. I will be ready in a minute." The abbess went outside to wait.

Claerwen wondered who would want to see her. She

pulled on her shift, then her overtunic, both new, clean and white, provided by the nuns. Then she suddenly stopped. It must be Marcus. No one else knew she was there. Unless Drakar had found out...

"No," she told herself. Drakar would invade; Marcus would visit. She pulled a comb roughly through her thick hair, hurrying, excited at the idea that he would come back so soon to see her. Tangles slowed her down and she groaned with impatience. She did not bother to put on shoes; they were still muddy from the long trek over the mountains.

Claerwen opened her door and stepped into the hall. The abbess silently led her to another room, and Claerwen wondered why Marcus would be waiting for her in a cell and not in the courtyard. The abbess opened the cell's door, then softly padded away, returning to her own chamber. Once inside, Claerwen could not believe her eyes.

"Julia!"

Her cousin lay on a cot identical to the one in her own room. In fact, the entire room was the same: whitewashed walls, a simple cot, a hardwood chair, a table, one wooden crucifix on the wall, and a tiny window. Another white overtunic and shift lay neatly folded on the chair. There were no other decorations or floor coverings. It was bleak, but spotlessly clean, like the white clothing.

Grania was awake, and her face was red and slightly swollen on the right side. She seemed tired and listless. Her old clothing was piled on the floor next to the chair. It was sooty and muddy, blood stains showing in patches.

"By the gods! What happened? Why are you here? How did you know I was here?" Claerwen knelt next to the bed.

"Olivia—" Grania reached to Claerwen's outstretched hand. She started to cry.

"What happened?" Claerwen asked again softly.

"It was awful. I'm not even sure I know what happened." Grania tried to sit up, to see her cousin better. "We were so afraid you'd been killed. We heard what happened at the market, and that somehow you had escaped. But we didn't know where you were. And then Drakar came to the inn to find out. He thought you were hidden there, that someone had helped you. But we didn't know and he wouldn't stop screaming. Then that other man came and they fought. Oh, it was awful!" Grania's words rushed out as the memories overwhelmed her, then she broke into sobs.

Claerwen slipped her arms around Grania and hugged her, dabbing at tears with a kerchief. "What other man?" she asked gently.

"The one..." Grania choked, "the one called the Iron Hawk! The one who poisoned us!"

Claerwen caught her breath. Slowly she rose, and leaned on the wall, staring out of the window. She had fully expected Grania to describe Marcus in his hunter's disguise. Many questions came to her, but she remained speechless as she pondered which one to ask first. Finally she chose, and frowned with dread at Grania. She asked, slow and distinct, "Where is Alis?"

Grania's eyes flowed with more tears. "She's dead."

Claerwen spat out her thought, "The Iron Hawk killed her, didn't he? Like he tried to kill us, for Drakar!"

Grania pulled herself upright in the bed. "No! Listen to me. He fought Drakar. He tried to kill Drakar." She could see Claerwen did not believe her. "It is true! They are enemies! Alis was killed when Drakar swung his sword at the Iron Hawk."

Grania stopped, thinking to herself. Then she looked up at Claerwen. "That must be how I got here! The Iron Hawk must have brought me. But why here? And where is this place?"

"I was told the mountains are called Eryri. That's all I know. Drakar must have found out I was here and told him. Then Drakar will be here soon, too."

"Unless the Iron Hawk has found Drakar first and killed him. He would have come by now."

"Or, Mar— " Claerwen caught his name in her throat. Hope rose inside her, that Marcus had finally trapped Drakar. She craved to tell Grania about him, but heeded his warning and held her thought. Perhaps he would appear soon with good news.

"What?" Grania asked.

"But why didn't the Iron Hawk kill Drakar there? I thought he was supposed to be so good." Contempt laced her tone.

"Oh, Olivia, you should have seen them. They were both so terrible. I have never seen such a vicious fight. Drakar came so close to being killed so many times, but he always managed to worm his way out of it. I don't know how it ended. I guess I passed out. A fire started somehow and there was smoke everywhere."

Claerwen looked over at the filthy clothing on the floor, now understanding why it was sooty, and bloody. The mud was from the journey to the convent.

"Did he tell the nuns anything when he left you here?"

"Not a word, I understand. I woke up in this room. I don't remember coming here. They said a stranger left me in front of the gates, rang the bell, and rode off like a mad man. When they said I was the second woman to be brought here, I told them my name was Julia and asked if Olivia was the other woman. When they said yes, I was so relieved. They told me you were ill and would not let me see you until you were better. Oh, Olivia!"

Claerwen continued to stare at the clothing. "Mad man, I should say. They are all mad," she muttered to herself.

"How did you escape?" Grania interrupted Claerwen's thoughts.

Claerwen continued to peer out of the window slit, wishing she could find a way to help Marcus, to keep him safe against Drakar and the Iron Hawk. She turned back to Grania, her face forced into a determined blankness. She answered, "A farmer helped me, and showed me how to get here. He told me the nuns would give me sanctuary."

Claerwen resettled on the edge of the bed and hugged her cousin tightly. She told Grania no more.

A fortnight later, a bard arrived at the convent, seeking a night's hospitality. Bards were very highly esteemed and this one was given as close to royal treatment as was possible for a simple and neglected religious house. They could not afford to offend the bard, as he could delegate them to the dregs of history through his witty songs. To protect a bard was to protect knowledge; these special men carried enormous quantities of history and technology in their memories, and they were among the few people able to read and write.

Everyone was invited to hear the bard sing and tell his stories. No one refused. A wide flagged ledge in the courtyard served as a stage, set with a simple chair. The hour was dusk, and several torches were lit, giving the yard a welcoming glow. As the convent's residents gathered, they chattered in hushed voices, eager for the bard to begin. Most had neither heard nor seen one before, knowing only that he was someone to be immensely enjoyed.

Presently, the man arrived, a small traveling harp under one arm. He wore dusty clothes, heavy boots, a long cloak, and a worn cap of dark grey wool, probably all meant to give the impression of having been everywhere in the world. He looked mysterious, as all bards were thought of, grey-haired and bearded, his face heavily shadowed under the hood of his cloak.

He sat on his stage, whipping back the cloak for freedom to play, also for the effect of making himself appear more dashing. After all, the audience was all women.

Then he began to tune the harp, slowly, carefully. He smiled, surveying the audience, gazing into a pair of eyes here, seeking a face there. He could hear the women whispering to each other. He smiled again.

"Good evening," he greeted them.

The women responded with polite answers.

He played sweet, melodious rolls of music as he continued to look into various faces, grinning charm out into the sea of white-veiled heads, a few uncovered ones interspersed among them. Seemingly satisfied that his audience was ready, he began the story of Leir and his three daughters. His deep, resonant voice matched the beauty of the harp, and soon he had the entire group enthralled, the tones rising and falling with the flow of the story. At the tale's end, the nuns applauded him roundly, and a few called for another story, this one for Cuchulain, another for familiar Branwen.

"He is very good, is he not, Julia?" Claerwen asked her cousin.

"Aye." The cousins stood at the rear of the watching group. Tired from their chores, neither felt like standing a long time to listen to the bard, but the abbess had persuaded them the cool evening air would be refreshing. They had never seen a bard before, and gave in to their curiosity.

"Come, Julia. We can see better over there. And we can sit down, too," Claerwen whispered. Grania started to protest, but Claerwen was already pulling her by the arm to a corner next to the ledge. They sat in the quiet shadows of the courtyard's edge.

"They will have an ague if we trample their plants." Grania remarked.

"Hush!" Claerwen scolded. She was only interested in enjoying the music.

The songs continued for a long time, the bard centering each one on a specific part of his audience. He made many of the group feel as if he was singing something special, just for that individual woman. He came to a romantic song, about a beautiful princess from Erin who was nearly lost by her lover when an evil giant kidnaped her. And as he began the song, he turned his face toward the corner where Claerwen and Grania sat.

"He likes you, Olivia," Grania whispered, mischief in her eyes. The entertainment had brought out her natural cheerfulness.

"Do not be silly!"

"He does. Look! He's gazing right into your eyes!"

"Hush, you see romance in everything!"

Grania sighed. The man smiled. Indeed, he was gazing intently into Claerwen's face, and she found herself in an unnerving return stare.

The song continued, building into a suspenseful climax. The hero was trying to rescue his heroine from the ugly giant by hiding her in an old Mithraen temple on the side of a hill at dawn.

Mithraen temple? On a hill? Claerwen realized she had not been paying attention, only dreamily listening to the man's voice. She began to concentrate intently on the words, staring hard at him. Suddenly, her mouth dropped open and her hand gripped Grania's arm.

"What is it?" Grania asked sharply, caught unaware by the sudden pain in her arm.

Claerwen did not answer. Marcus' eyes were watching her, the tiny lines around them crinkled up into a grin.

"Nothing, nothing," she whispered. "Just a cramp."

Mist soaked the air at first light. Nothing could be seen more than a few feet away. Claerwen was thrilled; the gods were protecting her by sending the fog. She silently crossed the walled-in square where Marcus had sung the night before, stepping lightly to the barred gate. No one was out yet as she pulled at the heavy oak door, opening it just enough to squeeze through, then pulling it shut again, hearing the latch click.

Although still very dark, the mist was a shade paler to the east, barely enough diffused light to show her the gravel track up the hill. The air was cold, but refreshing after so many days in the stuffy convent.

Claerwen found the temple easily. The ground at the entrance was extremely muddy, water having dripped from the clogging vines in the archway. Carefully, she pushed them aside and tiptoed around the mud puddle. Inside was dry, with only a hint of dampness. She shook water droplets from her new woollen cloak, glad to be wrapped in its warmth.

The temple was very dark inside; only a trickle of light eased its way through the vines.

"Marcus?" she softly called. No answer.

Disappointment set in, followed by doubt. She worried if

she had heard him right, had he truly meant the temple at dawn? Or had she only wanted to hear that, had she truly even seen Marcus, only wanting to be with him again. She had been so certain.

She realized how strongly she liked Marcus, how his rough wildness belied the steady, deep strength he radiated. Though she knew nothing else about him, his bold courage and quiet charisma told her enough that she could trust him implicitly. And she knew she liked the way she was almost uncontrollably drawn to him, and the way he kissed her and touched her.

Claerwen sighed, trying to relieve the tension building inside her. She disliked being alone in the dark temple. She knew she was probably safe, but worried that Marcus had not come. Huddling on one of the stone benches, she pondered what had happened to her.

She thought of life as a trap. One moment it all seemed so terribly important, and in the next, there was nowhere to go, nowhere to run. Marriage would have been a worse trap than the inn or the convent; at least marriage to someone like Drakar would have been worse. Was that all life offered, or did the gods have anything more worthwhile out there? And was that a question everyone asks sometime in their life, or do most people take it all for granted the way her mother had?

Claerwen stood and paced the floor, light slowly gathering strength outside as sunrise approached. She stepped on a pebble, hurting her foot, then picked up the offending rock. Pacing a few more turns, she threw it, hard enough for it to crack on the stone wall and drop in pieces onto the dusty floor.

"I would not upset Mithras if I were you."

Claerwen whirled at the voice. Marcus leaned casually in the archway, arms crossed, his cloak thrown back over his shoulders, the cap pushed forward. He grinned jauntily at her.

"I thought I had misunderstood," she said, rushing to him.

He opened his arms, the cloak hanging from them like flowing drapes, and he folded them around her. She leaned into him comfortably, and raised her face to meet his kiss.

"I wanted to talk with you privately," he said afterward, settling with her on one of the stone benches. He laughed, "I could have come dressed as a priest and 'heard' your confession, but I don't trust a religious house to keeps its ears closed."

She touched his hair, frowning when a powdery substance came off on her fingers.

"It's just ash," he said, still grinning. "My hair really is black."

Claerwen mused, "Unbelievable. I really didn't know it was you, at first. Everything was so different, even your voice. It was your eyes that gave you away." Then she blurted, "Have you heard what happened to Grania? And Alis, the woman we lived with?"

He let her tell him Grania's news. She finished, then added slowly, "I can tell by your face that Drakar escaped again. He will surely show up here soon. If the Iron Hawk knows of this place, so will Drakar." She sensed his frustration and a deeper uneasiness.

Marcus said somberly, "The Iron Hawk is not Drakar's man. And he did not bring your cousin here. He left her outside the burning inn. I found her when I went back into Caernarfon. When I left the town, to bring her here, I saw he had taken the heads of Drakar's men and stuck them on pikes outside the town gates as a warning to Drakar."

Claerwen's eyes opened wide, stunned by the gruesome description. She covered her mouth as her stomach wrenched, feeling sick.

Marcus winced at the pain his news caused. He took one of her hands between his, stroking it to comfort her.

Her brows arched down as she asked, "If he isn't Drakar's man, who *is* he? Whose side is he on? Why did he poison Grania and me, then pull her out of a burning building, and kill Drakar's men, but not Drakar? It makes no sense!"

Marcus calmly watched Claerwen's distressed perplexity, and quietly answered, "I can't say why. As I unravel the reasoning behind Drakar's behavior, perhaps the Iron Hawk's will emerge as well."

She studied his eyes. "You stay so calm, so level-headed through all of this. How do you keep from getting angry or upset?"

His mouth pressed into a flat line and he answered, "I've been doing this a bloody long time." He paused, and changed directions of thought, "Actually, this time I do not want to talk of trouble. I came to see you, to see how you are." He cupped a hand behind her head, feeling for the bump Drakar caused.

"It's much better. The headaches are gone. You've always been so kind to me. And I always keep getting in your way."

Marcus chuckled softly at her comment. "And why should I be anything other than kind to you? Claerwen, somehow I've gotten you involved in my 'business,' in spite of how I've tried to prevent it. I wish I could make amends."

"Amends! For what? You saved my life. You brought my cousin here. You've done so much for us already. That makes us more than even."

She smiled and studied his hands as they held hers. They were huge, husky and long-fingered, scarred from hard work. She realized then they were the same hands she had seen in the vision of Lord Ceredig's house and she understood how he had discredited Drakar. She said, "I wish so much there was something I could do to help you."

Marcus' face clouded, and he answered, "Just stay in the convent until I come to tell you Drakar is gone. Just stay safe for me."

"What are you going to do next?"

"You know all you need to know for now," he said, his voice stern, but he touched her face, gently brushing it with his fingers.

"Something bothers you very much, Marcus. Something you don't want to tell me, but I can see it in your eyes."

He bowed his head a few moments, then looked up again, his eyes locking with hers. He said, "It will come down to war between Drakar and me. Soon. If not within the next few weeks, then surely by Beltainne."

Marcus paused, hating what he'd just said. He watched Claerwen try to keep fear from showing in her eyes as she waited patiently for him to begin again. Grimacing, he spoke further, "Drakar continues to pull in Saxon mercenaries for Vortigern through Ifan and Gerallt, and Vortigern rewards him with their use. I've slowed them down, sabotaging their plans countless times now, but I just can't stop them. And if Drakar wins, the High King will take everything he wins from him. I doubt if Drakar even realizes that; his vanity is too large for him to see what's happening. Perhaps Drakar believes he is using Vortigern to gain power and intends to cross the king. Drakar will never win against Vortigern."

Claerwen drew a long breath, then asked, "If Drakar cannot win against Vortigern, then how can you win against both of them?"

"I have Cunedda's backing. And I know Vortigern will be coming into the area in the next few days. I have some ideas to play Drakar and Vortigern against each other, hopefully to distract them from us, perhaps they might even destroy each other."

"You don't really plan ahead much, do you?"

"It's impossible, because I never know what to expect, like when Drakar captured you. I was in and out, then back into that disguise faster than I've ever changed before," he laughed. "I figure it out as I go along, mostly."

"I've never seen anyone with such audacity, the way you confronted those guards!"

Marcus pulled a wry smile, then rose and strode to the archway, peering through the vines. "It's raining."

Claerwen followed him, and watched the large drops pattering the ground, splashing into puddles and starting rivulets through the scree.

Marcus suddenly turned to her and declared, "Claerwen, I brought something for you." He reached inside his tunic and pulled out a small cloth bag, placing it in her hands. "Ceredig was holding these for you. They were your mother's things. I sent for them."

She fingered the cloth, warm from being inside his tunic. "You did that? For me?"

His eyes grinned and he nodded.

"Oh, thank you!" She opened the bag and briefly checked its contents. "She never had much, most of it was purely sentimental, trinkets and jewelry my father gave her a long time ago. But I am so pleased to have them, Marcus. Thank you!"

Marcus saw sadness in her eyes in spite of her gratitude. His arms came up around her protectively and she pressed her face into his tunic. He pushed her chin up with one hand, gazing into her face.

"Claerwen, what's wrong?"

Tears hung in her eyes. She dragged in several deep breaths, trying to calm herself and dried her eyes on her sleeve.

"All my talk of war and politics has upset you, hasn't it? And then I remind you of your mother's death."

"I was thinking of Alis, the woman we lived with. I miss her. She was more of a mother to us than my own mother was."

"Damn," he muttered and hugged her closer. He spoke softly, "I'm sorry, Claerwen. Perhaps if I'd reached Caernarfon earlier, I could have done something to help her."

"'Twas not your fault," Claerwen countered.

Marcus grunted, grimacing his frustration. "I've tried to make things different. I've seen how men will always fight for the things they want from other men. I don't understand that myself, though I'm a warrior. I taught myself the art of the spy originally to stop the fighting, but it just never ends. I had hoped that war could be averted, through the right knowledge. But the knowledge comes so bloody hard, and rarely soon enough. If we could just win our freedom from the outsiders..."

"When the great future king comes." Claerwen's voice bounced softly from the stone walls.

"Eh?" Marcus responded.

She did not answer. She swayed slightly until her eyes

came into focus.

Marcus felt his stomach twist, realizing what had occurred. He grunted involuntarily, unnerved. "It happened again," he mumbled.

She looked up at him, her eyes questioning.

"Claerwen," he hesitated, his lips pressed and unpressed together, then he asked, "You spoke like that before, once in Dun Breatann, once here. Do you have what they call 'second sight?'"

"Second what?"

"Do you have visions? I think it's also called 'fire in the head.'"

"You know what it is?"

"I have heard of it. I've never been sure I've seen it till now."

She searched his eyes for a long while, then whispered, "It comes like a voice sometimes, telling me what to say, no... forcing me to say...things. Or like a dream. When I said the man on the road to Caernarfon told me what the Iron Hawk did, that was not true. It was a vision in the fire. He only guided me. I *saw* the Iron Hawk burn the homestead. I *saw* the bundle of papers you exchanged in Lord Ceredig's house. Marcus..."

She stopped when his lips pressed on hers. Her thought vanished as she moved her hands against the strength of his back, feeling knotted muscles beneath the leather tunic.

Marcus pulled his cap off, tossing it to the bench, missed, not caring. His big hands curled into her long, soft hair, then slipped around her slender waist; he felt he could wrap himself around her as if to completely envelop her. She clung to him, warming to his solidity and strength.

At length, their kiss ended, and he nuzzled her neck, kissing, tickling with his beard, one side, then the other. Claerwen tipped her head back, smiling, savoring.

"I wish I could stay longer, Claerwen," he whispered finally. "I wish..." He studied her face, an aching in his own.

She reached up and touched his brow, trying to remove the heaviness there. Then she smiled and drew him back into another indulgent kiss.

Afterward, his mouth flickered nearly into a smile, but the aching came back into his face. Then he dug into a pocket inside his tunic. He pulled out a ring, a copy of the large one he wore on his left hand and pressed her fingers around it. "If you need me, if anything happens, leave this in the basin of the spring above the temple. Keep it hidden always; you know why. If you leave it there, it will be brought to me, and I will understand. I will come."

Claerwen nodded, gazing at the ring. The gold glittered back at her, and she realized the rain had stopped. The clouds were lifting, brightening the temple. She looked up into Marcus' black eyes and saw years of loneliness in them.

Once more they embraced, naturally, as if they had always been lovers. Tenderly, Marcus kissed her cheek, telling her if there was any way he could, he would come back soon. She reached up and caressed his face, fascinated that out of his rough appearance came such gentleness.

"You have to go back now, to wherever it is you must go, I can see it in your face," she said very quietly, "I will miss you." She squeezed his hands and slipped out through the ivy before she would allow herself to give in to tears again.

CHAPTER 9

Eryri, Gwynedd
Spring, 467 A.D.

Days later, Marcus trudged slowly up the stone steps to the main hall of the fort. His head drooped, exhaustion dragging on him. He carried his sword and shield as if they were afterthoughts, such as a child might absently carry an extra piece of clothing that was too warm to wear.

The hall was empty, being the middle of the night. The heavy oak doors thumped shut behind him as he dragged his feet over the plank floor. He clanged the sword and shield on the table nearest the fire pit and stood still a moment, glowering fiercely, not at anything in particular, just needing calmness and silence. Then he sighed tiredly, and sat on the table's bench. Within seconds, he was asleep, his head resting half on his left arm, half on the shield.

Several hours passed, and first light crept softly into the hall. Marcus' father, Iorwerth, shuffled in through the rear door. At sixty years of age, shuffling was the fastest pace he could obtain anymore. He had been ill much of the last year, his body giving in to its many years, and he had reluctantly given his responsibilities to Marcus.

Iorwerth headed toward his sleeping son, a son he had

always been enormously proud of. "Marcus?" he called. He stopped across the table from him and stared at Marcus' dust-covered hair, then realized blood was crusted into dried mud on his right shoulder.

"Padrig!" Iorwerth yelled for his seneschal. "Good Mithras, what happened?" He came around the table, calling again for Padrig. Taking care, he woke Marcus, relieved that he was only sleeping. Padrig ran in from the hallway that led from the kitchen, saw the dried blood, and spun to fetch his ointments and bandages before Iorwerth could give the orders.

"Marcus, what happened?"

Groggy from sleep and exhaustion, Marcus looked into his father's eyes, momentarily confused, then winced.

"Padrig is coming. Let me look at your shoulder."

"It's only a graze, Da. Don't worry over it. It's Owein we must worry about."

"Owein? He is hurt, too? Where is he?"

"He's not hurt. But..." Marcus drifted off, a wave of tiredness and pain passing through him.

Padrig ran back in, a basket full of ointment vials and rags for bandages in one hand and a bowl of water in the other. Carefully, he stripped Marcus of his heavy leather tunic and shirt, then examined the wound. It was not deep, but was long and jagged, running a few inches down from the top of his shoulder. Skillfully, Padrig cleaned and treated the arm to protect it from fever and numb the pain, then wrapped it in clean bandages. As he packed his supplies, he said he would bring food for both Marcus and his father.

Iorwerth eased himself onto the bench opposite Marcus and asked again, "Now, tell me what is wrong."

"I do not understand." Marcus stared, pondering, mumbling mostly to himself.

His father cocked a ragged grey eyebrow.

"It makes no sense." Marcus slapped a hand on the table that made his gear jump. His eyes burned dark and grim when he looked into Iorwerth's face. He examined the shirt, cut and filthy, and tossed it back on the table.

Iorwerth waited for Marcus to gather his thoughts, watching his son brood, rise from the table and pace the floor. Finally Marcus confided, "Owein was to maintain the eastern border through the night. He was not there. Not one man of his patrol was there. It was like an open sea. Empty!" He pounded a fist on the table again. "I do not understand. It's just not something my cousin would do, no?"

"No, he wouldn't," replied the older man quietly, surprised by the news. "Have you spoken with him yet?"

"Only briefly. He came in when he should have left. So did the patrol assigned after his."

"Was it just a misunderstanding?"

"Owein decides the patrols himself. We all know that. And he double and triple checks, so that every man understands and remembers his instructions. Has he ever made such a careless mistake?"

Iorwerth shook his head in disappointment.

Marcus slowly pulled on his tunic, wincing. "I must go." Marcus reached to gather his gear.

"But you have to eat, boy!" Padrig blurted as he came in with a platter of food. He was nearly Iorwerth's age and had been with the family so long that they often forgot he was not related; he treated Marcus like a grandson.

"Son, you have been out there every day and night for weeks now. You cannot go on like this."

"I must, Da. I must if this is more than just a mistake." He asked Padrig to pack the food so he could take it with him.

His father asked, "What do you believe? Mistake or something more serious?"

They both avoided words like treachery, plotting, disloyalty. They did not want to associate such ideas with Owein, even in their minds. Not Owein, who was more of a brother to Marcus and a son to Iorwerth than Marcus' younger brother Taran had ever been, though no one ever dared admit it aloud.

"I cannot say yet," Marcus answered. He picked up the

sword and pulled it from its scabbard. He stroked the blade, almost sensuously, cleaning it with one of Padrig's leftover rags.

"What will you do?"

"For now, watch, wait. Not make assumptions. And I must be careful. If he is the problem, we can not afford to scare him into making a bigger problem."

"Aye, I agree. You have learned well, my son." Iorwerth sighed, tired, rising to help Marcus buckle the sword across his back.

"Please, Da, stay here by the fire."

"Aye, Marcus, I feel it will not be too much longer that I will be here to give this old fire pit my company."

"Nonsense!" Marcus shot back, ignoring his father's comment, but knowing it was probably true.

"You haven't told me how you were wounded."

"A bandit. He was alone and wore no badge. In my frustration with Owein and my tiredness, he surprised me. Then he fled so quickly, I had no chance to return the favor." He shrugged the bandaged shoulder. "I didn't give chase; the border is more important."

Padrig came with a pack full of food. As Marcus took it from him and picked up his gear, the front doors slapped open, setting the dust to flight. Marcus' brother Taran charged in, anger radiating from him like a smoke from burning green wood. Though he had a striking, chestnut-brown resemblance to Marcus, he carried arrogance and a disrespectful defiance as stubbornly as Marcus carried calmness and assured authority. The difference in their personalities became acutely apparent as Taran marched to Marcus and blocked him from moving away from the table.

"Where's Owein?" Taran demanded.

"On patrol, why?" Marcus glared stiffly at his brother.

"You are here, and you haven't heard?" Taran's voice was thick with contempt. "The storage buildings have been raided. Most of our supplies have been stolen or ruined. We barely have enough to get through spring now."

"Who did it?" their father asked.

"Probably bandits. Or Drakar's men. But there were no guards! They were gone!" Taran raved, waving a fist in the air, leaning his face close to Marcus. "It is Owein's fault! He set all the watches. He had control. And he failed. I told you, Father!"

Marcus and Iorwerth looked at each other, the same stern expression in their dark eyes. Marcus muttered, "It makes no sense."

"Damn right, brother! I say we haul him in and find out what he's doing!"

Marcus stared coldly at his brother. "We will wait and watch Owein before we make a bigger mistake." He explained the other incident to Taran and that he wanted to catch Owein by surprise instead of scaring him into further treachery or covering up what he had already done, if he was at fault.

"We have to do something now!" Taran flashed. "Are you out of your mind?"

"I agree with Marcus, son," Iorwerth interrupted.

Taran stared at his father. "Why? You always told us to keep an iron fist, to let nothing stand in our way, and let no one take away what is ours. Now you are just letting them get away with treason."

"Sometimes the iron fist must rule with discretion and subtlety, as well as harshness. I believe this is the time for subtlety. Listen to your brother."

Marcus concurred, "Aye, until we have evidence, we will not point fingers at Owein. We are not dealing with a stranger; he is a close part of our family. This could be a trap. Now is not the time to tear our family apart. What we have to defend is too important." Marcus glared steadily into his impetuous brother's eyes as he made his last statement.

Taran shifted irritably, his jaw working. Finally, he turned and strode silently back out of the hall. He detested the coldness of Marcus' black eyes.

Sunlight spread brilliant gold and green across the

mountains of Eryri. The magnificent early spring morning coaxed the first blossoms to stretch into the cool, incredibly clear air. Not a hint of the perpetual mist was anywhere. Ravens soared across the sky for the sheer joy of flight.

Marcus continued his patrol from the previous night, returning to the eastern boundary of his territory. Urging his horse into a canter, he put the problem aside to concentrate on his patrol. If he lost focus again, he could receive a far worse wound than the one from the night before. His horse made good progress, carrying him along a track that took him to a high ridge behind the fort.

Stopping momentarily, he watched below and across the valley, scanning up the other side to the crags beyond. Everything was peaceful. Dotted along the far border, he could see the standards attached to each of his warriors' spears. Each patrol seemed to be in its position. Marcus' lips pressed into a flat line, hoping that the last night's errors were only errors.

He clicked at his horse and continued upward, heading for another track that branched away and led above the pass. The air was cooler there, and its clearness magnified the entire vista. Patches of snow lingered in rocky crevices, melting into the muddy scree as the sun warmed them. Marcus knew it was probably only a false spring and that there would be more snow and ice before long, but the mild weather soothed his brooding.

He came to a jagged barrier of stone that jutted into the sky and he dismounted, then led his horse through a narrow passage. Except by accident, no one would know the gap was there. From the lower side, it looked like a solid wall of ragged rock. Carefully, he slipped through and came out into a large, bowl-shaped meadow, bare of trees, lined with hardy turf and strewn with moss-capped rocks. A small stream gushed down from the highest peaks, digging out a depression across the meadow's face and disappearing down into the pass below.

From the meadow, Marcus could see most of his territory. He intended to observe the movements of his patrols, looking for irregularities and contacts from outsiders. He had deliberately told no one where he was going, so no one would know from where he would be watching.

He let the horse trail reins and after a few minutes, sat next to the stream bank, laying his sword on the ground within easy reach. In the sun, his heavy tunic was too warm and he loosened the ties all the way down its front. After the stress of his constant patrolling, he let his mind wander to the fresh smell of the grass, the quiet munching of the grazing horse and the feel of the breeze on his face. He stared into the distance, watching the far crags, his eyes squinting into narrow slits against the glare.

Running a hand over two day's growth of beard, Marcus extracted one of several hidden daggers he kept on himself, this one from his right boot. He tested the knife's edge with his thumb, then scraped the stubble, carefully missing his long moustache. He raked his fingers through his hair, driving it back from his face as the wind blew it, thinking it was getting too long again and he needed to have Padrig cut it. He cleaned the stubble from the dagger with his fingers and polished it on the turf.

"Marcus?"

A small voice cut the serenity of the meadow and Marcus' stomach twisted sourly. Instantly he was on his feet, the dagger's blade between his fingers, his arm drawn back and ready to throw hard.

Then he froze.

Claerwen's heart-shaped face, wide-eyed and stunned, looked across at him. She went pale and dropped to the ground, covering her head with her arms.

Marcus dropped the knife, something he never did voluntarily. "Damn!" he said, and went down on his knees in front of her. He reached to her arms and raised her until she faced him. "Claerwen! What are you doing all the way out here? You're so far away from the convent; you shouldn't be out here by yourself. It's too dangerous!"

They stared at each other, stunned looks on their faces. Then Claerwen slowly began to smile as her fear drained away, breaking Marcus' sternness. She told him, "I had to get away from there. I couldn't bear it any longer."

"But at least you are safe there. You know this area isn't secure from Drakar. There have been a lot of bandits, too, lately." He stopped, realizing part of the reason he had come to the high meadow was to escape the fort's tension. He understood that she would want to escape the convent just as much. His lips spread into a grin, his eyes squinting amusement. He sat back and picked up the dagger, slipping it into his boot again.

"Sorry. That was a trained reaction to surprise. 'Be prepared or die,' my father would say. My temper has been getting the best of me lately." He stood up and helped Claerwen to her feet.

"I started out looking for healing herbs for the nuns. They are teaching me how to make medicines." She pulled out a leather pouch from under her cloak to show him.

As her eyes came up to his face, he was struck once more by their clear green-blue beauty. He studied her before he responded, noting that she again wore one of the simple white gowns of the convent under a loosely-wrapped dark brown woollen cloak. Part of her hair was braided and wrapped around the rest of her hair to keep it in place. She was barefoot, and carried her shoes by their laces, attached to a leather thong around her waist.

"You should talk to a man called Padrig, who lives with us. He knows all about healing herbs and things like that. He is the one who patches me up every time I get hurt." He rubbed the bandaged arm. "Is that why you came out so far?"

She shrugged, then said, "I just kept going; it is so beautiful up here. Then I saw someone was here. I almost ran away, then I saw it was you."

He smiled and scanned the distance, watching. Then he frowned at her, asking "Which way did you come?"

The sudden change of expression startled her, but she answered carefully and completely.

He considered her response a while, then nodded to himself as if satisfied. He invited her to sit with him while he watched the valley and the opposite cliffs.

"You are always thinking, Marcus," she said. "Always so serious."

He cocked a dark brow at her. His long hair blew across his face again, the sun glinting white highlights from it. His face did not move, but mischief sparkled in his eyes. Suddenly, he dropped a foot over the edge of the stream and kicked up, splashing water over her. She jumped up, shaking herself, and hopped away from him.

"Oh, you...you're crazy!" She started giggling when she saw his broad grin stretching with laughter. She ran to the water and slapped handfuls back at him.

"Whoa!" he yelled and rolled backwards, flipping himself onto his feet.

She was surprised at his incredible agility and exclaimed, "Why, you are faster than a diving kingfisher!"

Marcus roared with laughter. He kneeled back down on the grass, his sides hurting, gasping for air. It felt good to really laugh hard.

Claerwen sat down again next to Marcus, glad to see him relax. He appreciated her company like no one ever had, not even Grania. She enjoyed the warm feeling he gave her, especially when he grinned, showing broad, clean, even, white teeth. Thinking his smile was remarkably handsome, she suddenly realized he was wearing no disguise. She caught herself staring at his hair, far longer than it was that first night they'd met, shoulder-length and shaggier, loose and sensuous in the wind.

Marcus leaned back, laying on his side, propped up on one elbow. He used the slope of the hill to keep himself conveniently positioned as he watched across the hills while enjoying Claerwen's company. He did not want to send her away.

"Talk to me, Claeri; tell me about you."

She smiled with irony in her pale eyes. "My father used to call me that, when I was very little. No one else has ever used it; in truth, I don't think anyone else even knew of it. It's nice to hear again. You already know mostly everything about me.

Where I was born, how my family was lost. How we fled to Strathclyde and Lord Ceredig helped us. It's always been a simple life, working day to day just to survive. You know the rest."

"But you are much more than that. Tell me what you like to do, what do you want to do in this life? What do you hope and dream about? We all have hopes and dreams."

She tucked her bare feet under her gown, loneliness clouding her face. The feeling of a trap enclosed her again. Her lips curved downward as her eyes came up to lock with Marcus' and she answered, "Grania and I will have to decide soon if we will become Christian nuns. The abbess has told us that we must commit ourselves to the convent if we want to stay there much longer, or else leave. If we leave, we will have to find another refuge out of Drakar's reach." Her eyes dropped to the hem of her gown where it curled over her feet. She added, "That is not a hope or a dream. It is a reality."

Marcus frowned darkly at the turf in front of him and picked at the grass blades. "Mine was a stupid question. I know how limited your options are. It's taking too damn long to maneuver Drakar into the position I want him. And I wish I was in a position where I could do something to get you out of that convent, but I can't. Not yet."

"It is not for you to worry over. I have to be responsible for myself."

He thumped the ground with his fist in frustration. He had also wanted to ask her about her visions, if she had seen into the future, if she knew what would happen between them. But he hesitated, not sure he truly believed in fire in the head and not sure he wanted to know, if it was bad news. He decided not to ask, not wanting to stir up bad memories for her, as the visions he knew of had all been hurtful and disturbing. Instead, he sat up again and pulled open the pack of food, offering it to Claerwen.

They ate slowly, quietly, as Marcus brooded and Claerwen shyly watched him. When he handed her a wineskin of mead, she commented, "We served mead at the inn in Caernarfon, but we never drank it; it was too expensive to make for ourselves.

By the gods, that seems a long time ago already."

He was leaning back on his elbow again and looked up at her comment. He watched her swallow a long drink of mead, then hold the skin out for him to take. As he took it, he watched the wind draw her hair back and shake its full length as it floated down her back. She was sitting on her cloak, her knees pulled up and her arms around them, watching a golden eagle ride a thermal over the pass.

It was then he realized how much his attraction to her had grown; that his fascination was not a dream in the night or a feeling of pity for her troubles. He knew he had fallen in love with her the first time he had seen her; that deep in his mind he had fought against it, thinking they would never meet again and that she would never feel the same way. But the bond between them ran far deeper than either the danger he sought to allay or the distance of time they had endured.

He reached out and ran a finger along her cheek, brushing a stray lock into place. She smiled, sweet and guileless. He rose up and slid his arms around her, pulling her to him, and placed a gentle kiss where his finger had crossed her cheek.

Claerwen responded to his gentleness, crossing her arms behind his neck as he nuzzled her. She had never expected a man to be tender; she had assumed, rough in work, rough in everything else. She thought he looked and acted with absolute manliness, not any hint of falseness in his tough manners. Yet he was gentle and tender with her, a simple man expecting only simple replies to what he sought.

For a moment, Claerwen pulled back and gazed into his eyes. Then she smiled slightly and asked, "Was that beard you had when you sang at the convent yours, or was it fake?"

He looked confused at her question, wondering why she would ask such a thing, then laughed, liking the way she could pull him out of his brooding with a silly question or remark. He said, "That was mine. I shaved it off the next day. I didn't do a good job this morning, though." He rubbed his chin.

He took a handful of her hair and pressed it to his face,

breathing in its lavender scent, then leaned to her again, his mouth locking on hers. His palms slowly stroked her back its full length, caressing her in small, round movements as they moved down, then back up, giving her a warm, relaxed sensation. She hung onto him, moving closer until she had her legs twined around him. She felt her clothing coming loose as he untied the thin laces holding the front of her gown together, then the ties of her shift. The breeze moved warmly on her skin as he pulled the neckline far open. She saw his eyes drop to the ring he had given her where it hung on a thong around her neck. It rested in the valley between her breasts, and he arched her to him so he could press his face there, his lips exploring the warm softness of her skin.

Claerwen smoothed his hair, watching it shine blue-black in the sunlight, feeling secure in the hard strength of his arms as they wound around her. His face rose again and he grinned as the gown dropped down from her shoulders. Pulling her arms free, he placed her hands inside the loose opening of his tunic. She found a heavy mat of black hair on his chest and tangled her fingers in it, feeling perspiration underneath. As if opening a gift, she pulled the tunic from him. He winced slightly when he moved the bandaged arm.

"You've been hurt!" she exclaimed.

"'Tis nothing," he mumbled, pressing kisses into her palms and watching the fullness of her breasts as they moved with her.

"But your arm is bleeding!" She reached to the stained bandage.

Unconcerned about his arm, he pulled off his boots and tossed them aside. He grinned dreamily at her as she studied his face. He unwound her hair, letting it spread in the wind, reaching out to trail all around him. Getting up on his knees, he began caressing her again, his big hands slowly pushing her back into the folds of the cloak until she was laying down, his mouth urgently searching hers. He pushed the gown down her hips and legs, flinging it away onto the turf.

Claerwen understood what he wanted to do, though she

knew little of what happened between men and women. She watched him pause a moment, and she nearly shivered as the air wafted over her nakedness. His eyes drifted appreciatively over her the same way, taking in the curves of her breasts, waist and hips. One of his hands smoothed a winding path along her skin, and it came to rest between her legs, his fingers curling in to gently trace a pattern there. She reached to slip the ties of his breeches and he smiled again as she helped him to wriggle out of them.

He eased down, and she arched herself to him, savoring the feel of his weight on her. She ran her hands up behind his shoulders, squeezing her breasts to his chest and nuzzling her face into the side of his neck. Her lips kissed and moved under his ear, into his hair. He pressed himself into her slowly and carefully. He watched her face again, afraid of hurting her, but craving to go deeper and deeper. Her eyes opened and closed, alternating between surprise and fascination, pain and ecstasy. He worked with longing and she followed his lead, breathing long sighs of pleasure. She moved in rhythm with him, her urgency growing with an aching that took on a power of its own. His mouth came down on hers again, clamping her lips with hard but gentle strength. She dug her fingers into his flesh as the final push came, finding incredulous joy at the new feeling inside her.

Marcus lay collapsed, breathing quietly in Claerwen's ear, enjoying the warm smell of her hair and the sun on his naked body. She felt tiny under his weight, and he braced himself up to keep from crushing her. But instead of feeling smothered, she clung to him, delighted in the feel of his skin on hers and his manhood within her.

At length he stirred, and rose to gaze at her face. Her eyes were closed, a sweet smile on her lips. She looked so serene, he hesitated to move. Then her eyes opened, the pale green-blueness bright and clear. She reached her arms around his neck and he pulled her up with him as he got to his feet. He could not stop himself from watching her eyes.

Finally he whispered, "I know why you are called

'Claerwen.' It means bright, clear water. Because of your eyes. They are so beautiful, like the sea on a clear day."

He gathered her up in his arms and went to the stream bank. He waded into the water and perched on a flat, mossy rock, her on his lap. They washed each other with the refreshing, cold water, then retreated onto the turf to dry in the sun. Marcus tossed the cloak around Claerwen, to keep her fair skin from burning.

The afternoon grew late.

Marcus suddenly remembered why he had come to the high meadow. "By Lleu," he softly swore to himself. "I must go on. I have not been doing what I am supposed to. I am sorry." His eyes met Claerwen's with aching sadness.

"I understand," she whispered in return.

Quickly, they dressed. Marcus swung their belongings onto the horse, then he lifted Claerwen up. When he leaped up behind her, he asked her to show him how she had come to the meadow from the convent. He was still bothered that he had not seen her approach. Perhaps she had found a hidden path by accident, a path that was coincidentally connected to the problem involving Owein. Always thinking, she had said. Aye, he thought, he had to think. Or die.

"I will come back for you, Claeri," he said as they rode close in to the convent. His big hands stroked, crossing around her. "You already know that, fire in the head notwithstanding. I wish I could say when, but I can't."

She leaned back against him, tucking her head underneath his chin. She wished she could take with her the feel of his arms pressed around her, something to savor in the cold night when she was alone in her cell. She said quietly, "I wish you would let me do something to help you."

He halted the horse just beyond sight of the convent. He slid off and pulled her down to him and said, "Just be safe for me." Then he kissed her once more, long and longingly. After, he caressed her cheek with his finger and gazed into her eyes. "I do believe what you said before, that we have known each other for all time."

Claerwen squeezed her eyes shut to keep tears from filling them. When she opened them, she said softly, "I want to go with you, help you to fight Drakar." She knew it was a foolish thought; she was no warrior, but she hated the idea of becoming one of those god-cursed nuns as much as she wanted to stay with him. She was horrified that she would become bound to a religion she did not believe in and never allowed to be more than a friend to Marcus.

He was surprised by the depth of her commitment to him and he cupped his hand to her cheek. He answered, a little more sternly than he intended, "Just be safe for me, Claerwen. I must return home now. We have had a lot of trouble lately, which I must take care of as soon as possible. The gods' willing, I will be back soon." He kissed her again.

"Please be careful," she spoke, throaty with emotion.

"Farewell, my Claeri." He squeezed her shoulders and tried to grin cheerfully, as much to convince himself as to assure her that they would both be safe and together again. Then he swung himself up onto the horse, saluted her briefly, and galloped hard up the track, back to the fort.

"Marcus!" Owein called at his cousin's door.

Marcus was eating supper in the privacy of his house. "Come," he answered.

Owein entered, raking his fingers through his dark blond hair, anxiety crumpling his brow.

"We must talk, cousin."

Marcus looked up into Owein's solemn face, his eyes steady and exacting.

Owein pulled on his moustache, a lighter copy of the one Marcus wore, something he did when he was worried. He read Marcus' mind concerning the mishaps of the previous night. "Aye, I know what you're thinking. There is a new problem, far worse. The fighting is escalating dramatically now. And you were right about Vortigern. He is swelling Drakar's war band with

Saxons. We had another fight on the northwest border today. Of the dead, we found several of them." He paused, then added quietly, "War is here."

Marcus swore with vehemence. The northwest border was the only side he could not see from the high meadow. His eyes narrowed at Owein and he studied his face hard, as if to look down into his cousin's soul for the truth of the things he had been blamed for. He drawled, "I want a new code between us, Owein. Just between you and me. No one else. We will use it to station each part of the men where we need them and what they are to be doing. And I want this note sent to Cunedda when you leave here." Marcus went to a small table and scratched out a coded message on a small parchment, folded it, then sealed it. "We must mobilize the reserve men for the war band immediately."

"I have already done so."

"Good." Marcus stopped, his black eyes again boring into his cousin's. "Owein, a great deal of suspicion has been laid on you since yesterday. I hope it is only suspicion."

"I have no answers for you yet. I had switched the midnight patrol with the next one because the midnight watch was so tired; I thought they should get a few more hours rest. I sent a message to you."

"Message? I received nothing. Who did you send?"

"The man called Deinol."

"One of the mercenaries?"

"Aye, he's always been reliable and I've used him many times."

"Send him to me, I want to question him."

"Aye." Owein thought a moment, then said, "If you did not get that message, then others were disrupted as well."

"Either this Deinol knows something—"

A knock at the door interrupted Marcus. Padrig came in to retrieve the supper bowls.

"There is a message for you, Marcus. One of your hired men was killed in an accident a little while ago."

"Which man?"

"The one called Deinol."

Marcus and Owein stared at each other. They knew it was no accident. Marcus nodded at Padrig to leave them.

"We have a traitor among us, Owein. And it was not Deinol. Someone in this fort belongs to Drakar and Vortigern!"

CHAPTER 10

Eryri, Gwynedd
Summer and Autumn, 467 A.D.

As fighting escalated across the mountains, the abbess ordered her nuns to stay within the convent walls and keep the gate shut and locked. She reported that the local prince, from the nearby fort called Dinas Beris, had warned her of the danger from soldiers and bandits. He wanted the nuns to stay barricaded behind their walls, and he would send them supplies as he was able; but if the fighting became too perilous, he would eventually evacuate them to another location.

With the isolation, no visitors were allowed. No news was learned, except what could be seen over the timber walls. As the nuns rarely ventured far from the convent, most of them had little to adjust in their lifestyles. They cut back on the use of their stored food and supplies, hoping to stretch what they had farther so the prince would not be pressed for supplies himself. They converted the courtyard into additional gardens and planted as much as they could in the small space, hoping the conflict would be resolved quickly.

The weather returned to winter after the false spring, giving heavy, wet snow showers, endless mist, and harsh winds, continuing past Beltainne. The women huddled around meager fires, trying to conserve the dried peat. To distract themselves from the cold, they spent hours on their knees, praying in their chapel and reworking the gardens every time the snow melted. Gradually, however, warmer breezes combed the hills with gentle rain, dressing the mountains with brilliant summer greens.

Claerwen expected the isolation was coming after she sensed the uneasiness in Marcus when he left. She speculated that he was a high ranking military leader for the local prince, judging from what he said about being a soldier and spy, and that he had said his family held land, not owned it. She hoped he was as tough as he appeared to her, knowing that Drakar would be a difficult man to defeat. She had no sense for the extent of the prince's resources, but she took some comfort from what Marcus had said about Cunedda of Gwynedd's support.

Aside from studying the healing herbs, Claerwen spent her time learning the Latin chants that the nuns sang in the chapel. In the first days of the isolation, she drifted from one activity to another, no longer able to go out for the plants she had been collecting. She knew about gardens and raising crops and livestock, and could sew, embroider and weave already; she wanted to learn something new. The abbess suggested learning the chants after she heard Claerwen sing an old folk tune while she was helping to cook supper one evening. As the days passed into weeks, she grew lonely and worried about Marcus, and she tried to find solace in the haunting beauty of the music. She learned some of the meanings of the words, but she mostly just memorized the sounds.

Grania continued housekeeping duties, cooking and cleaning just as she had at the inn in Caernarfon. She missed the bustle of town life, but she enjoyed the company of the other women. She chattered easily with them, telling stories of inn guests and offering new ideas for meals. The nuns responded to her sparkling cheerfulness with rolling giggles, stifling their laughter with hands over their mouths when the abbess cast a stern look their way.

By contrast, Claerwen spent more and more time alone.

She chafed at the utter isolation, knowing it was safer that way, but found herself unable to control her fretting. She would perform her assigned chores, then retreat to the chapel to sing or to her cell to block out the others. She indulged in her loneliness, not because she enjoyed it, but because it was the only thing in her life she could seem to understand. She no longer slept well, lying awake for long hours, staring at the progress moonlight made on the wall opposite her tiny window. When she did sleep, her dreams were full of disconnected visions, none of which made sense. The fire showed her nothing of Marcus or where he was, what he was doing, what was happening to him, but she discovered she could sense his distress. At least she knew he was alive as long as she could feel his moods.

Grania watched Claerwen grow distant and decline into a dark brooding she had never seen in her cousin before. Not even her bitterness towards the Iron Hawk had made such a noticeable change in her, and Grania became worried. She followed Claerwen to her cell after supper one evening, and gently knocked at the door. When Claerwen did not answer, Grania pushed it open. She found her cousin lying in the dark on her bed, curled into a tight ball.

Grania lit a candle and pulled the chair to Claerwen's bedside. "What is wrong, cousin?" Grania asked, stroking her long hair back.

Deep hollows marked Claerwen's skin under her green-blue eyes. They were soaked, and when she blinked, more tears washed into the hollows. She did not answer.

Grania had not seen Claerwen so distraught since their family was torn apart by the Irish. She continued to stroke her hair and speak comforting things to her, but she felt she had to learn what caused her distress.

"Talk to me, Claerwen. Can you tell me what is wrong? What are you afraid of?"

Still no answer.

"Is it the convent? I know you don't like it here."

Claerwen shook her head, the movement so slight it was

barely discernable.

"Then what is it? Please, talk to me. Let me help ease the hurt you feel. Are you ill? Are you in pain?"

Claerwen shook her head again, roughly wiping away the tears.

Grania spoke, distress in her voice, "I see you sink away from us day by day. I see you watch over the walls, up at the mountains, listening, like you are waiting for something. Like someone should be—" Grania paused, then blurted, "It's not Drakar you are still afraid of is it? It can't be; he would have come by now if he was still looking for you. It must be someone else."

Claerwen squeezed her eyes shut and held her breath. She wanted desperately to confide in Grania about Marcus, what she felt, how she missed him, how she realized in the days after he left her at the convent that she loved him; and that she loved him not as someone who had conveniently rescued her or as a glorified warrior, but as a man who shared a deep bond with her, an intertwining of their souls, an enduring connection that spanned lifetimes. She had heard of such love in the songs of bards, but never hoped to find one of her own. Now she had, and her heart ached that she would probably lose the man before she could return to him.

"I cannot tell you," she hoarsely told Grania.

Grania was stunned at the sorrow in Claerwen's voice. "'Tis true then. You do watch for someone. Oh, Claerwen, if you want to unburden your heart, I will listen. I won't tell anyone."

"I can't, Grania. I'm sorry, I promised. I can't. Someday there will be a time when I can, but for now, please understand."

Grania pressed one of Claerwen's hands to her cheek and whispered, "It must be someone in the war of Dinas Beris. You must have met a man and fallen in love with him. By Lleu of the Long Hand!" Grania clamped her mouth shut and hugged her cousin. She asked no more questions.

More weeks went by, turning into more months, and Claerwen wondered if Marcus was still alive. The silence of the isolation dragged on her like a pall. She still sensed his soul, but her own depression clouded her judgement so that she became numb. Late summer closed in toward autumn and Samhuinn, and the skirmishes seemed to go on forever. Sometimes the battles came close enough to the convent to hear the shouts and cries and clash of spears on shields. These sounds disturbed her so much that she would take refuge in her spare cell and cry herself to sleep with the pillow wrapped around her ears. Morning would come and the day was faced with dread.

A fortnight before Samhuinn, a scream pierced the silence at midnight. Claerwen drifted out of her sleep, hearing the terrible sound, thinking she was still dreaming. But it came again. Smoke filtered into the narrow window.

"Fire!" she yelled. "Get up, get out of the building! Fire!"

In the dark, she quickly donned her clothing and ran down the hall, checking the other cells to see the other women were getting out of the building.

Flames had caught the thatched roof of a storage hut in the rear of the convent. A flaming arrow had started it, shot over the walls. Quickly, the women formed a bucket line from the well in the front courtyard to the burning structure, efficiently bringing the small blaze under control. The ever-present dampness greatly hindered the arson from progressing very far.

But then another flaming arrow flew over the wall. Then another, and another. Screams rose as they re-formed the bucket line, the water flying.

Then, suddenly, a man's head appeared at the top of the wall. He clambered up and over it, a spear in his hand and a shield strapped to his back. He wore the brown and black tartan of Drakar's clan. Another man came, then more on all sides of the convent. They were only a handful, but to the frightened women, they were too many, no matter how few.

The warriors rounded up the nuns, like so many sheep, into the front courtyard. Those who tried to run or hide were chased down and dragged carelessly back to the courtyard. The men did not say much, other than brief, sharp commands, but their intention was obvious. One young nun was singled out, torn away from the others and dragged to the center of the courtyard. She fell, whimpering. One of the warriors, apparently their leader, stood over her, and booted her a few times while he ordered her to stand. Finally, through her hysteria, she understood him and struggled onto her feet.

Seconds later, the leader roughly tore her habit and undershift away until she stood naked in the cold torchlight with everyone staring. He pointed at one of his men, indicating for him to take her into the buildings and do what he willed. Her screams rang through the air a long time afterward.

The other women cowered in their corner, wondering who would be next. They knew they would all get their turn. Several were ordered to go, under guard, to prepare a meal for the warriors. More women were taken away, and the remaining group grew smaller and smaller. Claerwen and Grania huddled in the back, wishing they could be absorbed into the timber walls.

Suddenly, Grania gasped, her tears ending abruptly. Whispering, she told Claerwen, "It is the Iron Hawk!"

Claerwen looked to where Grania gazed, a point on the wall near the gates behind the warriors. In the dark, an outline showed, in the shape of the strange, visored helmet.

Claerwen sucked in her breath. "*Y Gwalch Haearn!* The gods preserve us!"

The black warrior sprang over the wall and hid among the shrubbery. Moments later, he was many yards to the right, behind one of the invading warriors. He rose up and took the man down with a dagger, quickly and silently. He continued along the wall and disappeared into the buildings.

A few minutes later, the Iron Hawk returned to the courtyard. Claerwen could see he was studying the leader and the remaining warriors. She did not understand why he was killing the invaders; she had been certain he was one of them. Then she recalled what Marcus had said, that the Iron Hawk was not Drakar's man.

Whatever his purpose, she knew instinctively that a

distraction would help the warrior and, without hesitation, began to sing as loud as her frightened voice could carry. She started one of the Latin chants. She did not care if her voice screeched and broke, as long as it caused confusion among the invaders.

Which it did. They looked at each other, then held their torches higher and closer to the small crowd of white-robed women to see who made such a noise. They shouted orders to be silent. Claerwen kept going, gathering momentum. Some of the other women joined in. The leader became furious at Claerwen because she refused to stop singing. His face flushed and he yanked out a dagger, cocking his arm back to throw it. Abruptly she stopped, and waited for the knife to hit her in the throat. She closed her eyes, listening to silence of the night, when suddenly a piercing war cry drove through the darkness.

In the same instant, crackling lights punctured the dark sky outside the convent's walls. They resembled lightning, except the flashes seemed to flare upwards into the sky and carried low, echoing booms instead of crashing thunder. They lasted only a few seconds, but lit the courtyard enough to see the Iron Hawk advance, screaming with his sword circling wildly over his head. The women scattered back into their buildings, out of the way.

The warrior moved with speed and grace, and hideous accuracy. The leader died quickly, followed by the other men. No mercy was ever considered. Within minutes, he was done, nothing more stirred. Only the Iron Hawk's faint panting could be heard.

The mysterious warrior methodically searched all of the buildings. He found two dead nuns and another who had been raped, but was still alive. Doors were slammed open and shut as the man worked his way through. Every cupboard, closet, corner, and cell was inspected briefly. Even the damaged hut was not spared a perusal. In the last building, a last drape was push aside. Two pairs of frightened eyes stared up at the Iron Hawk. They belonged to Claerwen and Grania.

The Iron Hawk paused for several moments, staring back at the two women. They were surprised at his hesitation, they did not expect him to take more than a few seconds to make a decision. But now he stood quietly, pondering behind his mask, perhaps because one of these two women had created the diversion that insured the success of his retaliation.

He backed away, swiftly turning to leave.

"Wait!" Claerwen suddenly sprang up and tried to catch his arm, but she missed. The warrior hesitated, and in the time he spent watching her, she noticed that he wore the immense sword on a heavy belt that crossed his chest diagonally, the scabbard hanging along his left leg and the hilt easy to reach just in front of him. The pommel was shaped as a hawk, made of black iron.

The warrior suddenly turned and strode quickly out of the door. Claerwen called again, dashing after him, but Grania grabbed her hand and pulled her back.

"Don't be foolish, Olivia!" Grania begged.

"Let me go!" Claerwen shook herself loose and sprang for the doorway again. She ran out into the dark alley between the building and the outer wall, and saw the Iron Hawk running, preparing to leap for the top of the wall. She sprinted, launching herself directly into his path so that he could not make the jump.

The warrior saw her coming and stalled as she tackled him, gripping the heavy belt that held the sword. Her momentum pushed him against the wall, and he grabbed her and twisted, neatly dropping her onto the ground.

"Who are you?" Claerwen shouted at him as he came down on his knees next to her. She tried to sit up and reached for the helmet, but he roughly pushed her down again. She continued to shout, demanding, "Who are you? Why have you tried to kill me and —"

The Iron Hawk pressed a gloved hand to her throat, forcing her to be silent, then drew the sword with his other hand. He held the blade diagonally across her body, slowly pressing it down so that the portion nearest its tip rested between her breasts.

Claerwen stopped wriggling and held her breath while she stared up in alarm at the mask. The dim light from the courtyard merely silhouetted the helmet and she could see none of its features. She felt his fingers tighten under her chin momentarily, then loosen again, and the weight of the sword felt coldly heavy. She could see his breath steam out from underneath the mask.

A scream shrilled nearby and Claerwen rolled her eyes far enough to see Grania a few yards away. An instant later, the Iron Hawk whirled away, sheathing the sword in one quick motion and dashing along the wall. He leapt and gripped the top of the wall, easily hauling himself up and disappearing over the top.

The nuns spent the rest of the night in their chapel, praying and deciding what to do with all those bodies in the courtyard. There were nine of them, plus the two dead nuns. The abbess directed that the nuns would be buried properly according to their religion. But the raiders would not be allowed one of their Christian burials.

At daybreak, the abbess left the others to finish their prayers and sing their hymns. Someone had come to the gate asking to speak with her and she wanted to see if she could send for someone to take the bodies away.

An hour later, Marcus slipped quietly into the convent's chapel, seating himself in a dark corner at the back. A dozen nuns were gathered in a tight group, facing the simple altar, heads bowed in prayer. They were unaware of his presence.

He watched patiently. He had asked for Olivia, and was told she was in the chapel, but he could not tell which one she was. They all wore veils. Perhaps she was somewhere else, since he had never seen her wear one. He would wait until they were finished and ask.

As if they were of one mind, the nuns lifted their faces to the altar and began to sing. In harmonious perfection, a Latin chant filled the chapel, and its ethereal quality fascinated Marcus. The beauty of the voices struck him as the first positive thing he had ever felt about the Christians' church. He had always barely tolerated their preaching without listening, feeling their god and his gods were really all the same, that their holy books were propagandized stories from the ancient past.

The voices drifted away into a single voice, one of great sweetness and clarity, rich and full without any shrillness. Marcus watched this woman, very impressed with the sound even though he understood the Latin words and disliked what they said. Gradually the woman turned to her left as another nun joined in the chant, and Marcus realized the soloist was Claerwen. They continued, the others with them, building the sound higher and higher, and finishing with a long, final "Amen."

Ceremoniously, the nuns filed out a side door, one staying behind, kneeling at the altar. Claerwen.

She was bent over, surrounded by the voluminous folds of her wool gown. Her veil fell far over her face. Marcus thought she was praying at first, or crying, but she was silent and still, only staring.

He rose and strode noiselessly toward her, halting a few steps behind. Not wanting to frighten her, he deliberately moved one of the rustic benches, scraping it on the floor. She did not move or seem to notice.

"Claerwen?" he called softly. This time she visibly started, then jerked around.

"Marcus!" she exhaled, and rushed into his arms. "I thought I would never see you again!"

He clasped her tightly to his chest and pressed his face to hers. "It has been so long. By the gods, you're so thin. Have you been ill?"

"I have been so afraid for you! Oh, Marcus!" She flung the veil back and his mouth came down on hers in a kiss meant to satisfy months of longing.

At length, he pulled away and said softly, "Claeri, I must speak with you. Is there a place we can talk privately?"

Her joy sank when she saw the seriousness return to his dark eyes. Then she looked him up and down, realizing he was in full battle gear, his sword and a shield strapped on his back. She saw his hands were wrapped in bandages when he took off his gauntlets and he looked ragged and very tired, deep dark shadows under his eyes. She held her chin tensely as she mumbled that the chapel had a loft no one used. She led him up a steep, narrow stairway, and they settled in a small space hidden behind drapes and shadows.

He began, "I cannot stay long, so I will be brief. The war has stagnated on the borders. We battle back and forth, a little this way, a little that way. The convent is too close and now I feel it must be evacuated. It is no longer safe here."

She told him, "The nuns will never leave this convent. They will stay and pray, trusting their god will keep them safe. They are more stubborn than the Irish."

Marcus smiled with irony. "They will have to go further south unless we can force Drakar back. We are waiting for help from Cunedda. His mercenaries should have been here by now. Vortigern is backing Drakar as I suspected."

"You know what happened here last night?"

"Aye, and I thank Lleu you are safe." He touched her face. "I offered to take the bodies away for the abbess."

"The Iron Hawk tried to kill me again. This time with his sword. If my cousin had not come when she did, he would have succeeded."

Marcus searched Claerwen's eyes, incredulous shock in his face. "You can't be serious," he blurted. "Why would he do that when he just saved all of your lives?"

"I don't know! But that's what he did!"

"Explain to me exactly what happened."

Claerwen detailed the experience. She watched Marcus' face grow sternly analytical as she spoke. When she was finished, he said, "I think he was trying to warn you, not kill you, Claerwen. He was telling you to stay out of his way. If you don't, you could get yourself or your loved ones hurt or even killed."

"I have to know who he is."

"Claerwen, it doesn't matter who he is. What matters is that you are safe. And those around you whom you care for and who care for you. Leave it alone."

She recognized the finality in his voice and knew he

would not discuss it any further. Then he touched the veil, wondering why she wore one now.

She read his thoughts and sadness clouded her green-blue eyes. "I will take the final vows soon, Marcus. If I can't leave here, I have no other choice. And if I do take them, I will be committed to the convent."

His jaw went slack and he realized she would be lost to him. He ached inside. His voice came low and even, and he took her hands in his, "I had lost track of how long it's been. Then I will change my plan." He glanced beyond the curtain, scanning the chapel below to be sure no one had entered.

"I came here to ask you something, but first I have to tell you something before I can ask you." He paused again, taking a deep breath. "I have told you that I am mostly a soldier, and you know already that I am a spy as well, since that is how we met. I have worked for some of the kings within Gwynedd's alliance, Cunedda, Ceredig, and the kings of Cornwall and Rheged among others. Spying is more dangerous than soldiering. I am often totally alone, with no protection, no one to back me up, not like in a battle. I am away from home most of the time, and I have many enemies. It makes me a dangerous man to be around."

A door slammed downstairs.

"Marcus!" a male voice demanded.

"Damn! My brother. Something is wrong. Stay here," Marcus whispered to Claerwen. He rose and stepped through the curtains. Taran was already ascending the steps to the loft. They told me you were here with one of the nuns." Sarcasm stained Taran's voice. "Catting with a holy woman this time, eh?" His comment drifted away when Marcus crossed his arms over his chest and stared down at him with his coldest face. Taran shrugged indignantly and said, "I bring you bad news, brother. Father is finally gone. So, how does it feel, Prince of Dinas Beris?" Taran flourished a hand in the air and bowed, smirking.

Marcus exhaled long, then swore again.

"Great timing, eh, older brother? All we need is another funeral."

"Hold your bloody tongue. Your arrogance is disgusting. When did it happen?"

Taran looked bored. "In his sleep."

"Aye." Marcus stared at the family ring he always wore, and thought of the time when his father gave it to him when he was still very young. It seemed like a terribly long time ago and so much had happened since then. He felt suddenly very tired.

Sensing Marcus' distraction, Taran abruptly bounded up the last few steps to the loft curtain and pushed it aside. "Will you not properly introduce us, brother? My curiosity overflows." Taran nearly brayed, seeing that the nun was what he had suspected: young and pretty.

Marcus whipped around and grabbed Taran by his tunic, hauling him up close and staring him down hard. The smirk still did not leave Taran's face. The curtain was pushed aside enough for Claerwen to see them. She noted their resemblance to each other, except Taran had shorter and neater brown hair, and he had no moustache. What struck her more, however, was that their expressions were completely different. Marcus, even in anger, was cool and controlled. Taran had a restless pretension.

The brothers continued to glare at each other for more than a full minute, black eyes against brown. Claerwen could not see any change in either face, but at last Marcus said low and gravelly, "Go. I will return to the fort by midday." Then he released Taran, nearly throwing him down the steps. His brother left without another word.

Marcus met the confusion in Claerwen's eyes with a grimace.

"You are the Prince? Of Dinas Beris?" She had stood to come to him, but now she sat down again, astonished.

"Aye." He nodded, watching her reaction.

"I thought you were a military leader under the prince. The abbess never said your name. Why did you never tell me?"

He sat again and took her hands gently. "This is what I was starting to tell you. My name is Marcus ap Iorwerth. And now my full title will be Prince of Dinas Beris, of the land of

Eryri, in the kingdom of Gwynedd. I haven't been honest with you, but the reason I gave you before was true. I only wanted to protect you. The other reason I did not tell you was that I wanted you to care for me for just as I am, not for being a prince. I don't lead a life of glamor, not like in a bard's song. It's harsh, hostile, dirty, and cruel. You would be surprised how many offers I receive from families, noble and otherwise, to give me their daughters, only because I am...was...Iorwerth's oldest son. Those people have no sense for what they'd be getting into with me and how I live. The title carries very little significance; it's only hereditary and holds no power. I ignore it mostly. The only real power I have is as a spy. I have a reputation among the royalty of the Celtic tribes for being able to get into the impenetrable and out of the unbreakable, as they put it."

The surprise in Claerwen's face wore down into sadness again. He stopped talking, puzzled by her aching eyes.

"What is wrong, my Claeri?"

"You are going to tell me you will not be coming here any longer, aren't you? That I will never see you again. That you will send me and the other nuns far away." A tear traced its way down her cheek. Her green-blue eyes were iridescent and her long lashes wet.

He sighed and brushed away the tear. Gently, he took her face between his big hands and kissed her, one cheek, then the other. He pressed his brow to hers, and smiled lightly, then said, "The fire is not working for you right now. I was going to ask you to become my wife."

Claerwen's breath stopped in her throat and she felt suddenly hot. She was not expecting this anymore than learning his identity. She rose, unable to speak. Marcus came to her, turning her around, and he pulled the veil from her hair, dropping it on the floor. He leaned to kiss her again.

Suddenly she pulled away and spoke with stinging sorrow, "But I have nothing to offer you. I have no bride-price. Even this gown is borrowed. I could not be accepted as your bride. My family has no more rank. Oh, it is no use. I will still end up being a nun and I will lose you forever."

She hid her face in her hands, despair overwhelming her.

"Claeri, listen to me." He pulled her hands away. "Claeri!" He made her look up into his eyes. "I don't care about dowries and aristocratic protocol. I never have and I never will. That is part of why I didn't tell you who I am. I won't marry for political reasons or for greed. Other than the land and the fort at Dinas Beris, I am as poor as you are when it comes down to the truth. I don't need anything. All I want is you."

"You make it sound so simple."

"It is if you make it simple. But you cannot decide right now. You will have to think about it first. It is not an easy life. In many ways it would be easier for you to marry a simple farmer somewhere. Or be a nun. There is only me, my brother, whom you met," he pulled a face, "my cousin Owein, who doesn't talk much at all, Padrig our seneschal, you'll like him, and a few other men who watch the fort. It's not a village or even a settlement. There are a few families scattered on farms throughout the mountain and valley area surrounding the fort. Those people stay and make their living on the land for free. The only thing we ask of them is that they help defend the borders. They are tough and have been intensely loyal to us, most of them have been there for generations like my family has. We are probably the only land holders who do not charge a tithe for the use of the land.

"You must also remember that I am gone most of the time. The fort can be very lonely. There are no other women there, only a bunch of rough and rude bachelors. We raise and hunt our own food, just like the farmsteaders on the mountainside; I even do my own blacksmithing. We have no Roman luxuries, and the fort is cold and damp in the long and unforgiving winters. Snow can get deep enough that you cannot come or go for weeks, even months some years. But it is awesomely beautiful, too. It sits on a hill spur that juts out from a steep mountainside, high on a sheer cliff in a pass. When I stand on the ramparts and look across the jagged peaks, there is nowhere else on earth I could ever be."

Claerwen saw in his eyes how proud he was of his home and she recognized how he was part of the ancient mountains, and they were a part of him, as inseparable as her soul had become from his. He represented the immortal heart of his Celtic ancestors.

Claerwen smiled softly and said in a low voice, "I never had a real home before, only a place to stay. I don't know what it feels like, but I know it is something that has always been missing. I can see how Dinas Beris is a part of your soul, that something in you would die if you lost it. Just as something in my soul would die if I lost you." She laid her hand gently to his face, stroking the long moustache as it lay curving down the side of his mouth. "I will marry you, Marcus ap Iorwerth. And I will help you fight to keep Dinas Beris."

His eyes strained hard into hers as he stalled her, "You should not decide now. I don't think you understand; I am a very dangerous man. Even if Drakar dies today, I am still a spy, there will always be—"

"Do you want me to turn you down?" she interrupted.

He searched her face a few moments, then slowly smiled, and answered, "No."

She smiled back and said, "We are bound together, in our hearts and souls now. Whatever happens, I will marry you."

"Are you sure?"

"Aye. What we have has endured lifetimes and will endure many more. It is the way it should be. For all time."

He broke into a brilliant smile and embraced her tightly. "I will be here in a few days with mercenaries to evacuate the convent. I will take you and your cousin to Dinas Beris with me; prepare her to be ready. Oh, Claeri!"

He stopped talking to kiss her, then turned to leave, pulled her to him again, kissing her more, giving in to his craving to touch her after so many months.

CHAPTER 11

**Eryri, Gwynedd
Autumn, 467 A.D.**

"Olivia! Olivia, come here!" Grania hoarsely called, running down the hall towards her cousin's cell, her habit whipping around her. She reached the doorway and skidded to a halt, thumping the door closed behind her and bolting it. "They are here!"

"Who is here?"

Grania panted a few moments, catching her breath. Claerwen waited patiently, but became worried when she saw the fear in Grania's eyes.

"Who, Julia? The Iron Hawk again?"

"No." Her eyes widened. She hated to say it out loud. "Drakar is here."

Claerwen nearly choked, and sat down abruptly on the bed. "Oh, no, by Lleu! He can't be! What is he doing here?"

"He demanded a night's hospitality from the abbess. I was in the garden when he came, alone except for one manservant. I slipped away while his back was turned. What do we do now?"

Claerwen hid her face in her hands, trying to think. "I don't know, I don't know. If only—"

Grania listened at the door for footsteps, then turned back

to Claerwen when she did not finish her thought. "If only what?"

Claerwen went to the table and poured cups of water for both of them, then said, "I have to tell you something."

Grania sat on the bed and Claerwen joined her. Claerwen swallowed a sip of water, then started in a very soft voice, "Do you remember last summer, when I was so upset and I wouldn't tell you what was wrong?"

"Aye, you said there would be a time when you could tell me. Has that time come?"

"Aye, cousin. You thought that I had met someone from the war, that I was waiting for him. You were right."

Grania's brown eyes widened. "I was only making a guess!"

"I know, but you were right. I was so worried and so lonely, it overwhelmed me. He finally came this morning."

"This morning? Then he must have come with the prince's men who took those bodies away."

Claerwen almost smiled at the irony. "He plans to come back in a few days and take us out of here. The convent will be evacuated at the same time." Her eyes filled with tears. "If only he could have taken us with him this morning."

"Why is he able to do this? Where are we going?"

"To Dinas Beris."

"What? To the fort? Who is he?"

Claerwen hushed her cousin. "His name is Marcus ap Iorwerth. Did you see the man this morning who was wearing the brown leather tunic and had the huge sword strapped across his back?"

"The one giving orders? With the long dark hair and the moustache down to his chin?"

"Aye. That's him."

"But I thought I heard the abbess call him the prince."

"He *is* the prince. We are going to marry."

Grania caught her breath. Claerwen explained how she had met him, the other times Grania had seen him without knowing it, and why he had kept his identity a secret.

Claerwen pulled the ring out from under her shift and stared at it. "He told me if I ever needed him, to put this in the basin of a spring up on the hill above a Roman temple. I know where it is. But how can I get there without Drakar seeing me?" Then her eyes leveled with Grania's, horrified at herself. She asked, "And how could I send for Marcus, if Drakar is laying a trap for him? I can't risk his life like that."

"But Drakar will discover us, Claerwen. We don't know how many days before the prince comes again, if he is even able to come. Drakar won't wait that long."

Claerwen's face crumpled in sorrow at Grania's observation. "Drakar must already know we are here. He would never take hospitality in a convent without a reason like this one. He must have threatened the abbess, too, after what happened last night. She would never let him stay otherwise. He will search this place more thoroughly than the Iron Hawk did. We have to get out somehow, and go to Marcus."

"Do you know where the fort is?"

Claerwen looked aghast at Grania. "No, I've never seen it! He said it was in the pass, to the northwest." She shook her head. "We'd never make it there, through the fighting. We should go to the Roman temple and wait there, it is well hidden. Marcus would know to look there. If we are careful and hide our tracks, Drakar won't find us."

"The nuns will miss us at supper if we don't go soon."

"But Drakar will be there. We can't go."

"I have an idea," Grania said, and pulled the door open just enough to peek into the hallway. She saw two nuns coming towards her and slipped out, talked to them briefly, then slipped back into the cell. "I told them you were sick and cannot come to the evening meal; that I will take care of you and get us some food later."

Claerwen thought a moment, then said, "That should give us some time to figure out how to get out of here. I just hope Drakar doesn't come looking while they're eating."

Grania's face fell, not having realized the opposite effect

of what she had done. "Oh, no, I shouldn't have done that."

"It's all right, I think it was the best chance we have. I think we should stay hidden here until after dark, then I will get us some food from the cook house. Then we can sneak out of the gates and go to the temple. By the gods, I hope it won't be too late."

A storm was approaching by the time Claerwen thought it was safe to go to the cook house. She had watched clouds scud across the sky since Marcus had left that morning, and by the time the nuns had gone to bed, lightning was slashing down from them. She used the thunder to hide any noise she made as she crept out of her cell and out of the building.

Rain was already pelting the packed earth as she crossed the short distance to the cook house. The drops were huge and splashed mud up with each hit, quickly making puddles. Claerwen dashed inside, whirling in behind the door as she closed it on the horrendous din. Inside, it was not much quieter as strike after strike crashed overhead, great white splashes piercing through the shuttered windows to light the cook house brilliantly. Wind screamed through every crack.

Claerwen took off her cloak and shook it, tossing it over a bench, then yanked open the pantry door. As she reached a hand out to the shelves inside, she suddenly became aware of a presence next to her. A hideous face appeared out of the gloom by the pantry door, puffy and bilious, with protruding eyes surrounded by sunken dark sockets.

Drakar.

Claerwen screamed, backing away.

"No one will hear you," Drakar mocked, coming a step forward.

She glared hard at him, her rage rising swiftly. She wished she had Marcus' sword and the skill to wield it, but she knew she was no match against Drakar any more than she was against the Iron Hawk. In a sudden burst, Claerwen whirled away, springing toward the door she had come in.

He caught her arm before she could take two steps, and

jerked her around like a rag doll until she faced him. He still smelled, even worse than she remembered, his sour breath making her sick. He wound her long hair around one hand and pulled until her face came to his.

"You bastard!" she hissed through teeth gritted in pain. She thought her scalp was going to peel away from her skull.

Drakar's cruel, thin lips sneered. "What kind of words are those to say to the one you were supposed to marry? Eh?" He tugged her hair tighter when she tried to struggle. "I can break your neck, woman."

"You have no claim on me," she snapped. "That contract was broken. Traitor!"

He laughed at her, showing his ruined teeth.

"I don't care about that damn contract. Ah, but I will have you," he bragged, the words slurred. He was drunk. "This has been delayed long enough!" With that, he untangled his arm from her hair and nearly released her. But before she could realize and escape, he grasped the neck of her gown and jerked vehemently. The garment tore nearly to the hem and he knocked her to the floor as he pulled it from her.

Claerwen tried to scramble up, lunging again for the door, but Drakar was too fast. He raised one foot and tripped her, rolling her into the base of the fire pit. Then he bent over and took a handful of her undershift, ripping it halfway down its front. His cold blue eyes glared sardonically at her exposed breasts.

Terror filled Claerwen when she saw him discover Marcus' ring. Drakar hauled her up, gripping both her wrists in one of his fists. She fought, lunging and twisting, frantic to get away from him. But he kept her firmly in his grasp and picked up the ring with his free hand. He stared at it a moment, then recognized the Dinas Beris emblem. Rage replaced the derisiveness and he broke the thong off Claerwen's neck, cutting her. He flung it hard across the room, crashing it against the wall.

Then he began to laugh again, apparently amused by her frustration and the unintentionally sensuous movement of her body as the undershift gradually slipped away from her shoulders.

He backed her against one of the tables, at the same time easing his dagger from its sheath. She stopped struggling when she saw the blade, knowing she would die soon.

The blade was cold when it touched her breasts, flat against them, as if he were wiping something. She vowed to herself that Drakar would never have what she had given to Marcus. She would rather die.

Suddenly Drakar pulled her to him, lifting her off the floor, his ugly face between her breasts. She struggled again in earnest, trying to kick him and use her weight to dislodge herself from his grip. It only encouraged him.

Just as suddenly, he dropped her, nearly onto the fire pit. Reacting instinctively, she tried to leap up and run, but he stepped on the skirt of her shift and she sprawled on the floor. She had managed to grab a piece of wood from the fire pit as she rolled away and swung it at him. Drakar ducked and it missed, landing on the floor. Then he dragged her up against the table, pinning her again.

"Where is it, slut?" he demanded.

"Where is what?" She cringed that he was going to start that question again.

"Don't play that again with me, you little whore. Where is it?"

He bent her over against the table so hard she thought her back was going to break.

"You need a lesson!" he screamed when she refused to answer.

He picked her up, slamming her down on the tabletop. He pushed her back until she was flat and he climbed up, straddling over her, one hand pinning both of her arms above her head. Again the dagger appeared. He flicked it to her hips, catching the fabric of her shift with its tip. She felt it prick her skin and she jumped. Drakar grinned, pleased with his torture. He pulled the knife, dragging the cloth up her legs as he rent it all the way to the hem. A tiny trickle of blood stained the edges of the tear.

Drakar shifted his grip and repeated the act, first one side, then the other, until the shift was only tatters. At last, he put up the dagger. He laughed at her, full of sarcasm. He sneered, "It won't be long now. I'll have Dinas Beris, and the power of the treasure that you hold. Aye, you'll tell me where it is! And when my assassins come back, I'll know that damn prince will finally be dead."

Drakar sat back on his heels and grabbed Claerwen's ankles, pushing her legs up and apart so that her feet came up over his shoulders. His hands came down her legs, reaching towards her privates.

Drakar's reference to Marcus set off panic in Claerwen, even more than his rude hands. She screamed suddenly, a frightening, animal-like screech that could be heard even over the thunder, painful to the ear. Finding an enormous strength within her slight figure, she coiled her legs up and kicked Drakar in the chest. He fell backwards off the table, surprise on his face that she would still fight back. She rolled off the table and came after him, kicking him again, this time in the groin. He doubled over and she whirled away, lunging for the fire pit, still screaming. She sprang cat-like and grabbed another long piece of wood from the fire, swinging hard. This time she made contact, whacking Drakar across the face and neck. He fell cock-eyed and limp onto the floor. An ugly red and black ridge ballooned up and he smelled of burnt flesh.

Claerwen crouched, ready to hit again, but Drakar lay still. It was over. She dropped the wood back in the fire pit.

She ran to her cloak and dragged it on around her sore, cold body, tying it securely. She dashed to the door, but skidded to a halt. The ring! Searching along the wall, she found it and wrapped the thong around her fingers.

Then she sprinted out of the cook house, across the courtyard and out of the gates, into the blinding storm. The last thing she saw was a young willow bent to the ground by the wind, debris driving into her with the hard rain.

She never glanced back.

CHAPTER 12

**Dinas Beris
Autumn, 467 A.D.**

Marcus sat silently before the small table, brooding heavily as he listened to the gale beat his house's shutters. But for the glint in his tense, restive eyes, he was motionless, staring at a blank piece of parchment and an idle quill, seeing nothing.

Suddenly, he slapped the table with his palm, rose frowning, and paced to the window. The wind whistled in long, low groans between the shutters' cracks, causing the leather curtain hung over it to balloon out, ghostlike. A cold damp chill shivered on his skin as he turned and paced back to the table. A brazier stood nearby and he gathered warmth again from its glowing coals.

He muttered an expletive, irritated at the storm and that Cunedda's mercenaries still had not arrived. They had been promised and delayed too many times; he knew he would have to find a way to fight Drakar without them. Even if the hired men were on their way, the storm would delay them further. The roads into the mountains of Dinas Beris were impassable with so much rain and wind; they would be nothing but deep mud.

He chafed at the inaction he was forced to endure. He thought about going back to the convent to take Claerwen and her cousin out and bring them to Dinas Beris during the lull in the fighting. He did not mind the rough travel himself, but he fretted over whether or not Drakar would venture out as well. He feared Drakar might expect him to use the storm's cover for a special errand and follow him, thereby finding Claerwen.

Marcus swore again, and paced the sparsely furnished room. It was the main room of his house, round in shape, the fire pit in the center. Aside from the table and the brazier, there was a rustic bed built into an alcove along the wall and draped with calf-skin curtains and fur coverings, a comfortable Roman-style chair, another simpler chair, a clothing chest he had carved many years before, and a low copper-lined oak tub. A small anteroom was separated from the main room by leather curtains and served as an entryway for the main door. The walls were daub and wattle, the roof of thatch, and three windows were evenly spaced in the walls. The house was small but comfortable enough for a man of simple needs and who was gone from home much of the time. Function was more important than luxury in Dinas Beris.

Marcus concluded there was no longer any point in sending another message to Cunedda. Drakar would have it intercepted like all the others. His brows jagged down in consternation, knowing that without help, he would have to wait until after the war was over to bring Claerwen home. But if it was not over soon, she would be forced to commit herself to the convent permanently. He was certain she would not hesitate to break the church vows, but he disliked making her go through the hypocrisy of vowing faith in something she did not believe.

Marcus refilled the brazier and set it near the bed. He banked the fire pit and snuffed the lantern. Still frowning grimly, he removed his boots and laid down on the bed, hoping to catch a few hours of sleep.

Scraping interrupted from the door. Probably Owein, Marcus thought, sitting up again, listening. His skin crept. Owein would have announced himself within seconds.

Marcus slid back on the bed, noiselessly drawing the curtains around it. The gale roared outside, covering any sound he made. Unfortunately, the wind also obscured the intruders' noise. He crouched down and waited. In the occasional respite between heavy gusts, he thought he could hear creeping steps in the room. Slow and cautious at first, then more distinct and rapid, the steps searched the house. Then only the storm moaned.

The drapes across the bed suddenly whipped open, slapping back against the walls on either side. Barely reflecting the glow of the brazier's coals, two daggers loomed, poised high and hovering. Marcus laid on his side, facing the back wall of the alcove, knees drawn up, arms close in to his chest. He turned over slowly, groaning as if to imitate the draughts that inhaled through the shutters. Sweat shined on his face, and his hands worked at his belly. Through slitted eyes, he could see the daggers hesitate, then withdraw, two surprised grunts punctuating their removal.

"Somebody's already done it," whispered one of the assassins.

"Aye, we must go! Move!" One shoved the other toward the nearest window. Marcus turned over further, still groaning. A dagger hilt showed in the midst of a stain on his shirt. His breath escaped, then ceased.

"Go, man! Drakar will want to hear about this. Go!" They unhooked the shutter and scrambled out the window.

A few seconds passed and Marcus' eyes opened. Thunder rumbled over the fort as he rose and crossed to stand aside the window. He slipped just far enough to the window casement to see the intruders scale the ramparts and disappear over the wall. He slapped the shutters closed again, getting his head and shoulders wet from the blowing rain, then drew and tucked the leather curtains.

An instant later, the door smacked open and torchlight scattered the darkness. Swords clanged out, propelled by a half-dozen men. Marcus stood shocked, then relaxed as he watched Owein slide to a halt half-way across the plank floor. His cousin's face snarled, ready to fight, then evolved into dismay when he discovered Marcus in his stained shirt and damp hair, still holding a dagger hilt at his belly. They stared at each other, tension filling the room. Owein and the others fully held their breath, waiting for Marcus to topple over in a pool of blood.

A slight choking sound escaped him, starting Owein out of his trance. Then Marcus broke into a broad grin, followed by a roar of laughter.

"Cousin?" Owein queried, not understanding. Several guards made the sign against evil or crossed themselves. They put up their swords as Marcus continued to laugh at their stupefaction.

"Gentlemen, you are just a bit late." He held up the dagger hilt, showing that the blade had been broken off. "This and a little red ink and few well placed grunts create a good ruse."

Owein stepped forward, businesslike again. "Where did they go?"

"Out the window and over the wall. No!" He signaled them to halt. "Let them go. They were Drakar's. Let them think I am dead. This is the chance we have waited for. He will have to make his move now." Marcus paced the floor again, the stained shirt swishing grotesquely each time he turned. He still held the dagger hilt, unconsciously using it to emphasize his words. "With or without Cunedda's help, now we know Drakar will move in on us as soon as the roads are open again. And we will have surprise on our side, making Drakar overconfident. And by the gods, where have you been?"

Marcus' tone abruptly changed from optimism to anger. "Now, when we have be as precise as the stars, you are as sloppy as the mud in the courtyard! How did those two get into the fort? There are plenty of you to stop idiots like those." He pointed the hilt at the window, then flung it hard on the table where it bounced and slid to a stop just before falling off the opposite edge. "We are not playing games here!"

Owein reported, "They got in through the tunnel. Two of ours are dead."

"The tunnel? No one knows about that tunnel except us." He paused, glaring at the men one by one, his black eyes cold and unforgiving. "Whoever is selling us to the Saxons will soon be a head on a pike. No one, *no one*, will take this fort, not Drakar, not Vortigern, and not some bloody little traitor, by the gods!"

Marcus swung around, flinging off the ruined shirt and dragging the tunic back on. As he barked orders to the men to return to their posts, he pulled on his boots, checking their daggers, then buckled on the sword.

"We are going to inspect the tunnel, Owein. This foolishness must end, or we will all be dead before the week is out."

They jogged through the heavy rain, going across the compound to an obscure shed and disappeared inside. They inspected several barrels and some old tack that had been yanked aside to expose a small trap door in the floor. Marcus slapped the door's iron latch back and forth, then lifted it.

"There is no damage. That means someone on the inside opened it for them." Steps led down into the ground. The tunnel was an emergency escape route, one branch leading from the cellars and a second from Marcus' house. They joined, then cut down through the hill spur, emerging on a precariously narrow granite ledge on the southern side of the spur. The ledge was heavily overgrown by wild shrubbery and spongy moss. Without great care, a slip meant a long fall onto boulders in the river below.

Marcus and Owein descended into the cellar, the site of one of the guards' murder. Other men were just taking away the body; Marcus grunted acknowledgment as they passed, and waited for them to go up the stairs. A single guard remained, standing at the foot of the steps. Marcus eyed him warily, wanting to remember him in case of future trouble. Then he and Owein turned to an oak panel, hung over with nets of dried fruit and root vegetables. A bin holding dried corn that had been in front was pushed aside and the panel was ajar.

Owein remarked, "Whoever opened this for the assassins was probably the one who killed our men, eliminating his identity." He took a festering torch from a wall bracket and ordered the lone guard to let no one else enter the tunnel and let no one other than themselves come out, on pain of death. The guard nervously acknowledged his order.

"Just a boy," Marcus muttered as he and Owein entered the musty dampness of the narrow passageway beyond the panel. Sewage water reeked in the place, seeping between the rough stones and beams that supported the walls. Rats scurried before the light, scuffling away through greenish slime oozing across the floor.

The torch smoked profusely from the dampness, making their eyes smart. Slowly the two men crept further into the tunnel. The air was silent and dead; only the occasional dripping of water, the rats, and the hissing of the pine tar torch met their ears.

Gradually the floor sloped downwards and a slight draught began to suck the smoke away from them instead of hanging in the air. They moved onward, coming to a bend. They halted, hearing scuffling in the precedent darkness.

Marcus held up a hand to wait. The sound was different than the squeak and rustle of a rat. It came again and they listened for several moments, then overpowering silence drew in. Marcus drew a dagger; Owein pulled his short sword. Breathing could be heard now, ragged tired breathing. Then more scuffling. Marcus shifted the knife from one hand to the other and slipped out a second.

A soft moan followed by a tender thud echoed against the walls, then the silence returned. Marcus inched forward to the corner, his blood pounding in his ears, ready to attack. On his signal, he leapt out, both knives sharply ready, as Owein lit the corridor. But they met no resistance, nor did anyone back away from them. The only thing they saw was a bundle of rags tossed against one wall, soaking and filthy in the greenish mud.

Marcus quickly scanned the corridor, returning one dagger to its boot. Owein posted the torch in a handy bracket and would have put up the sword when he stopped and stared.

"Marcus," he grunted.

Marcus raised an eyebrow and followed his cousin's line of sight. The bundle of rags seemed to have rearranged itself slightly. Fingers, barely recognizable as such, showed among the mud and rags.

"By the gods my people swear by, what is that?" He slipped the other dagger into its sheath and knelt at the bundle, confused by its tangle. Studying the hand, he saw it was covered with thick mud and clutching something. The fingers were so cold and tightly wrapped around the object, he had a hard time prying them open.

"Not what, but who?" Owein asked.

"I can't tell. There's something wrapped around the fingers...there." He loosened the fingers from the object and held it up to the light. It was a ring on a thong. His gold ring. The one he gave to Claerwen to send if she was in trouble.

"Oh, Lleu, no. It can't be. It just can't be!" He worked and worked at the muddy, soaking rags, gently pulling and searching, trying to release their prisoner. Owein stepped closer, not yet understanding Marcus' urgency. Finally, Marcus discovered the hood of a cloak. Gently, he tugged at the sodden clothing that clung so tenaciously to its victim. At last the twisted, heavy cloth let go, freeing a deathly white, pinched face.

Owein watched Marcus' face register such utter shock and dismay that he thought his cousin had been kicked in the gut.

"No!" Marcus felt his breath sting his lungs. "Oh, my Claerwen."

"The woman you told me about? The one you will marry?" Owein knelt next to Marcus. "Are you sure?"

"I would know her anywhere." Marcus was totally confounded. "How did she ever get here? And like this?" He stared at Owein, then said, "I will take her to my house. Have Padrig bring food and supplies to me immediately." He scooped her up in his arms. She felt like a limp doll, frail and thin. He gave orders to Owein as he started back up the tunnel.

"Go in my house and move the chest away, so I can bring her up through that entrance. I don't want anyone to know she is here. Then rearrange all the guards. I want to know everyone's movements, from yours to Padrig's. No one is to leave the fort, tell everyone we are on full alert. No one, absolutely no one, must get to Drakar except those two assassins with their news. I will stay hidden in the house, since I'm supposed to be dead. Constantly shuffle the men; perhaps we can flush out our problems if they can not rely on being in the same place all the time."

Marcus was heating water for the oaken tub by the time Padrig came with baskets of food, bandages, salves and healing herbs. Owein followed, reporting to Marcus that the men were confused by the orders but had complied without question.

"Tell them I am preparing for the fight, as an excuse to stay out of the hall and the courtyard. I want everything to continue on as normal as possible, in case Drakar watches, which I'm sure he does. I will stay with Lady Claerwen as long as I can, then when it is time to go, I will sneak out and lead the fight to his surprise." He tested the water's temperature as Padrig poured a mixture of strained liquid made from several grains, bay leaves and lavender into the tub.

Owein watched his cousin, pulling on his moustache. He frowned heavily, thinking how Marcus usually handled problems with a calculated ease, but was worried how the woman distracted him. Finally he said, "I will see to the men." He wanted to say something more comforting, but could not think of anything worthwhile, clapped Marcus' shoulder, then left.

Padrig set aside his usual gruffness and eyed Marcus as he kneeled on the floor, holding Claerwen's limp form against him. "Son, do you want some help?" He was awed by the aching in Marcus' face.

"No, Padrig. Not until I have to leave. I will be all right."

Padrig squeezed Marcus' shoulder and left.

"What did they do to you, my Claeri?" he muttered when he was alone with her. "In the middle of the night, the worst storm in a generation of years has tossed you back to me. How did you ever find your way into that bloody tunnel?"

He swore to himself bitterly as he untied the sleeves of his tunic, tossing them aside so he could work more easily. He began to untangle the shreds of her clothing, pulling and unwinding the mess from her cold body. Once he got the cloak off, he pulled her long, matted hair together and back; it clung around her as if it was glued to her skin. Then he saw her gown was missing and how the undershift was torn and cut, only threads remaining to hold it together. Seeing there was no use to save any of it, he extracted his smallest dagger from one boot and cut the final threads. He peeled the muddy rags away, then lifted her gently, lowering her into the tub until the water was just under her chin.

With a soft cloth, he began to bathe her, his big hands slowly massaging her cold skin in the warm, milky water. He hoped the soothing warmth would waken her, but she did not respond, leaning against the side of the tub, her head resting on its lip. He pulled her forward, supporting her with one arm across in front of her and rinsed the mud from her hair. Pulling it aside, he saw the raw burn where the thong had broken. He saw several bruises down her back and began checking for broken bones. He rested her against the back of the tub again and moved around to face her, washing, rinsing, massaging. "By the gods," he mumbled when he saw the knife cuts. His eyes widened under his lowered brows as the thought crossed his mind that she may have been raped.

He looked into her face and saw pink had come into her cheeks and she stirred slightly, making a sighing sound. "Wake up, Claeri. Come now, wake up. It's Marcus." He reached out and supported her head, but she stopped moving again, her chin resting in his palm.

Finally, he lifted her out of the tub and laid her in a pile of soft linens. As he dried her, he applied one of Padrig's salves to the cuts and the burn on her neck. He felt himself become angrier with each cut and bruise he found, until finally he closed his eyes and whispered to her, "I'm sorry, but I have to know." He gently parted her legs then opened his eyes again. He let out a long sigh of relief; she was unhurt.

Marcus carried her to his bed, laying her down carefully near the back wall and spreading fur coverlets over her. Then he went to the fire pit and made a broth from a selection of herbs Padrig had left. He brought it in a small cup, dripping some into her mouth and rubbing her neck until she swallowed it, patiently doing it over and over until it was finished. He tucked pillows and covers all around her, then took a few moments to grimly watch her resting form. His mouth opened as if to speak, then clamped shut again and he swallowed hard.

Marcus reached to his sword that hung in wait on the wall over the head of the bed, touching it momentarily, choking down the rage he felt. He remained calm, but his black eyes glittered with hatred.

"Drakar did this to you, didn't he?" Marcus said softly. "He would not send hired assassins after me unless he was busy with something else he thought was as much or more important, not after vowing to kill me himself all these years. Damn!"

Finally, he pulled in a deep breath, forcing himself to think of rest. He pulled off his boots and stretched out on the bed, leaning his face against Claerwen's arm. He slept.

Marcus was up again at first light. Claerwen had not moved from the position he had placed her in. He went to one of the windows, stretching as he moved, and opened the shutters. Heavy rain continued to pound the muddy earth of the compound, and he re-closed the shutters. He wanted to leave them open for the fresh air, but the wind was blowing rain inside. Owein came shortly after, bringing food from Padrig and news that nothing had changed regarding Drakar. After inquiring about Claerwen, he told Marcus she would recover just because he willed it so.

Claerwen took fever at midday. It came slowly at first, sweat beading on her face, her hair dampened. Though never conscious, she would keen and whimper softly for long periods of time, as if in the throes of some ancient nightmare. Marcus kept her covered against the draughts and sponged her face until his cloth was soaked. Every hour or so he forced some of the broth down her throat until she either swallowed or coughed it back. Hour after hour, he sat watching her, his face lined in apprehension, his senses numbed to the outside.

By the second day, the fever raged within her body as if it was an evil spirit. She tossed and rolled with delirium, throwing the covers from her until she lay shaking and naked, soaked with sweat. Over and over, Marcus picked up the furs and sat on one edge while holding down the other side, trying to keep her warm. He watched in helpless agony as she would wear herself down and rest out of exhaustion, only to wind herself up again into new torture. In the quieter times, he fed her more broth and cool water, then tried to rest himself. Her illness knew no sense of day or night.

Marcus became irritable, running out of patience when Owein reported. He no longer concentrated on his cousin's words, making Owein uncomfortable. Owein silently worried that if Claerwen did not survive, Marcus would lose heart in fighting off Drakar, making Marcus as dead as Drakar was supposed to believe. Owein wished Claerwen would show some signs of recovering; he was not prepared to watch Marcus lose control in the midst of a crisis.

The morning of the third day brought no change. Claerwen had dropped weight, making her frailness even more pronounced, and Marcus could not see how she could last another hour. But she held on, fighting inside.

"You remind me of fragile crystal, but you are tough as iron and dragons, my Claerwen," Marcus told her. In frustration, he began talking to her, needing to keep his mind busy. He paced the floor, telling her about his life, his dreams, anything he could think of.

Evening approached, and the clouds began to break up at last. He knew he would have to leave as soon as the roads became passable, whether she was better or not. Craving to go, to finish the last battle, he dreaded leaving as much. He was afraid she would die.

Time was so heavy on his shoulders, he thought he could shrug it away. Light began to dwindle towards dusk. He went to the window again for fresh air, then sat in his chair next to the bed as usual, glancing his now practiced glance, to see no change. He pulled one of the knives from a boot and began to polish it, slowly, absently. It glittered in the brazier's coals, he scraped a thumb over its razor edge, returned it to the boot, vaguely satisfied. Then he pulled out another to polish, slowly, carefully. Glance to Claerwen. Polish, slowly. Glance...

And now stare. Her pale skin was not so flat and pallid. It had a more natural rose sheen and was dry. And her eyelids were moving.

Stuffing the dagger back into his boot, Marcus shot himself to the edge of the bed. Affectionately, he passed his palm over her forehead to one cheek. She was cool and dry, her lips colored now. The fever was broken. "By the gods, Claeri, come back to me!" A glorious grin spread across his rough features.

Claerwen felt she was swimming, floating, struggling to open her eyes. A voice in the distance sounded extremely familiar, but she could not place it. Confusion brought the sense of something terrible, but she could not place that either. One more effort and her eyes peeled open a slit, then closed again as if straining against sewn stitches. She wanted to raise a hand to push them open but could not seem to order her arm to move. She managed to twist her neck, helping to shake away some of the heavy drowsiness. A moan escaped her lips.

The familiar voice came again and she concentrated on it, finding its deep tone soothing. Finally her eyes released and her lids slid up painfully over their salty surfaces, seeing only darkness. She blinked a few times and gradually colors became shapes and forms, moving above her. One group of shapes moved more than others; a blob of black with more black above it, a paler color between. The voice came again, low and comfortable, calling over and over.

Claerwen stared at Marcus without seeing him; he could see her pupils constricting gradually as the western light suddenly burst through the clouds and the window, crossing the room. "By the gods my people swear by," he said softly, and he stroked her face again. Her eyes wandered over him, then finally settled on his face, studying.

"Marcus," she whispered, suddenly connecting his face and his voice. She gazed steadily into his eyes, pulling strength from him.

"Ah, my Claeri," Marcus reached for the ever-present cup of broth and helped her to sip.

"So...tired," she mumbled, a wave of fatigue and dizziness pushing over her. She struggled to keep awake, confused by the unfamiliar room.

"What is...this place?" she asked, her voice low and throaty.

Marcus smiled, "Welcome to Dinas Beris."

"Dinas Beris." She repeated, astonished, and scanned about the room.

"I don't know how you got here," he answered the next question he knew she would ask.

Her mind was not alert enough to sort out the confusion. She continued to sip broth, its warmth giving her strength, and she struggled to pull herself higher on the pillows. Then she realized she was naked. Her eyes shot up to Marcus' and she asked, "How long have I been here?"

"Three days."

"Three days. I can't remember..."

He held her hand, "You had a severe fever for three days. There is a tunnel below the fort; I found you there, half-dead, your clothing torn into filthy rags."

She stared up into his eyes, trying to remember. "I don't know. A tunnel...I don't remember a tunnel. I saw young willows flattened to the ground by the wind." Her eyes looked as if she was reading, trying to see the memories that were trapped in her mind.

"What happened at the convent after I left?"

"The convent...I just can't think."

Claerwen's eyes suddenly widened, a deep fear in them and she sat up abruptly. Her fingers dug into Marcus' arm, making him wince. "Drakar was sending an assassin to kill you! That's why I left. I had to reach you first, to warn you." She stopped, realizing too many days had already passed. "I am too late, but you're not hurt?" She looked him up and down to make sure he was not hiding any injuries. He reassured her he was fine, but his brows jagged down as he tucked a blanket around her shoulders. "Was Drakar there himself?"

"Aye, the same day you came, in the evening, with one man. He had the gall to demand hospitality, after what his men did the night before. If only he had been among the men the Iron Hawk killed."

Marcus' mouth curled inward with anger and his black eyes went cold. "Damn," he cursed. "He must have had me followed when I went to find you. If only I had taken you with me then. He would not have done all of this." He lifted the coverlet to show her the cuts and bruises on her hips. "It was worse before." The cuts were well scabbed-over, but he reached for the salve and applied another coating to keep them supple and less likely to break open.

"You have been taking care of me? All this time?" Her face was incredulous.

He smiled and nodded.

"But you have more important things to do than take care of me. What about—"

"There was nothing I could do until the storm broke anyway," he interrupted. He explained his ruse that fooled the assassins. Claerwen almost smiled, then frowned and said, "I hit Drakar with a burning stick from the fire pit. He will be livid when he comes after the fort."

Marcus snorted, "Like a hive of sting-bees!" Then he was struck by what she had said and asked, "If you left the convent on your own, how did you find the tunnel? It's impossible in the dark if you're not familiar, and extremely dangerous in a storm."

"I didn't know there was a tunnel. I didn't know where the fort was either; you never really told me." She paused, realizing what had happened, then whispered, "The fire led me to you."

Marcus raised one eyebrow. They stared at each other for several minutes, Marcus' skin prickling and Claerwen flooding with relief.

Finally, Claerwen broke the silence, telling him, "Drakar's still demanding to know where 'it' is. But this time he called it 'a treasure.' You haven't learned what it is yet?"

Marcus shook his head, answering, "No. There's been no opportunity."

"I just don't understand. I have nothing of value. Except the ring you gave me. But I didn't have that when they started looking at the farm. It has to be something else."

Her hand flew to her neck, feeling for the ring. She frowned, not finding it.

"It's here." He reached to a peg on the wall over her head and showed her the ring hanging on its thong. He watched her eyes grow comfortable when she recognized it, then go pensive again when she saw his huge, sheathed sword on the wall beneath it. He explained, "The sword is there when I am home, always within reach, even in the night."

"Be prepared, or die..." she echoed his thought. "You are going to go now, aren't you? I can see it in your face."

"Aye, this is the final fight, the one that will determine Dinas Beris' freedom." He gently squeezed her hand and rose to collect his gear. "Everyone except Padrig and four of the house guards will be leaving. Padrig will take care of you while I am gone." He pulled on a metal link shirt over his cloth shirt, then a long leather tunic that nearly came to his knees.

Claerwen pushed herself up on her elbows and blurted, "Marcus, I must go with you."

He stared at her, stunned. He could see her eyes were slightly out of focus, and he decided she spoke from disclarity left by the fever. He smiled and told her to rest.

She pulled herself up again and watched as he turned away, strapping a small dagger sheath under his left sleeve, then another onto the back of his belt. He turned again, coming back towards her, and she saw how his face had turned hard, the deep concentration of a warrior making his eyes cold. She declared, "I can not let you go without me! I *must* be there!"

Not responding, he took the sword down and buckled it across his back on a baldric. He went to the door and spoke briefly to a guard outside, then returned to finish his preparations. He took a gold torque out of a small carved wooden casket; it was made of several heavy strands of gold twisted together, gold dragon's heads on the ends that met in the middle front. He placed it around his neck and pinned on a long cloak.

"I have told them we are to leave immediately, Claerwen." He stood by the bed, watching her. Her eyes were still glazed, the pale green more noticeable that usual. His brows flinched in their heaviness; he felt a peculiar eeriness when he looked at her. He shrugged the feeling away and turned toward the door, but she lashed a hand out, gripping his arm.

"You don't understand, Marcus, I have to come with you! I have to be there!"

"No, woman! I forbid it!" He shouted more harshly than he wanted to, anger coming from his urgency to leave. His voice bounced off the walls and it frightened her. She had never been the target of his anger before. She eased herself back down into the covers and lay still, as if she was listening to something.

Calm again, Marcus gazed at her a few moments, then said softly, "I will be back as soon as it's over."

Claerwen held his gaze, seeing him almost as if he was a stranger. Then he swept out the door, a soft jingling with each heavy step.

The echoing voice within Claerwen's soul rang and pounded like ram horns and druid drums, calling louder and louder, until she clamped her hands over her ears.

CHAPTER 13

Dinas Beris
Autumn, 467 A.D.

Marcus stared at the confluence of rivers, far below, past the skirt of rocky crags, past the stand of trees, past the convent. The water sparkled with the sun that was rising behind him, over the top of the crags. He was nestled in a granite crevice that almost fitted him like a chair, out of the wind, but cold and still wet from the rains. The sky had cleared, giving hope for a fine day, but the dampness hung in the air like the cold water of the rivers below. Marcus leaned his spear on his shoulder so he could rub his gauntleted hands together.

The rocky slope was quiet all around him, but he knew his men were scattered there, hidden through the night like himself between the stones, prepared to pick off Drakar's men with arrows and spears as they would soon approach from the southeast. Unless Cunedda's mercenaries would suddenly arrive, they were on their own. He suspected Drakar had a full war band of Saxon mercenaries supplied by Vortigern, a contingent of three hundred men. Of his own, he had been able to scrape together just over one hundred.

"Marcus!" Owein called softly from above. He eased himself down to a spot almost behind his cousin.

"No sign of Cunedda's men?" he asked before Owein spoke.

"No."

"Then, so be it. We can't change it now."

"Hope Drakar comes soon, so we can get over with it." Owein muttered grimly.

"It will be soon enough."

"Likely your woman will be a widow before she even marries you."

"I didn't tell her the odds."

Owein grunted, "She can guess, cousin. She must have seen you when you left the house. Don't show that face to the men."

Marcus grimaced at Owein.

A boy barely into his teens was climbing down from above. He slid down into a hollow between two boulders where he was hidden, but could speak to the leaders.

"My Lords, one of the men caught a scout from Drakar. The war band is not far behind. They will be here within the hour."

"That is good." Owein acknowledged the news.

"Is the scout still alive?" Marcus inquired.

"Aye. They have him staked down on the other side of the ridge. A stinking Saxon." The boy turned up his nose as if he could still smell the invader.

"Good," Marcus said. "Go back to your station." To Owein he ordered, "Spread the alert."

The boy hesitated and Marcus raised an eyebrow when he did not leave immediately. "Sir, I must tell you something." When he saw he had Marcus' attention, he continued, "As I came around the ridge to report to you, Sir, I saw a man descending the slope around to the east, heading down towards the eastbound road. I recognized him as one who works with the equipment and horses."

Marcus studied the boy's face. He was the son of one his farmsteaders, from a family that had been part of the mountains nearly as long as his own. He knew the boy told him the truth. He clapped the boy's shoulder and told him he had done well. To Owein, he said, "Drakar will know our position. Order everyone back to the location of the third plan; to move immediately! Use the silent signals."

"The third, not the second?"

"If the man gave away our positions, they will expect us to go to the second plan, then the third. I never intended to use the second plan."

Owein grinned at Marcus' strategy, then vaulted himself up the slope, signaling the lines as he went. One by one, each man crept out of his hiding place and climbed up the crags, disappearing over the top ridge. Marcus sent the boy with them, then followed.

Beyond the line of the ridge, Marcus waited, watching his men spread out again. He had hoped to stop Drakar at the foot of the pass, using the advantages of the sun's glare and the steep, rocky surfaces unfamiliar to flatlander Saxons. But with Drakar knowing of those positions, he was sure Drakar would have attempted to surround them, driving them back down into the valley. They would be trapped in the narrow gap and massacred. By moving back along the upper slopes of the pass, Marcus could reverse the trap and easily surround Drakar's war band.

As the men swiftly resettled, he strode across the narrow plateau behind the ridge, heading towards a notch in the rock ledge. But Taran suddenly appeared, his cloak streaming out behind him in the wind. He blocked Marcus, and demanded to know why they were moving into the pass.

Marcus dragged Taran away from the ledge. "Will you get out of sight! That cloak is worse than a flag!" Marcus glared at Taran. "We are moving for tactical reasons."

"We were perfectly positioned. It's too late to move!"

"No it isn't. Why do you protest so much, Taran? Why?"

"Because you're going to lose the fort and make fools of us!"

Marcus reached a fist out and grabbed a handful of

Taran's tunic. "The only foolish one is you, if you delay me further. Is that what you want? Your arrogance and jealousy are getting tiresome, little brother. It is time for you to grow up and work together with the rest of us. Now get rid of that cloak and get yourself in position. Stop wasting time!" Marcus shoved Taran away and dropped down through the notch.

The mercenary war band hired by Vortigern and led by Drakar approached the foot of the pass. Marcus had left two scouts posted on the hillside to watch Drakar's progress. The warband halted and sent out three scouts of its own.

Immediately, Marcus' men relayed signals and warriors were sent, who silently picked off Drakar's scouts with daggers.

Marcus climbed down nearly to the road and perched on a flat-topped boulder to wait for Drakar. As he watched the communication signals, he learned the war band remained stalled along the river near the confluence, trying to decide what to do. Instinctively, he knew Drakar would not retreat, too proud to shame himself to Vortigern or the Saxons. Drakar would know the wily mountain men were drawing him into a trap. The Saxons would fight ferociously, like baited dogs, to make up for their lack of highland warfare knowledge.

The war band finally began moving along the road into the pass, Drakar and two huge Saxon sub-leaders in the lead. As they came into the narrow gap, the soldiers were forced to fall behind the leaders in a long, thin line, three or four across at the most. From his position, Marcus could see Drakar chafing nervously. Another message came; Drakar had not split his force to prevent being surrounded. Marcus grinned to himself and signaled for his men to close the pass as soon as the last Saxon was inside the mountain gap.

Marcus stood on the top of the boulder, leaning on his drawn sword. He could hear the rumble of three hundred pairs of Saxon feet pounding up the road, their muddy steps vibrating in the earth. As Drakar emerged into sight, Marcus signaled again. Instantly, an arrow hissed down, striking the road just in front of Drakar.

"What business do you have to enter Dinas Beris, Drakar of the traitors!" Marcus boomed out at Drakar, his deep voice ricocheting on the rocks.

Drakar's head jerked up, his eyes locking on Marcus' casual stance, the naked sword in front of him. The Saxon to Drakar's left moved to signal an attack, but Drakar stopped him.

"So, it is true what I hear. You are alive," Drakar snarled through his bad teeth.

"Ah, so it is true. And you have brought your playmates with you. You have not given up children's games yet, I see." Marcus deliberately layered arrogance into his voice. He wanted make Drakar talk, stalling so his own men could get into their positions.

"Do not play words with me, Prince." Drakar drawled the title with contempt. "You know why we are here. But why are you alone? Did your warriors desert you in your time of need?" Drakar laughed with insolence.

Marcus glared coldly at Drakar, "My truest soldiers turn out to end this foolishness. One of them is a woman who survived your stinking abuses to warn me of your assassins."

"And did she tell you what she did to me?" Drakar pulled up the neck of his mail hood and the cloth underneath. There showed a seething, angry burn left from the firewood Claerwen had struck him with.

"Ah, would that I had done so myself," Marcus said coolly.

Drakar grew impatient at the trading of insults. "Would that the little slut was here that I could slay her slowly and painfully as I will do to you, Prince of Dinas Beris!"

Marcus snapped, "So be it!"

Drakar snarled, then completed the challenge, "So be it."

Marcus ap Iorwerth rammed a fist into the air and screamed a horrible war cry that carried far into the pass. A pair of hawks rose, disturbed, and screeched their discomfort as they flew out over the mountains.

Marcus bounded off the boulder, leaping down into a

hollow behind it. As he landed, a shower of arrows rained onto the Saxons from both sides of the pass, wounding or killing many. The Saxons crouched down, trying to take cover, but the roadway was too narrow and treeless to afford them much. The men of Dinas Beris were high enough that they were able to keep the mercenaries continuously pinned.

The mountain warriors gradually worked themselves down the walls of the pass, their arrows unceasing and accurate. The Saxons barricaded themselves under their shields, occasionally heaving a spear up into the rocks, but they were unable to stand up long enough to aim well or throw hard enough to reach the Celts. Drakar's force was surrounded completely; any man who broke through the attackers was chased down and killed.

As Marcus' men had nearly used all their arrows, they had also nearly reached the road. Owein appeared and led those who were closest to the lower end of the road. They began driving in, squeezing the Saxons back further into the pass, using spears and short thrusting swords. At the other end, Marcus gathered his men and they forced Drakar back down. The mercenaries could only fall over themselves and their own dead, or try to climb up the steep scree of the pass where they were easily spotted and killed. Within minutes, the Saxons saw how they had been outsmarted and lashed out vehemently, trying to save themselves. Physically, they were well-advantaged to the shorter, stockier mountain Celts, but in hard-working strength, stealth, and using the mountains themselves to their advantage, the Saxons were purely lost.

By midday, it was over. The road was heaped with dead invaders, the river stained with their blood. The men of Dinas Beris took no prisoners. They stood solemnly watching the result of their careful planning, waiting for Marcus to declare an end to the hostilities.

Marcus climbed back onto the boulder he had staged the battle from and surveyed the carnage. He felt his stomach twist, bile churning inside him, but he refused to show it in his face. He stood proudly on the rock, his long hair flowing back in the wind and his sword raised high towards the sun. He took a deep breath, preparing to speak, when a shout came from behind him.

"There goes Drakar!" Taran screamed, pointing up the slope towards the top of the pass. "He is heading for the fort!"

"Leave him to me!" Marcus yelled, and without pause, leapt from the rock. He grabbed a spear from the nearest of his warriors and began a grinding charge up the hill. He crashed over the stony earth and through bracken that slashed at his chest and legs. He felt the power in his legs carry him higher and higher up the hillside, following Drakar deeper into the pass. As he approached the craggy heights, the slippery scree and the unevenness of the ground slowed him down. He could not see Drakar, but the man left a trail a child could trace. This is no mountain man, Marcus thought, grimness darkening his face.

Quiet descended as Marcus moved up the slope. It was topped by a rocky ridge which pitched down toward the fort's hill spur on the other side. All was silent from that way. Below he could hear his men's muffled movements as some of them trailed him. He subdued his own panting as best he could to listen. Drakar's track continued toward the ridge, plain and clear. Wary of a new trap, Marcus hefted the spear, ready to throw it, and crept upward silently. He knew Drakar was hiding somewhere, resting after the strenuous climb. Now would be the time to catch him. Marcus increased his pace, steadily gaining on the ridge. From the top, he could reconnoiter his position.

Suddenly the blatant trail gave out. No more muddy footprints or scattered rocks, nothing. Marcus knew he was running into a trap. But where? There was no time to spare thinking about it. He had to move.

In the instant he decided to gain the ridge, a dwarfed oak that jutted out from between two cracked boulders uprooted itself and spilled towards him. A great crackling and rustling rushed through the quiet air, and he felt the spear knocked out of his hand. In the next second, the branches fell all around, scraping him. A heavy one soundly rapped him on the left shoulder, knocking him flat. Stunned, but still alert, he rolled down and out from under the debris. He came up enraged and swinging his sword high over his head. He gave a terrible scream from deep within his soul, fully expecting to face Drakar and fight the last bloody struggle to the end.

But Marcus stopped, his sword still hanging in the air. His jaw dropped and he stared several full minutes. Owein, Taran and several other of his men raced up the hill and stopped behind him, stunned as well.

The tree that had fallen had actually only split. Drakar had climbed up it and was going to ambush Marcus from above. But his weight broke the branch he was perched on and the one below it as he fell. The lower branch was the one that had struck Marcus. The other never made it all the way down.

Marcus realized his spear had been wrenched away from him and held Drakar in the tree. Its tip had pierced his neck just above the collarbone, killing him instantly.

"By the gods my people swear by," Marcus whispered. He dropped the sword limply to his side. "Claerwen?" he called tentatively.

Claerwen stood, dazed from fire in the head, gripping the spear with both hands. She stared up, the sun bathing her tender, pale face, watching without seeing. A small stream of blood slipped down the spear shaft, running over her hands.

The other men made the sign against evil and retreated a few steps.

"Claeri?" Marcus called again. He could see the god was still in her and he was not sure if it was safe to disturb her. Strange light radiated in her eyes.

He saw she was wearing some of his clothing; she had taken it from the chest in his house as her own clothing had been destroyed. With so few people left in the fort, it would have been easy for her to leave and follow him. He was shocked that she had been able to climb the steep slope when she had been so ill.

Then he understood why she had insisted to come with him to the battlefield. He would have died if she had not come to save his life. She had seen it, and was driven by the fire, by the gods. And her love for him. He shivered and made the sign.

Suddenly, the trance broke. She backed away, becoming aware of her surroundings again, and looked up at the tree to recognize Drakar. She gasped, nearly choking at the way he died, then saw the blood on her hands. Her temples pounded with the pain of the departing vision. She looked like she was going to scream, her mouth open, still choking air.

Marcus ached, watching her agony, horrified at the outrageous way the gods had used her and thinking it was more of a curse than a gift. He watched her back away a few more steps, holding her bloody hands out and away from herself as if they were no longer a part of her. He could feel her pain and wished he could take it away from her. Then she swayed, her eyes closing. Marcus dropped his sword and caught her as she fainted.

CHAPTER 14

Dinas Beris
Midwinter, 467 A.D.

"Are you getting nervous?" Marcus grinned at Claerwen.

She nodded and shivered in the cold morning air. "But I still think this will be such a grand surprise for everyone. I am so glad you thought of it!"

Owein entered the great hall, stamping snow off his boots. "The druid is here," he announced. "He is in the guest house, preparing. Most of the people seem to be coming, in spite of the cold."

"We have a lot to be thankful this Midwinter," Marcus said.

"I have never seen a Midwinter celebration," Claerwen returned.

"This won't be very elaborate, compared to some I have heard of, but I think it will be fitting. We haven't had one since my grandfather was alive. Padrig would remember them." He crossed to a window and pulled back the shutter and leather curtain. He looked up at the mountain that rose behind the fort, sharply steep, rising from just beyond the last bank and ditch defense line. It was sheer rock over most of its slopes, with no cover to hide approaching outsiders. There was a terraced path cut into one side that led to an ancient oak grove at the summit. The trees looked like a heavy halo ringing the top.

"Before the Romans came, druids had regular ceremonies there for the mountain people. You will see there is a single standing stone, in the center, like the ones in Avebury or the Giant's Dance on the Great Plain in the south, only this one's smaller." He closed the window again.

"I hope we don't all freeze to death out there!" Taran strode into the hall. Marcus rolled his eyes. Just once, he wished, Taran could be gracious.

"So wear an extra cloak," Owein mumbled and went to the door. "I will see if the druid is ready."

Marcus nodded and picked up cloaks for himself and Claerwen. He wrapped hers around her shoulders, his hands lingering there in a light squeeze. He thought she looked so lovely.

Like everyone else, she had on new and extra nice clothing. Her gown was a soft, thick, green-blue wool, the same color as her eyes, only a rich, darker shade. She and Grania had made it themselves, embroidering the edges with a Celtic knotwork pattern in silver thread. The cloak matched it, having the same pattern around the hood. He could not stop smiling at her while he threw his own on.

"This looks so good on you!" Claerwen pinned Marcus' brooch on his cloak as he adjusted the torque around his neck. She and her cousin had made the cloak for him as a Midwinter gift. It was dark blue and they had made a row of gold decorations on the front where it draped across to close. She took a step back to look at her finished work and pressed her fingertips to her mouth. Pride glowed in her eyes as she admired how handsome he looked, thinking how it suited him.

Owein came back through the door, followed by the druid.
"It is time," announced Owein.
Marcus held his hand out to Claerwen and said, "My Lady?" She took his hand and they followed Owein and the white-robed druid outside.

A layer of snow on the ground had frozen hard and crunchy in the night. The sky was very cold and clear, glowing softly in the east. The ceremony, by tradition, was to be held at sunrise. The druid began singing, clear and sharp like the cold air, his voice carrying easily over the pass between the mountains. It was a call to assemble. He walked out of the fort's courtyard, down the path through the banks and ditches, to the terraced walkway. Marcus and Claerwen followed him, echoing the ancient song of the druids. Behind them came Taran, Grania, Padrig, and Owein. Out of the mountains surrounding the fort came the people of Dinas Beris, the families and loners who had defended and were defended by Marcus ap Iorwerth.

They moved up the mountain to the grove, singing all together in the way the Celts have always loved to sing. There they assembled around the edge of the clearing in the grove, the druid in the center by the standing stone.

He lit a torch and raised his arms to the sky, chanting in the ancient Celtic tongue. The dialect was old and difficult to understand, but the people knew he was calling to thank the gods for keeping the cycles of the earth and the seasons turning. It was the end of the season called Samhiunn, the death of the old year, and they celebrated the rebirth of the earth, the spark of life in the seed of the new year. At precisely the right time, the druid dramatically waved the torch and lit a pile of firewood laid before the stone. The sun peered over the horizon at the same moment.

The druid then began a long chant, reciting the history of Dinas Beris and its people, the descendants of whom surrounded him. It reconfirmed their places there on the mountain, that they belonged there and they belonged together. The fire dwindled down as the sun reached up above the horizon and the holy man finished his chant.

As the druid backed away into the shadow of the standing stone, Marcus stepped forward. The people cheered him and many began to kneel before him, until all were kneeling. He stretched his arms out to them, the handsome cloak flowing out like a waterfall behind him.

"I am glad you could all come here today." He paused and went to some of the older people, helping them rise. It embarrassed him to see people kneeling to him in the snow. "Please, be comfortable. There is no need for high protocol. We are here to celebrate and remind ourselves that the gods have protected us, bringing us to our victory. There has not been a Midwinter celebration since my father's father's time and we would like to propose that we bring back those celebrations. We have much to be thankful for now."

The people stirred, nodding their appreciation for the prince's initiative. They had deeply admired his father, but Iorwerth had grown distant from them due to his ill health. Until now, they had not had much contact with the younger Marcus. So far, they liked what they saw. He had vowed to not change the titheless land policy his father and grandfather always stood by and he had shown himself a true and courageous leader, an outstanding warrior.

Marcus continued, "Today, I also want to introduce you to Lady Claerwen, who has been a part of our victory, as you know already." He held his hand out and Claerwen joined him. Her shyness embarrassed her, but the crowd cheered heartily. When Marcus squeezed her hand, she smiled at the people.

"If you will indulge us, we have asked the druid to marry us here, now, as part of this Midwinter ceremony. As you know, weddings are usually held at the Beltainne festival in the spring, but we thought it would mean more to us, and to you, if we completed our pledge of marriage now."

Hushed "ahs" and grins of approval circulated among the people. Marcus and Claerwen turned to the standing stone and the druid reappeared before them.

Another chant was begun, a recitation of the ancient marriage laws. Marcus and Claerwen bowed their heads in reverence to the words, words of the gods. They held hands, their breath streaming in the cold air. As the druid finished his recitation, he waved his arms ceremoniously to the lightening sky. The sun rose a little higher and burst through the gap in the trees where the path cut its way, warming the couple and the standing stone in its light.

Marcus turned to Claerwen and spoke softly, "I wish to give you a token of my soul." He pulled a ring from his little finger. Her eyes widened as he continued, "This ancient Celtic ring symbolizes our ancient bond, but its beauty is no match to yours." He smiled, his dark eyes glinting in the bright sunlight. "That bond has never been and never will be broken. Ever and forever, we are united."

Claerwen was visibly moved by his simple words. He slipped the ring onto the third finger of her left hand. How could she match such a lovely thought? Then she looked up into his handsome face, his dark hair gently moving in the cold breeze and pulled the ring she had for him from her thumb and placed it on his left hand's third finger. Slowly she said, "You know me down to my very soul and have seen beyond. This ring represents the circle of our lives, the intertwining lines are the intertwining of our spirits. There is no beginning and no end, and likewise, we are forever linked to one another. Ever and forever, we are united."

They stood for a long time, fingers intertwined and gazing into each other's eyes, the sunrise glowing only on them in the shadowy grove as the druid sang the celebration chant. The gods had blessed them.

The people slowly slipped away, most heading to the fort to celebrate with drinking, music, dancing, and storytelling. They followed the druid down the mountain, happy from the rituals that bound them all together. The druid began singing again, this time a cheerful song. The people joined in, their voices fading away down the hillside, back to the fort.

Grania shivered from the cold in spite of the warming sun. A sigh escaped her unconsciously, and Taran turned briefly to her, an eyebrow raised in amusement. His lips grinned and she became aware of his attention, responding with a tentative smile of her own. She thought, he is so different from Marcus, yet curiosity chewed at her to know if he had a sense of romance and passion like his brother. She felt her stomach flutter, then turned to follow the druid and the others down the mountain. Taran came after her, followed by Padrig and Owein.

Marcus and Claerwen lingered a few moments longer, waiting to be alone. At last, he took her face between his hands and kissed her.

The family gathered in the great hall of the fort for toasts and food, talk and drink. They seated themselves around the biggest table, set with enough food and drink for ten weddings. The people of the clan surrounded them, filling the hall and spilling out into the courtyard.

"I told Padrig not to overdo it," Marcus mused, grinning at the display.

Taran poured wine for everyone at the table, then sat down by Grania. "We haven't eaten this much in years," he said, looking over the spread, trying to decide where to start.

Owein sat on the other side of the table from Taran, a bit away from the others and sipped slowly on his wine. He watched each face over the rim of his goblet.

Padrig came in from the kitchen with another huge wineskin and set it next to Marcus.

"Sit, Padrig," he told the old man.

"Nonsense! I have work to do!" Padrig winked.

"'Nonsense,' he says. Sit, I say!" Marcus pulled on Padrig's tunic until he finally sat on the bench between himself and Owein.

"Oh, if you insist," he laughed.

Marcus stuck a goblet in his hand and told him to relax, have some drink, and let someone else worry about the kitchen for one day.

Padrig gulped a couple of swigs. He thought a moment, then held his cup in the air and thumped his fist on the table for attention. He said, "I wish I was good at fancy words, Marcus, but there is just a simple old fool I am, who has followed your father and his father and now you all my life. I have grieved at both of their passings and rejoiced in their's and your victories...and will do so until my own passing."

Marcus put an affectionate arm across the old man's shoulders. A lifetime settler of Dinas Beris, he helped Marcus keep the feeling of a connection to Iorwerth and those of previous generations with his vivid stories and memories of their lives. Now he ran the household, did the cooking, and patched the men up whenever he was needed.

"You've got a long way to go, old friend," Marcus told Padrig. "And now you've got more of us to take care of."

"Aye, but that will be a pleasure, Marcus, you lucky buck! Why would such a lovely lady want to marry an ugly old hound like you? And I hope she likes all that damned hair of yours!" Padrig rumpled Marcus' hair like he was still a little boy. He giggled as he retreated toward the kitchen, picking at his own very sparse hair, the others laughing with their cups raised and thumping the table for another toast.

Grania sipped wine slowly, watching Claerwen enjoy Marcus' affection from over her cup's rim. She felt lonely, in spite of the friendly atmosphere. Used to the bustle of Caernarfon and then the steady companionship of the nuns, she had found the fort lonely, its few occupants and the scattered homesteaders constantly busy. She admired her cousin enormously, proud of the way she had fought so hard for both of them, defying Drakar and the Iron Hawk, then succeed in marrying the man she loved. But in the few weeks since arriving at the fort, Grania had remained mostly alone, watching Claerwen glow in glorious contentment with Marcus' blatant affection. Even after regaining her strength, Claerwen spent most of her time with him, working alongside him to help prepare for the winter. Grania sighed again, happy for their romance, sad for herself.

"It's snowing again," Taran said, sliding down the bench closer to Grania. Surprised that he would pay any attention to her, she smiled briefly in reply. He had barely acknowledged her presence and she did not like the perpetual sarcasm he radiated.

Taran watched Grania's face, one eyebrow twitching in slight consternation at her apparent preoccupation. Again he grinned, and asked her, "Do you like to dance?"

Grania looked at him full in the face this time, and she saw his usual arrogance was gone. She blushed and said, "I don't know how."

"I can show you, if you like."

Before she could answer, he turned and yelled over his shoulder, "Hey, Marcus, play us something on that harp of yours. Something we can dance to!"

The others cheered in agreement. Taran pulled Grania out to the floor in spite of her protests. He held her hands and led her around the open space, stepping in time with the tune, teaching her simple steps. Soon he had her laughing and swirling around with him. Marcus deliberately stepped up the tempo, making their feet fly and twirl until they nearly fell down from dizziness.

Marcus turned the harp over to Padrig the next time the old man came in from the kitchen and told him that he was the official musician for the night and the cook house was closed. He was going to dance with Claerwen.

Marcus sprawled in his favorite chair by the fire pit of his house, his legs stretched limply before him. His right hand rested around the base of his wine cup that was on the small table next to him. His eyes sleepily watched something in the fire, their blackness softly grinning and glazing from too much alcohol. Slowly he raised the cup to his smiling lips and sipped, then gently replaced it on the table. The sun had gone down and he was glad he could finally retire to his house.

Claerwen stood before a long bronze mirror, unpinning her hair. It rolled down like a great splash of water as she shook it loose. She could feel Marcus' eyes watching her and turned to him. She still wore the green-blue gown and it flowed around her like fine silk. Because it felt so good, she had not changed clothes.

"Come." Marcus held out a hand. It wavered slightly.

She came to him, moving smoothly across the room and

sat on his lap. She put her arms around his neck; he wrapped his around her slender waist.

"Did you make this?" He fingered a lacy cloth he just noticed was on the table under his cup.

"Aye," she answered. "My mother taught us how to do that."

"It is beautiful." He paused, his eyes wandering over the various items in the room that had appeared in the weeks since she had moved in. "Like you." He kissed her hand. "By Lleu, but I'm drunk!"

Claerwen laughed. "It's been a long time since you had any rest, after all we've been through and then all the work to prepare for winter. You deserve it."

"Ah, but you helped as much as anyone. Even helping me in the smithy when no one else had time, by the gods!" He tossed down the last of the wine.

She rose to take away the cup and he stood up to stretch. "I wish I could take you abroad, Claeri, to southern Gaul or Iberia where it is warm in the winter. Did the cold weather bother you today? I was afraid your fever might come back. This cold fort is no place to recuperate from such an illness."

"I am fine! Don't worry so much. The illness is gone and I am strong again."

"It just seemed to take so long to get over."

"But it is over. Now stop worrying." She patted his chest and giggled, "You sound like Padrig."

"As long as I don't look like him," he teased and hugged her to him.

She snuggled her face into his chest, breathing in his scent. Slowly, she untied the laces on his tunic and pulled it from him, dropping it on the floor. Then she opened his muslin shirt, pulling it out from his breeches, and ran her slender, warm hands over his muscular back.

Marcus picked Claerwen up, whirled her once around in the air, then dropped her lightly back on her feet. He kissed her as he pulled the ties of her gown apart. It opened and slipped to the floor, her shift following. He dropped the rest of his clothes and picked her up again, taking her to the bed. He laid her down, nestling her in deep, comfortable pillows and fur coverlets, closing the drapes against the night air.

She reached up and caressed the hard muscles of his arms as he climbed over her on his knees. He grinned widely, his long hair hanging shaggy around his face. He began to explore her with his big hands, tracing tender, intimate patterns on her skin. His lips followed the paths of his hands, then slowly wandered their way back to find her mouth with long, luxurious kisses. She wrapped her legs around him and tangled her fingers in his hair as his manhood rose into her. They loved each other without holding back anything, the celebration of their marriage bringing them a deeply cherished joy and satisfaction.

Some time later, they lay quietly tired, curled together and relaxed. Claerwen traced the shape of Marcus' nose and lips with her finger, memorizing every curve and line, smoothing his long moustache where it flowed around the corners of his mouth.

He turned slightly, propping his head up on an arm and faced her. The dim light left from the banked fire pit was just enough to show him her face as they lay with their legs intertwined. He studied her, soft and glowing in the darkness, her pale eyes calm.

"You have a question, but you are afraid to ask," Claerwen whispered.

He smiled a moment and continued to study her face. "I could never try to lie to you, you would know before I could even say it."

She smiled and smoothed the hair on his chest. "What is your question?"

"I don't want to make you sad; it's our wedding night."

"You couldn't possibly make me sad tonight."

He drew one of her legs up, till it crossed over his belly, her foot hooked behind him, and he caressed its softness, then finally asked, "What is it like, the visions you have?"

She drew a long breath, but before she spoke, he

interrupted.

"I wanted to ask you a long time ago, but it always brought back such disturbing memories and made you sad. But it's..." he paused.

"...made you curious," she finished for him. "It's very hard to describe. Sometimes, it's like watching a dream; sometimes, it's just an idea that comes into my head, a compelling idea. Sometimes it's words, a name, or merely an image."

"Does it happen all the time?"

"No. But it's always there, like a presence behind a drawn curtain...no, like swirling clouds waiting to part for the sun, ready to burst out. And when it does, it takes over. I don't know what I'm like when it happens. I usually only remember it like a fading dream, if I remember anything at all. It's very draining and there's always pain when it leaves."

"A headache?"

"Aye. You have seen me when it happens. What am I like?"

Marcus remembered her face when she killed Drakar. It still shook him. He licked his lips and told her, "I have never seen anything so terrifying. To go into a battle, outnumbered by better warriors is less frightening to me. Your eyes have an eerie light in them; they seem to glow on their own, not bright, just a soft glow. Sometimes it is in your whole face. Then you sway like you're in a trance. If you speak, there is a tone of authority that is unshaking. You could probably bring Vortigern himself to his knees if you spoke so to him."

"No!" she frowned at him.

"Aye! The gods were so strongly in you that last time, I was afraid to call you or touch you, lest they would destroy you. The power is that great. Only a druid could hold that kind of power."

"I don't hold the power. The god does. They will not destroy me. In fact, I find it almost comforting. Perhaps, because I have always known it, even without realizing what it was. I didn't really understand until the man on the road to Caernarfon seemed to open up the power to that vision. He has a power far stronger than I do."

"Who was he?"

"I don't know. His name was Lord Emrys. We never saw him again."

"Emrys." Marcus rolled the name around in his mind, but it was not familiar. "I hate the way it uses you."

"Do not be afraid for me. It is there for a purpose and I think I would feel like a part of me was dead if I lost it. It cannot hurt me. But, since Drakar died, I have had no visions, no voices, nothing."

"Maybe the purpose has been served and the gods no longer need you to have the power."

Claerwen traced her finger along his chin and shook her head. "The power is still there. I believe it lies dormant until it is needed again. As you cannot give up the constant defense of this fort, the power of the fire cannot leave me either."

Marcus watched Claerwen's face a long time after she stopped talking. She appeared to be thinking, her eyes pensive and searching. Wanting to distract her, he ran his hand over her neck and shoulder, then down along the valley between her breasts to where they pressed against him. Finally her eyes came up and smiled at him.

"You have a question this time, no?" he asked.

Her eyes went pensive again and she answered, "Aye. I was trying to remember what happened when Drakar died. I still can't."

"You don't know what happened? You never told me you didn't."

"We have barely spoken about any of it since then, as if we tried to sweep it all away. That's not like you, Marcus."

"You're sure you want to talk about it now?"

She nodded. He briefly detailed the battle and how she had suddenly appeared, saving his life. He was silent for a few moments, then spoke again, "You are right, Claerwen. I did try to forget, for a while. What it did to us. And even though Drakar is dead and his death forfeits whatever he could have told about this treasure, there are others out there who know of it and will try again to find it. We will never be safe until we know what it is and why they want it. Drakar never would have told me what it was anyway. I had an idea to use one of my disguises and trick him into telling me, but I never had the chance to try it."

Claerwen told him, "Of that night, I remember seeing Drakar in the tree, dead, over and over, like a dream. The only thing I know for sure is that I woke up sometime, I think it was nearly morning because it was almost light outside. I felt tired and sick, probably from the fever still, and started to go back to sleep. Then I felt warmth next to me and when I turned my head, I saw you were lying next to me, sprawled out naked and sleeping. There was a bruise on your left shoulder from where the tree hit you, so I knew that it was true, Drakar was dead. There was a peacefulness in your soul like I had never felt before. I could see you were not otherwise hurt, but I was surprised to be back here in the house."

"Surprised? Where else would I take you?"

She smiled, almost shyly.

He cocked a brow at her and grinned, "Have you been listening to the Christians too long? We still follow Celtic law here. You and I created a marriage pledge when I came to see you in the convent chapel, when we agreed to marry. Under such a pledge, a man and woman are allowed to live together, as long as they marry within a year and a day. If they don't marry, the pledge is voided and they must separate. Because neither you nor I have any elder relatives, we were free to decide for ourselves, with the blessing of the local authority, of course."

"And you are the local authority?"

"Of course!" he laughed. "Sometimes that title is worthwhile. I still have to answer to the druid and to a consensus of my people, but there was never any question in this case."

"The contract my mother made for me was completely different."

"Aye, Strathclyde has had different influences brought into their laws, although it is possible to make a similar contract in Gwynedd. Does it bother you, the way I handled the pledge?"

Her head moved back and forth and she smiled broadly, "Oh, no, it was perfect. Now I understand. I was surprised when no one said anything about me living in your house. Grania asked once, and said the nuns would be mortified at us. Then she giggled."

He laughed at the implication she referred to, thinking on the many nights they had kept each other warm with their lovemaking. He pressed his rough cheek to her soft skin, rubbing lightly. His broad palms spread across her back and he stroked her comfortingly, then he rolled onto her again, his mouth searching for hers. He whispered, "I do cherish you, my Claeri."

Padrig swept away the last of the crumbs, his feet dragging his tired body around the room. Since Marcus and Claerwen had gone to their house, he and Owein decided to clear the platters and cups and wineskins away to the kitchen, a few of the clanswomen helping. Finally, declaring an end to the day's work, Padrig tossed the straw broom into its corner, wiped his hands on his tunic, and told everyone to go home, then trudged off to his quarters.

Taran was still in the hall, lounging on a bench with his back leaning on a post and his feet propped up on the table. Grania filled his cup with more wine, and they giggled like a pair of young children over some silly joke. Taran nearly fell off the bench and spilled his cup on the floor.

"Oh, no! I'll get you more!" Grania cried, still laughing.

"No, no. It's all right, I think Padrig will come back to throw us out soon anyway." He laughed some more. "Come, I will walk home with you." He paused, and looked sadly into the empty cup, then back up at Grania. They burst out again in another round of giggles.

He stood shakily and he wrapped her hand around his arm,

patting her fingers. She leaned on him, her own legs wobbly. They wove their way across the hall and out into the courtyard of the fort. The quiet night air hushed them.

Grania shivered in the dark as they headed to the small house that had become her home, and Taran put an arm around her shoulders. Taran pushed the door open for her and lit a candle to show the way.

"You have given me a glorious time tonight, Lady Grania, like I haven't had for a long time." He swept an imaginary hat off in a deep, graceful bow to her. She giggled and hiccoughed, dizzy from drinking too much.

Taran laughed at her, waving a finger in the air. He tried to land the finger on his lips to hush himself. "We don't want to disturb the prince, do we?" he whispered in fun. "With all that intense practice in the last two months, he's got to give her his best performance now that he's finally married her!"

"Oh, absolutely! Oh, shhh!" she giggled again and imitated him.

"I interrupted them once, you know. He must have just about been ready to crawl inside her when I knocked. He came to the door dressed only in his loincloth and his anger. You should have seen his face! And she was just whipping the bed curtains closed."

Grania giggled again, twirling around the room as if she was still dancing.

Taran caught her arm and tried to dance with her, his eyes fogged over from the drink. He said soothingly in her ear, "You know, you really are very pretty." His lips touched her hair, moving it to tickle her ear. She turned her face to his and their lips brushed. She seemed to steady a bit, and he watched her glassy eyes. She would sleep soon, he thought to himself, and a wry grin pulled up one corner of his mouth.

"Taran," she sighed, looking into his eyes, hypnotized suddenly by them. She leaned toward him, intoxicated by her own romantic imagination, and wanting to be as lucky as her cousin.

Taran's arms went around her, encouraged by her

drunkenness. She reached up around his neck and pulled herself to him.

"Taran," she said again and he hushed her with a kiss, soft at first, then hard and demanding. She responded, letting herself be carried away.

Surprised by her intensity, Taran was amused. He lifted her onto a table, kissing her, telling her gentle compliments meant to send her off to sleep with sweet dreams.

But Grania continued to cling to him, hooking her legs around him. Was she more lucid than he thought? He let her untie the front of his tunic and shrug it off him. Then her hands dropped to fumble with the ties of his breeches.

Propelled by his own sense of fun, Taran grinned sardonically and loosened the neck of her gown. She had his shirt open and was rumpling the hair on his chest, kissing it. Taran found he did not want to stop and pulled her gown and shift down to her waist. In the dim candle light, he could see her small breasts rising and falling with her strong breathing. He caressed them, his thumbs kneading her nipples, then he sprang up onto the table and straddled her. He swept everything off and roughly pushed her back.

She shivered with excitement and she pulled him down to kiss her, hard and rough.

Then as suddenly as Grania had become aroused, the wine took over her senses, and she drifted off into blissful oblivion, still mumbling Taran's name.

Annoyed, Taran laughed and called himself a fool. He backed off the table, staring at Grania's half-naked body. Then he smirked and pulled the gown the rest of the way from her, flinging it onto the floor. He strode once around the table, studying her, then stopped and smirked again. He ran his palm heavily from her neck down between her breasts, over her belly and gripped hard between her legs. "Maybe next time, little one," he whispered, pinching hard, then withdrew his hand. He swung his tunic over his shoulder and snuffed the candle on his way out.

Chapter 15

**Dinas Brenin and Ynys Môn, Gwynedd
Winter, 468 A.D.**

Dinas Brenin loomed out of the gathering twilight. Compared to Dinas Beris, this fort was enormous. Its setting on a hill spur was similar, but originally it had been set up to house a true war band. It was nearly in ruins now, not used since the height of the Roman occupation and the stone and timber walls were neglected and crumbling. The timber from the watchtower that had been over the gates was missing, torn down and used by local people to repair their own holdings.

Marcus rode an old mare up the track that led to the stronghold. He was once more disguised as a bard, wearing traveling clothes, his old grey cap, and the small knee harp tied to the back of his saddle. He had again greyed his hair and moustache with ash.

"Who goes there?" came the familiar cry at the gate. A young mercenary blocked the entrance, his pike diagonally across the entrance. He looked Iceni to Marcus, a tribe from the east that had been battered countless times by invaders.

"Your humble servant, young man," said Marcus to the soldier. More a boy than a man, he saw, once he got closer. "I seek a night's hospitality. I am a traveling bard." He made himself sound tired and older than he was.

"A bard?" the boy asked in excitement. "Welcome, my lord." Pride radiated from him as he welcomed his special guest, his curiosity brimming over to hear some news. "I will show you to the guest house. Please excuse how this place looks. There are plans to rebuild it soon, but there has not been time to get started."

"Don't worry about me, son." Marcus grinned at the boy's enthusiasm. "What is your name?"

"I am Ulfa, my lord." Ulfa called to another mercenary to take over the gate post while he showed the bard to the guest quarters. "This way, my lord."

Marcus was shown to a simple hut, not unlike several within his own fort. He asked Ulfa to take his horse to the livery and give her an extra feeding of oats.

"Yes, my lord," Ulfa said enthusiastically. He paused as he took the mare's reins from Marcus and asked more shyly, "Will you be singing tonight, my lord? The High King always enjoys music and news."

Marcus showed a hint of surprise, replying, "Vortigern is still here? Aye, if he so requests."

"Oh, I am sure he will. I will announce your arrival immediately. May I ask your name, my lord, to give to the king?"

Marcus proudly stretched to his full height and said in his deepest voice, "Tell him the bard Marthan is here, and would be pleased to sing for the King if he so desires."

Ulfa grinned broadly and bowed, then dashed away toward a larger building in the middle of the compound.

Marcus felt a chill of excitement run over his skin as he watched Ulfa disappear into the building. His black eyes squinted into a smile the rest of his face hid.

It was after midnight by the time Marcus finally flung himself into the bed Ulfa had prepared for him in the guest house. He was exhausted. The cold air had strained his voice and stiffened his fingers for harp playing, but the soldiers kept asking for more songs, more news. He was also disappointed. Vortigern had not shown at the performance. He slept hard and dreamless.

Sometime just before first light, Marcus woke, disturbed by some noise he did not really hear. Then suddenly his mind kicked him fully awake and he sat up, his hand gripped on a dagger just under the bed covers.

Ulfa was pouring fresh water in a basin for him. Marcus watched him for a moment and relaxed. He slid the dagger under the pillow and swung his legs off the bed, stretching.

"Good morning, son."

"Oh, I am sorry, Lord Marthan, I did not mean to wake you."

"I was awake anyway. It's time for me to move on."

"Is there anything else I can get for you, my lord?"

Marcus shook his head, then said casually, "I did not see the High King last night."

"I heard that he unexpectedly left the fort late yesterday." Ulfa paused, curling his mouth and coming closer to Marcus. "I should not say so, but there is a rumor that the High King went to Ynys Môn to consult with druids," he whispered.

"Druids?"

"Aye, sir. He is very superstitious. Whenever he is not satisfied with the advice of his magicians or priests, or whomever he is consulting at the time, he throws them all out and brings in another bunch, stranger than the last. Now it's druids. I don't know when he'll be back."

"Well, how about that?" Marcus chuckled to himself.

"May I bring you something to eat, my lord?" Ulfa asked.

Marcus was deep in thought, but nodded to the boy to bring the food. This was going to take longer than he thought. Ynys Môn was across the strait northeast from Caernarfon. He already knew there were still druid gatherings there from his own spying. This could be interesting, he thought, and began planning.

The old horse drudged slowly through drifts reaching halfway to her knees. Her breath plumed and curled from her muzzle as she labored up the road, the last weary leg into Ynys Môn's druid hideaway. The wind blew stinging cold off the sea, filling the night air with the smell of coming snow.

The druids' shelter was not much more than a few timber huts in a protected lee of a hillside, ringed off by a thick stand of ancient oaks. They had been driven underground centuries before by the Romans during the occupation. A secret society had scraped by, persecuted and banished. However, in the years since the Romans had left, the group had been experiencing more freedom. People wanted to go back to the old beliefs and rituals that were deeply rooted in their ancient heritage.

Marcus rode up to the main hut, which seemed to guard the rest of the structures like a mother duck shielding her babies. He still wore his old traveling clothes, but the small harp was hidden away in his rucksack. He had further greyed his hair, moustache, and even his face, then darkened the tiny lines around his eyes and the heavier creases down from his nose. He rode the horse slowly, sagging in the saddle, head bowed, arms limp, legs listless.

A man appeared on the step before the hut, a spear in his hand, suspicion clear on his face. He called a demand for identification. Intruders were extremely unwelcome.

Marcus did not answer him. He made the mare trudge up to the man and stop. At once, he slid sideways to the ground, sprawling in the snow, face up and eyes closed.

The guard stared in amazement at first, then saw how grey and pale Marcus' face was in the dim torchlight filtering from the doorway. Camp policy was to turn all strangers away, but this old man needed help, thought the guard. Against his better judgement, he dragged Marcus into the hut, laying him on a pallet by the fire pit. Then he sent a youth to take care of the old horse. The guard thought that she looked like she was in about the same shape as the old man. What were they doing out in the miserable weather? And here of all places? Well, let the Grand Druid worry about that.

Many fires blazed within the grove of ancient, knarred oak trees, trailing smoke that swirled up among the bare and grotesque branches. It was midnight and the time of the new moon. Snow lay ankle deep where it had not been trampled or melted to slush by the fires.

A dozen eerie-faced, hooded figures chanted in a circle around the biggest fire, swaying, making a soft and sensuous sound, rather like a humid summer breeze, so incongruent in the freezing air. More robed men appeared ghost-like from the surrounding shadows, joining in the chants. One led a pig on a tether.

Two figures stood in contrast to the others. One was apparently the head priest, well adorned with gold decoratives and a long staff. The other was the High King, Vortigern. The king was positioned away from the main activity, probably to keep him from learning too much, but he was still close enough to understand and feel included in the impending ceremony.

Vortigern had come, high-strung with excitement over the promise of a prophecy just for him, but he was not prepared for the blatant display of magic. Other soothsayers, priests, and wizards had flaunted their talents for the King many times, but none came close to the dynamic energy emanating from these robed holy men. No answer from his previous encounters had ever given him satisfaction; now, Vortigern shuddered inwardly. These druids must hold the highest power. They should have the answer to his questions.

The pig was brought to the circle's center, a flat granite slab laying near the fire, then tied securely. Swaying in a trance, the head priest waved his staff over and around the pig. A wide, deep bowl was placed before the nervous animal, which began to bawl as it sensed its impending doom. The holy men paced in a circle, forming hand signals significant to the ceremony's scheme, their chanting rising to a frantic level.

A very still, robed figure appeared next to and slightly behind Vortigern, beyond the firelight. He did not chant, but simply emerged silently from the deepest shadows. Vortigern became aware of the watching presence next to him and jerked his head around. All he could see were dark, shadowed eyes and a grey moustache. He looked questioningly at the shrouded face, which nodded a slow, deliberate acknowledgment. Vortigern felt a chill shake him involuntarily, and a runnel of perspiration slipped its way down his back. He reckoned the man was there to guard him in case he panicked.

The chanting was reaching a feverish quality now; the pig was terrified. Then, with a swirl of robed arms, the head druid flashed out a long dagger and deftly slit the pig's throat. The animal bawled horribly, blood gushing down its chest, spilling in and around the grail. It fell, twitching, then died.

The priest lifted the bowl and ostentatiously carried it around the circle. The holy men began a soft chant again.

"They are calling the gods," a low, monotone voice spoke from the shadows next to Vortigern.

The king jerked visibly, startled out of his intense concentration. He turned and stared at the hooded figure. Vortigern felt anger rising within his misery, not knowing what to do about the mystery of the druids' actions. He waited for the man to speak again, but was met only with a pair of black, chilling eyes. The King turned back to the ritual, nerves taut to anything the strange interpreter might do or say.

The high priest came back to the circle's center and raised the bowl high, offering the sacrificial blood to the spirits, then spilled a libation to them on the earth. Dazed, he chanted and swooned in the ancient language, then drank from the bowl.

Vortigern thought he was going to retch. He wanted to run, but felt like his feet were rooted to the ground more deeply than the oak trees.

Minutes passed and the chanting faded, rose again, and faded. Abruptly, the priest began shouting, "Beware! Beware!" then drifted off to mumbling again.

Vortigern was shaking, but not from the cold. His fear became paralyzing. He was afraid to look at the robed man behind him.

The high priest shouted again, "Beware! The white dragon shall swallow itself! The red dragon and the great bear shall free us from the white scourge!" Then he went silent. He stalked off, the others following him, taking the sacrificial remains with them to be buried.

Vortigern, confused, turned again to the robed man. "Is that all? What did it mean? They told me nothing I came here for."

The man, still speaking low and monotoned, answered slowly, "You have been told everything you need. You are to end your dealing with the Saxons. They shall destroy you and themselves as well. They are the white dragon."

"But they help me stabilize Britain against outsiders."

"*They* are the outsiders. They will dessert you when the red dragon rises up against you. No Saxon, no treasure, nothing will ever save you."

"You know of the treasure? You know where it is?"

The interpreter stared coldly at Vortigern. "The treasure is sacred, not to be defiled by hands soiled with your own people's blood, as yours are."

"It belongs to me!" Vortigern hissed through gritted teeth. "Only me!"

"The treasure belongs to the red dragon. You must never challenge the dragon's strength. You will never stand against it."

Vortigern glowered fiercely at the interpreter, trying to control the rage choking him. The prophecy was not what he had wanted to hear. He puffed himself up, trying to intimidate the robed man, but could not shake the unnerving eyes that drilled into him. Finally, Vortigern asked, "Who are the red dragon and the great bear?"

The interpreter continued to stare, then spoke again, "The red dragon is the Welsh."

"Hah!" Vortigern sneered. "I've heard this before!

They're only a bunch of rough, unorganized mountain men. They don't know how to fight."

"Be warned again, High King. The gods know that the stealth and cunning of the mountain men make them easily capable of slitting your throat in the dark of the night. They are able to move unseen and unheard. Remember, the Iron Hawk is a Welshman."

The interpreter's eyes became increasingly unforgiving. Vortigern backed up a step, nervously biting his lower lip at the mention of the Iron Hawk.

He asked in a low voice, "Is the Iron Hawk the great bear?"

The man hesitated a moment. "The Bear has not arrived to reveal his face and the gods do not say his true name yet." Before Vortigern could ask again, the interpreter said, "Heed the warning of the gods, High King. Heed the warning, or you will find your head in your own hands. It is time to leave." The man turned and disappeared into the black night as new snow began to fall.

"Well, where is the old man?" The head priest, now more simply dressed, bullied the man who had taken in the disguised Marcus. The guard shivered at the awesome sternness of the druid.

"He was here. See, the pallet he used. He looked nigh to death when I brought him in. Just fell off his old nag like a sack of potatoes."

"He's not here now. And you know better than to let a stranger into this camp."

"He needed a healer. He can't be far. Perhaps he took a fever and is wandering about somewhere here."

A young fellow rushed in, excusing himself. "The old horse is gone too, my Lord. And Brithnen, the interpreter, says somebody thumped him on the head. He was not at the ceremony with the rest of us. He woke up in one of the huts."

The high priest scowled at the other two. "Is Vortigern still here?"

"No. He left without a word, just as he was instructed to do immediately after the ceremony."

A wolf howled in the near distance. "I will go after the old man, or whoever he was," the guard said, already looking to his gear.

"No." The priest held up a palm toward the sky. "I believe mother wolf will help rid us of the problem. Listen."

More howls echoed from the wood.

"That old horse will not get very far; she was no fake. The wolves will have her down before he reaches the ferry to the mainland. And if they don't, the storm that's coming will."

"What about the High King?"

"Nothing. Vortigern is a fool. He will hear only what he wants to hear. He is doomed and knows it, but will not give in or admit it." The priest suddenly looked tired. He rubbed his long hands together and told the others to make sure the shutters were tight, a blizzard was on its way.

The wolf howled long and lonely in the night.

CHAPTER 16

Dinas Beris
Winter, 468 A.D.

Claerwen sat on the floor before her loom, sorting spindles of thread into groups of colors. She spread them on the floor around the loom, then rose and stepped back to consider if the colors were placed correctly for the pattern she wanted. She hummed lightly, and toed a pair of spindles with her bare foot, pushing them to slightly different locations until she was satisfied with her arrangement.

Smiling, Claerwen paced across to the fire pit to poke at the fire, then went to check on the small personal pantry she kept in the house. Finding only one half-full wineskin left, she decided there was time to hurry across to the kitchen for another. After slipping her feet into a pair of clogs, she yanked the heavy door of the house open.

Wind struck her face unexpectedly; the afternoon had been cold but calm. Now, thin, streaking clouds scudded in from the west. Taking her cloak from its peg, Claerwen skipped down the steps as she wrapped it around herself, and headed for the rear door of the kitchen house. Before she was half-way there, Padrig appeared from the other direction.

"I need another wineskin before Marcus comes home,"

she said as he approached.

"It's going to be a blizzard, Claerwen," he declared before she could continue.

She halted, knowing he was not exaggerating. He could read the signs as accurately as the wild creatures of the mountains.

"See if you can find your cousin, and get her to help in the kitchen. I've got to get Owein and Taran to secure the fort before dark," Padrig ordered.

Claerwen whirled and ran towards the small house Grania lived in. As she approached, she heard voices laughing inside. She guessed Taran was there and she grimaced. She never could get used to his constant arrogance, and she bristled whenever it was aimed at Marcus. And in the six weeks since the wedding, she had watched Grania spend more and more time with Taran. She could see some of Taran's attitude coloring Grania's words and actions, and Claerwen wondered how deeply Taran's influence would take its toll on Grania's gullibility.

Claerwen lifted her hand to knock, but paused when she saw Owein coming towards her. He signaled at her to wait. As he approached, his fingers ran nervously through his long dark blond hair, then pulled on his moustache. She came down the few steps to wait for him.

"Is Taran in there?" he asked quietly, his dark eyes tense.

"Aye, I can hear them laughing."

"Don't disturb them," he advised.

Claerwen frowned, surprised by Owein's words. "We need their help. Padrig is worried about the storm."

"I know. But you don't want to disturb them. I can handle what needs to be done with the house guards."

He turned to go, but Claerwen gripped his sleeve. "Why, Owein? You don't want me to know something?"

A shrill peal of giggles came from the house, then what sounded like furniture thumping.

"What are they doing?" Claerwen started up the steps.

"No, Claerwen. Please." Owein stopped her, leading her

away from the house by the arm. "I was going to wait for Marcus and tell him, then he could tell you. But I think you can guess what they're doing. He's suspected it's been going on for a long time."

Another thump bounced inside the house and they turned towards it. Owein's face was lined with disgust. He muttered, "I'm sorry for your cousin. He will make her miserable one day soon." He strode away.

Claerwen retreated slowly to the kitchen house, disappointed, but not surprised by Grania's actions. She found Padrig sitting on his favorite stool, peeling potatoes. A wooden bucket caught the skins as he neatly stripped each one, quartered it, and tossed it into a cauldron of hot water over the fire pit. A pile of carrots waited its turn. The kitchen was quiet except for the rasping knife, the bubbling water, and the plinking of potato quarters hitting the water.

"I will help you," Claerwen sighed as she pulled a bench next to him. Silently, she hoped Marcus would come home before the storm arrived. She had expected him to be home that afternoon, and now the realization that she had not seen the depth of Grania's involvement with Taran distracted her. Her face furrowed into a frown.

"I thought Grania was going to help with this."

Claerwen locked eyes with Padrig, wondering if she was the last one in the fort to know. She replied, "It appears she had to do something with Taran instead."

Padrig snorted. "So, it grows obvious. Marcus was afraid Taran would take to her."

"I get the impression Taran does this a lot."

Padrig frowned at Claerwen and asked, "Can you bear to hear the truth?"

Claerwen nodded, holding her gaze steady. Padrig grinned approval at her directness. "Taran likes the excitement of courting women. And your cousin is exactly the kind of woman he likes to court. She is naive and very vulnerable, believing anything he tells her, no matter how rudely he says it. And because she believes everything he says, that fans along his vanity. He likes the sound of all his own fancy words.

"By itself, that isn't so bad, but Taran lacks the courage to back what he says. If he promises her something, he won't go through with it. As an example, Marcus often uses him as his ambassador. Taran excels at diplomacy, as long as Marcus produces the services or goods promised. Together, they work very well. Oh, Marcus could do well enough on his own, but he recognizes Taran's talent and wisely uses it to his advantage, saving him time to do other things."

"Like spying?"

"Aye, that most of all."

"Isn't that dangerous if Taran agrees to something Marcus doesn't want?"

"It could be, but Taran is a good man in spite of his blasted sarcasm and arrogance. He and Marcus do love each other, although it doesn't seem like it sometimes. Taran has always performed exactly as Marcus instructed him. In fact, I believe Marcus is going to send him to Conwy when he comes back. Your cousin won't like that much."

"Owein said Taran would hurt Grania soon."

"Aye, that will probably happen, unfortunately. But your cousin doesn't love Taran anymore than Taran loves her, and that will make the break quicker, once he gets bored with her. Or she gets bored with him."

"You've seen this happen a lot, haven't you?"

Padrig sighed and tossed a handful of potato quarters into the cauldron, splashing water over the rim. "Aye, that I have."

Claerwen and Padrig worked on, mostly in silence, another hour passing.

"Claerwen!" Grania's voice shrilled from the hall.

Claerwen and Padrig exchanged glances as if to say, now she comes, when supper is nearly ready.

Grania stopped in the doorway. "We have a visitor. One of the patrollers met him on the road as he was coming in and offered him supper. But with the storm coming, I think we should ask him to stay. Should we put him in the guest house?"

"Aye, that is fine enough," Padrig answered.

"Thank you." She turned to bound out again.

"Grania!" Claerwen called. "What is his name? Who is he? What was he doing out on the road?" She was irritated at her cousin's shortness.

"I don't know. I didn't see him. We can find out at supper." She ran back through the hall.

Claerwen rose and went to the hallway that led to the hall. "She always looks like she's running, even if she's standing still," she observed, then helped Padrig serve the meal.

With Marcus gone, supper was quiet. Claerwen fidgeted and picked at the food in front of her. Owein was more taciturn than usual, eating quickly, then sitting by the fire pit, oiling and polishing weaponry. Taran and Grania chattered incessantly, their voices droning like bees against the straining silence of the hall.

The visitor arrived late for supper, apologizing for his tardiness and introduced himself as Rhun. At first glance, he was rather plain. Though tall, he was thin, with deep-set blue eyes, a long broad nose, thin lips, hollow cheeks, and hair of a nondescript brown. His clothes, though well made, hung on him, as if he had lost weight in his travels. He looked to be about thirty years.

But once Rhun sat down and became acquainted with the others, they discovered his smile was his most disarming feature, his blue eyes startlingly full of sparkle. Accompanying that, he had a gift of chatter that ranged from simple trivia to accomplished storytelling. The man could talk on just about any subject at length, with wit, intelligence, and great ease. Rhun's voice was soothing, never becoming rough or monotonous. Even Taran looked impressed.

The wind blew hard outside, rattling the shutters. Claerwen listened to it, her face lonely in the dim lantern light. Padrig, who had been deeply concentrating on Rhun's chatter, suddenly saw the look on her face. He quietly got up with the excuse of clearing the table, going to her. He squeezed her shoulder and told her not to worry.

"He's not going to make it back tonight, is he?" she whispered to him.

"He'll be fine."

"I think I will go to my house." Padrig patted her arm as she slowly got up and slipped out.

"Oh, oh!" Rhun paused as she left without a word. "I think I have offended the lady."

Padrig fibbed, "I don't think she is feeling well. She asked me to give her apologies to you and to tell you that you are very welcome to stay."

"Ah, I hope she will forgive my chattering. I do get carried away."

A house guard came forward to refill Rhun's ale cup and asked him to continue the story he had been telling. Others thumped the tables in agreement, and Rhun went on, late into the night.

The storm sent ice and snow streaming against the fort. Cold sneaked into every crack and chink. The fire pits were kept filled and hovered over.

Claerwen tossed and turned, alone in her bed. No matter how much mead she drank, she could not sleep. She could not get comfortable. First she was too warm, then too cold. Finally, she dragged herself out of the bed and sat in Marcus' favorite chair. She stared into the fire, hoping a vision would show her where he was, but she could not open herself to the gods.

A knock rapped lightly on the door.

"Come," she called tiredly.

The heavy door pushed in, snow and wind with it. "It's Padrig. May I come in?"

"Oh, please, do," she called and lit a candle. "You couldn't sleep either?"

"No. I brought some tea, lots of camomile."

"Oh, thank you." She was genuinely pleased and eagerly took a cup from him. It warmed her hands.

He grinned, glad he could at least make her smile.

"Claerwen, dear," he started as he sat on a stool by the fire pit, his own cup between his hands. "Don't make yourself sick with worry over Marcus. He can take care of himself. He's probably taken shelter somewhere out of the storm and will come home as soon as it clears. You know how resourceful he is. There is no one like him in the world."

Claerwen could see the pride in Padrig's eyes and smiled again, taking comfort in his words. "Aye, I have seen how he works. I just can't stop worrying."

"I have an idea. Tomorrow I will begin to teach you what I know about poultices and such. You already understand a lot of the healing methods from the nuns, so I thought you might want to learn more. That will take your mind off waiting."

She nodded her head. "I am glad you want to teach me. It will give me something to do, something useful."

"In the spring, when the snow is gone, I will introduce you to the homesteaders around here. I usually go once every moon cycle around to all of them, to see if anyone needs medicine or a treatment, or anything. Now, in the winter, I usually mix up a new stock to use."

"I wish Grania would find something like that to keep her busy."

"What does she like to do?"

"She never seems to show interest in anything very long. She will do something for a while, then drop it and do something else. Nothing ever gets finished."

"Have you talked to her about it?"

Claerwen shook her head. "She hardly even talks to me anymore, since she is with Taran so much. She's changed a lot, grown distant."

"I think that will pass soon enough."

"Even before she was with Taran, she barely talked to me. It's as if she ignores me, or is angry with me. I know she hates living here, in spite of how she seems to like Taran. She'd rather be in a place like Caernarfon."

Padrig thought a moment, then slowly smiled a little. "I

don't think it's anger. I think she is afraid of you."

"Afraid? Why?" Claerwen was amazed.

"What happened when Drakar was killed was a very mysterious thing. We all believe in the power of the gods, but it is very frightening when that power comes so directly into our daily lives like that. Do you understand what I am saying?"

"Is everyone scared of me? Owein, Taran, the clan?"

"Aye, I think so. That is why I want to take you with me in the spring. It will ease some of that fear."

"Why aren't you afraid of me?"

Padrig chuckled. "I have lived long enough in these mountains to know, like Marcus, that things will happen no matter what we do. It is the nature of things. Fire in the head is part of that nature."

"Marcus said it scares him, but more because of the way it uses me. He is afraid for me."

"He is afraid of losing you. He loves you more than life, Claerwen, more than these ancient mountains. He would do anything for you. He sees things through the power of his intelligence and the strength of his soul. And though he accepts the truth of the fire, he cannot understand it the way you do."

Claerwen wiped a stray tear back. "He's so strong and full of courage. And I couldn't even face a guest tonight."

"It's all right to miss him, Claerwen. That's not a sign of weakness. Marcus told me how you stood up to Drakar. I don't think you realize how much courage you do have. Or how proud Marcus is of you. You are still a little shy occasionally, but I see you losing it everyday. When you need strength, you find it. And I believe you are a perfect match for Marcus."

Claerwen finally smiled. She appreciated Padrig's quiet wisdom and hugged his hand to her cheek. They talked long into the night.

The blizzard howled three days and three nights, snow building into enormous drifts that iced over into hardened dams. Owein, Taran, the house guard, and even Rhun continuously swept and shoveled paths and roofs. They threw snow over the ramparts, finding no more space to pile it in the courtyard. It choked windows, doors, smoke holes, the gates, even the ramparts.

Rhun continued to entertain the fort's residents every evening, which helped ease the sense of isolation. Taran and Grania continued their laughter and teasing, punctuating the hall's smokey air behind Rhun's chatter. Owein silently paced the fort, checking and rechecking the security of the grounds and the house guard, scowling when he came within earshot of Taran. Padrig and Claerwen spent most of their time sequestered in the kitchen, studying their medicines.

By late afternoon of the storm's third day, the blizzard began to break up, but continued in fits of icy rage throughout the rest of the day. The wind dragged on, moving drifts capriciously from one side of the fort to the other. Owein, Taran and the house guard began the clean up.

Claerwen was in her house that afternoon, mending one of Marcus' old shirts, a job that never seemed to end. As soon as one garment was fixed, another one presented itself for work. Marcus was hard on his clothes, but much of his work at home was tough and physical. When he could, he would strip and work in just a loincloth, though many times cold weather or the protection of clothing was necessary. Claerwen never complained; she had never been able to afford new clothing very often and always tried to repair what was torn. Every garment was considered precious.

Claerwen folded the shirt and placed it neatly in the carved chest with the rest of Marcus' things. She closed the lid and before she rose from her knees, stroked the piece of furniture lovingly, wishing he was there.

She got up and slowly wandered out of her house and across the courtyard towards the hall and the kitchen. As she crossed, she saw Owein chipping ice from the steps leading up to the ramparts. Taran was helping, using a torch to loosen the ice as they worked their way up the steps.

Turning back towards the houses, she abruptly halted,

hearing Grania's voice coming from the open door of the hall.

"I've seen you before!" Grania said. "You were at the inn, in Caernarfon!"

"Ah, you remember me, then. You were worried about your cousin, I believe. Was she the woman I had heard about?" Rhun answered.

"Aye, she was. And you were right, she did escape. Six weeks ago, she married the man who helped her, and he turned out to be the prince of this forlorn place."

Rhun laughed and said, "And she is the lovely lady with the sad eyes, who waits for her man to come home?"

"Aye, she does. Perhaps if he ever gets home, she will stop moping around."

Claerwen pressed her lips into a line of irritation, recognizing Taran's attitude emerging in the tone of Grania's comment. She was equally irritated that Grania spoke so freely to a stranger, even if she had met the man before. She realized that though Rhun had been amiable enough, whenever he spoke, it was about neutral news outside Dinas Beris, or it was centered in subtle conversation about the person he was talking to. Otherwise, he was still a stranger to all of them. Claerwen took a step forward, thinking to intercept Grania's continued conversation.

Suddenly, Owein's ram horn pierced the cold air. Claerwen's head jerked up to see him on the ramparts, blowing the gathering call as hard as he could. Taran was beside him, shouting orders at the house guards. Claerwen ran a few steps into the center of the courtyard, staring up at Owein. Finally, he released the horn, letting it hang on its thong around his neck. He spotted Claerwen watching him and signaled her.

"I saw him, beyond the first bend of the river! Marcus is coming!" To the men, he yelled, "Get your shovels and sledges out again. We have to open the gates and clear the road. Marcus is coming!"

She had never heard Owein with so much excitement in his voice.

And Marcus was coming home!

CHAPTER 17

Dinas Beris
Winter, 468 A.D.

"Hurry! Hurry up! Dig! Faster!"

Shouts ricocheted across the freezing air of the courtyard like dozens of arrows shooting every which-way.

Owein, Taran and the house guard furiously dug through the massive drifts blocking the gates. They used anything they had that could move snow, hacking at ice dams with metal bars and sledges.

Claerwen, wrapped tightly in her cloak, followed the track Owein had made up to the ramparts. She had strapped on leather leggings under her long skirts for warmth and to keep her dry. She gathered the trailing skirts and climbed up. From there she could see down the pass into the river valley for several miles. It looked completely different under the deep snow. She had never seen so much before. The woods seemed thinner because the smallest trees were completely covered and the taller ones were dwarfed. The sky was incredibly sapphire blue next to the piercing white of the snow.

Then something moved far and away below. Claerwen watched, her eyes aching from the brightness, until she recognized a man struggling against the hip-high powder. Her mouth slowly dropped open and she felt her breath stream out as if to reach across and give strength to him. Marcus.

Then another movement caught her attention. Further away, a creature followed. Then another. And another.

Suddenly, Claerwen shrieked. The men nearly dropped their tools as they stared up at her.

"Wolves!" she screamed. "Owein! There are wolves behind him!" Her words lashed out like hurtled stones. She half-ran, half-slid down the pile of snow back into the courtyard, her skirts getting soaked. Her arms and legs already felt stiff from the damp cold. She ran to the gates and took up a shovel.

"He cannot out-run them. The snow is too deep!"

"Claerwen, go back inside! Let us do it. It's too cold for you out here!" Owein yelled at her as he worked.

"Nonsense!" was all she replied. She struck the shovel into the drift and heaved, flinging snow with long, determined strokes.

Gradually, the gates were cleared. They yanked on the iron latch, but it was frozen solid. Taran held the torch to warm it while Owein pounded on it with an enormous sledge, the metal ringing painfully in the air. Finally it gave. They inched open one massive door far enough to file through.

The men swarmed out, trampling through the drifts. They did not take the time to strap on snowshoes, and they ran as fast as they could, following Owein as he thrashed out a path. They were fresh and eager for activity and flung, fell, jumped and dug their way down from the embankments. If the situation had not been so serious, they would have found it amusing.

Once they reached the flat area between the last bank and the mountain of the standing stone, the men fanned out and down into the valley. Whooping and hollering, they greeted Marcus as they passed him, charging at the wolves. Suddenly they had weapons, daggers and rocks in their hands, ready to hurl. Owein was screaming some horrid war cry.

Claerwen followed the men, trudging through the packed path they made. She saw the wolves pull up short when Owein began his bellowing. Excitement rose in her and she hurried on, plunging and scattering white powder all around her. She heard cries and yips come from the wolves as the rocks stung them.

She could see Marcus. He was standing still now, his feet facing the fort and his body twisted back to see his cousin, brother and clansmen driving back the animals. Then he turned back toward the fort. His clothes were soaked through and frozen stiff. Several days growth of beard and his moustache wore a heavy coat of ice. He had a woolen kerchief wrapped around his head and neck, the old grey cap smashed over it, and the hood of his cloak over the hat. The hood drooped sadly over his eyes. He carried an old ragged rucksack, a bedroll, and his sword slung over his back. He took a few steps, then stopped, took a few more, stopped again.

Claerwen was running now, finding strength in the rhythm of her steps. Her stride lengthened and she hung onto her wet skirts and the cloak to keep them out of her way as she pumped and forced her way to him.

Finally, she was there. He nearly fell when she reached him, his legs weakened from fighting his way through the deep snow. She leaned him against her, holding him up while she dropped the gear from his shoulders.

"Marcus, oh, by Lleu of the long hand! What's happened to you!" she cried. Unprepared to see the condition he was in, she was horrified. She wrapped her cloak around both of them, and dragged his right arm across her shoulders to support him. He was barely conscious and she was not sure he even recognized her. He shook violently and his eyes were out of focus, deeply bloodshot. She hugged him to her, her arms around his middle, and began pulling him with her toward the fort. She talked incessantly, trying to make him understand he was home and would soon be warm and dry and fed. At the same time, she was assuring herself that he was really there, and he would again be the same man who had left several days before.

The wolves reluctantly retreated into the woods, and the men turned to rescue Marcus. But Owein stopped, watching

Claerwen pull him along, already nearing the gates. He held a hand up in signal to the others, and they gathered around him.

"I have never seen a woman like that one before, cousin," he said to Taran. "Any other man would have collapsed and his woman gone to crying, sitting back by the warm fire and waiting. This one has brought him in all by herself." He pulled his hood up tighter around his ears and led the men back to the fort.

Claerwen struggled along, bringing Marcus to their house. The few short steps up seemed like a mountain to climb, but she braced herself and pulled him up and forward until his legs followed. He was breathing hard as if his lungs would burst. They trudged through the anteroom, then finally into the main room, where his legs gave out and he went down on his knees, dragging her with him. She tried to ease him carefully the rest of the way down, pulling him towards her, but she had to let him fall. He was too heavy and her strength was nearly finished from half dragging, half carrying him.

"Padrig!" she screamed as she rolled Marcus over on his back. She knew Padrig was on his way, or that one of the other men would get him if she called.

Before she could shout again, Padrig was there with a heavy basket of medicines, telling her what to do. "Get this wet clothing off him. We have to check for frostbite immediately. I wonder how long he was out there." He worked furiously as he gave her directions.

"Looks like he was out during the entire storm. Damn!" she swore, working at his leggings. They were so icy and stiff she could not get them untied.

Padrig looked at her and grinned. He never heard her curse before. He jumped up and threw more wood on the fire pit to raise the temperature of the room.

"Here." Padrig slipped one of the hidden daggers from a boot he pulled off. "Cut the ties. And be careful. He's got more of these somewhere on him. He's always a walking arsenal."

"I know." She thought back to the time he nearly threw one at her. Finally the leggings loosened, the ice melting onto the floor. His skin was red and very cold.

"Get his feet out and check them. If the toes look like they have burns on them, it could be frostbite and we have to treat them right away by rubbing snow on them and then with some of this ointment." He pulled a small jar from the basket. "I will check his fingers."

"They look red and wrinkled, but not burned."

"Excellent, let me see, aye, you are right. See, his hands look all right as well. He is lucky. His face is a little sunburned, but not frostbitten. Here, let me mop up some of this water." Padrig rubbed the plank floor with rags. He chuckled and said to the unconscious Marcus, "You melt faster than a snowman, my boy!" He handed Claerwen another rag and said, "Try to dry his hair some. We've got to get the rest of this wet stuff off him."

"I didn't think it would be so bad," Claerwen said, pulling on Marcus' tunic.

"He is very, very lucky. He was not dressed well enough, but he had oilskin in his boots and gloves. That's probably why he didn't get frostbitten. I wonder what happened to the horse he took with him."

"How long will he sleep?" she asked.

Padrig helped her sit him up so she could peel off the tunic and shirt. She stayed behind him and wrapped her arms around his chest, letting him slump back on her while Padrig stripped the breeches off.

"I don't know, but I would say from now through the night and maybe part of tomorrow. Now, do this while I dry him off." He showed Claerwen how to massage Marcus' muscles. "It will help warm him, stimulate him from the inside. Good, that's it." He pulled a heavy fur cover from the bed, throwing it over Marcus, and told Claerwen to keep massaging him. He hung a small pot of water over the fire pit and tossed several kinds of herbs into it, measuring with quick, expert hands. He reviewed each ingredient with Claerwen as he worked, reinforcing the studying she had done.

"We will lift him into the bed, and you can keep doing

that for a while. Then, try to get him to swallow some of this every half hour. It's the same broth he gave you when you were so sick."

Together they lugged Marcus into the bed, covered and tucked him against draughts. Padrig showed Claerwen how to pull him up and forward enough to slip the soup into his mouth, then rub his neck until he swallowed it.

When Marcus was settled and sleeping comfortably, Padrig stretched his old arms and legs, tired from the work.

"I will go tell Owein and Taran he should be all right before long, but that he will sleep through the night and no one is to disturb you." He took one of Claerwen's hands and squeezed it, "Don't worry. He'll be fine. You know what to do. I will bring you some supper in a little while."

Claerwen shut the door and went back to sit with Marcus. He was stirring and she would have loved to see him open his eyes, but Padrig had said the sleep would be better. If he woke too soon, he could have a lot of pain as his body warmed up. She sat on the edge of the bed and watched his face move in some dream, rubbing his left arm, then the right one. He seemed to drift in and out of one dream to another. She worked back and forth over him, kneading his muscles, then fed him the healing broth. Padrig came and went, bringing supper, and told her to change her wet clothes; she would not be much help to Marcus if she got sick again. She had completely forgotten to change.

At midnight Claerwen put more peat on the fire pit and gave Marcus another sip of broth. He was coming around again, though he still had not truly wakened. This time he moved more, his mouth opening and his breathing heavier. Finally his eyes slit open a little and he tried to pull himself up.

"Hush. Rest now," Claerwen whispered to him. "You are home."

He stopped, still half sitting up, trying to open his eyes further.

"My Claerwen," he mumbled, then dropped back down. He rested quietly after that.

The next morning dawned clear with a strong sun that finally brought warmth. Already, the great drifts had begun to melt.

Unable to talk with Marcus yet, Owein set to work with the house guards at clearing the courtyard and the entry road of enough snow so that they could function normally. He hoped by nightfall his cousin would be awake and well enough to talk.

Taran was restless as well, fidgeting to be out of the fort, but Grania did not want to stay inside alone.

"Then come with me," he invited her.

"Where?"

"You'll see," he teased her. "Dress warm."

He was in the courtyard flinging a blanket onto his horse when she ran back from her house, pulling a cloak around herself. Her reddish hair streamed out like a cloud behind her. Taran grinned sardonically as she came to him and he lifted her onto the blanket, then leaped up behind her. He kicked the horse into a trot out of the gates. He slipped his arms around her waist, guiding the horse with his knees. They rode on silently, crossing into the woods to the north of the fort.

"I want to show you something," Taran said as they wove through the trees, following a path only he could see. Shortly, they emerged in a tiny clearing, an ancient abandoned stone hut in its center.

"It was *hafod*, a summer dwelling, probably was used by hunters at some time," Taran told Grania as he waded through deep snow, kicking it away from the door. "I found it about three years ago and repaired it. I claim it for my own now. This is where I come when I want privacy."

He had new kindling and peat already waiting in the small fire pit. He lit it, and a plume of smoke gently rose to drift out of the smoke hole. He also had blankets, feather-stuffed mats and utensils stored in a small chest. A long, narrow, flat topped log served as a bench and table.

"Come, sit with me." Taran pulled Grania by the hand and tucked blankets around them for warmth.

"You had this planned?" Grania asked, surprised.

Taran leaned to reach a wineskin and uncorked it with his teeth while he stroked her hair. After taking a long swallow, he placed its neck to her lips, helping her to drink. He set the skin down, then pushed her back roughly, kissing her hard. Sly mischief showed in his eyes.

"What more do you have planned?" Grania giggled, grappling Taran, driving herself into his grip. Clothing littered the *hafod* within minutes. And as quickly as their desire was approached, it was spent.

"Have you ever made a pledge?" Taran asked afterward, his breath softly tickling in Grania's ear. He reached again for the wine, and she took it from him, taking a deep swallow.

Grania rolled up onto Taran, her cloud of red hair floating around them. Her soft brown eyes deepened as she smiled and whispered, "What sort of pledge?" She nuzzled and rose up enough to make sure he saw her naked breasts, then pressed herself tightly against him, trying to arouse him again.

"A serious pledge," he answered, responding by turning over onto her, crushing her beneath his weight. He could see the wine was reaching Grania's senses.

"Is that why you wanted to come here? To have the privacy to make a pledge?" Grania's eyes brightened, breathing hard under Taran's weight.

"Aye, little Grania," he breathed and pushed himself into her again. She gasped as he dug his fingers into her flesh, jerking in pain as he charged vehemently inside her. But she did not cry out. Instead, she clung to him, gritting her teeth into a wide smile, pressing back, and feeling the cold air tingle her sweating skin where he was not touching her.

Their grunts and moans dwindled down into sighs of satisfaction. Grania beamed up into Taran's face, smoothing his hair back from his brow. "I accept your pledge, Taran."

Taran's eyes held Grania's for a long while, his face serious at first, then evolved into a chuckling smile. He rolled off her, picked up the wineskin and drank long. He offered it to

Grania as he pulled a blanket over them and reached to throw more peat on the fire. Grania drank again then snuggled down against him, vastly happy.

Marcus continued to sleep, through the day and into the second night. He seldom stirred. When he did, Claerwen dribbled the broth into his mouth and made him swallow. Sometimes he would involuntarily spit it back out. He took no fever, to her relief, but the tiredness held onto him like a pall. She had stayed up all night tending to him and by the end of the second day, she was nearly sleeping upright. Padrig offered to take over for her, but she refused. He went away, muttering she was as stubborn as her husband.

Past midnight of the second night, Marcus was sleeping very peacefully, prompting Claerwen into finally realizing she had to rest. She changed into a loose shift, climbed over and curled up next to him, planning to nap for an hour. In seconds she was asleep.

Morning came bright again, streaming in through an eastern window. Claerwen suddenly wakened, realizing she had neglected Marcus throughout the night, giving in to her own fatigue. She sat up and turned, kneeling to lean over him. Then she smiled, relieved. Color was in his face now, good strong color. She felt his face and chest. He was dry and warm, no fever. She could not keep from smiling.

She tiptoed over him, trying not to disturb him. She slipped her bare feet over the edge of the bed, and dropped down to look in a storage space underneath the bed frame. The door stuck, and she yanked on it till it released.

"Blasted thing," she mumbled, didn't find what she looked for, then pressed it shut again. Still on her knees, she stretched up to look over the edge of the bed to see if she had bothered Marcus.

Two glittering black eyes stared back at her.

"Find any gold down there?" Marcus asked, his throat

very hoarse.

She was so startled, she jumped back and sat down hard on the floor.

"No gold, eh?" Marcus winked. Then he burst out laughing. "The look on your face is priceless!"

"Oh, Marcus!" Claerwen scrambled up and launched herself into his arms. "How long have you been awake?"

"Just now, I guess."

"How do you feel?" She picked up a waterskin and climbed over him again. She settled beside him, tucking the shift around her cold feet.

"Very tired. But not bad. Hungry. Weak. Very thirsty."

Claerwen helped him to drink. "I have some food here for you." She started to get up again, but his hand came up to press her shoulder.

"Please...stay like that. I just want to look at you. I want to always remember what a lovely sight it was to wake up and see your face, just as it is right now. It feels so good to be alive, and home, and see my lovely wife."

His hand reached around behind her neck and he pulled her down so he could kiss her. Her hair tumbled over him and he scooped up handfuls of it as he folded his arms around her.

"How long have I been home?" he asked when he released her. As she sat up again, his hand caressed her shoulder, casually dropping the side of the loose shift down her arm. He grinned, his finger tracing the edge of the shift where it crossed low over her right breast.

"Nearly two days," she smiled, mischief sparkling in her eyes. She pulled the shift up.

"I don't remember coming in. Where did they find me?" He played with her fingers, making her move until the shift fell again.

"You were about a half-mile away, barely still walking. Owein and the other men had to chase wolves from behind you. Then I brought you in."

"Wolves?" He thought a moment, but could not

remember. "You brought me in?"

"You were barely conscious, and by the time you were in the house, you had passed out. You slept ever since."

He pushed himself up, swinging his legs over the edge of the bed. He leaned back and kissed her again. "Incredible," he grinned once more, glancing down her shift.

Standing up, he found his legs unable to hold his weight, and he fell back onto the bed, into Claerwen's arms.

"Are you sure you're ready for this?" she asked softly in his ear as she hugged him.

He whispered, winking, "I really have to use the latrine." He stood and tried again.

As he wobbled across the floor, he continued to tease her, saying, "One step at a time, eh? I think I've got it now. Don't go away and don't get dressed, I'm coming right back."

Marcus coaxed Claerwen to sleep most of the day; he could see she was exhausted by her vigil. He continued to rest, sitting in his chair by the fire pit, casually dressed in loose breeches and a long-sleeved wool tunic. He spent the time alternating between carving patterns in a piece of wood and dozing, his feet stretched out on the hearthstones.

By evening, Owein returned to the fort and Padrig sent him to Marcus' house.

"Where's Taran?" Marcus asked.

Owein answered, "He went out this morning, took Grania with him. They're not back yet."

Marcus grunted. "And he always complained about me catting around." He looked up at Claerwen when he realized he had just insulted her cousin and apologized. She was working at the loom and looked back at him, but gave no indication of anger, just a thoughtful sadness. He slightly raised an eyebrow at her lack of reaction.

"She knows, Marcus," Owein confided.

"Damn," Marcus muttered. "I'd hoped it wouldn't last this long."

"You could have told me what you'd suspected," she

chided him mildly, leaving the loom and coming to him. She sat on the floor to warm herself at the fire pit. Marcus leaned his leg against her back.

Owein said, "We've had a guest. Came the day the storm hit. Called Rhun. He's been here ever since."

Marcus frowned, pulling on the rough fringe of beard on his chin, considering if he should leave it or shave. He asked, "Has he said when he will leave?"

Owein shook his head.

"Do you know where he came from, where he is heading?"

"He says he was going to Caernarfon."

"But he was alone?"

"Aye."

"Marcus," Claerwen interrupted, turning around on her knees to face him. "I heard something that really bothered me about him, just before Owein saw you coming home."

His eyebrows went up as she told him what she had heard between Rhun and Grania. Leaning forward, he frowned into Claerwen's face. "What does he look like?"

She described him.

"He was at the inn after Drakar captured you?"

"He must have been, from what Grania said to him. I'd never seen him before. I'm sure I would remember those blue eyes, they're very unusually bright."

Owein stood, coming forward into the light of the fire pit. "You know who he is?"

Marcus gritted his teeth, his brows slashed down in suspicion. "I think he is one of Drakar's spies. He was probably planted at the inn to learn if I'd brought Claerwen back there and hidden her. I had Drakar running around for days, thinking we were somewhere in or near Caernarfon, when we were in the mountains the whole time."

"I thought you had seen Drakar, the second morning," Claerwen asked, confused.

Marcus grinned slyly, "No. I said Drakar was following

my false trail, and when I came back that night, I said he was heading back to Caernarfon. What I didn't tell you was the horn you heard was Owein, signaling me to come home so he could give me information about Drakar's location. I never actually saw Drakar, but I always knew where he was."

Padrig knocked, interrupting with supper.

"What should we do about Rhun?" Owein asked as the meal was laid out on the table.

"Rhun's gone," Padrig said.

"Gone!" Marcus stood up, leaning heavily on the back of the chair.

"Aye. This afternoon, without a word."

"Damn. Then I'm probably right about him. I may even have seen him before, and that's why he doesn't want to be around when I'm well enough to go out." He sat down hard again in the chair, sighing heavily.

"Do you want me to go after him?" Owein asked, fingering his sword's hilt.

Marcus considered the request, then said, "No. He and whoever he's going to will be expecting one of us to follow him. I suspect he's going to Vortigern, and since you, Owein, were the only one I told where I was going, he can't tell Vortigern anything about what I was doing. All they can do is guess. So, for now, we wait. Let them come to us. Increase the watches and keep the gates closed. We can lay a better trap than they can."

After Padrig left, Marcus told Claerwen what he had set out to do, then detailed to both how he had followed Vortigern to Ynys Môn on the day the storm began.

Marcus grinned and started laughing as he continued, "You should have seen him, Owein. You would have rolled up laughing! He was shaking like a blade of grass in a summer gale."

"What did you do?" Claerwen asked.

He leaned forward, trying to rub the tiredness out of his legs and said, "I infiltrated the druids' camp and took the place of one of them at their meeting. They were prophesying for him. So I...er...glorified the interpretation the way I wanted."

"You did what?" Claerwen was aghast. "You would have been killed if they found you out! I thought you only listened in on conversations for information."

Marcus smiled at her and stroked her hair affectionately. "Spying is a lot more than just listening at windows, like I was doing the first time we met." He winked at Owein. "Cousin, here, could tell you some really spooky things I've done."

Owein nodded in agreement. "Did you get it through his dull head to leave us alone this time?"

Marcus pulled a kerchief over his head like a hood and made his coldest face and the monotone voice he used, "I told him the Iron Hawk would slit his throat in the night, and no Saxon would help him."

Owein snorted a laugh. "By the gods, that would have been worthwhile to see. But did he believe you?"

"For a while, perhaps, but he'll go back to his mercenaries soon enough." Marcus looked at Claerwen, touching her face with his fingers. "I tested him about this 'treasure' that Drakar spoke of. He says it's his, but I didn't have the chance to get him to say what it is. Soon enough, he will come looking. That may be why Rhun was here."

"We have to find out what it is," Claerwen muttered.

"Aye," Marcus agreed. "Before they come looking."

"Where did you shelter in the storm?" Owein asked.

"I didn't. It came in when I was trying to get out of the camp. I had to run like a bloody fool to get my horse and get back to the ferry. The ferryman was gone, so I crossed alone. They nearly caught me. But wolves were howling and I bet they thought either predators or the storm would take care of me anyway. By the time I crossed the strait, the horse was too tired to go on, especially in deep snow, so I let her go near Caernarfon. Then I came on home."

"Why didn't you stay somewhere, or go into Caernarfon?" Owein queried.

"I could not risk being identified by anyone, especially so close to the island."

"Then you were out in that blizzard for all three days and nights?"

"Aye. Even if I could have found shelter, I didn't have enough food. And I couldn't know how long the storm would last, so I kept moving. I made snowshoes by tying short branches together, but they kept breaking. That was the longest journey home."

Claerwen swallowed, staring at him. "You could have died out there."

He was quiet a moment, his black eyes deeply serious. "Aye, it was a gamble. With very steep stakes." Then he looked up and smiled, "Ah, but 'tis good to be home."

CHAPTER 18

Dinas Beris
Spring, 468 A.D.

"Who are you going to see in Conwy?" Grania's voice shrilled like cracked brass bells.

Taran's face stretched into a grimace, not attempting to cover his impatience. He slapped down the tunic he was folding and turned to her. "Cunedda, who else?" he snapped.

"That's not what I heard Owein say. He was telling Marcus you were going to see some woman called Blodwyn."

"Owein talks too much. And you don't mind your own business."

"Owein hardly talks at all. And only when he really has something to say." Grania stopped, studying Taran's face.

He turned away, concentrating on his packing. She stalked around in front of him, then suddenly reached out to abruptly push his arm, making him look up at her.

"It's true, then, isn't it? It's true what your brother said a long time ago, that you go after women like it was a nasty habit. I didn't believe him. You aren't even denying you're going to see a woman!"

Taran scowled, his anger rising. Her shrillness was hard to tolerate. "I'm going to Conwy to talk with Cunedda. Marcus needs me to go, now that the snow is clearing and while there is still time before we have to start the spring planting. I have to settle with Cunedda about the problems last summer."

"Why can't Marcus do it? He is the one who should go. He is the leader of this miserable fort!"

"He's been home barely a fortnight and he still has a hard time just to walk up the steps to the ramparts. Besides, I am the better negotiator." Taran completely agreed with Marcus' opinion of his abilities as an arbitrator and his vanity was certainly not going to deny it.

"You pompous..." Grania's face went deeply red. "You still haven't denied it!"

"I don't have to deny anything. Get out of my house! I don't need you in my way all the time. You're worse than a lost calf. Go on! Get out of my house!"

"But you pledged—"

"Pledged what?" he sneered with mockery.

She stared in horror at Taran. "I thought...I thought you meant..."

"You thought. You never think. It's time you grew up some, little girl. The world does not depend on you and what you want. We all have to seek what is best for any of us. I'm going and that's the end of it."

"All right! Go! But don't bother coming back for my sake, you arrogant fool! I won't be here waiting for you."

Taran laughed harshly, the perpetual sarcasm stinging in his words. "And where are you going to go? Back to the convent? That's right, 'little Sister Grania.' No, you'll be here. If you do go, you will find nothing but trouble and the Iron Hawk will have to rescue you again."

"He wouldn't be able to find me."

"He did before."

"You would send him after me? Why? You don't want me. You just used me. Like you use everything and everybody else!"

"Even if I knew the Iron Hawk, I would not bother to send

him for you. It would not be worthwhile to waste his time...or mine either!"

She flung her hand up to slap him, but he blocked her arm and jerked it aside. He stuffed the rest of his things into a pack and stalked away without another word, his contempt showing in his swaggering strides.

Claerwen was on her hands and knees in a small patch of soil along the eastern wall of the fort. Turning over the cold, mushy soil, she yanked out weeds and debris emerging from under the melting snow. Up to yet, no one had ever called the patch a garden, but she did, and was determined to make it into one.

In the short time since he'd begun to teach her, Claerwen had already learned more of healing from Padrig than from the nuns. She was amazed at the extent of his knowledge and sponged it into her memory as fast as he could show her his methods and mixtures of medicines. In the new garden, she wanted to grow many of the herbs and healing plants he used, making them more easily available.

Padrig had done most of the gardening for the fort, along with the house guardsmen. The family also traded work and other goods for food from their clansmen across the mountains. Because the fort supported only a few people and the thin, rocky mountain soil was not well suited for crops, farming was never a large operation. Most of the men hunted for meat, so very few domestic animals were kept; only cows or goats for milk, sheep for wool. The mountain women foraged for edible plants to supplement their diets.

Claerwen wondered now if any plants still grew in the garden she had kept at the homestead in Strathclyde, however wildly, or if the Iron Hawk's fire had destroyed them along with everything else. For a moment, she felt the old anger swell inside her; she still could not forget the Iron Hawk's cruelty. And she still wanted to know who he was. If she never came face to face with him again, she hoped at least Marcus would someday learn his identity and why he had tried to kill her.

Claerwen stood and slapped her soil-covered hands together to dislodge the worst of the dirt, then washed them in a nearby bucket of water. She studied her work, drying her hands on a rag and pondering how she should arrange the plants. There was not a lot of room, but she was already planning to ask Marcus if she could dig up some of the unused portions of the front courtyard to make additional space.

The fort had been quietly peaceful that morning. All the men except Padrig and two reserve house guards were out patrolling. Claerwen had seen Taran leave, rushing out on his big stallion. Shortly after, Marcus had ridden out, planning a short patrol to ease the boredom of his recovery. Claerwen caught movement from the corner of her eye, and saw Grania walking slowly toward her.

"Grania, come look at my new garden!"

Then Claerwen saw how Grania's face was tracked with tear streaks. She went to her, and as she reached to take Grania's arms, the younger woman broke into sobs.

"Oh, Claerwen, he's gone!"

"What happened? Who is gone?" Claerwen was alarmed.

"Taran. He's gone. Oh, what am I going to do now?"

"Come, sit with me." Claerwen pulled her cousin to an upended barrel she used for a seat. "He's coming back within a fortnight. Did he not tell you so?"

"Aye, but...Claerwen, I thought he wanted to marry. He talked of a pledge. Now he denies he ever did."

Suspicious, Claerwen asked, "What did he say, exactly?"

When Grania finished, Claerwen sighed, wishing she had Padrig's wisdom.

"Grania, listen to me." She took her hands in her own. "It sounds like he tricked you into believing a pledge was made. You agreed to it, but he never really did. He would have had to ask Marcus for permission to make the pledge legal. He didn't do that either. I'm sorry, Grania."

"Why, why did he do this to me?" New tears flowed unheeded.

Claerwen winced, knowing the difficult truth.

When her cousin did not answer at first, Grania's face came up to stare at Claerwen.

"You knew what everyone else knew, didn't you? You knew Taran was going to hurt me and you knew I was too stupid to see it. You were too busy playing the 'Queen of Beltainne' with your husband to care about me!"

Grania's fists clenched and unclenched. She stood and turned fiery-eyed to Claerwen, then shrieked, "I hate him! By the gods how I hate him! He wasted everything we had. I thought I could come to you for help and all I get is a lesson in law."

Claerwen struggled to remain composed in the stinging indignities of Grania's childishness. She had tried to offer the truth of the situation, but Grania had twisted it into hindrance more than help.

Claerwen stood to face her cousin and tried a more soothing approach. "Taran will be back soon, Grania. If he does care for you, he will seek your forgiveness for his harshness. If he doesn't, then you have not truly lost anything but some time. Taran may be arrogant, but he is not evil."

Grania's voice went low and hoarse, "You didn't hear him. The way he said it. What he said. To him I am no more than so much rubbish. And your face tells me you don't believe Taran ever cared about me. Just like everyone else in this miserable place. Oh, I hate this place and everyone in it! I just hate it!"

She turned and marched swiftly away, toward the gates, aching to leave.

Grania wanted Taran to hurt the way she hurt, wanted him to be shocked when he returned, to find she was gone with no trace. She wanted him to come looking for her and not find her, and hurt because he would realize what he had lost. He and all of those other self-righteous people. No one cared, no one! Of course, he was right, she would probably live at the fort the rest of her life. It was truly not fair that he was right. She wished she could disappear.

The anger in Grania's strides and the stricken look of her

face brought stares from the clan people whom she passed as she pounded her way out of the gates and down the sloping road toward the river. However, no one paused to stop her, even though an unescorted woman outside the fort was seriously frowned on due to the potential danger. The people had become too well aware of her shrill, volatile temper. While they saw Claerwen as the calm, kind woman, a little too shy and serious sometimes, they cringed when Grania took her moods to the extreme, a little too publicly.

Claerwen watched her cousin walk away from her, feeling guilty and depressed. She had been sharper than she intended and had not wanted to lecture her, but she could not have said it any clearer. Grania had not had much experience with men and, Claerwen hoped, this lesson would be the beginning of a new maturity.

Claerwen started to follow when she saw Grania was heading out of the gates, and called after her. She ran several yards but saw no use in continuing when she realized she was being disregarded. Grania trotted down the road went left, disappearing around the bend. Claerwen believed she would not go far, having no penchant for either exercise or missing supper.

Moments later, Marcus rounded a copse of young willows from the opposite direction, cantering in on one of the husky Welsh grey horses that Owein raised and trained. He was surprised to see Claerwen waiting for him.

"What's wrong?" he asked as he eased down from the horse and saw the frustration in her eyes.

She leaned her brow against his solid chest and sighed. "Taran broke with Grania, just before he left, and she's terribly upset."

"I saw her walking down the road. Should I go after her?"

"I'm sure she won't go far. Let her be for a while. She needs time to think. Did you know she thought he wanted to marry?"

Marcus' brows went up and his voice deepened, "Marry? Taran? Hardly."

"From what she told me, I think he may have tricked her into believing he'd made a pledge with her. And now she's angry with all of us because we all knew it would happen and didn't tell her."

Marcus' face filled with irony and he said, "Of course, she doesn't realize she never would have listened to any of us. He put his arm around Claerwen, and they walked slowly toward the buildings, the grey following. "I wouldn't worry, Claeri, she'll get over it. But if she's not back by evening, let me know and I will go find her."

She nodded in agreement with his offer, then said, "Her spunk is becoming a fickle willfulness and it worries me. She is changing, and not for the better."

Marcus caressed her shoulder comfortingly, and kept his opinion of Grania to himself.

Grania's mood swept over her like an ocean swell, engulfing her, sucking her down. She felt as if every shred of her pride and dignity was destroyed. Tears ran unheeded as she marched her way to the river. Reaching its banks, she was not able to decide which way to go, which frustrated her further. She finally headed downstream.

The end of the path came and went, and Grania followed the riverbank, a natural flat shelf at the bottom of the long, deep, narrow valley. Eventually this shelf gave out to sheer cliffs rising sharp and high to the sky, and she had to move up and away from the water. She found a place that was not difficult to scale and emerged atop a spur-like hill that overlooked a long section of the valley. She stopped there, suddenly giving in to exhaustion.

Grania had not realized how far she had come and only vaguely understood where she was. She guessed she had walked for a pair of hours, but she did not really care as thoughts crowded her overwhelmed mind in the recurring pattern of Taran's lies, Claerwen's unsupportive response, and her loneliness in the fort's isolation.

Grania found a level, rocky surface at the outcrop's summit and sank to her knees. There she cried long and hard, letting tears fall into the dust, ripping out handfuls of newly sprouted grass to fling in anger over the cliff's edge, pounding fists as hard as she could stand against anything worth hitting.

Her foolish display continued until the last of her energy was spent and she sat still in the sunlight. Like the end of a thunderstorm, she laid down and drifted off, the tantrum disappearing in sleep.

Sometime later she woke, tired and hungry. Her feet and legs hurt with vengeance, not used to walking so far or with such ambition. And now she was faced with walking all the way home. That thought nearly broke her into tears again. The sleep had done some good, giving her calm and rest, but the pain of Taran's insults dragged on her mood badly. She thought about staying there, forcing someone to come looking for her, teaching them to not be so cruel. But she knew Taran would not be the one looking and he was the only one she really wanted to hurt.

She slowly rose to her blistered feet and painfully began to move down the hillside, back toward the river. Then a drop of water struck her face. Startled, she looked up and realized clouds had moved in. "Oh, wonderful, rain," she grumbled, picking up her pace. She knew she could never beat it home, but urgency pushed her to limp and slide her way down the hill. The unfamiliarity of the area made the way back to the fort seem much longer and frightening. She angrily slapped back at shrubbery that snagged at her clothes and scratched her hands as she descended. More raindrops, huge ones, crashed down from the sky, quickly soaking her and the soil. Her shoes were simple, everyday footwear, not meant for long outdoor journeys and they slipped easily in the mud.

She neared the bottom of the hill, and her speed had increased to the point that she was almost running and not able to control her descent. She tried to slow, but her momentum pulled her down. At the slope's base, the brush cleared, showing where rainwater was streaming down in runnels, filling puddles just before the riverbank. The spring grass had not taken hold there, and when Grania reached the spot, she sprawled headlong, sliding through the puddles and onto the grassy riverbank. By then, the rainstorm was in full spate.

Grania sat up and realized she was not hurt, only streaked with mud. Crying again, she rose and attempted to use the rain to wash the muck from her. She managed to clean some of it, but her dress would be reduced to rag duty once she finally got home. "Home," she blustered to herself, "How can that place be called home?" She stamped the wet earth and cursed her bad luck.

Then, suddenly, she froze, listening. Was that a voice calling? Who would be out here?

She listened again. The rain pounded the earth, confusing sound. Grania shivered in her wet clothing. The sun had been warm, and in her anger, she had not thought about taking a cloak; now she was getting chilled. Shielding her face from the rain, she peered into the misty distance, looking for anything that moved. Again she shivered, this time from fear. She realized she was far from safety.

Out of the wooded slopes, upstream from where she stood, came a single horseman. From a distance and through the rain, she could see he wore a simple leather cloak, draped over much of his horse as well. The cloak's hood was pulled low and dripped profusely from its sagging edge.

"Hullo!" he called, waving. Grania was rooted on the riverbank, too surprised to move. He came on slowly, the horse plodding carefully through the mud. She didn't know if she should run or wait; but knowing she could not outdistance a rider, she decided to wait. At this point in her life, she felt it no longer mattered what happened to her.

"Hullo!" he called again, expecting an answer. Grania tentatively waved. Her sniffling slowed as curiosity overpowered her; she wanted to know who the stranger was. He stopped a few yards in front of her and lifted the edge of the hood.

Rhun sat there, smiling at her.

Grania's jaw dropped, then shut again. She was so

surprised she could not even greet him. Instead she asked, "What are you doing here? I thought you'd left."

"I changed my plans."

"You are going back to Dinas Beris?"

Instead of answering, he asked, "Are you all right? I saw you fall from up there. 'Tis a shame about your pretty dress."

Rhun jumped off the horse, and came close to her, to see if she was hurt. He briefly examined the cuts and scratches on her hands.

"Come," he said, guiding Grania to a thick pine tree and pushing his way through its branches. He pulled her with him, making her stand near the trunk and out of the heaviest rain.

Grania gazed up at him. She had not realized how tall he was and he towered over her slight form. He took one of her scraped hands in his, gently wiping dirt and blood from it with his own kerchief. Then he soothingly kneaded it, massaging the cold and pain from it.

Grania felt suddenly warm.

"Thank you," she said softly. "Why?"

He ignored her question, demanding, "What in the gods' names are you doing out here alone? Do you know how dangerous it is? You nearly fell into the river!"

She pulled her hand from him and said, spite in her voice, "I know. Everyone seems to want to preach to me today."

"I am sorry, it was not my place to say so." He took her hand again and kissed its fingers. He pushed the hood back and at the same time, the sun struck through a gap in the clouds, catching in his eyes. They sparkled brilliantly blue, startling Grania. She stared into them, noticing how raindrops clung to his lashes.

Rhun looked up, dropping the hood down. "The rain is stopping."

Grania shivered, then abruptly raced out from the tree limbs. "I must start back. They will be looking for me soon."

"Wait!" Rhun lunged after her, catching her hand. "Where is Taran? Why are you out here all by yourself?" This time he asked gently.

Grania's mouth twisted as she considered what to say, not wanting to admit her foolishness. She finally said, "Taran left to go to Conwy. I was upset. I did not think."

Rhun looked surprised. "You look like you were more upset than for what you tell me." He lifted her chin and saw the shame in her brown eyes. "He is the fool, I believe."

Grania smiled, relieved when Rhun asked no further. She gazed again into his startling blue eyes, and saw no arrogance, no sarcasm, no criticism, no impatience. It was then she realized what a heavy pall of stress Taran had created in her.

"Can you take me back to the fort?" she blurted, tiredness overwhelming her.

"I can take you most of the way."

Grania did not understand. Her confused expression made him chuckle.

"I will explain, and you may find this either strange or funny. Come, ride this poor old horse with me." He helped her mount, then climbed up behind her.

"You don't know that I was requested to leave Dinas Beris," he said in a tentative tone.

"The prince told you to leave?"

"No. I never saw him; he was too ill yet. Taran ordered me to leave. Because I criticized how he treated you. Of course, he didn't like my comments."

"You defended me?" Grania was astonished.

"Aye. I was disgusted by his manners. I told him so and he told me to get out."

"That sounds like Taran."

Rhun chuckled. "I decided to comply, rather than upset the prince's household. I had to go on to Caernarfon anyway. But then..."

He stopped, the quiet of the mountains drawing in on them.

Grania twisted around, looking up into his face to see why he went silent. "Why did you come back?"

"I wanted to know if you were all right. I couldn't bear the way Taran treated you. So I came back, to see you."

Grania silently considered Rhun's words, not certain if she should believe him. She bowed her head, studying his hands as they held the reins in front of her.

Finally he asked, "What will you do now?"

"I don't know. I don't want to stay where Taran is. But I have nowhere else to go. Unless I find a way to keep myself, I'm dependent on my cousin and her husband."

"I have a suggestion. Ignore Taran when he comes back. Make him swallow his pride when he sees your dignity in the face of his arrogance. He tried to hurt you, but don't let him. Carry your head high and walk past him. If he tries to insult you, pretend he is only whistling into the wind."

"What happens when I start to cry because I'm not brave enough?"

"But you are brave enough, Lady Grania. You don't need to be afraid of Taran. Men like him are afraid of women."

"Afraid? You must be joking!"

"No, I'm not. If he had the courage he talks about, why hasn't he married a long time ago? Once he gets a woman interested in him, he runs in the other direction."

"I wanted to be lucky like my cousin, but I wasn't."

"You will be, Lady Grania. In time, you will be. It wasn't easy for her either, in the beginning, was it?"

"No. But she was luckier than most, because Marcus has more grit than most men, I believe. He never gives up."

"He must care for her very much."

"Oh, aye, they have a very special bond between them. The kind bards sing about."

Rhun chuckled at Grania's romantic reference. He clucked at the horse, urging it into a trot.

They rode to within a half-mile of the fort, arriving in late afternoon and staying within the fringe of woods, out of the patrollers' sight. The sun had shone the rest of the day, drying their clothing. Grania calculated what she would have to say to explain her disheveled appearance, but her mood was so improved from the morning that she anticipated a minimum of fussing would be made over her.

"Are you sure you cannot stay at the fort any longer? Taran will not be back for a while," Grania coaxed as they slipped off the old horse.

"I dare not. Taran would find out when he comes back and I don't want to subject you to his anger again," Rhun countered.

"You've given me much good advice. And helped me a great deal by going far out of your way. Why?"

Rhun fidgeted with the reins. His eyes dimmed as he looked down, loneliness in them. Then he looked up again into Grania's face, their blueness brilliant again. He took her hands and pleaded softly, "I want to see you, Grania. Very much. How can I do that?"

She was surprised and thrilled at his words and how he said them. She thought a moment, then her eyes brightened. "I know of a place, it's perfect. There is a stone hut above here that no one uses. A trail leads to it, starting not far from here; I will show you where it begins. You can stay there."

"Will you come to see me?" He held her shoulders and looked down into her soft brown eyes. His face took on a soft, pondering look, meant to haunt her memory. He leaned, tentative at first, then more assured when she did not back away.

He kissed her.

She held her breath, unsure if she should continue. A sprig of fear sprouted, but she denied its growth. "It will be difficult to find reasons to go away from the fort all the time."

"You will find them, I am sure." He kissed her again.

"How will you find food? Should I bring some to you?" She looked for excuses, still not sure if she was getting into more trouble.

"Do not worry about me, I can take care of myself. Just come, Grania. Come to me whenever you can." He kissed her once more, embracing her tightly to him. She felt weak in his arms, her better judgement telling her to go against what Rhun presented to her. But she wanted his companionship and was unwilling to fight her conscience. Rhun's gentleness was like a great salve against the pain Taran had inflicted. Silently, she vowed that Taran would not know, nor anyone else, and she would have the satisfaction in her own heart that she had found something better than Taran's arrogance.

As Grania held onto Rhun, she realized she had been attracted to him since his arrival at Dinas Beris, ignoring it because she thought she was in love with Taran. Now she wondered if she had ever been in love at all. That attraction had been very different. Rhun stirred something in her she thought of as mature, even sophisticated, and she wondered if it was the same mysterious bond that Claerwen held with Marcus. She savored the secrecy, scheming to herself to see Rhun everyday if possible. And maybe one day, he would love her enough to take her away.

Grania briefly explained how to reach the *hafod*, then bade him goodbye. Before letting go, Rhun leaned to lightly kiss her again. But before his lips met hers, she stretched up and whipped her arms around his neck.

He saw her eyes sparkle just as they closed, her mouth clamping onto his in eagerness. Then she tore from him, bounding away down to the fort.

Chapter 19

Dinas Beris
Spring, 468 A.D.

Grania had no chance to slip away without being noticed until midday. Before she left, she sneaked into the kitchen and concealed two loaves of fresh bread in a basket while Padrig was out on an errand. She saw Claerwen was deeply engrossed in her garden, then darted out of the gates when the guard was distracted. No one was on the road, and she ran for the trail to the hut, avoiding the watchful eyes of the patrollers.

Eager to meet Rhun, Grania hummed lightly. She was complacent, as if she had never been through the tears, the despair, the arguments, the discourse on behavior. She wished she had been able to start out earlier, intensely glad to be away from the dismal fort, always feeling trapped there in its oppressive loneliness. Even when the men were home, they were always working or in the hall talking and drinking together. Nor could she seem to resume her closeness to Claerwen; her cousin's time was always consumed with Marcus or Padrig.

Grania had no compunction whatsoever regarding her rendezvous with Rhun at Taran's private hut. Her resentment had projected into a belief that she had the right to take and use anything she thought Taran wasted in return for his ill treatment of her. She believed that she deserved the use of the tiny stone hut as he neglected it most of the time, and it suited her situation regarding Rhun perfectly. She never paused to think what would happen when Taran returned or what he would do to her or Rhun if he found someone living there under her guidance.

As she neared the hut, she smelled roasting meat, and she realized how little she had eaten since Taran had left. The fresh bread she carried smelled delicious, intensifying her hunger. She hurried, a cross of nervousness and excitement spurring her towards the hut.

Grania called at the doorway and received a quick answer. Rhun was turning a spit of partridges hung over the small fire pit. He grinned broadly at her as she exclaimed delight over them. She set her bread on the hearth stones to warm.

"You are too generous, Lady Grania," Rhun said, holding a hand up to draw her to sit with him.

"'Tis nothing." She immediately felt the same strong attraction as she gazed into his blue eyes. He returned her gaze, watching her face become dreamy. He leaned a little closer, as if to tease her with a kiss.

"Your timing is perfect," he said, snapping the spell with his cheerful, ingratiating tone. "Share with me?"

Grania nodded cheerfully as he filled a chunk of the bread with torn pieces of the partridge. She took it like a greedy child.

They lingered over the meal. Rhun was an excellent cook. He explained that he had spent much of his life alone abroad and had to fend for himself, including cooking. He complemented the bread, saying it accompanied the partridges very well. Grania wished she had made it herself, but she admitted that either Padrig or Claerwen had made it.

"Come, pretty Grania, talk to me," Rhun smiled when he had finished.

"I wish I could stay," she sighed to him.

"Please, just for a short while? It's lonely here."

Grania smiled, sympathizing. "I know. 'Tis so lonely there as well. I will try to come earlier tomorrow, but it's not easy. There's no crowd to hide in at the fort. They notice an absence too easily."

"Tell them you are going walking and that you will stay within the patrol boundaries where you are safe. They'll get used to it. They will think you are trying to cope with Taran's argument."

She thought a moment, frowning. Then he took her hands in his and held her gaze again, a slight, wistful grin curving his lips. Her mouth went dry and her eyes widened.

"I will be here tomorrow, as soon as possible," she breathed huskily to him, almost compelled to say it.

"And I shall be waiting."

He bent to kiss her hands, gently and politely. She was awed again by his mildness after Taran's tense arrogance. He squeezed her fingers in farewell.

The next few days patterned themselves after the first. Grania always brought food to complement Rhun's hunting prizes. Her visits began by mid-morning and lasted longer each day, stretching nearly to the evening meal, when she would romp back to the fort just in time to appear at supper.

Rhun's kindness astounded Grania, rekindling her sense of romance and assuaging her bitterness at Taran. Rhun stirred a fascination in her she had never encountered. She attempted to memorize the many stories and adventures he entertained her with, watching every detail of his face as he spoke, smiled, and laughed; she was entranced by its expressiveness. By definition, he was not handsome, but his laughing charm and startling blue eyes more than made up for any lack in looks.

True to Rhun's word, Grania's long daily absences became expected. By the end of a fortnight, both the people of the fort and the people of the mountains became deeply engrossed in their spring work, generally ignoring Grania's activities. However, with the large burden of work to be done, the people gradually grew resentful of Grania for shirking her share of it. For generations, they had traded skills and helped each other, no one being over-burdened or lacking in a necessity. Though spread thinly across the wild hills, they were a tight-knit clan that worked well together and no distinction was made between prince or farmer. Each worked just as hard and received just as much.

Claerwen was puzzled that Grania appeared to enjoy spending so much time alone, especially after complaining so bitterly about the loneliness of Dinas Beris. As the family and house guards gathered in the hall for the evening meal, Claerwen watched Grania arrive and seat herself apart from everyone else. She rose and approached her, settling across the table from her cousin.

"The spring work is going well," Claerwen began. "Padrig is taking me around to all of the clan's homesteads. He is introducing me to them as he checks with each for any medicine they may need."

"That's nice," Grania answered, not paying much attention.

"You should come with us, Grania. You would like the community feeling of the clan. Once they know who you are, they begin to lose their natural suspicion and welcome you. For the first time since we left fled from the Irish, I feel like I belong."

"No thank you, Claerwen."

"Grania, why do you spend so much time alone?" Claerwen slipped her hand around her cousin's wrist, tying to break into the young woman's inattention. "You liked Caernarfon and the convent because of all the companionship. You could find the same thing here if you take a short time to look for it."

Grania finally looked up into Claerwen's eyes, then gazed briefly beyond. She saw Owein come in with two other men, brushing bits of wool from their tunics that had clung from shearing sheep and goats. Then she saw Marcus stride in, wiping his hands and arms with a rag after working at the forge, his sleeveless tunic still open. As he scanned the room, looking for Claerwen, Grania quickly excused herself and rose, hurrying for the kitchen.

"Good evening, lovely lady," Marcus greeted Claerwen, kissing her cheek as he straddled the bench next to her.

Claerwen shook her head as she watched Grania walk away.

"What's wrong?" he asked as he tied together the front of the tunic.

"She must be more upset than she shows. I tried to talk her into coming with Padrig and me, but she only wants to be alone. I don't understand."

"She runs away whenever I come. Do I remind her so much of Taran?"

Claerwen turned to him and smiled, "No, I think she doesn't like to watch us." She ran her hand along his muscular arm.

Marcus grunted, grinning at her, then looked up and stared across at the front doors. His brother had walked in and dropped his traveling pack on the floor.

Marcus rose, striding across to greet Taran. A round of chatter stirred as the others noticed the arrival. Padrig began bringing food as they took their places at the table, mead pouring all around in welcome.

"You're doing well, brother, since I left," Taran commented, eying how easily Marcus was able to move now.

"Aye, I have been lucky. Tell us of Conwy, Taran. What says Cunedda?"

Taran stood again, holding his drinking horn in the air, everyone else following his example. "To a success! I wish it were bigger, but that is the next step." Everyone cheered, drank, then settled into noisy talk.

Taran launched into a detailed account of his meeting with the king of Gwynedd. He presented an elaborate apology to Marcus for not sending the needed mercenaries. They had worked out new codes and messenger routes between Conwy and Dinas Beris, in the hope of preventing future miscommunications.

"We discussed Vortigern at great length. He has stalled importation of more Saxons, but Cunedda feels this will not last long, as we have sensed. Vortigern's British support continues to erode and he is continually becoming more dangerous; not because of himself, but because the Saxons are more plentiful and stronger than ever. Cunedda suggested that we seek stronger alliances directly with Cornwall and other kingdoms in the south. I agreed, and if you do as well, I will set out immediately to accomplish these needed alliances."

"You would be gone quite a while. Two months, perhaps, or more?"

"Aye. I would not go if it looked like last summer's trouble. But with Drakar no more, and Vortigern stalled for a while longer, this would probably be the best time to go. What do you say, Marcus?"

"I agree. When do you want to leave?"

"I will rest here for two or three days and gather the supplies I need. I want to accomplish this before Vortigern has a chance to reach any of them."

"Aye, then so be it. Owein, have you anything to say, or ask?"

Their cousin shook his head, taciturn as always. Negotiation did not interest him though he well understood its necessity. He was a warrior down to his soul, arms and battle were the games he played best.

The meal was finished long before Taran ended his report. The scraps had been taken away and the drinking horns refilled from a fresh skin of mead. The three men remained, analyzing Taran's mission. The house guards retired to the barracks to await the next watch, and Padrig disappeared into his quarters at the rear of the kitchen house.

Claerwen knew Marcus would stay late, planning with Taran and Owein. She rose and slipped outside, seeking fresh air. She strolled around the courtyard, then decided to look for Grania, wondering if her cousin had eaten in the kitchen with Padrig or taken food to eat alone in her house.

Claerwen knocked at Grania's house, but received no answer. She called twice, then left, going back to the kitchen.

Padrig poked his head out of his doorway when he heard Claerwen rustling in the kitchen. He told her Grania had heard the men welcome Taran home, and he had caught her standing behind the curtain that covered the kitchen doorway, peering across at Taran. "I told her to either go in or out, but at least stop blocking my well-worn path so I could gladly wear it out some more!" Padrig chuckled. "Then she took her meal to her house. I assume she ate it there."

Puzzled, Claerwen went back into the hall. She waited in the kitchen entry for Marcus to look up.

"Claerwen?" he broke off his discussion and rose, alarmed by her expression.

"I can't find Grania," she said quietly when he came to her, trying to keep Taran from hearing. "I think she's gone out of the fort again."

"No," Marcus shook his head slightly. "The gatesman would have immediately reported it to me, or Owein."

"I saw her go in her house..." Taran said, coming forward, "...just a while ago, when I went to the latrine."

"She didn't answer when I knocked and called."

Taran rolled his eyes. "She's either asleep or ignoring you. Don't worry about her. She's probably found another man to play with by now."

Marcus spun around and caught Taran's tunic in one fist, dragging him back across the hall away from Claerwen. He hissed, "Speak of your own exploits, brother. Comments like that are not of any use, not in front of my wife. And even if it were true, it's no longer any of your concern, after the way you treated her."

Taran shook himself out of Marcus' grip, a smirk on his face. "Your woman's got you crawling for her, doesn't she?"

Marcus' face went cold. "I can still cast you out, Taran. Remember that."

"You need me too much. You need those alliances, and you know I can seal them better than anyone, including yourself."

"I would rather fight alone for our freedom than chain our home and people in your shrewish arrogance." Marcus glared at Taran until his brother turned and strode away, picking up his pack as he went out the door.

Claerwen moved alongside Marcus, slipping her hand around his arm. "You would cast him out?"

Marcus scowled heavily at the door as he spoke, "Aye, if I have to. He knows it, too. He will watch his tongue for a time, but the arrogance will creep back in, then I will have to threaten him with banishment again. My father had to threaten him several times. But one thing is certain about Taran, he is extremely predictable. He likes his comfort too well to give it up for banishment."

Marcus sighed harshly, then his face eased into calmness again. He looked at Claerwen and said, "Let's go to bed."

Grania never mentioned Taran's return to Rhun. She arrived at the hut earlier than usual the next day, however, and he sensed her agitation, guessing it to himself. She attempted to hide her high-strung attitude by showering attention on him, cooking a special morning meal for him and cleaning up afterwards.

Taking advantage of another glorious spring day as warm as Midsummer, Grania coaxed Rhun into hiking up and over the ridge above the tiny hut, down into the next valley. She walked with him as if she had known him many years, her arm crooked in his, chattering like a sparrow. Rhun carried a rucksack of leftover food, intending to snare a pair of ptarmigans to fill out a meal.

By midday, they reached a remote meadow and stopped, tired from the steep walk. Rhun quickly set the snares and hung the other food safely high in a tree. A tiny stream ran through the meadow, where Grania stopped to soak a kerchief and wash her face and hands. Humidity and the exertion made them feel tired and lazy.

Rhun stood watching her back as she bent over to rinse the scarf out in the water and smiled. He thought, such a tiny little thing, she is, a little round, but so pleasant. He softly approached, and settled beside her.

Without speaking, she dipped the kerchief once more in the cool mountain water and offered it to Rhun like it was a prize. He smiled, watching how her face was soft and prettily colored, the rich background of greens and tawnies behind her complemented her complexion perfectly. Her fingers clung lightly on the kerchief as he took it from her. He wiped his forehead and neck slowly, watching her face. She locked into a penetrating gaze with him, her brown eyes wide and sharply alert. Unconsciously, his breath quickened, the scarf falling forgotten on the sweet-smelling grass.

Grania felt herself compelled to touch Rhun's face, stroke his hair, caress his features as if they were priceless ermines or gold. His eyes seemed bluer than ever, as if competing with the sky itself. She pulled herself up, kneeling, and put her arms around his neck. She did not smile, but neither was her face serious. She seemed driven to seek something, and she was not conscious of what it was; in fact, her mind was quite blank. She only knew she was drawing closer and closer.

Her lips met Rhun's and she was drifting away from the real world, drunkened with the sensuous craving of her own imagination. She rubbed her face on his, trying to breathe in all of his manly smell, her hands stroking and urging. She climbed into his lap, knees hooked around his waist and clung there.

Rhun did not hesitate. His response was equally instinctive when he understood she was beyond recalling to reality. With practiced dexterity, he untied her tunic and shift, and pulled them from her. Still clinging, her lips fused to his, her eyes closed, her body arched into his. She perspired freely, her nakedness shining, fragile yet eagerly strong.

Rhun rolled over backwards with her, hoisting her up to kiss her breasts and belly. She groaned with pleasure, yanking off his clothing as she continued to kiss his chest. He barely was able to remove his breeches before she knocked him over to roll several times together across the grass, reveling in the rich turf. Delicate! Rhun reminded himself of what he had thought earlier. This little woman has the compulsion of a wolf! He chuckled lightly at himself.

They grappled fiercely, rolling together in tangled fury. Grunts and pants rumbled through the air, a curious counterpoint to the spring bird songs, breeze-rippled grass and leaves, and the soft slither of the stream. Shortly, he released inside her and their breathing eased into the soft, relaxed sounds of sleepers. Her eyes still closed, she almost smiled, drifting into a dream. Rhun covered her from the sun with a light cloak.

He briefly washed in the steam, dressed, and left to check the snares.

Chapter 20

Dinas Beris
Summer, 468 A.D.

Claerwen stared at the cloth she was embroidering and sighed tiredly. She was seated in Marcus' favorite chair, pulled up to the west-facing window, trying to catch the last of the evening light. But it was slipping away like the breath of her sigh. Her needle held still and she was paralyzed in her decision of what stitch she should do next.

Instead, she found herself thinking of the danger Marcus faced in his work. Taran had completed his ambassadorial trip in the south and was home again; and now Marcus was planning his next espionage mission. Discussions had been continuous over the days since Taran's return. Marcus would be gone a minimum of four weeks, more likely six, and he would be in constant danger, samples of which Claerwen had seen too clearly. She had gone alone to her house, not wanting to listen to the men talk anymore. Though she had seen Marcus' bold courage in facing down Drakar's soldiers and knew he was strong and smart, she also vividly remembered how he had suffered through the blizzard.

Claerwen tried hard to control her thoughts by keeping a tremendous schedule of work from sunrise to well past dark each day, but the closer Marcus' departure approached, the more unnerved she became. Others sensed the moodiness she tried to escape and were sympathetic, having watched her cope with his absence before.

Padrig tried to comfort her, but she overrode his words with forced cheeriness, telling him not to worry. Once she reached out to Grania, needing female companionship and asked if she could come with her on one of her daily outings. But Grania turned her away, preoccupied and possessive of her secret relationship with Rhun. The rejection stung Claerwen's feelings.

The sun fell below the mountain ridge beyond Claerwen's window and she watched a tear drip onto the back of her hand. She wiped it away, but another soon replaced it. Her face was very still and very sad, her eyes overflowing. She was barely breathing. She had accomplished much work during the long summer day but felt no satisfaction. Only tiredness, and the dreaded anticipation of loneliness.

The house was as quiet as the mountains. The evening was warm and she watched the utter stillness of it through the window without seeing it. She did not want to move, not even blink, not even breathe. She was afraid she would begin to weep and never be able to stop. Finally, she took a deep breath, exhaled slowly, and wiped away the tears. She tried to relax and gain control of her nerves, drawing on the serenity of the evening.

"Claeri?" Marcus' low voice interrupted the hushed atmosphere. He stood in the doorway, his presence filling the room. Startled, Claerwen twisted in the chair to see him. He smiled until he saw the pain in her face.

"Claeri? Why are you here all by yourself?" He came forward and sat on the edge of the carved chest next to her.

When her eyes came up and locked with his, they gazed steadily, their green-blueness iridescently beautiful.

Marcus' lips pressed into a flat line, stretching out and down, then he said quietly, "I know, I will miss you, too."

Claerwen finally smiled, running her finger along his moustache. Then she went solemn again and whispered, "Let me go with you."

His brows dropped and his eyes grew intense as they searched her face. "You're serious."

He rose and paced to the window. Then he turned back to Claerwen, astonishment on his face when he saw her expression had not changed. "You truly are serious," he repeated. He took her arms, pulling her up so she was away from the fading sunlight, and stared into her eyes.

"It's not the fire, Marcus. Not like last time."

"Claerwen, this will not be a holiday. I cannot even consider taking you with me."

"I don't expect it to be easy. I know what danger you will be in. I've seen it. I want to help you. I know how much Britain's freedom means to you."

Marcus closed his eyes, aching inside. He exhaled roughly and went back to the window. "When I warned you before we married, you accepted that I would be gone much of the time. Claeri, I wish things were different, but I can't change who I am and what I must do because of that."

"It's not that, Marcus. I do understand. No questions asked. And I agree with what you do, why you must go. But I want to do more than just wait for you. After what Drakar and the rest did to us, I cannot sit here doing nothing anymore."

Marcus stared out the window, watching the darkness close in. For a long time, he was silent. Claerwen stood behind him, watching his wide shoulders. Finally, he spoke, his voice very deep and quiet, "When I warned you, Claeri, I should have warned myself as well. I didn't realize how hard it would be to go."

He turned from the window and Claerwen came to him, her arms slipping around him. He tucked her head under his chin, his hand smoothing her long hair. He said, "I cannot consider taking you with me, Claerwen. It's too dangerous and you don't have the experience. You would have to know instantly what to do, what to say, know whose face belongs to whom and whose side they belong to. I've been doing this nearly ten years now.

There's no time to teach you what I do now by instinct."

He paused, his hands idly stroking her back, then he added, "Even if I would quit, a spy is always a target to the day he dies."

Claerwen leaned her head back to see his face. "You would never quit because your work is so much a part of you, like the mountains, like Dinas Beris. I see how your eyes light up when you discover something important, or when you see an opportunity that will help you achieve what you seek."

Marcus studied her face, and he slowly smiled, the lines around his eyes crinkling deeply. "If I ever have to make a choice, though, between you or anything else I have or I do, I would choose you, my Claerwen."

She smiled at last, hugging him tightly.

Tiredness swept over Claerwen like the strong westerly winds that race across the sea. She had tramped through the mountains all day, making her medicine rounds. Now she was back in the cook house with Padrig, stirring the "must" of mead that was beginning to ferment. He was sorting hops to add while she stirred the concoction with a large paddle.

Dark circles underlined her eyes and her face was pale and slightly shiny with sweat. She continued to force herself to keep busy. Marcus had left a week after their talk and it was three weeks since he had left. Late summer had come and the heat was unusually heavy and lasting, making Claerwen's loneliness that much more oppressive. The stale air trapped between the mountains laid like a pall within the high ridges. For once, the mountain people wished the cold mists would return.

"Can I help?" Grania's voice asked from the doorway. Padrig looked up sharply, surprised at the sudden appearance of the one person least likely to ask.

"Certainly!" he exclaimed, "Come here and—"

The paddle slapped hard against the oak tub. He and Grania stared. Claerwen's face was as grey-white as a snow sky and she sat hard on a bench that luckily was directly behind her.

"Claerwen!" They both ran to her before she could fall further. Her eyes were open but not focused, more greyish than usual. Within moments, her senses returned.

"What happened?" she asked.

"You tell us," Padrig chided her fondly. "You're so pale."

Grania brought cool water and a soaked kerchief to wipe her face. Claerwen shook her head to clear it.

"It must be the heat. I'm so tired I almost feel sick."

"You haven't felt well for a fortnight now," Grania said. "You shouldn't work so hard." She stroked her cousin's hands with the damp rag.

Padrig gazed intently into Claerwen's face, then took her chin to turn her head to each side and back. Then he grunted to himself and grinned.

"Grania is right. You will have to stop working so hard. And you will probably not feel well for some time to come."

Claerwen looked at his grinning face through the haze of her weariness. He would have laughed at the strained way she stared at him if he did not know how poorly she felt. She fussed to herself, trying to understand what he was talking about.

Suddenly Grania squealed, "Of course! Cousin, you are with child!"

Claerwen scanned from one face to the other, not sure if they were teasing.

Padrig told her, "You have the same look in your eyes that Marcus' mother had when she was carrying a child."

Claerwen pictured Marcus' face in her mind and how he would react when she would tell him. Suddenly, a long-suppressed joy welled up inside and burst through her depression. She smiled brilliantly, and hugged Grania and Padrig to her, telling them how proud Marcus would be.

"I'm getting worried Padrig," Claerwen remarked quietly. Padrig looked across the kitchen table, eyebrows knit. Four weeks had gone by since her pregnancy was discovered, seven since Marcus had left.

"He is overdue," he returned. "Probably just a delay. Like last time."

Claerwen was edgy. It was late evening and they were finishing the daily chores. She was queasy all the time from her pregnancy, not just in the mornings. "Last time was too close," she snapped, rubbing her forehead.

"Go to bed, Claerwen." He squeezed her hand.

"I'm sorry, Padrig. I just feel so...so out of control."

"Go to bed. Come." He helped her get up and led her out of the kitchen and through the hall.

The courtyard was silent but for the steps of the guards patrolling the ramparts. Dim light came from some of the houses and the torches in the yard. Claerwen and Padrig walked slowly through the still darkness, silently appreciating each other's company.

They halted as a shout came from one of the guards. The man was on the rampart near the gates and he fell from the walkway, crashing to the courtyard floor. Padrig ran to him, turning him over. An arrow stuck out of his chest.

"By the gods!" he muttered, then began shouting the general alarm. "Go inside!" he yelled at Claerwen, pushing her back towards the buildings.

Taran raced out of the hall, followed by the off-duty guards. Torches flared up throughout the compound. Grania followed the men out, asking what happened. Shouting filled the air from all directions. Padrig huddled the women together, pushing them back to the buildings.

Suddenly, showers of arrows stormed over the ramparts, skittering over the hard-packed earthen yard as they fell. They missed any targets they had been intended to strike. Owein and Taran spread the men out along the walls and began firing back.

"Look!" Grania pointed in the direction of the higher hills. Smoke poured up into the black sky, illuminated by flames from below.

"They're burning the homesteads!" Padrig cried.

"Who are they?" Grania queried.

"I don't know, but we're in a bad way."

"We must get the spare arrows and spears ready for the men!" Claerwen shouted, pulling Grania and Padrig with her towards one of the storehouses behind the hall. But when they turned the corner, they stopped, their faces astounded. The storehouse was on fire, too. It could not have been burning very long, one of the guards would have seen; but it and its contents were already too well destroyed to be of any use.

More arrows whizzed overhead and the three crouched along the great hall. They darted to the nearest door and whipped inside, slamming it shut behind them. Then they bolted all the window shutters. As they reached the last window, they stopped momentarily to watch. Soldiers were coming over the ramparts and fighting the house guards with swords. One man stood out from the rest, wearing a strangely visored helmet.

"The Iron Hawk!" Claerwen hissed. "Damn him! He will burn the fort! Why?" She looked at the others, too stunned to say more.

She took a step towards the door, but Padrig caught her arm. "No, Claerwen, I know what you're thinking, but we have no chance against him," Padrig ordered her, his eyes drilling into hers. "We will get some cloaks and leave by the tunnels from under your house."

"Where will we go?" Grania wailed.

"I don't know, but we have to leave. Now!"

"What about Owein and Taran?" Claerwen asked.

"We will have to trust the gods. Marcus will never forgive me if I don't get you out of here. Now, go!"

They sprinted the few yards to Claerwen's house and slammed the door shut, bolting it. They grabbed up cloaks and a few essentials, only what was easily carried and absolutely necessary. Padrig took some of Marcus' spare daggers and a small sword.

They peered through a slit in the shuttered window, seeing

more men come over the walls. The gates were opening. Men from the homesteads could be seen bitterly fighting on the road below. Fire was everywhere.

"There are so many of them," Grania whispered.

"Let's go!" Padrig yanked back the carved chest to reveal the trap door. He pulled it up, exposing cut stone steps that led down through the house's foundation.

But Claerwen stood rooted, staring at the small bag containing her mother's trinkets, not remembering how it came to be in her hand. Her fingers squeezed it, feeling the details of the items within. She knew Padrig was shouting at her to move, but she could not pull her eyes away from it.

"Hurry!" Padrig snapped, forcing Claerwen to look up.

Her mind suddenly cleared and she tied the bag to her belt as she followed him and Grania down the steps. Shouts roared at the outside door.

Padrig handed Claerwen a candle to light, then slapped shut and bolted the trap door. He pushed the women down the tunnel and told them to keep back. He picked up a metal bar and wedged it behind a beam that held back rocks and gravel in a space in the walls and ceiling. The beam was meant to be released in an attack, causing the debris to block anyone from following through the tunnel. He lugged with difficulty at the heavy beam.

"They're going to find us before it gives out!" Grania cried.

"Help me!" he yelled at them.

"Listen! Voices!"

A familiar voice was shouting to search the house above.

"It's Rhun!" Grania cried. "We're safe! Claerwen, he will help us." She started for the steps, but Claerwen grabbed her arm and jolted her back.

Padrig heaved at the beam again, and it finally gave, falling aside. They jumped back as clouds of dirt billowed out at them.

"Run!" he ordered, coughing and cursing the tunnel.

Grania refused to move, angry at Claerwen. "Rhun will

help us!" she repeated.

Claerwen groaned, exasperated. Then she shouted at her cousin, "Don't you understand? Marcus said he was one of Drakar's spies!"

"But—"

"Not now. We have to run. Come!" Claerwen dragged Grania deeper into the tunnel.

Above, Rhun's voice shouted louder.

"I want the Princess," Rhun was ordering in Irish. Do what you want with the others, I don't care." He laughed roughly. "Now that proud Marcus ap Iorwerth is dead, we can figure what we are looking for is here with his woman." The laughter continued, fouling the air.

An instant later, the secret door slammed shut. The invaders had seen the source of escape had been permanently blocked. Rhun commanded, "Go to the other entrance. We'll head them off. Get me that woman!"

Rhun carried the visored helmet under his arm.

"If Rhun knew about the tunnels, then we will have trouble at the other end. We will have to fight our way out," Padrig said as he re-lit the candle, blown out by the dust cloud. They groped their way along the low, damp corridor of escape. There had been no time to think of picking up a torch; but, Padrig thought, perhaps the small candle was more to their advantage. If anyone was waiting for them, any light or smoke would announce their approach that much sooner.

The three clasped hands together with Padrig leading through the blackness. He was familiar with the tunnel's turns and drops as it approached the clinging hawthorn clump, and he led them quickly through. A dim difference in light showed them the tunnel exit. All was silent. Padrig tried to indicate through hand squeezes for the women to be quiet, he would go first, expecting trouble. Claerwen blew out the candle and set it on the ground. They could not see each other at all.

Padrig went forward. His sword had been drawn before their descent into the cellar; he had no worry about the sound of pulling it. Claerwen slipped out a dagger. She and Grania were barely breathing. Padrig reached the exit. The shrubbery was thicker than ever, blocking the way. A quarter moon lit the area enough to see shapes, but if someone was lying in wait, he would have full advantage over the escapees.

Padrig threw a tiny stone in the direction of the track leading away from the exit, along the spur's cliffside. Nothing reacted. He threw another, a little further to indicate progress along the track. Still nothing. He listened intently for a few minutes, but could detect no breathing or motion. Absolutely nothing.

Worried, he knew they had to go on. The invaders would not take long to find the way through the other tunnel from the cellar. He went back to the women and spoke in his softest whisper.

"I hear nothing, but I can not be sure. It is too dark to see. We must go before they come from the other tunnel. Stay close to me and be very alert. Be ready to run, but be very careful on the ledge. The brush will make it extremely difficult to pass, but we must move fast." He squeezed their hands again in reassurance and for luck, then moved forward, the women huddled in behind.

They crouched low at the exit and crawled their way through the shrubs. Nothing stirred around them. They could hear shouts in the distance from the fort and down along the river. Every rustle of leaves and branches made them wince, knowing their position was extremely vulnerable. They moved uncomfortably along the ledge, up the side of the spur. As the track rose, light from the distant fires lit the path more, allowing them to move more quickly. Padrig desperately wanted to disappear into the woods but the slope to either side was too steep. They stopped frequently to listen, but never heard a sound close enough to represent a threat.

The track reached the top of the spur and leveled out into a wider trail that led back to the fort in one direction and to the river road in the other. At the junction, Padrig led the women into the wood. He started to breathe easier, the heavy cover welcome. He did not understand why no man had been posted against their escape, and he guessed Rhun did not know where the tunnel came out. They walked several hundred yards when, suddenly, Claerwen stopped.

Bright flashes streamed before her eyes and pain shot through her head. She swayed, and the others, who had not noticed at first, ran back to her. Then a dark figure leaped from the shadowy trees, landing exactly in the spot where Padrig had stopped and turned back to Claerwen. Padrig whirled and swung the sword, the soldier in him acting instinctively. It bit the arm of the dark figure and a scream escaped. The blow, however, did not disable the man. Padrig's aim had been off-guard and at his age, too slow.

As suddenly as they came, the flashing lights in Claerwen's head left, leaving her sight clear and sharp, even in the dark wood. She saw the figure back away and shift, then begin a new attack. Padrig was not fast enough to catch the swinging sword squarely with his own, but he parried it awkwardly, preventing serious damage. The blade caught his hand, weakening his grip, but he was too enraged and frightened to notice. Claerwen screamed, distracting the attacker, giving Padrig more time to recover. Then she realized she still held the small dagger. Without thinking, she rushed at the figure, and in the final few steps before reaching him, she threw it.

Padrig was poised to strike again, then stopped. The man laid prone, unmoving. Claerwen's dagger hit its mark perfectly, piercing the man's throat.

"Marcus did not exaggerate when he said how cruelly the fire uses you. By all the gods my people swear by, I have seen nothing like this." He knelt by the body and pulled the dagger free, then wiped it clean. He looked up at her, dread serious. Her face was still glazed over. He could barely see her in the gloom of the forest night, but he could tell the gods still held her.

Visions passed like lightning across her mind, none staying long enough to show its meaning. Fire, another fort she did not know, screaming people running, a quiet mountain tarn, Marcus' face, a magnificent jeweled sword flanked by a gold torque and grail on one side, a crown and spearhead on the other, a darkly hooded Christian monk, Marcus' face again, more fire. All passed and were gone, most left unidentified and apparently unrecorded in her memory.

Claerwen's vision cleared again and she saw Padrig looking up at her. Other than Marcus, he understood the power better than anyone she knew, even though he never had experienced it himself. A fierce headache gripped her but she ignored it, and she took the dagger back from him.

"Your hand, Padrig," she said quietly. Automatically, she reached down to the hem of her tunic, ripped a length of it off, and wrapped Padrig's hand. "When it's daylight I will try to find some marigold and willow bark for it." Her face was still calm.

"It's back, isn't it?" he asked softly.

He sensed her nodding in the dark.

"Grania, come," Padrig gathered the girl to them. She had stayed back, watching in paralyzed horror at the events. Not only had the attacker severely frightened her, but the fire alienated her completely from Claerwen. She had seen it work before through her cousin, but not with such utter brutality. The girl trembled violently, making Padrig pull her along.

By daylight, Padrig calculated their whereabouts, but he could not recommend a trustworthy direction to proceed. They stayed deep in the wood, avoiding contact with anyone. Movement was slower than they wished, but traveling through dense mountain woodlands for two women and an old man was not easy.

In general, the odyssey led them in a southerly direction. North toward Caernarfon and west near Dinas Brenin were too risky because of Vortigern's close ties. East was too unknown and more mountainous, so south appealed the most. Claerwen and Grania knew no one there. Padrig had traveled as a young soldier, but it was many years since then. He speculated the people he remembered were probably long dead as he had already out-lived everyone else from his own generation.

They had no tools to cook with, and even if they had, they dared not to make cooking fires to mark their location. All their food was taken raw from the plant, gathered as they walked. They also had to stay near streams for water; they had no way to carry it. And because of the lingering summer heat, they needed water often.

As the days passed, the shock of the attack wore off and each began to analyze what had happened. Padrig and Claerwen were not surprised that the fort had been attacked, but they were stunned at the connection between the apparently mild-mannered Rhun and the Iron Hawk.

Claerwen understood enough Irish to know what had been said about Marcus. Her instincts did not sense he was dead; however, she understood there was a connection between the sacking of the fort and Marcus' overdue homecoming. She desperately wished she could open herself at will to the fire, but she felt absolutely no more intervention by the gods. She clutched her belly as she walked, hoping they would at least protect her child.

Padrig was angry. The ease with which the fort had been taken did not make any sense to him. So many men would have been noticed, even at night. And codes, service routes, everything significant to their defense had been changed, several times, since Rhun had left.

Grania was stunned into confusion, not understanding Rhun's actions. Since she had begun her relationship with him, they had grown steadily closer. She thought she knew him very well, and never considered that he had the least interest in the fort. Now she began to realize he had deceived her horribly.

The days passed slowly. Because they had no definite destination and a huge lack of confidence in the future, the journey became endlessly tedious. Luckily, they saw no one, but Padrig was aware of the possibility they were being followed. He tried to set a brisk pace, as brisk as his weary legs would carry him. He gently cajoled the women to keep moving. Hungry and tired, they trudged onward.

Claerwen tried to keep Rhun's declaration tucked away and forgotten, but she often found it pushing its way back into her mind along with his foul, derisive laughter. As a distraction, she took on the responsibility of searching out the roots, leaves, vegetables, and fruits they could eat, fiercely trying to concentrate on locating as much and as varied food as possible.

Grania stopped speaking. She remained in an apparent state of shock, silent agony mirrored in her eyes. She stared into space and merely followed the others' lead without question. She neither cried nor showed any desire to communicate. She ate what Claerwen put in her hands, but rarely finished. Padrig and Claerwen worried but felt it would pass in time when they found a refuge and the girl had a chance to sort out her feelings.

Claerwen did not know how much Irish Grania understood; the language was very similar to their own. She thought part of Grania's shock might have come from what Rhun had said, but she was not sure. If not, she wondered if her cousin had overhead her and Padrig talking about the attack one night when they thought she was sleeping.

A week passed. They were weakening from not eating enough. Claerwen's pregnancy was draining her strength as well. She forced herself to eat, trying to keep her energy up, but she often vomited much of the food. She guessed she was about three months along and wished she had some of the medicines from her supply to ease the sickness.

Night was falling again and they needed to find a place to camp. They had made a priority of finding a good campsite; it had to be sheltered and the right size for the three of them to huddle together. It also had to be safe from predators.

Light was fading fast, and they had not yet found a resting place. Claerwen was experiencing another bout of sickness and asked to rest a few moments. She leaned against a tree, her forehead dripping with perspiration, her stomach ready to heave again. Padrig said he would scout the area for shelter, a place nearby looked like a good possibility. Grania followed him like a puppy.

Claerwen sat on a fallen tree trunk, exhausted and ill, burying her face in her arms. The forest was quiet except for birds singing above. She could hear Padrig's steps circling the area, Grania's following his. A rustle of leaves above indicated a breeze in the treetops, and Claerwen looked up.

A low snarl punctuated the rustling leaves. She squinted her tired, scratchy eyes, staring at a dark patch above. Padrig was wandering back towards her when her eyes widened and she froze.

"By *Lleu Llaw Gyffes*," she said between her teeth. She was staring at a jet black panther. Padrig halted and grabbed Grania, ordering her to be absolutely still. For a long time, they stayed motionless, Claerwen staring into the panther's eyes, the cat staring back.

She could sense the animal's soul as she looked in his eyes. She saw his intelligence and felt his courage. As they watched each other, Claerwen felt the power of the gods briefly connect her spirit with the panther's, then release it again. It was as if they had come to an understanding of each other's ways.

Gradually, he slipped down the tree and his silent, graceful steps led him away.

Padrig could feel Grania shaking within his grip. She made no sound, not even a whimper, but tears streamed down her face and she trembled violently. Without warning, she broke away and ran maniacally in the opposite direction the big cat had taken, her reddish hair streaming behind her.

"No, Grania! Not yet, it's too soon to be sure if it's gone!" Indecision delayed Padrig, he did not know what the best solution was. Finally he decided to go after her, he could not just let her run. They might not find her again.

Claerwen had watched Padrig make his decision. Momentarily, she waited, looking in the panther's direction. Quietly, she started to follow Padrig, trying to break into a run. Then she slowed down, pain violently shooting through her.

The forest floor came up and slammed into her face.

CHAPTER 21

Mid-Wales
Summer, 468 A.D.

A strong staleness stung in Claerwen's nostrils. As she awoke, she was not sure if she was dreaming the smell or if it was real. Her eyes slit open, and as they focused, she tried to scan her surroundings. The light was dim, making it hard to see, but she thought she was in a loft, close in under a poorly thatched roof that let draughts rush in from outside. She laid on an uncomfortable straw-filled mat, and she wondered what other live creatures were in it. Cautiously, she turned her head side to side, trying to gain her bearings. The dim light glowed from beyond the edge of the loft; she figured it was evening or night.

Claerwen shifted to make herself more comfortable. Suddenly, choking pain shot inside her. Sweat drenched her immediately, and dizziness clouded her senses. Scanning across the space for someone to help, she barely could see another mat in the opposite corner, a person sleeping on it. She strained to see, and recognized Grania's red hair tumbled across an old, worn blanket draped over the mat.

"Grania!" she attempted to call, but her voice only sent a hoarse whisper. She gathered breath to try again, but the effort brought more pain. She moaned low as it ground through her.

Footsteps clattered up a ladder from below and Padrig's head popped up from the loft's edge. He quickly crossed to her and knelt, holding a cup with hot liquid in it.

"Drink this. It will ease the pain and make you sleep." She sipped and nodded, recognizing some of the contents' taste.

She looked long and fondly at her faithful friend. "I'm going to lose the child, aren't I?" she asked in a strained whisper.

Padrig hung his head, bobbing it up and down. "I am sorry, Claerwen. There's nothing I can do for you, but wait."

She sucked in her breath, long and slow, and turned her head away to cry. She spoke, trying to convince herself there was a purpose to the pain and loss, "I will tell myself the gods need it to be so. It is not time yet for a child. But, oh Lleu, how I wish I could keep something of Marcus within me until I find him again. It is so hard to let go."

"Perhaps if you didn't try to hold on so hard, the passing would be easier," Padrig suggested gently, aching at the sorrow in her words.

Another pain passed through her, making her arch her back against it. Her body shook until she thought she would burst with the spasm.

"Drink more, Claerwen. And rest, now. Rest as much as you can."

She glanced at Grania and looked back at him inquiringly. The drink was beginning to work; she was drifting.

"I gave her something to sleep, too. She will be fine," Padrig answered the unspoken question.

"What is this place?" Claerwen's words slurred.

"A miller took us into his home. It's a very poor settlement, just his family lives here, but they are very kind."

"Thank them for me...please...Padrig." She fainted.

Claerwen slept for another day and two nights. When she woke again, the pain had lessened and the dizzying nausea was gone. She was grateful for Padrig's help, thankful he was a good healer. She nearly felt refreshed in spite of the grogginess.

She lay thinking, searching her memory for a long time,

but could not recall how she had come to the miller's loft. She remembered the wood but was confused, not understanding why they had been there. Unable to concentrate, she looked up into the mildewy thatch, noticing light seeping through it. The loft was still dim, even though there seemed to be bright daylight outside.

Claerwen turned her head sharply, suddenly remembering the other mat where Grania had slept. It was empty. She wondered where Grania and Padrig were. She could not remember the miller, either, or anyone else. She guessed she must have slept a long time.

She studied her memories of the forest, and abruptly recalled the panther. And walking down hillsides, through bracken and thorny gorse. Scratchy tree branches that stuck out and whipped her face. Stumbling over stones and roots, scattering scree and great hordes of leaves. Chasing Grania. And pain.

Claerwen scratched herself, wishing the bed would be fresher and more comfortable. She also wished she could bathe, wrinkling her nose at the staleness pervading the air. Slowly, with great caution, she pushed herself up until she was very nearly in a sitting position. She stuffed the mat in behind herself for support. No pain cut through her, and confidence lifted her morale. She settled back, and decided everyone else must be at their chores, letting her rest in privacy.

A noise came from below, followed by footsteps.

"Padrig?" Claerwen called, her voice still not strong, but able to carry better.

The steps paused, then shuffled around.

"Halloo!" she called again.

The steps continued, heading away.

Claerwen did not understand why the person would not answer. She thought it might be an old person who had lost their hearing or a shy child. She tried to boost herself up more to see past the edge of the loft, to catch a glimpse of this person.

She was too far back to see much, but the top of a door frame in the opposite wall was visible. The steps appeared to be heading in that direction. Claerwen strained to see, pushing her elbows into the mat.

The door opened and a flash of red hair was carried up by the wind blowing through the breach.

"Grania!" she called sharply. Pain shot abruptly through her again. It had been severe before, but this time it cut her so she cried out involuntarily.

"Grania!" Claerwen screamed. She gripped her belly, pushing on it as if to shove away a plunging, turning knife. It ground through her, relentless and agonizing. She slipped back down on the mat, writhing onto her side and curling up. She screamed her cousin's name over and over, until the girl finally came up the ladder.

Grania's face registered only blank shock. She had no understanding of Claerwen's immediate danger or needs. She merely stood, silent and wide-eyed, next to the mat.

Claerwen felt terror welling up within herself, a fear of what was happening, that was as powerful as the pain. With a ferocity borne along by the dreadful fear, she made herself lunge an arm out far enough to grapple Grania's wrist. Her nails dug deep into the younger woman's flesh, causing blood to spurt where the skin broke. Animal-like strength came to Claerwen and she yanked Grania closer, nearly wrenching her arm from its socket.

"Get Padrig!" she hissed at her. "Now!" She cried out in agony again.

Grania could not rise. She drifted like a cloud suspended in the sky. As Claerwen began to momentarily recover from the violent contraction, she found strength again and lashed out, slapping the girl hard across the face several times.

"Grania! Come out of your stupor! I need you! Now! I am losing this child and if you do not get Padrig, or someone, I will die. GET PADRIG! GO!"

She screamed again. The pain, the terror and the anger mixed and were propelled out into horrible groans. Slowly, blackness descended, smothering her. Within it, she felt the horror gradually drain away, the darkness soothing, mothering her. She was suspended in a vast space, drifting, sometimes her feet going first, sometimes head first. A dim light was in the distance and she thought it was getting closer, or she was getting closer to it; she could not tell the difference. A piper was playing, a haunting tune she had never heard. Then she changed her mind, thinking the piper was signaling instead of playing a tune, in the same way Owein blew the ram's horn to announce riders approaching the fort.

A woman's soft voice spoke, echoing from the direction of the dim light. Claerwen could not tell what she said, but the voice was familiar.

Then suddenly, Padrig's voice was cursing. He sounded far away, too, and very angry. Claerwen wanted to see him, talk to him, but she could not find him. She reached out and groped in the darkness, but could not connect with him. She wondered why he was so angry.

She felt warm, too warm, wet, sticky. Then she was floating again. She did not remember lying down, and she could not understand why she had to start over again, floating in the darkness. Then a coolness soothed her, making her feel clean again. The light was getting closer and the pipes louder, the voice, too. The voice was humming a song, familiar from her childhood.

Claerwen realized she was listening to her mother, that she had opened a path to *Annwn*, the Otherworld. She stopped, appalled that she could sense her mother's soul. She hung suspended in the darkness, staring at the dim light, trying to see Linor.

Then she realized that Marcus would be there if he had been killed. Her bond with him would have pulled their souls together; she would never hesitate to go to him.

"Claerwen," her mother's voice called.

"No!" Claerwen shouted back. She felt herself breathing hard, fighting for control. She had to go back; she could not be trapped in the Otherworld. She had to find Marcus.

"Claerwen, come," Linor called again.

"No!" Claerwen screamed. "You trapped me before, you

will *not* do it again!" She struggled against the flow of the darkness.

Padrig's voice interrupted. He was still cursing. She had never heard him so angry before.

"Claerwen!" She heard her mother call again, but much further away.

"Marcus!" Claerwen screamed with her whole soul. "Marcus! Where are you?" Her strength was fading. She could no longer hear her mother or the pipes. She only heard the echo of her own voice as it drifted away with the dim light, calling for Marcus, over and over.

Then all was silent.

Several days passed and Claerwen slipped in and out of consciousness. She slept in a feverish, dreamless haze, sometimes awake enough to sip some of Padrig's meat broth, but more often too weak to do more than just breathe shallow, ragged puffs.

Padrig stayed by her constantly, worrying himself into a frenzy. He coaxed and cajoled Grania into bringing him the necessary ingredients and utensils to use for Claerwen's care. He checked and rechecked everything she brought him; he knew she was perfectly capable of performing the tasks he gave her, but her withdrawn state of mind continued, even deepened, and he was not sure of her competency. It disturbed him deeply, but Claerwen's needs took priority.

Gradually, after a good fortnight of constant nursing, Claerwen showed fledgling signs of recovery. Her alertness returned, though speech was limited to single-word answers. She continued to sleep most of the time, but it was true sleep from weakness, not comatose. Her progress was incredibly slow, but day by day, he could see her fight back against the debilitation. She lost weight until bones pushed against her skin, and her hair lost its luster. Padrig fed her as much as he could every two or three hours, day and night. He was reminded of feeding an infant, small and helpless.

Time also supported the healing process. Autumn had arrived by the time Claerwen was able to walk around and eat normal food again. But strength came only very slowly. Each day, she walked as far as she could to build up stamina, then came back to the miller's tiny home to sit exhausted by the fire pit. Padrig cautioned her endlessly against over-tiring herself; he was afraid fever and infection would return.

But the long walks in the fresh air gradually rebuilt her strength. She explored the small valley from end to end, side to side. She learned the settlement itself contained only the miller's extended family. It had been a larger group before, but the decline of society after the Romans left had isolated them and their numbers dwindled. They were incredibly poor, relying on nature to feed them. They pooled everything they grew, much in the same manner the people of Dinas Beris had, and split it equally. The loft where she had been sleeping was in their barn.

While she walked, Claerwen gathered as many herbs, wild fruits and vegetables as she could carry. The activity kept her busy during her recovery and kept her mind occupied against having to think about where she would go once she was well enough to travel. She also wanted to be useful to these kind people who could not afford to have taken in her and her two companions. She knew Padrig could help contribute to his own keep, but she and Grania had been burdens to them.

On a cool, breezy autumn day, Claerwen moved briskly along a deer run across the valley floor. For the first time since losing her child, she felt energy surging through her. Rather than stopping periodically to gather roots and other edibles, she decided to take advantage of her vigor to exercise harder.

Claerwen also wanted to think, without distractions, of a way to reach Grania. She needed to break down the wall of emotional isolation the girl had built around herself. Frowning as she strode, she pondered heavily, unable to guess what had caused her cousin to be so remote, so stone cold. All morning she asked herself questions of how to help Grania, but she found no answers.

Frustrated that she could not resolve the problems Grania presented, Claerwen cleared her mind and concentrated on enjoying the beauty of the land and the turning colors of the leaves. She stopped to rest by a stream and ate a small meal she had brought with her, supplemented with wild apples growing nearby. The place she had picked was warm, protected from the wind and she smoothed the sun-warmed grass with her hands, breathing in its sweet scent. Suddenly, she remembered the day she discovered Marcus sitting by a similar stream, resting, his handsome grey horse grazing in the meadow. She smiled softly, remembering how he had loved her.

"By Lleu, how I miss you," she ached. In her mind, she could trace every detail of his face, the lines radiating around his glittering black eyes, his long moustache framing his sensuous lips, his tanned face, his shaggy black hair that she loved to tangle her fingers in.

She felt tired suddenly, and leaned her head back, sighing. "Ah, Marcus...where are you? What have they done to you? How in this world do I find you?" She spoke, wishing the gods would answer her. But no answer came.

The walk back to the miller's was slow and painful. All her energy was gone, replaced with sorrow. She clutched her hands low on her belly, cramping again, and muttered, "Padrig will probably give me another lecture, saying I try too hard to get well." She sighed and pushed on towards the house.

Grania sat on a bench in front of the house, staring at nothing, as always. As she approached, Claerwen scowled from her dark mood, tired and disgusted of the waste she saw the girl was making of her life. "Well, this is enough," she said to herself before she reached the house. "This has to end once and forever."

Claerwen sat on the bench next to Grania. The girl did not move, not to speak or even nod a greeting.

"Grania?" she called, starting softly, gathering her thoughts. She pulled the girl around until they faced each other. Grania's steady gaze dropped downward. She refused to meet Claerwen's eyes.

Claerwen continued, "What is it, Grania? We have waited and waited for you to come back to us. It is time now."

Grania gave no answer. She did not even make an expression to indicate she had heard.

"Grania, can you hear me? Why do you go on this way? Is it because Taran hurt you? Or that we lost our home again?"

Still no acknowledgment.

Claerwen gripped Grania's shoulders and spoke so closely that she could not ignore her. "We will find a home again. And Taran is better lost, you must see that now. Grania, speak to me. Do you know how much you hurt me and Padrig when you do this? Do you hate us so much?"

She lifted the girl's face and shook it. "Listen to me. Talk to me. What is it that hurts so much that you can not tell me?"

Anger boiled under Claerwen's tired, cool countenance. She thought Grania was playing a childish game meant to gain sympathy. But Claerwen wanted communication, her sympathy was used.

"Grania, I have lost my home, too. You must understand how much that home meant to me. After hiding all those years from Drakar, to find Marcus and then lose him again, do you know how bad that aches in here?" She made a fist over her heart. "And then to lose the baby, the only thing I had left of him? Do you think that was easy?

"But I will take what has happened and go on with it. We all have to. And I will figure out where we will go from here. Do we stay and try to make a life among these simple people? Do we go on to somewhere unknown? Or can we go back, if there is a place to go back to? It is my responsibility for all three of our lives and a very heavy burden, very frightening. It is a decision I don't want to make, but I must, and soon."

Grania still did not answer, but she was shaking, her eyes closed. Claerwen watched her, her resolve to survive making her strong against Grania's self-pity. "Talk to me, damn it!" She jerked Grania's shoulders again. "Talk to me!"

A whimpery cry came from Grania as she plunged

upwards in an attempt to run away. But Claerwen was faster and caught a flailing arm. She lost her temper and yanked her cousin back, then slapped her face. "Stop feeling sorry for yourself for once in your bloody life, girl! Talk to me!"

Grania's legs went limp and she plunked down on the ground. A torrent of pent up tears broke loose, streaming haphazardly down her face. She pounded her fists on the soil, her long red hair blowing fitfully around her. She looked like a madwoman.

Grania wailed hysterically. Claerwen sank down and pressed arms around her, encouraging her to release her emotions, to finally say what hurt so much that she could not bear to tell anyone. Gradually, Grania began to sob apologies over and over.

"It was all my fault. I am so sorry...so sorry...so sorry."

"What was your fault?" Claerwen probed gently, rocking her back and forth.

"It was all my fault. Oh, what have I done? What have I done? I must be so evil..."

Claerwen waited, not understanding Grania's lamentations.

"I have caused all this." Grania's eyes finally came up and met Claerwen's. Her tear-filled brown eyes were focused and squinted, full of deep anguish, but somehow more alive and coherent than ever.

"Caused what?"

"Everything. Everything we lost. It was me. I have killed all those who died. I caused the fort to be taken." Her voice dropped, breaking. "I killed your husband. I killed your baby."

Claerwen stared hard, unprepared for the confession.

Grania continued, "I hate myself. I should never have been born. I was trouble from the first day I took breath. I cannot ask forgiveness because I do not deserve it." She sobbed, her face in her hands.

Claerwen was astonished. Involuntarily she asked, "Why?"

Grania's weeping sharpened, bitterness edging it.

"Because of Rhun."

"Rhun?"

"And me. Claerwen," she looked up again, then her eyes closed tightly. "Rhun and I...were lovers. When Taran left, Rhun came back to see me; it was the day I ran away. He was so kind and sweet to me. I had met him once before, he stayed at the inn after you left there. It felt so good to confide in him. But it was all a trick. You were right. It was all a trick. He always found a way to bring our conversations so they were about the fort. Or the people. He was always interested in what they were doing. And I was so stupid, I told him everything they said. He used me to listen in on the plans and signals and codes that they talked about. He used it to take the fort from us. Oh, dear Lleu, what I have done is too evil." Her words collapsed into a wail.

"By the gods," Claerwen cursed. She was physically and mentally shaken from the revelation, as if a blow had struck her. "That is why you insisted on the daily walks alone last summer and why you stopped fussing about Taran so quickly, isn't it? And it's why you stayed in the hall in the evenings around the men when you had no interest in their talk before. Marcus was certain Rhun was one of Drakar's spies and that he was supposed to draw Marcus or Owein away from the fort. They would have attacked then. But Marcus didn't fall for that trick. It never occurred to any of us that Rhun was hiding out there."

Claerwen was struck then that if Rhun had been a spy for Drakar, he must be working for Ifan and Gerallt, or even Vortigern, those who had backed Drakar, and that would have made Rhun's alliance with the Iron Hawk more credible. Her skin prickled.

Claerwen felt both intense anger and sorrow for Grania. Her cousin had been used as cruelly as the gods used herself. Though Rhun had obviously been a man to distrust, her cousin seemed bound to find trouble. Claerwen felt the gods were trying to teach something, but she could not find the lesson.

They sat together a long time into the evening, Claerwen rocking Grania in her arms, until at last Padrig came looking for them. He helped Claerwen take Grania to bed and gave her another herbal brew to make her sleep.

Storm clouds boiled in throughout the night, riding fast on the wind and heavy showers threatened by morning. The air was full of static, and the handful of people reflected it in the urgency of their work. Claerwen and Padrig helped the miller's family prepare the morning meal, when one of the boys knocked insistently at the door.

Padrig answered, opening to the breathless, wind-blown youth.

"I am sorry, sir," the boy stammered.

"Come in, boy, and sit down. Have you run far?"

"Aye," answered the boy. He eyed Claerwen and Padrig nervously. They looked at each other, not understanding his apprehension.

The miller asked him where he had been and what was wrong.

"From the north wood, Uncle. I have bad news for the Lady and the Master."

"Go on," prompted the miller when the boy hesitated.

"The other lady, she...she is..." His brow wrinkled and he look as if he would cry.

Claerwen brought him a cup of hot camomile and sat down with him, taking his hand. Her warm voice reassured him and he calmed.

"I am sorry, my Lady, but the other woman who came with you...she is dead."

A gasp hissed around the room.

Claerwen went pale and Padrig grabbed her shoulders, afraid she would faint.

"She...she hung herself in the wood. With her own belt." He hated to say every word. "My brother is bringing the body in now." He was relieved to get it all out.

"By all the gods my people swear by," Claerwen

whispered. "She was just waking when I left to come here this morning. She said would be along shortly. But we were so busy here, I didn't notice she hadn't come. I never would have thought she'd give up." Claerwen's eyes squeezed shut in guilt.

Padrig sat next to her, slipped his arms around her in compassion. The family offered sympathy, each member taking her hand for a few moments, then quietly settling nearby to keep her company.

Claerwen graciously acknowledged the kindness of the others, but she still felt terribly isolated. Not one member of her own family was left. They were all dead or lost, only the gods knew where.

CHAPTER 22

Mid-Wales
Autumn, 468 A.D.

"Padrig. I am leaving."

He stared at Claerwen, his brows arched in astonishment. "Leaving? Leaving for where?"

"I must find Marcus."

"But Claerwen," he lowered his voice, trying to ease the words out tenderly, "Claerwen, Marcus is dead."

"No, Padrig. He is alive. He's out there, somewhere, and I have to find him. I will be leaving as soon as I have the right equipment to take with me."

"But you can't go alone. Winter is coming. You have no idea where to look, even if he is alive."

"Then come with me. Help me."

"Claerwen, be reasonable. I am too old to go. Getting here from Dinas Beris was almost too much. I have to stay. Please, do not do this!"

"I must, Padrig, my loyal friend. I must find Marcus."

"You have not seen him in the flames. The fire has told you nothing, even whether he is alive or dead."

"Then I must at least know what happened. I must go."

"Claerwen, please, at least wait until spring. Do not go

now, so late in autumn. You cannot travel in winter. Please!"

"I am sorry Padrig. I have no choice."

Tears came to the old man's eyes. "I have never begged anything of anyone in my whole life, but this I time I do. Please do not go. Please!"

She chewed on her lip, hating herself for hurting Padrig. Only Marcus had loved her more, but in her soul she knew she must go. She looked sadly at Padrig and said, "There is no other decision for me. Dinas Beris is lost and I have no place with the miller's family. I must learn what happened to Marcus, even if it is only to bury his bones and his sword."

Claerwen carefully began gathering the gear she would need to travel. This time she wanted to be well prepared. Once the miller's family learned of her goal, they began to help her locate the items necessary for a long trek. She had never told them she was a princess or where she had come from, not wishing to use the title for gain. Her natural charisma and the difficult loss of her family had endeared her to them, prompting them to willingly contribute to her supplies. Their Celtic sense of romance and passionate loyalty made them dig into their already thin reserves in order to help her succeed and be able to say they had helped.

She started by assembling clothing more suited to the outdoors and long-distance travel. Long skirts and heavy cloaks were completely inappropriate. To replace them, she found worn leather tunics and breeches used by the local boys and saved for future siblings' use. However, no more boys had been born since the youngest ones had outgrown the clothes. She converted and repaired them to fit her. She shortened the tunics to a mid-thigh length and patched the breeches with scraps left from the tunic. She was given knee-high boots, which she double-soled with heavy rawhide and oilskin scraps, then lined with sedge grasses mashed into a felt-like material. Next, she made a muslin shirt and a lining for the leather breeches from her own undershift, to guard against chafing. Someone brought her a sheepskin cap.

The miller's grandmother came to the house one evening as Claerwen worked on her garments. The old woman suffered from rheumatism and Claerwen had treated her with tisanes and poultices, relieving much of the pain and stiffness. In gratitude, the woman brought a large tanned hide, uncut and soft. With great dignity and pride, she presented the skin to her, telling Claerwen she would miss her gentle treatments and good company.

Confounded, Claerwen said to the woman, "I cannot take this from you."

"Please, you must have it. I will not use it. After the many years I have spent in pain, I want to give you something in return for the relief you have given me. Please take it. I am proud to have known you, Lady Claerwen."

Claerwen held the lovely hide reverently. "I will be so proud to wear this. It will make a wonderful overtunic with sleeves, for when it gets colder, and there will be plenty left for many other things."

She and the woman looked long and admiringly at each other. They swiftly embraced. The old woman shuffled off, back to her house, tears in her eyes. Claerwen made an addition to her mental list of preparations; she would leave extra supplies and instructions with Padrig for further treatments.

The hide provided the overtunic Claerwen needed for winter, as well as traveling pouches, thongs for sewing and scraps for future repairs. While she cut and sewed diligently, she had Padrig gather the tools, food, medicines, and other items she would take with her, all essential for survival.

Carefully, she checked and recalculated, packed and rearranged, planned and resolved every piece of clothing, every tool, every morsel of food. She tested her pouches' weight and their distribution, reattaching their straps until they could be carried comfortably for long periods. She took only foods and medicines she knew she would not be able to find to supplement her diet along the way. She had the miller sharpen her small dagger. It was not top quality, but it was suitable for cutting material for snares and traps, cleaning game, and eating. Among all of her possessions, she prized it the most. Without a good knife, survival would be extremely difficult. Nearly equal to the knife's value was her flint and iron set; fire was as essential as water and food.

Within days of her announcement to leave, she was ready. At first light, she stood in the common area among the huts, the miller's family huddled around her.

She looked like a wild creature from beyond the northern border, north of Hadrian's Wall, clad in her skin clothing, all her long hair braided and tucked into the old cap, her various pouches slung across her shoulders. She felt strange, with everyone staring at her, but the mood was one of understanding, not criticism. They were proud that her path had crossed theirs. And as she would leave them, they would pray to all the gods to give her safe passage in her journey.

Except Padrig. He was heartbroken that she would risk the dangers of the wild mountains alone and with no definite destination or direction. He hung back from the small crowd, fretting, wringing his hands, feeling a thousand years old. As he watched Claerwen say farewell to each person, it struck him how she had overcome her shyness and developed a charisma like Marcus; though, where he had a sincerity of charm and friendliness, she had a soft kindness about her.

Sadness washed his eyes as he noted her beauty, still apparent through the masculine clothes. He felt so old and tired. Marcus was gone, now Claerwen would go as well, and there was nothing he could do to stop her from stepping into her own misfortune. He felt deeply guilty to let her go, but he had begged and begged, to no avail. Finally, the night before, he had given in and he embraced her, saying farewell.

As she said goodbye to the people, he could not bear to watch her walk out of the valley alone, to be forgotten. He drank in one last look of her lovely face, as she spoke softly once more to the miller's grandmother. Then he turned and disappeared tearfully back to his chores in the miller's house.

The first few days out were approached and tested

gingerly. Claerwen knew Marcus had gone south, into the country somewhere near the holy settlement of Ynys Witrin, the Glass Isle, also sometimes called Avalon, but she did not know exactly where, either by name or location. She figured she would head toward the holy shrine, then delve carefully for information to fix his position.

The problem was, he had not told her the nature of his espionage and she knew he would have been in one of his disguises, making identification extremely difficult. She knew every piece of gear he took with him, but she also realized his resourcefulness would have led him to use materials available where he was, things she would not recognize. This bothered her immensely. She might ask for him as a traveling bard when he was dressed as a peasant or servant. She had no way to know. If he had been involved in a battle of some kind, stories of it might be easy to come by. However, if Rhun had staged an ambush instead, then no word might ever surface.

She had to try. The gods had gone completely silent again; no visions were in the fire, the water, or her dreams. Yet she knew she was being pushed somewhere. She wished desperately she could understand where that was.

She felt lost at the outset and her conviction wavered. She knew she could survive; she had the basic skills, knowledge, and resourcefulness. It was the loneliness and feeling of abandonment which peeled away her resolve. She looked for clues from the gods along the way, but saw nothing to lead her in the right direction, nothing made her feel closer to Marcus.

Eventually, logic took over. She kept to the southbound roads, paralleling them from the mountain ridges above, far enough away to remain undetected by other travelers on the road itself. She rarely saw anyone; very few people were abroad so late in the season. They were all home preparing for winter. Then she wondered where she would be herself this year. "One step at a time," she muttered to herself. If she needed to shelter for the winter, she would worry over that when the time made it necessary.

The days became routine. Claerwen rose with the sun and quickly made a rather heavy meal, leftover from the previous evening's supper. She wanted to cook only once a day, preferably in the evening. The fire she made would be for warmth and protection from predators, as well as preparing enough food for a day's cycle. Breakfast was meant to last most of the day, supplemented with forages.

She spent most daylight hours traveling, broken by frequent stops. Foraging did not slow her down much; she developed an almost automatic watchfulness for useful plants to eat. She planned her meals as she walked, filling the leather pouch she used for food by late afternoon. She ended her daily trek about an hour before sunset, locating a good campsite and quickly setting a pair of snares. Then she would arrange her camp, collect any creature she had snared, cook, clean, arrange the next day's supplies and store her goods high in a tree, away from prowling animals. Finally, she would burrow into her bedding and quickly find sleep, exhausted from the day.

As the days passed, the loneliness drained her. She looked for ways to release the tension, but found no success. She felt like a person who had gulped down an entire skin of wine and could not get drunk. She could not even cry. The tension ached physically in her neck and jaw, making her feel half-strangled. So she sighed heavily to ease her snarled stomach, loaded on her traveling pouches, and trudged onward.

Claerwen reached Ynys Witrin a little over a fortnight after leaving the miller's settlement. The holy shrine had been easier to locate than she had anticipated. The ancient holy stone monument sat atop a distinctive tor that had guided her for many miles. The name meant Glass Isle, because the tor looked like an island amid the smooth-surfaced marshes surrounding it. The marshes rose and fell in cycles, cutting off access to the tor during certain times of the year; narrow causeways across the fens were the only paths into the area. The place had always been a holy shrine, and the marshes had protected it well. Even the Christians had begun to try converting its pilgrims to their way of thinking.

Claerwen skirted the swamps, not wanting to actually enter the village. She needed information to track Marcus, but she was at a loss as to where to begin. She was afraid to approach people because she did not know what kind of status she had, fugitive or otherwise; and her situation of traveling alone, dressed as a boy, would raise too many unwanted questions. Also, the dialect there was different. Though very similar to her own, she was not confident of her ability to communicate. She did not have Marcus' remarkable ear for language and accents outside of her own country.

Claerwen decided to explore the area east of Ynys Witrin, mostly rolling plains. It was more populated and active than her remote homeland. Cover was harder to find in the open fields, so she stuck to hollows, river valleys and wooded areas as much as possible. She learned to camouflage herself, to blend in with her background like a hunter. She also realized the physical strength she had acquired along her journey enabled her to move quickly, easily, silently, finding she could run long distances if she paced herself correctly. Traveling became a game of learning to move without being seen. Her hunting skills improved as a sideline of this activity, observing how animals hid themselves to hunt or keep from being hunted, then following their examples.

And then it occurred to her that Marcus used his disguises as camouflage. If he had gone to Ynys Witrin, he probably would have been disguised as a holy man. Whether druid, Christian, or other priest, she could only guess, but now she was certain she sought a holy man. She asked herself where would a holy man be traveling to upon leaving Ynys Witrin, and logic told her he probably would go to another religious center. The largest was the Giant's Dance out on the Great Plain to the east. He might have headed there, completing the mission he set out to perform somewhere along the way. Or he might have gone to any of several other places, like Avebury, closer than the Giant's Dance.

Excitement surged through Claerwen. She felt like the gods were beginning to guide her again and this discovery had entered her mind as bright and clear as the fire ever had. Energy filled her and she took off in a flying run towards the river. She wanted to follow it east and try to find Avebury. She knew the Giant's Dance was somewhere beyond; hopefully she could pick up Marcus' trail and eventually catch up with him.

Claerwen ran swiftly, her soft leather-soled boots hushing her steps as she darted through the wood along the river's edge. There was not much bracken to slow her down, and she felt so marvelously renewed that she needed the exercise to vent her energy. The wood eventually thickened, forcing her to slow down and then finally walk. She came over a short rise and followed the land as it dropped down into a small ravine, the river also dropping by a short falls. The day was getting long-shadowed and she began thinking about finding a campsite. The hollow looked like a good spot, and she proceeded eagerly down the slope.

What she saw stopped her abruptly. First, it was the awful smell. Then she saw the dead horse. And beyond it, another; and then a skeleton with a very rusty sword struck through it. She shivered violently. Her impulse was to go back up the slope and go around; the place felt incredibly evil. But she had to look; she knew she had to.

With extreme caution, she crept down the hillside, circling the horses, and picked her way towards the skeleton. The sword was several inches into the ground through the ribs. There was nothing left to identify the poor soul. She scanned the area for more bodies. There must be, she thought, if more than one horse was there.

A bony hand was perched against a log, the arm leading down into ferny overgrowth. She approached, afraid to look. Her stomach flounced and she backed away, the face frozen in a ghastly scream and still decaying.

Claerwen turned aside, waiting for her stomach to settle. After a few deep breaths, she began to look for more bodies, wondering what had happened. She took a few steps towards the river and stumbled on a rock, glanced at it, then stopped to look more closely. It was not a rock but something else, half buried in the mud and ivy, mushrooms growing on one side. She kicked at it, loosening it, and picked it up.

Claerwen held the object up to the fading light. It was a helmet of heavy, formed leather, an odd visor riveted to the front. "The Iron Hawk?" she gasped. Involuntarily, she dropped the helmet as if it would burn her hands. "The Iron Hawk. But what happened here?" she asked herself softly. This battle would have to have happened at least as long ago as the attack on the fort, by the degree of decay. Who were these men? The Iron Hawk's? Is he one of these dead, too? Curiosity overshadowed Claerwen's fear and she began searching in earnest for clues of the men's identities.

In all, she found six bodies, all in nearly complete decay. There was very little other debris left from the battle other than the helmet and the sword; only scraps of clothing. She speculated that bandits had taken anything of value and easy to remove. Unable to discover who they were, she decided to move on quickly and find an evening shelter before it got darker. She felt sick and wanted to leave, needing to get the horror of the bodies out of her mind before she was ill. She headed upwind from them as the last glint of sunlight pierced the trees. For an unknown reason, she turned for one last look at the grisly scene. The light caught on something metal in the scrub around a tree trunk. Claerwen stared, but she could not figure out what it was and went back to investigate.

A dagger had been thrown and was wedged into the trunk, having missed its mark. Claerwen only briefly looked at it, unconcerned, even disappointed. She almost walked away, but curiosity made her go back. The handle was old and wrapped in worn, smooth leather. She had seen that handle before, many times. Last winter she had watched Owein polish and oil that old knife a hundred times. She wondered, was one of these skeletons Owein's? Was he victim or victor? And worst of all, was Marcus here?

There was no evidence that either of them was among the dead. But she knew Owein well enough, no matter how little he spoke, he would never leave behind his favorite dagger. Marcus had said it was lucky for him.

Sorrow struck Claerwen, her buoyant excitement was shattered. The easy sureness of finding Marcus was replaced by the foreboding that in reality he would be among these awful bones. She wanted to grieve for these men, though she was not convinced that she had known them, either as friend or foe. Either way, it saddened her.

Claerwen went back to the abandoned helmet and picked it up again. She was struck then that she no longer felt a need to cry, as if all the years of trouble had hardened her. She had all the grief and pain within her heart, but she accepted its presence, no longer needing tears as an outlet to ease her burden.

She tucked the helmet into a spare pouch, then pulled the dagger from the tree and put it away, too. Then she turned once more toward the riverbank and went upwind. She would have to hurry to find a campsite before dark. She trotted slowly up the far side of the hollow and came into a much thinner wood. She saw another depression in the land ahead, perhaps making a good place to camp.

Eeriness pervaded the air. Claerwen wanted to be further from the death, but she could only go far enough to avoid the smell as darkness fell. Then suddenly, the sound of crunching twigs and leaves interrupted her plan. She froze, listening.

It was too clumsy for an animal. Experience had taught her the differences in sounds and she knew the predator was human.

She backed into a tree, melting into its branches.

CHAPTER 23

East of Ynys Witrin
Autumn, 468 A.D.

Claerwen watched silently as two men approached. She was sure they had not seen her, but she was not certain if they had heard her or sensed her presence. She waited patiently, wishing for the gathering darkness to come sooner, shrouding the wood and making her invisible. There would be no moon in the night and once dark, she knew she could elude them. But for a while, she would have to wait.

The strangers looked like mercenaries. They were heavily armed, though horseless. Claerwen wondered on whose side they belonged, the local prince, Vortigern, the Saxons, or if they were traveling to join some chieftain's war band. Whatever they were, she did not want to test their loyalties.

At first they did not speak, but she could tell they were looking for something. She noted how they listened intently, nervously jumping at any small sound. They stopped directly in front of her, several yards away, and began whispering to each other for what seemed like an interminable length of time.

Suddenly, they moved towards her hiding place. Again they stopped and spoke low. This time she caught a few words in Welsh. Gradually their voices rose enough to be understood.

"...Dinas Beris. With the Iron Hawk dead, he can't get in the way anymore."

"Aye, but that doesn't help if we don't find Marcus ap Iorwerth's woman. She's the key to the treasure."

"Vortigern's placed her under fugitive status now, so everyone on this bloody island will be looking for her."

"She's disappeared like a faerie, not a trace anywhere. Just like her husband."

"Ah, he's dead. Vortigern saw to that. She's probably dead, too, decayed in a ditch like those back there."

"They never found his body. You know he's a master of disguise. He's probably sitting in Vortigern's court laughing behind a false face right now."

"That's nonsense. Marcus ap Iorwerth is dead, so stop worrying about him. We have to concentrate on finding the woman. Go on!"

The two men moved away a few yards, then stopped again, still arguing, but too softly to hear anymore.

Claerwen was appalled at how the search for the unknown treasure had escalated. If Marcus was alive, he would be under fugitive status as well. But she knew Vortigern would have him killed on sight, not wanted for capture like she was. She had to find him, and without leading anyone to him.

An owl hooted above Claerwen in the tree. She winced, anticipating her doom. But the sound echoed among the trees and was confusing; the two men stared a while, then let it pass. Finally, they began to move off, slowly, like grazing deer, trying to be silent and cautious of the dark.

A few more paces, a few more...

Claerwen's feet had cramped from standing still so long and she began to flex her ankles, trying to waken her feet. They tingled and she carefully picked each one up and put it down, alternating, until they relaxed. By the time she could move easily again, the strangers had reached the heavier wood.

Silently, she slipped out. She knew she would either have to travel a fair distance away to avoid the men or find a good hiding place for the night. Unfortunately, she had not been able to reconnoiter the area and it was too dark to negotiate much movement or search for campsites. She would not be able to light a fire, either, and she decided to return to the same tree, crawling into its lower branches, pulling them together, and pinning them with stones. Then she dug out a depression big enough to lie in comfortably. She lined her bed with soft humus and covered it with a skin tarpaulin. She ate a quick, cold supper and succumbed to her daily exhaustion.

Morning brought no further sign of the two men. After the encounter, extreme caution became Claerwen's priority. She suspected they had been there to inspect the battlefield.

She traveled steadily for several days, intensely keeping herself hidden, jumping at the slightest movement of any creature. At the same time, she desperately desired someone to talk to, if only for comfort and understanding; yet she was terrified at the thought of a chance meeting with another person.

Each night, Claerwen made certain she was fed and bedded down by dark. She made few fires, using them only when necessary to cook enough to last a few days. Her food gathering and storage skills became incredibly efficient. She watched the wildlife of the woods, following their instincts to supplement her talent for finding food and shelter. She developed a cat-like walk, hunting with stealth and speed, and she learned to make herself invisible, as if she had become truly part of the forest. Her eyes watched everything, her wariness complete, her reflexes astonishingly quick, her senses alive and acute. Any people she saw were circumvented and watched with a deepening distrust from a large distance.

In time, her obsession created a mental stress that hurt her more than she realized. Although it honed and polished her skills, it also created an irrational fear. She became easily spooked, seeing ghosts in treetops, human faces on animals, omens in the way birds flew or the shapes of clouds. Her mind slowly was beginning to lose its sense of reality.

Claerwen crossed out of the comforting cover of the

woods, finding plains and moors as she continued east. She skirted their edges as much as possible. The weeks of traveling began to take their toll on her, depleting her strength. Her pace slowed and she became neglectful of caring for herself. She trudged on, drunk with exhaustion, eating haphazardly, sometimes too tired to eat at all. She began to neglect finding proper shelter in the evenings, falling asleep where she dropped.

The weather had been mild throughout Claerwen's trek, though fairly cold. Wind was the worst, and the occasional frost overnight. Now the first winter-like storm was crossing the island and Claerwen failed to anticipate its coming. It was not severe, mostly wind and clouds, and she had certainly been out in far worse, but she was not of a mind to fight her way through it. A heavy mist rose, complicating her sense of direction and she did not have the presence of mind to stop moving and seek shelter until it passed.

As the wind buffeted her, Claerwen's exhaustion drove her into a deeper delirium. She had climbed a ridge and was stumbling down a long slope into the center of a field. In the heavy, swirling mist, she thought she was seeing an array of enormous ghosts, all dancing around her.

Not understanding if they were part of a vision or real, Claerwen tried to dash away, but they came at her, closing in. Suddenly, one touched her. She tried to push it away, but it pushed her instead. It was rough and scratched her hands.

She ran again, sensing danger, but she could not determine which direction meant safety. She had to escape, they were closing in again, like giants looming, iridescent in the pale, glowing light.

Panic suddenly gripped Claerwen, and she darted from side to side, unable to avoid the ghosts. Each time she thought she saw a gap to escape through, one thrust itself in her path and she pulled up, choking for air. She whirled around again, then finally a new avenue opened itself and she turned into it, running full tilt. Beyond, the plain opened wide like a yawn to the east, a forest beyond. But as Claerwen dashed along the avenue, the ghosts closed in once more.

Suddenly, a different figure stepped in front of her. It was tall and dark, like another stone, but it reached out with arms and grabbed her. Claerwen struggled, trying to swing fists at the figure, but she had no more strength. Gasping for air, she went down onto the wet grass, then into the black of unconsciousness.

"Lady Claerwen," a voice drifted to her out of the mist. "Wake up." It was so far away, calling again and again.

Cold sunlight washed her face and she opened her eyes. She felt comfortable, too comfortable to move.

"Good to see you again," came the voice once more. It was just above her.

She sat up, dashing away the comfortable feeling.

"You!"

Lord Emrys grinned at her. He was mixing something in a small wooden bowl. "Aye...me again."

His smile disarmed her first reaction of surprise and suspicion. She curled her feet under her and rubbed the sleep from her eyes.

"What happened?" she asked calmly.

"I think you were confused by the mist last night. I saw you going in circles here, so I stopped you. Then you fainted, from exhaustion."

She stared at him in confusion, then began to scan around her. She saw they were camped at the edge of the forest she had seen and below was a broad field. Surrounding the field was a circle of enormous standing stones.

"What is this place?" Claerwen asked as she rose to her feet. She took a few steps down the slope, awed by the massive stones. She realized they were her ghosts, still eerie, but less frightening with daylight and the absence of mist.

"It is called Avebury," Emrys told her.

Her eyes widened and she took a few more steps.

"You were looking for this place?" he asked.

She nodded, scanning across the entire area as she spoke to Emrys, "Aye. I thought there would be a village here. It's not like Ynys Witrin at all, just a lonely stone circle in a field."

"You are disappointed," Emrys remarked. He studied the way she was dressed and curiosity filled him.

"No. They are magnificent," she murmured as she studied the massive stones. Finally, she came back to the camp and saw Emrys had neatly piled her pouches next to her bedroll. He offered her a small tin platter of food, and she realized how hungry she was, gladly accepting the food.

"It must be late afternoon," she said finally, after finishing the meal and washing it down with strong tea. "I guess I was awfully tired."

Emrys nodded. "You were delirious."

She looked into the man's eyes and remembered how he had introduced her to the vision in the fire all those years ago. Several ideas struck her in the same instant.

"Is it a coincidence that we meet again, or was this planned?" she asked him sharply.

Emrys was surprised by her directness. "You are not the shy young woman I met before." Then he smiled again. "When you journey into the path of gods, only they will show you why things like this happen."

His answer confused her at first, then she said calmly, "You were drawn here. For a purpose. As I have been."

Emrys studied Claerwen's eyes several moments, then replied seriously, "Aye. You begin to understand the power, Lady Claerwen. It has grown dramatically in you these past years."

"It comes and goes, sometimes very powerfully, other times it is as if it had completely left me. When I wish it was there, I cannot open myself to it at all."

"You will never be able to command the fire. I cannot, and," he grinned wryly, "I've been told I have one of the greatest powers of the fire in Britain. But the gods know when you need the power and will show you only what must be shown, no more than that. It is not to be wished for, only to be accepted when it is necessary."

Claerwen considered Emrys' words, deciding he made perfect sense for what she had experienced. Then she asked, "If both you and I have been brought her for a reason, then there must be something we both need to learn here."

"Aye, I believe you are correct."

Emrys stood and indicated for Claerwen to follow him. They walked down to the stone circle, stopping just outside its perimeter.

"There is a place of power, there, in the center of the circle. I believe we will find the purpose of our meeting there...if you and I are willing to seek that knowledge."

She gazed into the circle and shivered. She recalled the panic she felt the night before. But her need to find Marcus was more intense than the fear, and now she knew the gods had been holding her there.

She watched a while longer, then turned to Emrys and said quietly, "I am willing." He could see the light in her eyes glowing.

They walked to the center of the circle and turned to face each other. In that instant, the sun set and darkness fell. Claerwen could see the light in Emrys' eyes now, as she had before, and understood why people feared her when they saw it. But she calmed herself, and let the gods take over.

She could feel the power in the earth rise underneath her and it radiated from Emrys. It came into her and she felt her arms raise involuntarily to the sky. Her eyes were closed, but she could sense Emrys' arms rising the same way. The stones glowed slightly, as if in the aftermath of a lightning strike. She felt she was leaning back, her face to the night sky. Then she and Emrys stepped back, away from each other a few feet, and a glowing aura of power emerged between them.

Claerwen saw men riding horses in from the sea. Their leader was dressed in the Roman style, tall and proud. They rode many miles northward until they met another group of men. Vortigern's men. They fought, long, hard, bloody, then chased the high king's men into a fortress. Vortigern was dead, his men were dead, burned in the fortress, burned to the ground.

The vision was hidden behind swirling clouds for a few moments, then reappeared. A dingy, dark room opened, showing filthy walls of stone, empty but for a pile of chains to one side. Then the Iron Hawk was riding fast across the mountains of Gwynedd, swinging his flashing sword round and round over his helmeted head. And Claerwen saw herself, high up somewhere, calling in the dark, but she could not tell what she called.

The vision faded slowly. Claerwen and Emrys tried to hold onto it, but the gods left, slipping back into the earth. As Claerwen opened her eyes, she saw Emrys gazing at her, the amberish light in his eyes fading. The night was pitch black now, but as they looked up, another strange light glowed in the northern sky.

"It is the flashing of *Y Gwalch Haearn's* sword," Claerwen mumbled. She turned to Emrys and asked, "Do you know who he is?"

"No. No one knows. The gods have not revealed him."

"I heard two soldiers say he was dead. But he's not, is he?" She watched the aurora, unable to stop.

"No, he's not. Is he the one you seek?" Emrys watched her.

She returned his gaze, her face solemn and proud. "Who are you?" she asked.

Emrys was struck by Claerwen's calm dignity that covered her suspicion of him. He studied her lithe figure, clad in the boyish clothing, her long hair braided and reaching down nearly to her knees. He thought she would make a magnificent princess, or even a queen. Finally, he smiled, and said, "My name is Myrddin Emrys. The man in the Roman clothing is my father, Aurelius Ambrosius."

Claerwen's mouth opened in surprise. At last she understood who this mysterious man with the fire in the head was. She involuntarily stepped back a pace. "Emrys...Ambrosius. Of course, the same name in two languages. You are Merlinus

Ambrosius! The one sometimes called Merlin the Enchanter?" Chills ran over her skin. "My Lord!" She went down on one knee in deference to him.

"Please, there is no need. We have become intimate enough friends by now to dispense with such nonsense. And please, just call me Myrddin. I prefer the Welsh version." He chuckled at her sudden formality and raised her by the elbow.

"Then, your father has taken the High Kingship back from Vortigern?"

"Aye, the battle was at Doward. Vortigern is dead."

Claerwen turned back to stare at the sky. The aurora continued, glowing brighter, then dimming, brighter again. Claerwen could not shake the feeling that it was the flashing from the sword in the vision. She watched until her eyes ached.

"*Y Gwalch Haearn,*" she mumbled. Myrddin brought her a cup of some brew.

"This will help your headache. You must have one, there always is after the power leaves." He paused, thinking about the vision, then frowned and asked, "Whom is it that you seek, Claerwen? Did you see him in the vision?"

She shook her head slowly and answered, "No. But his face was not among the dead." She accepted the cup. Then her eyes leveled with Myrddin's and she spoke with clarity, "Have you heard anything about Dinas Beris, in Gwynedd? About what happened there in the summer?"

"No."

"The fort was sacked by the Iron Hawk and a group of warriors." Claerwen watched the standing stones as she spoke.

"The Iron Hawk? But he always works alone. Always."

Claerwen's head jerked around to look at Myrddin. She asked, "A false Iron Hawk? Using the disguise to place blame on the true *Gwalch Haearn*?" She paused, and he could see her mind working, trying to understand the vision. "Then it makes sense, that the gods show he is still alive. Then I must go north."

Myrddin reached a hand to touch Claerwen's shoulder. His face was full of questions.

"What involves you with Dinas Beris? I know that the prince who rules that fort is a spy, allied with some of the same Celtic chieftains that my father is allied with. I've never met the man, but I've heard he is incorruptibly loyal to freeing Britain of the Saxon scourge. Is he the one you seek?"

Claerwen smiled, her face wistful in the glow of the aurora. "Aye," she said softly.

"Vortigern had him under fugitive status, which makes him a dangerous man, Claerwen. Even with Vortigern's death, the status has not changed. And he could be nearly impossible to find. He's extremely elusive. Why would you seek him?"

She smiled again, more broadly. "He is my husband."

Myrddin stared at her, stunned beyond speech. Finally he asked, "You married Marcus ap Iorwerth?"

Claerwen nodded.

Myrddin exhaled sharply, then nearly smiled. "I'm not surprised, that you would marry a man like him. Tell me what happened."

Claerwen told Myrddin of the sacking and how she had fled. Her voice softened as she finished, saying, "I heard the man called Rhun say that Marcus is dead, but I do not believe it. Though I have not seen him in the fire, he is the mate of my soul, and he is not dead."

"Then you will go north? With winter coming on? That is too dangerous."

"I must go, Myrddin. If the Iron Hawk is looking for this treasure, he may know where Marcus is and think I am there as well. I have to reach Marcus before the warrior finds him."

Myrddin shook his head, debating to himself if Claerwen was the most courageous or most foolhardy woman he had ever met. At last he said, "In the morning I will leave for Doward, and I will speak with my father. He will lift the fugitive status from both you and your husband. But, beware, Claerwen, it will not bring you safe passage. Not from those greedy for the treasure, whatever it is, and certainly not from the Iron Hawk."

"I know, Myrddin. And I thank you, for your help. Know

that you and your father will always have our allegiance."

Claerwen also refused Myrddin's offer of an escort from his father's war band help find Marcus ap Iorwerth for her. She told him that alone, she could find him more easily, and without leading anyone else there.

Reluctantly, Myrddin conceded and said, "Then you had best get some rest, because it will be a long, difficult journey." He turned away, frowning deeply, to stoke up the campfire.

Claerwen slept soundly.

By first light, she was preparing to set out. Her head still ached, but she felt calm and steady again. She looked at the sky, clear and pale, calm and cold. No shining lights, not even a cloud. But she still knew she had to go north. Far north.

She said goodbye to Myrddin Emrys. At first she felt stiff and formal, knowing he was the High King's son, but as she looked into the man's face, she realized how much he had helped her and how their power connected them. She knew they would be life-long friends. Impulsively, she hugged him. He softly wished her luck as he returned her embrace and kissed her cheek.

Myrddin sadly watched her lithe form slip into the forest and disappear, and he fiercely hoped she would survive.

Claerwen covered territory quickly. She still did not know exactly where she was being led to, but she could feel the gods pushing her along.

She foraged and hunted as she traveled, not stopping long for anything other than the barest necessities, still staying away from roads and settlements as she no longer needed to be near them to seek information.

The spirit within drove her hard and fast. She ignored the aching in her legs, the blisters on her feet, her tired back and shoulders that carried her gear. She held her hope and vision like a warm blanket around her, not daring to think of anything else.

She crossed through long forests, skirting open plains and farm fields. She welcomed the sight of the spine of mountains that ran northward through Britain, loving their beauty and solitude. She strode with long, full steps up and down valley walls, crossing rivers, running when she felt she was moving too slowly.

Claerwen came upon Hadrian's Wall. It was abandoned as were most of the Romans' structures. She climbed up at a high point to scan the land beyond. Strathclyde lay to the west, Brynaich and Lothian to the east. Not wanting to enter Ceredig's territory, she slid down the embankment on the far side of the wall and moved on, staying just to the east of the ridge that divided Strathclyde and Brynaich.

Claerwen had been traveling steadily for more than a fortnight by the time she crossed Antonine's Wall, the boundary with the Picts. She felt she was slowing down, and began to force herself to keep moving. She did not know much about the Picts except that they were supposed to be wild, unfriendly, and covered themselves with blue woad and tattoos. She continued to avoid being seen, casting wide detours around any human activity.

Exhaustion was returning to Claerwen's body and she fought with herself over whether she should rest or continue to follow the arduous path she was compelled to take. By the end of another week, the highlands of Alban loomed before her. She sat and rested for a few minutes to admire their stark beauty. She was not sleeping well at night anymore, and every step struck sharp pains through her legs. She had lost weight again because she was not eating enough to maintain it against the physical hardships she endured. Food was scarcer in the northern hills and she was ignoring her own needs.

And winter was in the air.

The afternoon brought in a miserably cold gale from the northwest, stinging ice coming with it. Claerwen decided she would have to seek shelter early, before the storm hit, but the mountains stood cold and stiff before her, offering no caves or trees to protect her. She could not stay in the open, and she could smell snow coming. Lots of snow.

Claerwen gathered her gear and headed for a gap in the first ridge of the mountains. She hoped there would be a place on the other side more suitable to hide in until the storm was over. She ground her way up, glad she had rested and eaten. Her lower legs ached with the cold wind, so she stopped again briefly to wrap them in another set of leggings. They felt better, but every step still hurt as if the bones were rubbing together.

The climb up the ridge took her a long time, but she finally reached the top and stopped to survey the next valley. It was partially barren and rocky, the slopes covered with scree. A thin forest sloped down one side, and a projection of rock shaped like a basin jutted out of the trees and overlooked the small valley. In the basin was a tarn, dark grey from the scudding clouds that preceded the storm. Its water rippled in a steady stream of cords from the wind that nearly blew Claerwen off the ridge. To one side of the tarn was a tiny crannog, a small fortified building built on an artificial island. It looked abandoned.

Claerwen approached the tarn, stalking it from above. She had seen no one for days and did not want to meet anyone now. She slipped down closer, watching the crannog intensely. It looked old and disused, its main door slightly ajar, bobbing in the wind.

Claerwen moved closer. The roof was partially caved in on one side, but the other side looked fairly solid. There was no coracle to cross the water. She could almost taste the comfort of the building. She crept back and forth above it a second time and became convinced it was empty. Then she took up a position to see through the gap of the door. Nothing moved. Slowly she crept closer, listening, feeling the air, sniffing for scents. Instinct told her it was safe.

She crept down to the edge of the water and tested it. It was very cold and probably would form ice soon. She had forgotten how close winter was coming on. She did not want to swim across and get wet with the cold weather. And she could not find a boat. But there was a log floating at the edge of the tarn, small enough for her to pull out and steer. She waded in the water's edge, pulling it around and aiming it at the island. She hoped it would not roll over and dump her in the icy water; it was bad enough getting her feet and aching legs wet. She sat down on the middle of the log, wrapped her feet under it, and kept herself and her gear low and balanced. She hand-paddled slowly, using her arms as balances, and gradually she drifted across the narrowest part of the lake to the island.

Sedge grass grew thickly around the shore and made it hard for Claerwen to land her log. The fatigue in her body increased with the cold and she finally abandoned trying to beach it. She waded ashore.

She crouched to one side of the main door, next to the leather hinges and pushed gently. It creaked a little and swung in. All was dark and a musty smell floated out. It looked like no one had been there for a terribly long time. A frayed pallet sat next to a dusty hearth; a small stack of firewood, some ancient tools and a lump of unidentified debris were against the wall. Claerwen heaved a sigh of relief and closed the door, latching it securely against the wind. She peeled her pouches from her shoulders and unwound her bedroll onto the pallet. Night was falling and she had no desire to eat; the pain and fatigue had withered her appetite to nothing. She would worry about food in the morning. Perhaps it would be a good place to stay to rebuild her strength, then decide how and when to carry on.

The storm hit in the middle of the night, waking Claerwen from a coma-like sleep. The wind, rain and snow shook the tiny structure and she hoped the gods would leave the remainder of the poor roof attached. Sleet or hail was falling in the roofless room. After listening for a long time, she realized sleep was not going to return yet and decided to cook a meal.

Lighting some of the dusty firewood in the hearth with her iron and flint, Claerwen savored its warmth and dryness. She realized she had not set foot inside any structure since leaving the miller's house, nearly two moons' cycles. She also realized how spoiled she had become with normal amenities, even in a remote place like Dinas Beris. The fire grew and warmed, making the room almost cozy. Quickly, because there was little wood to burn and the storm would probably have soaked everything outside, Claerwen spitted a small piece of dried meat leftover from her last meal and heated it over the flames. She rummaged through a pouch and smiled when she found a small, wrinkled potato she had dug up a few days before and was saving for a special meal. She placed it carefully to roast, thinking this was just the right occasion for it. She sucked on a handful of dried fruit while she waited for the meal to heat.

It was not much food, but it had been so long since she had eaten properly that her stomach was shrunken and not able to hold much. She was quickly satisfied. Then exhaustion swept over her again, and she banked the fire and crawled back to her bed, diving into another deep, dreamless sleep.

The moon strung light intermittently across the crannog's interior, clouds scudding anxiously past its shining face. The wind still blew in sharp gusts, but it was dying along with the storm. The air grew colder. The contrast between the shadowy darkness and flashing moonlight was stark and eerie.

Claerwen woke to the dancing light and had to think to remember where she was. It had been dark before; she was not sure if it was still the same night, or if she had slept through a day and into another night. Shrugging to herself, it did not matter anyway. She lay thinking, glad for the rest and the peaceful safety the crannog gave her. She listened to the trees' soughing in the wind and watched the patterns the moon made on the walls and objects around her. Lost in no apparent thought, she stared at the pile of tossed off items comprising the debris along the wall. It suddenly came to her mind that the object crowning the lump was a cap, old and raggedy-edged.

It was dusty and mud-caked, barely recognizable as anything more suitable than a cast off rag. She reached to pull it closer for examination. It was torn from the edge half-way to the crown. Dark grey once, it had been of fairly good quality. She threw it back on the pile.

Claerwen yawned and stretched, wondering at the time. Her legs still hurt, almost more than before, now that they had stiffened during sleep. She rubbed them, wincing. When she was more rested, she would dig through her pouches and find a salve to ease them.

Then something made her pick up the cap again, and she turned it over and over in her hands, her thoughts wandering. The inside of it was sweat-stained. It must have belonged to some peasant, perhaps a poor herder who once occupied this tiny place. She thought of the time Marcus had come dressed as a simple harper wearing a similar cap. She looked at the one in her hands. Similar shape, that one was grey, too. With the same frayed edge on the crown. And a nick above the seam, just like this one.

Claerwen's mouth hung open and her breath became thin. She stared and studied the cap, searching for more details. She brushed and scraped off some of the mud, finding a familiar scar along the crown. Aye, it was the same old cap Marcus had used so many times.

She closed her eyes, remembering the dashing figure he had struck in the Mithraen temple's entrance. She ached to see him again, to hear his voice, feel his fingers tracing along her throat. Then she opened her eyes and saw again she was not dreaming. The cap was real.

"What have they done to you?" she spoke aloud hoarsely. "The Iron Hawk found you first, didn't he? I'm too late." Memories crashed through her mind, and she suddenly remembered seeing the crannog before in a vision. "Did it mean I would find where you died, where you were finally killed?"

She stood, hugging the cap tightly, crushing it, pacing to and fro with it across the room. She keened her grief, not with tears, but with a soft wail like the wind draughting through a narrow slit. Everything was gone, her family, Grania, her home, probably she would never see Padrig again either. They were all gone. Vortigern had his revenge, and Drakar as well, though they would never know of it. So all this journey was meant for was to bury Marcus' bones after all. Padrig was right. It was only to seek her own misfortune.

Her sorrow swelled and billowed like water overflowing a dam. She held her breath until her lungs burned and she felt dizzy and disoriented. Still the tears and weeping could not come. She crashed onto her knees, scraping them into the dirt floor, then hurled the cap down and pounded it with ineffective fists. That held no satisfaction either. She ventilated hysterically, keening and anguishing, letting her convictions be destroyed by her despair.

The moonlight continued to constantly shake and mingle the shadows in brooding patterns. Then a flash of lightning crashed overhead as if to destroy the crannog and the very mountainside it was nestled in. Claerwen, still on her knees, pulled herself upright, flung her arms in the air.

"MARCUS!"

Her shriek emerged from the thunder, carried far and away above the storm, disturbing the night creatures. It seemed as if the forest itself shuddered in fear of the cry, swaying back and away.

Claerwen drooped, spent; and darkness descended again. Her long, wild hair fell loose over her face and streamed down around her like a wooly, tangled cascade. She felt the darkness like a cloak; clouds covering the moon again, but she did not care. She sat there, silent and motionless, not hearing, not wanting to live.

A soft scraping noise broke the quiet. Numbed to the core, Claerwen realized the wind had died and there was no other noise except the new sound that disturbed the uneasy peace. Her eyes rolled up slowly, and she tentatively looked through the curtain of her hair. It was still dark, very dark, like a hood had been put over the tarn, yet she could tell the moon was shining brightly through one of the window slits. Why was it so dark?

She felt a presence. She thought the gods should take her now to the Otherworld. For failing to find Marcus before he was killed, her life should be forfeited as well. Let them take her, she resolved, caring no more.

The darkness moved; it was at the doorway. The shadows crept and the scrape came again. Now Claerwen looked up, seeing the shape advancing on her, inch by inch. She thought she was past fear, but this presence chilled her to the soul. It shuffled and slipped, ever so slowly. There was no face, no feature of any kind. Was this what Beli Mawr, the god of death, was like? Or the one the Christians called Satan?

Involuntarily, she edged backward, though she knew there was no room to flee. She stared and stared, trying to see a face, but only a black hollow showed. Her hands touched the pallet and she halted. Well, it was a good time to die.

The figure moved closer and the glowing moonlight lent it further shape. It was hooded, wearing an old, ragged, billowing soutane of a deep brown homespun, an equally ragged cloak over the soutane. She saw that it leaned heavily to one side, the end of a makeshift crutch exposed among the folds of the sloppy, ill-fitting garments. She had also heard a saying about a "Grim Reaper." Perhaps this was he, and she wondered why she remembered all those odd sayings now. It never occurred to her that this might be the owner of the crannog, or at least another temporary occupant like herself.

The shadow stood just beyond a window slit, just out of the moonbeam that streamed in. It no longer moved, and only stood facing her as she cowered before it. Not understanding why it hesitated so long, Claerwen wondered if it was trying to make up its mind what to do with her. She wished it would get on with its duty, whatever that was to be. She pushed back her unruly hair, to try to see a face, but still could not distinguish anything under the low, wide hood.

"Claerwen?" A low, hoarse voice spoke her name. She barely heard it. It was not the authoritative voice she expected to hear to take her away or send her into the next life.

"Claerwen?" The voice tried to be clearer, but was only a little stronger, a little more urgent.

The figure lurched, heavily dependent on the stick, and scratched forward a few inches more. The moonbeam struck it, casting sharp contrasts on the head and shoulders. This was no apparition, no ghost. But the hood still hid the man's face.

He coughed, a deep, horrible cough, choking on phlegm. Claerwen rose, unsure what to do. Her instinct as a healer shook some of the overbearing fear out of her, and she wanted to help ease the obvious pain in which the man was encompassed. But the feeling of evil still pervaded the air and she still sensed a trap.

The fit passed and the hood faced her again. But this time it had moved back a little. She could see a dim face, emaciated by illness and hunger, overgrown with a dirty, unkempt beard. She could see cloudy eyes boring back into her own, holding her still. He shifted his weight again, uncomfortable on a bad leg, and the hood moved back a hair's breadth more.

Now she could see the eyes clearly; the moonlight struck them as her flint and iron could spark dry tinder. Like two pieces of obsidian, Marcus ap Iorwerth's eyes held her own.

It could not be, she shivered involuntarily. It must be an apparition after all, and she almost felt disappointed. She dared not blink, else she would lose the vision. *Oh, to be cursed with fire in the head, how cruel the god is to show me this, when I know it will only vanish again.*

She reached out a hand, afraid to touch, afraid the vision would disappear. But she had to know. Her fingers burned to know. She reached further, a little further, for the hood. Her forefinger grazed the edge, and she drew back as if scorched. But it was there. So she reached again. Now she pushed on the hood, brushing it back with her palm until it fell behind his neck and his head stood naked in the moonlight.

"By the gods my people swear by," she whispered, "it can not be. Marcus..." Her voice cracked and she could speak no further, it was too hard. The crutch fell, clattering and unheeded.

They crashed into each other's arms.

CHAPTER 24

**The Highlands of Alban
Winter, 468-469 A.D.**

"They said you were dead," Claerwen whispered. "I knew it wasn't so."

Tears rimmed Marcus' red-shot eyes, his brows wrinkled in knots that were painful to see. His voice cracked and squeaked when he said, "Tell me I am not dreaming. Tell me it is really you, my Claeri."

Claerwen stroked his beard with her palm. Her lips hung open, a tender "ah" escaping them. "Aye, 'tis me, 'tis me." She lovingly held his face in her hands, afraid to let go lest he should disappear in a puff of mist.

She smiled brilliantly, the moonlight sparkling her, and he was again awed by the stunning beauty of her green-blue eyes. He stayed absolutely still, wanting to remember her so for all of his lifetimes.

He clung to her, unsteady on his feet, half leaning against the wall, half on her. Then she realized how tired and ill he looked. His face was pale, waxy skin draped haphazardly over bone, and his eyes were sunken and slightly out of focus. His cheeks, though covered by the scraggly, unkempt beard, were very deeply hollowed. His hair was equally unkempt and had grown long past his shoulders.

"How long has it been since you've eaten?" she asked.

He hesitated a moment, confused out of his reverie, and queried, "What?"

"When did you last eat?"

He thought a moment, then replied, "I don't know."

She looped one of his arms across her shoulders and eased him carefully onto the pallet. When he sat, he drooped. She was afraid he was going to faint, he looked so weak from illness and hunger.

"There is a lantern there," he told her, indicating the pile of odds and ends, "but I have no fat to burn in it."

Claerwen retrieved the lantern and examined it in the moonbeam, then rifled through one of her pouches. She found rendered lard leftover from the last time she had cooked and deftly packed some of it into the pocket, then stuck a wick into the center. With her iron and flint, she lit a twig and held it to the wick. Shortly, a warm glow emanated throughout the room.

"Is there more firewood nearby?" she asked.

He did not answer at first, but she could see he was thirsty. She dug out a tin cup and filled it with water. He drank noisily.

She searched the rest of the crannog and returned briefly with an armload of wood, dry enough to use, having been tossed into corners by the wind. Within minutes she had a fire crackling and a pot of simmering water full of herbs, fat, dried bits of meat and vegetables.

Marcus responded to the heat and the smell of the herbs. He had been sitting, only half-coherently watching her. His interest perked up as she stirred and tested the concoction, softening the meat so it would be easy for him to eat and digest. She continued to search through her food pouch and found the last of her ground meat powder, pouring most of that into the soup. Soon, it thickened, becoming similar to the soup Padrig had nursed her with after her miscarriage. She poured some in the cup and held it so Marcus could sip.

"Let it cool some," she warned.

"It's been so long since I had anything warm to eat, I would welcome my tongue being burned just to taste the heat." He sipped, letting it trickle down his tongue and throat, savoring every drop.

But he was interrupted by the cough before he could finish, nearly sloshing the soup. Claerwen took the cup back from him until he stopped.

"I will try to find cherry bark in the morning to take that away." She silently thanked Padrig and the nuns for her extensive knowledge of herbs and cures; he was spitting up blood with the phlegm. "Out with it," she ordered, making him spit into a rag.

Claerwen fed him more broth and made some simple barley cakes to soak in it, until she felt he had enough. She would not give him more, no matter how hungry he was. She did not want him to bloat and vomit it all back up.

"Rest for a while now, my love. You will feel better soon." She helped him to lay down.

"I want to know how you came to me, Claeri." He hung onto her arms, pulling her down to him.

"There will be time enough for that. Sleep now." Claerwen gently kissed his brow and covered him in her own blanket, then banked the fire and blew out the lantern. She watched as he gradually closed his eyes and drifted into sleep.

In the dark, she sat very still next to the pallet and listened to his rough breathing, her eyes willing strength into the rhythm of his chest as she watched it rise and fall with great effort. She reached out to gently smooth a piece of his long hair that fell over the edge of the pallet. The severity of his condition horrified her, but she bowed her head in the darkness, allowing herself to feel a moment of joy at finding him at last.

He was alive!

By the gods, he was alive!

She laid down on the floor next to him, tucking her hand around his arm, so that if he moved, he would wake her. Shortly, she fell asleep.

Claerwen was awake again by first light. Most of the snow had thankfully passed to the north. She needed to scout the area and gather as much food and fuel for heat as possible before winter began in earnest. She judged the year to be well past Samhuinn, by the position the sun took upon its rising and setting. When she had begun her quest, she had kept a record of the days, but she lost track after the encounter at the battlefield in the south. She felt it was two-thirds of the way between Samhuinn and Midwinter, give or take two days.

Claerwen emptied all of her pouches and packed them onto her shoulders, then she slipped out of the building. She searched the entire island, gathering anything that was usable as food, firewood, or medicine. Within a short time, all the pouches were overflowing. She returned inside the building and piled the items in a corner to be sorted later.

Marcus was still sleeping soundly. She speculated it was the first good sleep he had had for a long time. She bit her lip, wishing she could see him wake up and smile at her with his black eyes sparkling. But he needed sleep, so she went outside again.

She scanned the valley from the shore of the tiny island, walking all the way around again. She could hear a stream bubbling in the distance, from across the bowl-shaped hollow, coming down from beyond the forest's edge. She decided she should probably cross the tarn and explore it the next day. The trees thinned and ended halfway around the hollow, majestic rocky mountains spreading out before her. They were banded with dozens of shades of rock, magnificent as any jewels. It was desolate, but the beauty of the mountains' starkness touched her. She wondered if this place, like Avebury, was a place of power.

Misty light filled the crannog, making it look almost smoky. The fire pit was banked and glowing, the cooking pot still over it.

Marcus woke to find himself alone. He looked over at the

fire pit and recalled the night before. Had it all been a dream? Chills shivered him.

"Claerwen?" he called as loud as his hoarse throat would allow. Panic filled him, propelling him to sit up. "No, no, it cannot be." He rose, heaving himself off the pallet. Pain seared his chest and left leg. "Claerwen!" he tried to shout. A violent spell of coughing took him over.

As the spell eased, he groped for the makeshift crutch and staggered for the door, calling her name over and over. He ignored the pain, clutching a wad of the soutane over his chest, and pushed himself to the door. The cold air hurt his ears.

"Claerwen!" he yelled.

He drooped over the crutch, tremendous sadness overwhelming him. She was gone. She was not real after all. It was just a dream again. Only the pain was real. He shook uncontrollably, grieving over his mistake.

"What is it, what is wrong?" her voice called.

She was running to him, surprised to see him standing there. Before she reached him, he fell, toppling limply to the cold, wet turf. She was holding another bundle of firewood but she threw it aside to run to him. Dropping to her knees, she skidded to a stop.

"I'm here, I'm here," she soothed as she pulled him up, dragging him into her lap. He sprawled there, breathing in short, painful gasps, muttering unintelligibly. She was stunned by his incoherent state of mind. What had happened in these several months, she could not reckon.

She tugged Marcus up and pulled him back into the crannog. He was not so tall or big to start with, but he had always been solid and muscular. She was amazed now that she had the necessary strength to nearly lift him to his feet. She could feel ribs, front and back, with deep valleys between, sharp hips protruding beneath the ragged soutane. She resettled him on the pallet. Turning to reach for a cup of water, she was stopped by his hand suddenly gripping her sleeve.

"Please don't go," he whispered, desperation in the words.

She held the cup to his cracked lips. She had never seen fear in his eyes as she did at that moment.

"I thought you had gone, Claeri."

"I am here, my Marcus, I am here." She kissed his hand, hugging it to her cheek, and felt it shaking. "You must rest now, so I can make medicine for you, to make you well again. I will not be far."

"I have to see you," he pleaded.

She leaned to embrace him, covering the anguish she felt. She kissed his cheek and said softly in his ear, "I will leave the door open so you can see me. I need the firewood and the plants I gathered."

He seemed to settle down, but she was not sure he really understood. She eased herself out of his grip, moving the short distance to the hearth, and heated another cup of meat broth.

"Can you drink this?" she asked, offering it to him.

"Aye," he answered, sipping it willingly.

"I will lay out some snares tonight. Perhaps I can catch some ptarmigans," she said, trying to draw his attention away from his pain.

"You hunt?"

"Aye. I needed to learn how." He gave her the cup and laid back, pondering her answer.

She began preparing a strong poultice to draw out the cough and bloody phlegm. She sang and hummed a motley selection of melodies to make her presence more noticeable while she hustled back and forth, staying in his line of sight as much as possible. He lay awake, but not very alert, trying to watch her.

When she was ready, she told him, "Marcus, this poultice will draw the pain from your chest and warm you through. With care, you should feel better within a week."

He did not answer, but he watched her with his haunted, hollowed black eyes. They disturbed her, not because of his illness; she knew how to cure his pneumonia. She sensed there was something else, something more hurtful behind his aching eyes. She hoped that once the physical pain was gone, the mental pain would fade away with it.

Claerwen untied the old soutane carefully. She was appalled at the condition he was in, and steeled her face to keep from showing it. His once bronzed, well-muscled chest was nearly caved inward, the black hair thinned and matted. She bathed him gently, out of a pail of water. This refreshed him, and he cooperated with her directions of which way to move or roll to complete the bath. Then she plastered the thick, gooey poultice onto his chest. It was hot and she saw him wince, but he said nothing. As she finished, she swathed it over with a soft doeskin bandage.

"Now I want to look at this leg," she said as she tied his garment. She lifted the hem up his left leg. The knee was red and swollen, fluid bulging under the skin.

Marcus explained, "An arrow caught me there. I tried to treat it with marigold, like I remember you doing, but it just will not stop hurting."

"It needs to be drained. I will have to lance it, drain it, and let it heal over once more. It will be very painful."

"So be it," he returned.

She ejected a short breath and rolled up a piece of cowhide. "You can bite down on this. I'm going to tie your arms and legs to the pallet, so you won't accidentally move and disrupt the surgery." She pulled out some spare thongs from her supplies and reached to wrap the first one around his left wrist.

Claerwen stopped, the thong dangling from her hand. "Marcus? How did you get this?" She picked up his hand and examined his wrist. It was encircled with scars.

He stared at his arm, then raised the other. The right wrist had matching scars. "They look like rope burns." He frowned at Claerwen. "I don't know how they got there."

She was surprised by his reaction, but decided to wait for further answers. She tied his hands down, using the soutane's long sleeves to protect his damaged skin. Similar marks were on his ankles. Swallowing nervously, Claerwen realized he must have been held prisoner during the months he had been gone.

She prepared her dagger in the fire, disliking this part of her work, but respecting its necessity. She would not risk losing Marcus to a fevered wound. Grimacing, she deftly slit the healed-over injury.

Marcus strained against the ties, his head jerking roughly back and forth with the pain, the cowhide clenched in his teeth. But within minutes, Claerwen had the wound drained and salved with a willow bark and marigold mixture to ease pain and fever. She rushed, trying to cause as little discomfort as possible, bandaging the knee firmly.

"Get these ties off me!" Marcus hissed suddenly. His lower jaw was shaking.

"Of course." She was stunned by the strange expression on his face. All of the pain he was feeling was overwhelmed by his abrupt need to be released from the bonds. She slit the thongs with her dagger.

Marcus sat up half-way, but Claerwen stopped him from rising further, afraid he would tear apart the wound.

"It's too soon, Marcus. Drink this and lay down. It has willow bark for the pain, and cherry bark for your cough." She held the cup to his lips again.

He calmed, the fear in his eyes retreating. He drank, then dropped back on the pallet. "If I did not know you were the best healing woman in Britain..." His voice trailed off. Though he sounded gruff, she thought he was trying to tease her.

"I need to examine you, to see if anything else is wrong. I'd like to do it now, but if you are too tired, I can wait until tomorrow morning," she offered.

He had pain in his eyes, but his admiration for her business-like attitude showed through it. He replied, "Do it now, Claeri."

Claerwen found no other wounds or signs of internal injuries or illness. However, as she untied his loincloth to take it for washing, she found several marks in the skin of his groin. She pressed her fingers lightly on them and asked if they hurt.

"No, what is it?"

"Do you know how you got these? They weren't there before."

He pushed himself up to see and frowned. "I don't remember them. What are they?"

She stared at him and said, "They look like burns. Like somebody touched you with a burning stick. Like you were...tortured."

He stared back at her, shaking his head. "I don't know." He swallowed and studied the marks, trying desperately to remember. Claerwen pressed her fingers to them again, and he drew his breath in sharply.

"Did that hurt?" she asked.

He stared up at her again and answered, "Not when you touched me. But I have a sense of pain associated with them."

"You remember pain?"

"Aye. But not how...or why," He tired suddenly, and laid down again. Claerwen let him sleep.

"Talk to me, my Claeri. Take my mind away from this itchy plaster you put on me."

It was late afternoon a few days later. Claerwen had gutted and cleaned several small game birds she had snared and was roasting them over the small fire pit. Bannock cakes sizzled on a hot, flat rock on the hearth stones, and a pot of root vegetables hung simmering. Marcus was improving steadily; she had fed him continuously with her herb and meat soups, every few hours, day and night. He responded remarkably. He still refused to tell her how long he had gone without eating; she suspected he had given up hope and stopped looking for food, knowing his illness would have soon killed him.

His knee continued to bother him tremendously, and she knew she would have to drain it again. To distract him from some of the pain, she persuaded him to let her wash his hair. He could not remember how long it had been since he had a comb and she could not get hers through the mass of tangles. She decided to try washing it first, rinsing it with a solution of dried nettles. She patiently worked at it, and gradually smoothed it out. It was as uneven as the frayed hem of his soutane and she was amazed at how long it was. She trimmed it in layers the way he usually wore it, the longest just even with his shoulders.

Claerwen offered to shave the beard, but Marcus said he wanted to keep it; it would help keep his face warm in the coming winter. He consented to let her trim it, and as she began to carefully scrape the excess from his neck, she found more scars, similar to the ones on his wrists and ankles. Her eyes widened and she looked up at him.

"By Lleu, what did they do to you?" she mumbled, putting down the knife. She studied his neck, pressing gently to learn the extent of the scarring.

Suddenly, Marcus gripped her hands and shoved them away, and he glared hard at her. His eyes flicked back and forth, not truly seeing her.

"What is it? What are you remembering?" Claerwen asked gently, gritting her teeth from the pain in her hands. In spite of his illness, the panic he projected gave him strength in his grip.

Just as suddenly, the image he was trying to recall disappeared. "Damn!" he ejected, laying down again.

"What did you see?"

"It's gone. I'm not sure what I saw. When you held the knife, it reminded me of something. Just a feeling. A sense of...pain. I only recall pain. Nothing else. No faces, no voices, no reasons."

He shook his head as if to dispel the eerie feeling, then turned on his side to watch Claerwen. His eyes were focused and intense.

"How did you come to me, Claerwen?" He reached out and pulled a long, tossed lock of hair. "You are such a wild thing now, almost like one of the Old Ones, the Ancient Gods, if only you were dark like them."

She turned her heart-shaped face to him, her eyes pensive.

Before she could speak he said, "It was the fire again,

wasn't it?"

She nodded, her graceful lashes shadowing her eyes.

"Tell me what happened, Claerwen. All of it." He had not felt like talking until now, and though she dreaded it, she was relieved to finally unburden herself. She began with the sacking of the fort, what she had heard Rhun say, the false Iron Hawk and his death, her flight with Padrig and Grania. Her eyes remained downcast when she told him of Rhun's intrigue and Grania's unwitting treachery.

Marcus remained composed, only occasionally interrupting with a question. Claerwen was surprised he took it so calmly. He asked, "And where is Grania now?"

Claerwen hesitated, then said softly, "She is dead. She took her own life out of bitter shame."

A wordless "oh" traced his face and he sat up, tired of lying down.

"Done is done, I suppose," Claerwen philosophized. "I am sorry, Marcus. I feel responsible for the loss of the fort. I could not, or did not, control her."

He countered, "She was not your responsibility. The fort was mine, and all who lived within its boundaries and influence. It is my failure." He winced as he moved his bad leg to a more comfortable position.

Claerwen cringed at the pain he felt, both inwardly and outwardly. She continued her story, "There is something else I must tell you."

His dark eyes gazed into hers, waiting for her to go on.

"I was with child when you left."

He continued to stare, and she could tell he was trying to count the months.

"I didn't know until three weeks after you were gone. The pregnancy wasn't normal from the beginning, and I miscarried about a fortnight after the sacking." She wished she had not started to tell him, but now she had to finish. She spoke slowly, each word precise and heavy, "It was just too hard, the traveling, no food. When I lost the child, I nearly died, and I was sick for a long time afterward. Padrig saved my life. I am sorry."

She watched him realize what she meant, and his face crumbled into heartache. She thought he was going to weep and she hated herself for telling him. She wrapped her arms around him, wanting to take away the pain she had caused.

"I have been such a fool," he said, sitting limply. His arms came up around her. "Such a bloody fool..."

She shook her head, and said, "You are not a fool, ever. Tell me what happened to you." She traced her finger along his moustache.

He took her hand and his fingers fidgeted with hers. "There is not much to tell. I was headed for Ynys Witrin, meaning to find a more permanent way of dealing with Vortigern before he could bring more Saxons into Gwynedd, or even into Britain. I wanted to seek counsel with Aurelius Ambrosius; he calls himself the Count of Britain now. He and his brother Uther were raising an army in Armorica, across the Narrow Sea, and should have landed in Britain by then. They will try to drive out Vortigern and his Saxons. My plan was to pledge loyalty to him, and a degree of the same from Cunedda as well. I also held information that would have been valuable to him to gauge the strength Vortigern has across Britain."

He paused to drink and cleared his throat. The cough had subsided substantially, though it still racked him from time to time.

Claerwen stated, "He succeeded against Vortigern. In a battle at Doward. Vortigern is dead."

Marcus was stunned. "So soon?"

"Aye. Did you know Ambrosius has a son?"

"Aye, he is called Myrddin. He has been working with the Celtic chieftains to prepare for Ambrosius' arrival, mostly in secret. A peculiar man, I was told. I've never met him." He drank again.

"The man Grania and I met years ago, the one called Emrys, who took us into Caernarfon, is the same man. I met him again in Avebury, on my way here. He is Myrddin Emrys, or

Merlinus Ambrosius. He has the power of the fire very strongly, like nothing I have ever experienced."

Marcus muttered, "Merlin the Enchanter. That must be why he was described as strange." He cleared his throat again and continued, "I never was able to meet with Ambrosius. Unfortunately, he had not yet landed on the south coast by the time I approached Ynys Witrin, so I was forced to wait. I didn't actually enter the village. But someone followed me out of the marshes and I was ambushed."

"To the east of Ynys Witrin?" Claerwen asked.

Marcus scowled. "How do you know?"

"I went to Ynys Witrin, looking for you. Then I figured out you must have been disguised as a holy man, probably going from one holy shrine to another. I went east, heading for Avebury, and I found a battlefield. Do you know who ambushed you?"

"No. There were at least two, masked. They looked like common thieves. I was disguised as a priest. But knowing now what happened to the fort, they had to be Rhun's men. I should have changed my disguise, but I didn't. By Mithras, what a fool I was!"

"How could you have known?"

"I'm a spy, Claerwen! I'm a walking target, all the time. I have to know. Because I wasn't careful enough to change, I lost everything. I can never make up for the pain I've caused you and everyone else." He pounded a fist into a palm, anger flushing his thin face.

"What happened in the ambush?" Claerwen asked, trying to distract him.

His lips curled in disgust. "I was hidden along the road to spend the night. They must have followed very carefully and quietly because I had no sense of them at all. No sound, no motion, nothing. I even ate a cold supper, no fire, then rolled in under a fallen tree I sheltered over with branches. As it got dark, an arrow hit just above where I laid. Well, it was either play dead or run. Playing dead was too risky because they probably would have run me through with a sword just to make sure, so of course, I ran...straight into a sword fight."

Claerwen's eyes widened and her brows frowned in horror.

"He was a fairly good swordsman, but I knocked his weapon from him and booted him over a stone ledge. Then the archer got off another shot and got me here in the knee. The impact spun me around and I fell far down a ravine."

Marcus stopped for a few moments, then looked up at Claerwen. The haunted look was plain in his eyes again. "I can't remember anything after that. Absolutely nothing. I don't know how I got here or where this place is."

He drifted off, lost in thought.

Claerwen said, "This place is somewhere in the highlands of Alban."

Marcus looked up sharply at her. "Alban! So far north? Damn! You came all that way, for me? All alone?"

She smiled slightly and nodded.

His mouth worked, amazement in his face. Then finally, he smiled back, the first time since she had found him. He reached out and touched her cheek with his thumb, stroking the softness of her skin. "You still believed in me, when everyone else thought I was dead?"

"You are the other half of my soul, Marcus. As long as I sense you are alive, no matter where you are, I will find you. The gods..." Claerwen stopped, remembering the vision of the Iron Hawk. Her smile faded slowly into a frown.

Marcus stroked her cheek again, and asked what troubled her.

"It is widely believed the Iron Hawk is dead because of the false warrior Rhun used. But when I met Myrddin at Avebury, he and I entered the power of the stone circle. There was a vision, and we know the true Iron Hawk is still alive. The vision showed he was going north, or was already there. That was when I knew I had to go north, too, to find you, before he did."

Marcus raised one eyebrow and nearly smiled again. He

asked, "The gods have not shown you who he is?"

"No. When I found that old cap of yours," she pointed at it, "I thought he had found you first and killed you."

"He's not been here that I know of, Claeri."

"With Vortigern dead, I wonder if the Iron Hawk is behind the search for this treasure."

"Impossible," Marcus ejected, then asked, "Why would you think it would be the Iron Hawk?"

"If the gods showed me he was going to the far north, he must be looking for you, and probably me as well. There is no other connection."

He reminded her, "The Iron Hawk always works alone. Always. He would not work with others, such as Drakar or Rhun. No, I doubt he is behind it." Marcus' mouth flinched, then pressed into a flat line. Then he asked, "Where was the false Iron Hawk killed?"

"In the battlefield east of Ynys Witrin, I found six bodies and two dead horses. I could find nothing to identify them. Except for two things." She reached to rummage in the pile of items she had dumped out of her pouches. She carefully pulled out the Iron Hawk's helmet.

"There were two mercenaries looking for me; I heard them talking while I hid. They said the Iron Hawk was dead." She hesitated, her face very solemn.

Marcus took the helmet and studied it. "What was the other thing you found?"

She reached again, and extracted a folded piece of rawhide. "This," she said, and held it up, pulling back the leather to show him Owein's dagger. "It was struck into a tree."

Marcus stared in horror at the knife. He swore low and cruelly, muttering his frustration that he remembered nothing. Then he rose awkwardly to limp outside.

She let him go, watching silently as he plodded painfully out towards the shore.

Claerwen decided not pursue him with more questions. She had another speculation that she kept to herself about

Owein's fate. At first she had thought it was far-fetched, but the more she thought about it, the more credence she gave it. She wondered if Owein was the true Iron Hawk, and had left clues at the battlefield to mark his own death and that of the Iron Hawk's, leaving himself free to resurface under another identity and continue the search for the unknown treasure. Suspicion of Owein's loyalty had been cast before, and Owein's taciturn nature and singleness of interest in warrior activities lent well to the Iron Hawk's silence and swordsmanship. Claerwen wondered if Owein's solemn face hid such a secret, deceiving even Marcus.

She would approach Marcus with those questions later, but not until she had more evidence.

The evening sky was turning towards dusk and showing signs of coming snow. Marcus had been gone nearly an hour, and had not eaten supper. Claerwen kept food warm on the hearth stones for him, hoping he would return to eat, and she was getting worried. She had lost her own appetite when she saw his reaction to her news, but now she was hungry and wanted to eat with him.

She pulled on her overtunic and set off tracking him. Within minutes, she found him at the shore on the opposite side of the island, leaning on a tree and staring down into the water.

"Marcus?" she called softly.

She startled him; she had approached too softly, used to walking without making sound. He turned and clumsily tried to wield his crutch into a club. For a full minute, he stared at her, his face frozen in an expression that combined recognition and bewilderment. He seemed to be watching something, not seeing Claerwen in the path of his vision.

"Marcus?" she asked, touching his arm. "Are you in pain? Or are you remembering something?"

Finally, he dropped the stick, shaking himself out of the trance. He licked his dry lips. "I am sorry, Claerwen. You are more wild and stealthy than a panther."

"Nonsense," she reacted, then, "A panther!" She was surprised by his choice of words. "How odd."

He raised his eyebrows at her remark.

"Just before I lost the child, the last thing I saw was a panther, deep in the woods. He was a beautiful, black, sleek panther. I felt his soul and mine connect, just for a moment."

Marcus felt his skin prickle. "And now you move like one, hunt like one." A hint of fear crossed his eyes as they leveled with hers. "The druids would say the panther became your spirit helper. You have a tremendous power you don't even know you have. You could be accepted by the druids, to become a shaman." He almost backed away from her.

"Well, I don't want to be a shaman. All I want is for you to come eat something so you get well and strong again." She felt his face for fever. "You should come inside, out of the wind and the cold. You still have a long way to go to get well." She smiled and hooked her hand in his arm, intending to lead him toward the crannog.

He stalled, sinking into brooding, his dark eyes scowling at the stones on the ground. He confided, "I wish I could remember something, anything, how I got here. I don't know what this place is called. No other soul has crossed here that I am aware of since I have been here. It looks like it is awfully old."

"It is such a long way from anywhere. How did you cross the water?"

"There was a dug-out canoe, but it drifted away a few days before you came."

Claerwen had not seen it, and guessed it was wedged somewhere in a swampy spot. Then she realized why he had given up hope and how long it probably had been since he had eaten before she arrived. He could not cross over to find food.

He was thinking out loud when he interrupted her thoughts and said, "I think I've been here since about the middle of autumn. I have lost several weeks." He turned to her, his hands fingering the scars on his neck and sorrow shrouding his face, "What did they do to me?"

Then he suddenly pulled her to him, looking in her fiery green-blue eyes. This time he saw directly into her soul. "I thank the gods you found me," he breathed into her ear, and he clasped her tightly against his chest.

Claerwen hugged him back with all the compassion of her being.

Silently, with their arms wrapped comfortably around each other, they went inside.

A light snow began.

CHAPTER 25

**The Highlands of Alban
Early Spring, 469 A.D.**

Six weeks passed. While Marcus continued to recover, Claerwen spent the days gathering winter supplies, scouring the forest for as much food as she could carry back to the crannog. She made a small raft of fallen logs so she could float easily across the tarn. She also found a source of peat for fuel and cut many great slabs, taking them inside to dry. It snowed off and on, but not in much abundance, giving her more time to prepare against cold and hunger.

Time, patience, and Claerwen's strong poultices nearly cured Marcus' pneumonia. He still coughed heavily on occasion, but he no longer wheezed or spit phlegm and he began to feel much stronger. His knee, however, did not heal properly. He could not walk on it at all, and it was badly swollen again. Claerwen decided she would have to lance it once more to drain it. When she told him, he agreed to the surgery, but he objected fiercely to being tied down again.

She threatened him with the worst of possibilities: "Marcus, I have to tie you down. If you move accidentally, I could cut you so badly you could lose that leg. You know what pain can do. It can make both the strongest and the weakest of people lash out. I've got to drain it again; it could become fevered and I would have to take off most of your leg. Is that what you want?"

"I can't let you tie me down." He stared at the scars on his wrists.

"You remember something about those, don't you?" She reached to touch his arm, but he pulled away, the bewildered expression coming into his eyes again. "What is it, Marcus? What do you know? Or are you afraid to tell me because it is too awful to say?"

He brooded silently, studying his wrists. Then he spoke, his voice very low, "I can't tell you because I still don't know. You said once that sometimes the fire gives you only a sense of something that's happened or will happen. It's like that. Maybe I have the fire, too."

Claerwen smiled ironically, and sat next to him, leaning on his shoulder, then said, "You do not have the fire. I could tell, the way Myrddin knew I had it."

"Then what is it? What is this foreboding I get when you touch the scars?"

"Perhaps, if you were so badly injured or sick, or both, you might have been unconscious, or delirious, so much of the time that you weren't aware of what was happening. You may never remember. It looks like you were a prisoner."

"If I was a prisoner, how did I get away? How did I get here? It makes no sense."

Claerwen sighed, knowing she had to find a way to drain the knee; it was not just the leg he could lose, he could die if the tissues began to rot. She dared not waste any more time trying to convince him to be tied down.

Marcus brooded over supper without much talk. Claerwen watched him fight within himself as he chewed slowly, paying little attention to the meal or her. He rinsed the food down with a cup of hot brewed herbs. She did not tell him she had laced the usual ingredients in it with belladonna, to make him sleep through the surgery. He sat drowsing on the pallet and gradually dozed off, leaning against the wall.

Claerwen eased him down and stretched him out on the bed, then quickly set about the job she needed to do. She had the tools already at hand, and she tested that he was totally asleep by pinching him several times. He did not waken.

Within minutes, the knee was slit, drained and bandaged neatly, the tools cleaned and stored. Claerwen stood and watched her sleeping husband, breathing sighs of relief. She had been able to perform the surgery more carefully and thoroughly this time, and she wished she had used the belladonna the last time. In her examination, she found that the true damage was limited to only one side. The tough connecting sinews had been partially severed on the outside behind the kneecap, but everything else seemed normal. The drainage would ease the pain and hopefully start the healing process. She felt that Marcus would always limp some, but the other tendons and muscles would compensate with increasing strength for the damaged ones.

Marcus slept through the night and woke with a headache the next day at sunrise.

His eyelids rolled up over dry eyes and he blinked in confusion several times. Looking about, the crannog was cold and quiet, frost lining the window sills. The holiday of Imbolc would be coming in another day, he thought. How strange it will seem, here in the quiet mountains of the north with only the howling winds and wolves for company.

And Claerwen. He turned on the pallet and watched her sleeping in her usual place on the floor next to him. He took a handful of her long hair and wrapped it around his fingers, smoothing it, savoring its softness. He smiled slightly, thinking if his knee would stop hurting long enough, he felt well enough at last to make love with her.

He kissed the handful of hair and released it, letting it fall gracefully among the rest of her hair, splayed out around her peaceful face. "Ah, my Claeri," he whispered, "I'm a lucky man to have a woman like you."

He watched her a few more minutes, then grunted softly. His left eyebrow went up slightly and his lower jaw came forward as he decided, "I will take you home again, one day, Claerwen. Somehow, I will find a way." His heavy brows came down as his eyes hardened, and he stared out of a southern window slit.

Marcus wanted to get up to relieve himself and began easing to the edge of the pallet. Carefully, he shuffled his legs over the side, then he suddenly noticed the bandaging had been changed. Confused, he did not remember Claerwen changing it the day before. He leaned forward to examine it. The swelling was down. And the pain was far less.

Raising his eyebrows in surprise, he reached for his crutch and stood. Maybe extra willow bark was in the tea last night, he thought. But then there would not be this headache.

Marcus returned from outside to find Claerwen awake and rekindling the hearth fire.

"How is it?" she asked, smiling, dipping her head towards the knee.

He stopped, confounded. "What did you do? I can't remember."

"I put belladonna in your drink to make you sleep. I think this time it will heal properly." She also explained the results of her examination.

"Why didn't you tell me you were going to drug me?" he snapped. "I've lost enough of my memory already."

"I couldn't risk your life any longer," she responded quietly.

He was stung by her words, and realized she had saved his life again.

Imbolc came and went with no celebration. A week later, Claerwen removed the last bandage from Marcus' knee. The swelling had stayed down and only an ugly scar remained. It would fade in time. She told him, "We need to start exercising this leg now. Can you put weight on it and see if there is pain and if it will hold you?"

He stood, balancing between his crutch and her shoulder,

saying, "It still aches all the time." He let go of her shoulder and stood momentarily with his weight distributed equally between both feet. The left knee was locked straight, the right slightly flexed for balance. Like a child's first step, he smiled, and she was delighted. But suddenly, new pain shot through the knee and it collapsed without warning, toppling Marcus into Claerwen's arms. The crutch slipped and clattered against the wall and they fell together to the cold packed earthen floor. At Midwinter, she would have been able to support him, but he had put weight back on, and he was too heavy for her to catch.

Marcus cursed bitterly as he rolled off Claerwen, his dark hair hanging over his eyes. She could see he was sweating beneath the heavy beard and long hair. Then he abruptly clamped his mouth shut and sat up, staring again at the scars on his wrists. His black eyes glared at them with a loathing that frightened her.

"Shackles," he said quietly, "They were iron shackles, not ropes." He sat staring at them for a long time, thinking, forcing his mind to remember.

"I want to hunt a deer, to have smoked meat, Marcus," Claerwen declared softly that night over supper. "We need a better supply of meat because the game is getting too scarce." Her snares were more often empty now, or stolen by the wolves.

Marcus looked tiredly into the hearth fire. He had not heard her. He had been walking around the crannog for the last two hours, doggedly exercising his knee, trying to strengthen it, in spite of the pain it brought him.

"Marcus?" she called.

He started, shaken out of his thoughts.

"I was concentrating on the shackles. I was hoping it would bring back something else, but I'm just as blank as ever."

"You struggle so hard."

"I must, Claerwen. I have to know what happened to me. I may not remember yet, but my soul does. It's in there," he thumped a fist on his chest, "and I will find it."

She was afraid he was trying too hard, that his efforts would set him back, both mentally and physically. Since the pneumonia had subsided and he had discovered how little he remembered from his ordeal after the ambush, Claerwen watched him become obsessed with regaining his strength and digging into his mind for answers. If he injured himself from over-working the knee, she knew his stubborn nature would make him work harder, increasing the risk of a deeper, more permanent injury.

"Marcus, I need your help," Claerwen disrupted his thoughts. When he finally turned to her, she explained again about the deer hunt.

His lips pressed together as he considered her request. "We have no weapons other than our daggers. How would we kill a deer, even a small one?"

She saw his attention was already drifting and she blurted, "Help me to choose a tree to cut and make into a bow and arrows. You know how. You said you made many of them.

"Have you ever shot? I can shoot, but I can't stalk the animal yet."

"I can stalk it. We will just have to make the bow small enough for me to handle."

"But it must be strong enough to bring a deer down, and then it would probably too taut for you to draw."

"Then we will have to design it so that it will accomplish the purpose, no?"

Claerwen kept Marcus focused on the hunt, discussing ways to shape and carve bows and what materials were easily available. By engaging Marcus in long, detailed discussions, Claerwen discovered she could pry him out of his brooding.

Suddenly exhausted, Marcus began yawning, ending that evening's discussion. He laid down and watched as Claerwen cleaned up and banked the fire. When she came around to arrange her bedding on the floor by his pallet, Marcus reached an arm around her, pulling her into a kiss.

"I thought you were tired," Claerwen teased.

"Not that tired," he grinned, then said, "I have missed

you." He loosened her tunic and pulled on her shirt, running his hands underneath, kissing her neck.

Claerwen unlaced the soutane and slipped it off his shoulders, and rubbed her face in the hair on his chest. When she moved up again to kiss him, he turned over with her, coming off the pallet onto the floor. She locked her arms around him, hugging tightly, enjoying the feel of his weight on her.

But Marcus suddenly grunted. He pinned Claerwen's arms down and pushed himself up. His eyes strained in the darkness, his brows slashed down over them, making them look intensely appalled. He gripped Claerwen's arms until she cringed and cried out, but he would not let go.

"Marcus," she called, trying to break his concentration. "Stop it!" She struggled under him, unable to shake him loose. He was absolutely still, staring into the darkness somewhere above her head. She knew he was trying to pin down another memory and she did not want to disturb him, but his fingers dug into her arms so hard she thought he was going to break the bones.

"Marcus, stop!" she cried again, louder. He still did not hear her. Then she nearly screamed as his grip tightened more, unable to take the pain.

Marcus jerked his head down, and saw that he had bruised Claerwen's skin under each of his fingers. "Damn! What am I doing?" He backed off her and sat up, holding his hands out in the air, afraid to touch her.

"What did you see?" she asked, taking his face in her hands.

He blinked, surprised at how she ignored the pain in her arms. Then he looked down at his bare chest and said, "I was naked. Shackled and naked. Struggling against the shackles. A long time, but I don't know how long." He was shaking, out of tiredness and from the memory. He swallowed hard and studied the pain in her face. "I'm sorry, Claeri. I can't believe I hurt you like that."

His jaw worked up and down, struggling to say more, but not able to find the right words. Finally, he dragged the soutane up and retied it.

Claerwen reached to comfort him, but he jerked back. "No, Claerwen, I don't want to hurt you again!"

She slid her arms around him anyway and held him, her warmth gradually easing the pain of the memory. She coaxed him to lay down and he slowly responded, easing into his blanket on the pallet. She laid down on the edge of the pallet, keeping one arm closely hooked around him, her head resting on his arm.

Marcus knew she was trying to restore his confidence, that she trusted him to touch her. He closed his eyes, but remained awake, still trying to remember more, still afraid he would hurt her again. He felt Claerwen's hand curl into his hair as she fell asleep, and he marveled at the depth of her compassion.

In the morning, they crossed the tarn, heading into the wood to search for the right wood for a bow. Resting at frequent intervals to ease the stress on Marcus' knee, Claerwen continually chattered about the deer hunt. She was afraid to talk about the night before, not wanting him to drift back into his obsession.

"Yew would be good material, but there is none here," Marcus observed. "But I think these birch trees would work very well." He hulked around them, studying. "Unfortunately the wood will not be seasoned; the bow would retain its resiliency much better and longer if it was, but we can't help that. What I haven't figured out is how we'll cut down the tree. Between us we only have three small daggers and they will not fell a tree very well."

"There is flint near the river, over the first ridge. We can make stone tools."

"Do you know how to knap flint?"

"No, but we can figure it out, I think. As long as we can make a sharp edge on a piece of flint and attach it to a handle, we can get our tree. I will make a sledge so I can move the wood and stone that is too heavy for me to carry."

"I can help."

"Your knee isn't ready, Marcus. I will not risk injuring it again."

He looked at her with curiosity, then asked, "Where did

you learn to do all this?"

"From watching you. How you work, how you puzzle things together."

He touched her face, smiling slightly, and said, "Padrig was right, that you have an enormous strength underneath that fragile surface. I'm not surprised. Only proud."

Claerwen hid the urgency she felt about hunting the deer. They were extremely low on food and she had not been able to trap any game for several days. She watched Marcus' continuing struggle to learn the truth about his imprisonment and she hesitated to burden him with her problems. She understood that he had to know what happened to him, even though his obsession and sudden changes in mood frightened her.

Instead of worrying him, she contrived to use expeditions for the flint and wood as ways for Marcus to exercise his knee and prepare for the hunt. She did most of the cutting and carrying, not minding as long as the preparations went forward and his health improved. She also had him accompany her on foraging trips when the weather was mild. Even though it took more than twice as long as normal to complete a chore, she would seek his advice, or company, or help just so he would come along.

It took several tries to knap the flint into a properly shaped piece for an axe, but they finally succeeded between the two of them. Claerwen started the piece, shaping one of the split cobbles she brought back from the scree slope. Then she flaked off a series of chips around the edge, trying to make a blade, but she could not get the shape right. It ended up too thick around the middle and the tapering edges too steep to be effective for cutting.

"I have not done this myself, but I remember an oldtimer from my grandfather's military camp who made tools." Marcus took the piece from her and set it on an old tree stump she was using as a work table. He studied it a good while, then picked up one of the hard stones she used as hammer and chisel and said, "I think he did this." He had her hold the chisel against the flint at nearly right angles and struck the chisel with the hammer rock. A large piece came off, leaving a platform on one end. Then he turned the flint upright with the platform on top and struck it again, splitting it neatly down the middle. He now had two equally sized pieces. Then he had her turn each piece while he chipped flakes around the edges of the cut side. When the edges tapered to a smooth enough line, he tested the sharpness with his thumb.

"This is better than I thought we could do," he said, and he smiled up at Claerwen, the lines at the corners of his black eyes crinkling up.

She grinned back at him, thrilled to see his eyes sparkle. The scattered memories of his imprisonment had left him deeply serious, and she treasured his rare smiles.

Once they discovered efficient ways of preparing the flint, Claerwen decided they could use some other tools along the same line. She had Marcus make several axes of varying sizes. She wanted to save their daggers from wearing down through heavy use and to use the stone tools instead for things like scraping hides and cutting small firewood.

In between tool-making projects, they cut the birch trees for the bow and arrows. Carving and shaping the bow was much simpler than knapping flint and it was ready very quickly. They made piles of arrows and fire hardened the tips on most of them; the rest they fitted with flint arrowheads. Claerwen crossed over the tarn and hiked to the stream to collect a pouch full of fine sand; they used it to smooth the weapons nicely.

"I have been saving feathers to flight the arrows," Claerwen said, pulling out a small bundle full of bird feathers plucked from previous kills. She had also collected stems of old nettles, which provided strong, thin fibers to tie the feathers to the arrows.

"Tomorrow, I will hunt the deer," Claerwen declared as she finished a large bundle of arrows. "This is enough."

"You've been so urgent about doing this. Why?" Marcus asked. "In another week I could probably hunt myself."

She sighed, her face flinching. "We need the food. I didn't say anything because I didn't want you to worry. You have enough to fret over."

"Ah, Claeri. You could have told me." He paused. "It's really that bad?"

"Aye. But, no matter now. I am ready. There's a deer run across the tarn, that goes up along the stream. I'll leave before first light."

"I'm coming with you."

She wanted to tell him to stay, that the hunt would be too hard on his knee. But she did want him to come, for his company, his help. She felt selfish, but she knew he would stubbornly insist on coming anyway. She smiled and ran her finger along his moustache. "I'm glad you want to come."

"Oh, no!" Claerwen cried. She stood at the door of the crannog, holding the lantern out to see.

"What is it?" Marcus limped to her side. "Oh..." More snow had come in the night, heavy enough to spoil the hunt.

"I wanted to get a deer before the next storm," she pouted. "I hope it melts so I can go tonight." She turned back inside to scrounge together the morning meal when she halted and stared at him.

"What's wrong?"

"Look at you!" she grinned broadly, brushing back her long hair tangled about her face. She reached out and took both his hands in hers. "Look at you! You're standing on your own!"

He had walked the few paces to the door, unaided by his crutch or her arm.

"Is this something you've been practicing or did it come of its own?"

He flexed the knee, waiting for pain to cut it, but none came. He weighted it and stepped a few times, and though stiff, it held. "Maybe I can hunt for you."

Claerwen laughed and said, "This is wonderful!" She pinched him playfully on the arm. "There is a good chance you will walk almost normally."

"You think I'll always limp?"

"Guessing? Aye, some, but not badly."

"Can I fight?"

Her stomach twisted. She was not prepared for his question. "I don't know."

Marcus was surprised by her sudden change. He raised an eyebrow and said, "You know there will always be some fighting."

She leaned her face into his chest, slipping her arms around him. "I know. We've been through so much, I wish we could just stay here, alone."

Marcus hugged her, his face solemnly still.

The day stayed cold, keeping the snow from melting. Claerwen was forced to ration the food they had left until they could hunt. By the second morning most of the snow had been blown away. The weather turned cold again and hoarfrost clung thickly on the trees.

"Tracking will be easy," Claerwen remarked. "I want to catch one at the stream, so we don't have to carry it a long way back. Hopefully the weather will stay cold enough to hold the frost and any fresh tracks in it until we have our kill."

Marcus had cut a new walking stick for himself from the birch used for the bow and arrows, replacing his clumsy crutch. He carried extra arrows in one of Claerwen's pouches. "You could track me for a thousand miles." he said, looking back at the wide trail his soutane, cloak, and stumbling walk left.

"Then at least I will always know where you are," she teased with an impish grin.

He grunted and hitched up the pouch on his shoulder. "Maybe we should re-cut this ugly old thing into some decent breeches and a tunic for me, if it will hold together."

Claerwen suddenly halted, signaling Marcus to freeze and be quiet. They were nearing the deer run from the downwind side and she listened for movement along the trail. She moved on, cat-like now, approaching silently and carefully through the wood and light bracken. She could see the stream sparkling beyond the trees' edge. No deer were there and she debated if she should wait there for them or follow the run up to the feeding grounds. She signaled Marcus to come and he stumbled forward as quietly as he could.

"I have to go forward to see if they have been here yet. If not, then we should wait here until they do. Otherwise, I suggest we go on up to where they feed," Claerwen whispered. Marcus nodded, agreeing.

She slipped away into the shadows and came within a few yards of the deer run. No tracks showed in the deep frost between the edge of the trees and the water where the deer liked to drink and roll. She studied the signs for a few moments, no other predators were apparent by sight, sound, or smell.

She appeared before Marcus as quickly and shadowy as she had left, startling him. He could never get used to the stealthy way she had about her, in her boy's clothing, and it unnerved him almost as much as her power did. They decided to wait.

A quarter hour went by, and the first deer sauntered its way down the hill run to the water. It stopped, scenting the air and watched a few moments, then headed toward the stream. Minutes later, two more followed.

Claerwen began creeping forward, bow strung and an arrow pulled from the pouch she had converted into a quiver. Marcus admired her ability to stalk, as graceful as the panther, he could not hear her footfalls. He thought, she must carry enormous strength in that slender, supple body, to move so carefully, so controlled. He wanted to watch her shoot; he knew she could do it. He waited for her to reach her position and he crept forward himself, to try to glimpse her.

Claerwen crouched just inside the cover of the trees, her bow ready, her arrow nocked. Her camouflage was excellent in the shadow-dappled bracken, yet she had a clear sight to the deer. She did not want to kill one of the magnificent, beautiful creatures, but the meat, fat, skin and bones would give her and Marcus many good solid meals, useful tools, supplies and new clothing.

She drew and took careful aim. She held her breath and the deer she wanted froze. Something had caught its attention. An instant later, she loosed her arrow, trying to catch the animal before it ran. The bowstring sang, raking her arm as it flung the arrow true. But in the same instant, the deer leaped in a wide arc and was dashing with its companions back up the deer run, over the hill and into the next dale. The arrow plinked harmlessly into the stream, lodging in the reeds on the opposite bank.

"Damn," she swore to herself as she watched the little clods of slush-mud settle where the deer's hoofprints were.

She stood and stamped her foot in frustration. Marcus limped down through the trees and reached her moments later.

"Well, now we will have to follow them, probably many miles, or find another deer run," Claerwen said, and stalked off to retrieve her arrow. As she walked back, she saw renewed pain creasing Marcus' face. She dropped the arrow and ran to him.

Leaning heavily on his stick, he said, "I lost the deer for you. I slipped and fell because of this damned knee; it gave out again. I spoiled it for you."

"Then I will try again. Please, don't feel bad. If I gave up every time I missed a kill, I never would have learned to hunt. I never shot an arrow before we made these."

"You would have hit it the first time. You are so good, Claeri, you don't even realize how good you are." He leaned over to rub the knee.

"Rest a while," she told him.

"No. I'm ready now."

She saw his stubborn pride in his eyes and her mouth pressed into a smile. "Then, so be it!"

They followed the deer run up and over a short series of hills and came to a hollow with a tiny tree-lined water course draining through its base and a small clearing above on the opposite hill. There, the three deer had come to a stop and had resumed grazing. It was midday by the time they reached the spot. Two of the animals were munching grass in the open, the third was lounging under a nearby oak.

"This is our chance," Claerwen whispered. "I will circle around behind it." She tested the wind with a wet finger. "From that way, and strike from there." She pointed to a group of rocks above and to the right of the oak. Marcus nodded agreement.

"I will stay here. I promise not to move this time."

"Wish me luck?" she signed, kissed his cheek, and slipped off.

To Marcus, it seemed like eons before he could see anything happen. He never saw her movements as she circled round the clearing. Every time he thought he could see her at the rocks, he stared and stared and could not be sure. The air was still and coldly fragile; he wished he had thicker boots. But he held himself rigidly still and waited.

Then, a soft "twang" came from the distance, followed by a "fffffffwmp," and a small, hurtful cry. The grazing deer leapt and raced away. The deer under the tree tried to rise and took a few ragged steps. Another "ffffwmp" slipped through the air, and the animal fell, shook a few times, and died. Claerwen had made her kill.

By the time Marcus stumped his way across the dale, Claerwen had removed her arrows and had bound the animal's legs together. She pulled a long, twigless branch through between its legs, preparing to haul it back to the crannog.

"We have a long way to take this, but it will be worth the effort," she said to Marcus, who watched her with fascination.

"You hunt better than most of the men of Dinas Beris!" he said, his admiration plainly showing.

The animal was not a big one, but it was heavy for Claerwen. She had planned on dragging it back to the tarn, carrying one end of the bough on her shoulder and letting the other end drag. But as she lifted one end with a heave and a grunt, Marcus propped himself solidly on his good leg and heaved up the other end.

"Like you said, it's a long way back. Just go slow and on as even ground as you can find." He took up his stick from where he had slung it in his belt and was ready to go.

They stopped every half mile or so to rest Marcus' knee, which was aching badly. Claerwen wanted him to stop helping to carry the dead animal and save his knee, but he refused to drop it, saying they would be home sooner. The winter day was growing short and they needed to safely string the deer up in a tree before nightfall. He had been watching her tire, her legs shaking under the weight of her load. He shifted the branch further back on his shoulder, trying to take more of the burden from her, using his walking stick to steady himself. He started to sing softly, his deep baritone encouraging Claerwen that he was able to carry the load.

Within a half mile of the tarn, Marcus suddenly stumbled and fell, dropping the kill. The lurch nearly knocked Claerwen down; she was forced to drop her end of the branch. She ran to him; his face was twisted in pain.

"Ah, damn," he groaned. "This knee will just not work."

"It's too soon, Marcus. You must stop and let me carry it the rest of the way in."

"It goes along fine for a while, then it just goes limp. No warning, just limp like an old rag and then the pain comes. Damn, I hate this!"

She stroked his hair out of his face and wanted to hold him, comfort him, but she looked up and saw something that made her heart stop.

"Marcus, do not move. There is a wolf up there behind us." She swung off the bow and quickly strung it, easing out an arrow.

"Don't be foolish! If you only injure him, he won't lay docile like the deer. He will attack for sure!"

"It's too late, he wants the deer."

"Let him have it, he probably has friends out there."

"He is a loner. I've seen him before. Move out of the way. Go! Go!" She drew the bowstring back and shot. The arrow flew straight and hard, catching the wolf in the shoulder. It snarled in pain and intense anger, but was stunned only briefly. In the time it took to recover its senses, she had another arrow ready. Again she shot, this time it found the beast's throat. Blood spurted and stained its chest and the snow it stood over. The wolf screamed but still stood and made to charge. Fear stood out like a crown on Claerwen's face and she shivered, but she reached again for an arrow. Again she fired, but she missed.

"Get your dagger! He's going to charge!" Marcus was shouting. He had both of his knives out, flashing in the sunset light. He swore in frustration because he could not stand; the knee was collapsed under him and he could not straighten it out enough to heave himself onto his feet.

The wolf charged, streaming blood, making one last daring attempt to avenge the damage done to him. Claerwen dodged in the last instant as the dizzy wolf plunged. He missed her. She spun around and nocked a fourth arrow, but could not fire. Marcus had thrown himself, a dagger in each hand, over the wolf and was bearing each down into the animal's neck. The beast squirmed and roared in bloody agony. Its head ripped back and around, trying to slash Marcus with its fangs, and in one last great effort, it rolled over, flinging Marcus with it. It stood unsteadily and tried one more time to charge Claerwen. This time she fired and struck him again. In a few more seconds, the courageous wolf died.

Marcus rolled over and sat up, sweating, the wolf's blood soaking his hands. Claerwen dropped her bow and ran to him. He was stunned and looked at her with pained eyes as she took the two bloody daggers from him. She reached to slip her arms around him, but he suddenly yelled, a long, harsh scream like the war-cry he led his men into battle with.

Claerwen stayed crouched in front of him, staring at his face. His eyes squinted into dark slits; his teeth were barred and gritted. He was remembering something again and she waited, appalled at the horror in his expression.

Gradually, the tension in Marcus' face released and he looked at Claerwen, recognizing her. "They were Saxons. I was singing, to keep myself awake. Bloody, filthy, stinking Saxons. Two of them. In a Roman villa, I think, somewhere. I don't know where..." He drifted off, trying to remember more.

Claerwen washed his hands and arms, then wrapped the cloak he had flung aside around him.

The deer and the wolf provided enough meat for the rest of the winter and into the spring. Claerwen made Marcus new clothes of the skins and a handsome mantle from the wolf's fur. She also made new leggings of the fur, to top his boots.

"By the light, you look fine, my Prince Marcus!" she declared when he tried it on all together. She made him go outside in the bright, morning sunshine so she could see the full effect. She admired how well he had recovered his trim muscularity. His black hair and beard were set off handsomely against the mottled black, white and greys of the wolfskin mantle. The deerskin breeches fit him closely to the legs, which had filled out and were well-formed again.

"If only I still had my sword. I feel naked without it in spite of these fine things you made me." He walked slowly to the shore of the tarn, limply slightly. Claerwen followed him and watched as he gazed into the distance toward the south.

"You want to go home, don't you?" she asked, curling her hands around his arm. "I have seen you watching, into the south, so many times."

"Aye, Claeri, 'tis true. I want to go as soon as the roads are dry enough. We won't be safe here much longer, either. The Picts will find us eventually; they won't let us stay." He looked into her face and said, "I made a vow to you, at Imbolc, while you were asleep. That I would find a way to take you home. I am going to find that way, soon. But I need your help, Claerwen, before we can go."

"My help?"

"Aye. I have to know the rest of what happened to me, between the ambush and when you found me here. I must know."

"But you may never remember. How can I help?"

"Fire in the head."

She frowned up at him, not understanding.

"Through the fire, maybe we can see what happened."

"But I don't control it, Marcus. If the gods do not want to reveal something, they will not show it. The power may not even come into me if I try."

"I know. And I know how much it takes out of you every time and I know I'm not being fair to you. But I need to learn the truth. Please, will you try, for me?"

"Are you sure you really want to know?"

"I must know. I am a spy. I rely completely on my memory for information, facts, faces, political and military maneuvers, all things that can affect the status of what I do. If I can't remember someone's face and I run into that person, it could mean my death. Or someone else's death. I *have* to know."

Claerwen sighed, and pondered his request, pacing along the shore. She was afraid. Afraid to know, afraid not to know, afraid to ask the gods. She turned back to him, studying his face.

"Please, Claerwen. I am afraid, too. The pieces that I do remember trigger such strange reactions that I can't trust myself. I haven't been able to make love with you because I'm afraid I'll hurt you again. I miss you, Claeri, I want to be with you again. I want to be able to touch you and not be afraid. I've got to free myself somehow."

She took his hands and held them to her lips as she gazed into his eyes. She wished it was so easy, to merely look into the fire. But she understood his desperation, and she missed him just as much. Lightly, she lightly kissed his fingers, one by one. Then she whispered, "I treasure you, Marcus ap Iorwerth, more than I ever knew it was possible to love someone. I will try for you."

CHAPTER 26

**The Highlands of Alban
Spring, 469 A.D.**

Claerwen built a new fire, outside the crannog. She was not sure what else to do. She remembered Myrddin's words, telling her it was impossible to invoke the gods, that they only come of their own will. But the place of power in Avebury's stone circle had brought on a clear and stunning vision. She hoped that she could create a place of power on the crannog's island.

Instinct told Claerwen to build the new fire, large and powerful, on the earth, outside in the open air. She watched the flames shoot up, wondering what to do next.

Like a sudden draught of warm air, Claerwen felt the gods stir within her. The power sprang, smothering her mind and soul, visibly moving her as if someone had shoved her slightly. Her eyes blinked slowly a few times, the glow of the power filling them. Then they held steady, gazing without seeing the fire.

Water, she suddenly knew she needed water. Her head turned slowly to the right and she stared at the tarn, its cold water rippling before the colder night air. A few moments later, her head turned back to the fire, her hands reaching for the laces of her tunic.

Marcus watched from the crannog's wall, leaning on a

ragged tree. He had hoped Claerwen would find a vision in the fire, and he expected to experience the same eerie feeling he always got when he saw it take her over, but he was utterly stunned by her actions.

He saw Claerwen slip off her clothing until she stood completely naked in the cold evening air. The dusk was fading quickly, and she turned away from the fire, walking toward the shore of the tarn. Her figure was dimly silhouetted by the dying twilight, and the bonfire glared harshly into Marcus' eyes so he could hardly see her. He stared, his mouth dropping open in astonishment as he watched Claerwen wade into the tarn, crouch down to immerse herself, then rise again, emerging with water streaming. He moved forward from the tree almost involuntarily, so stunned that he thought he might be dreaming.

Claerwen went to the fire, slowly lifting her arms, palms upward. Her wet hair hung all around her, clinging to her body, reaching nearly to her knees. Droplets ran down her legs. Her arms went higher, as if to pluck stars from the sky. She began a seemingly incoherent chant, and slowly paced around the fire, facing it.

She circled three times, so slowly that Marcus thought something had gone wrong. Her face was glazed over, and her skin was slightly reddened from the heat of the blaze. As her hair began to dry, strands of it floated around her, wafting on the warm air. She continued to chant softly, then as she completed the third circle, she stopped and went silent.

Abruptly, she crumpled and fell unconscious onto the wet turf.

"Claerwen!" Marcus yelled and sprinted to her. The gods were gone, leaving her cold and limp. He scooped her up and carried her inside, nestling her onto his pallet, tucking covers around her. He ran outside again to kick sand over the fire, but was astonished to find it had already gone out by itself. He muttered a curse, then grabbed Claerwen's clothing and trotted back inside.

He approached Claerwen silently, wishing now he had not

asked her to seek a vision. His mouth pressed into a tight line as he sat on the floor next to the pallet and smoothed tangled, damp hair from her face. Her skin felt unnaturally cold. He spread more covers over her, added peat to the fire, then stripped and slowly eased himself onto the pallet, afraid to disturb her rest. Curling himself tightly around her, the heat from his body gradually gave her warmth.

Claerwen dreamed fitfully in a heavy sleep, as if drugged with belladonna. She knew she was dreaming, discordant pieces leftover from the vision she had sought. None of them made sense. She tried to follow, even tried to rearrange them in her mind, but they slipped away like water drops on grease, squeezing themselves into oozing shapes to fall helplessly away from beneath her eyelids.

A voice called, rough and disturbing. At first, Claerwen thought it was part of the dreams, then realized it was separate and she was coming fully awake. She listened, straining, unable to claw her way out of sleep.

The voice screamed, loud and harsh, propelling her sideways with its force, and her eyes jerked open. She found herself clinging to the edge of the pallet, naked and clutching the edge of a blanket, staring at Marcus. He was naked as well, sprawled off the other edge of the pallet, his hands in fists over his head, in the midst of a long, hideous yell. He abruptly came awake and sat up, staring again at the scars on his wrists.

"Lightning," Claerwen said softly. She watched Marcus' eyebrows flinch.

He was panting, but did not look up.

"Water," she whispered.

He still did not move.

"The Iron Hawk."

Marcus turned his head so sharply that his long hair swirled around and slapped against his face.

"What were you dreaming?" she asked. She reached for the lantern and lit it with a twig from the hearth.

He was sweating, breathing hard, and taking a long time

to sort out his mind.

Claerwen repeated the words, the comfort in her voice calming Marcus, "Lightning. Water. The Iron Hawk."

He winced in bewilderment. Finally, he licked his lips and said, "I was in an abandoned Roman villa, on a high hill, my arms shackled over my head, an iron ring around my neck, more shackles on my legs. I was naked. They beat me, over and over and over, breaking off the arrow shaft that still stuck out of my knee. There were two of them, big, ugly Saxons. A third man spoke British; he was dressed in black, giving them orders. I did anything to stay awake, sing, recite bard songs, think of you." His brows came down, heavily shadowing his eyes. "What did you say before?"

"Lightning."

"A thunderstorm. Aye, a thunderstorm, with lightning." He looked down at the burn marks in his groin. "These are from the shackles. Somehow...somehow the Saxons were driven away, the other man as well. I got loose and lightning struck the villa. It went through one of the irons...it was close enough that it burned me." He ejected a sharp breath and stared again at Claerwen. "You saw that in the vision?"

"I only saw images. The first one was lightning. Then water."

"Water...a river? Or the tarn here? I don't understand."

"It felt big."

He reached for a waterskin and drank a long swallow to clear the dryness from his mouth. He poured some into his palm and smeared it with his thumb, then shook the remainder off. "Water. It was the sea. The villa was on the Saxon shore. There was a boat, somehow I was on the boat; but I was so bloody sick and hurt. I wanted them to stop at Dun Breatann, but they weren't going there. I think I was unconscious most of the time. I still don't remember landing, or how I got here from the sea."

Claerwen said, "The sea is just beyond the ridge to the northwest. You must have crossed from there somehow to reach the crannog. I went over that way, only once, when I went out alone. We've only gone to the southeast side to find food and hunt, because it's easier. The sea's not far, just difficult to get to."

Claerwen stopped, incredulous at the ordeal he had been through. "By the gods, Marcus, what you have survived!" Then she remembered the third image. "Was the man in black the Iron Hawk?"

Marcus had calmed, his face full of his normal good sense again. He leaned back against the wall, pulling Claerwen with him.

She settled comfortably in his arms and sensed he was finally at peace with himself, the brooding done. But she turned in his arms, asking again about the man in black.

Marcus shook his head slightly and leveled his eyes with hers. "No. He was Vortigern."

Claerwen caught her breath in her throat. "The High King?"

"He tried to make me tell him what I knew about Ambrosius, about what I was doing. He knew who I was."

"You were betrayed!"

"Aye, by Rhun, I'm certain. I told Vortigern nothing. I didn't even give him the satisfaction of crying out when they beat me."

"But why did I see the Iron Hawk? You're sure it was Vortigern?"

"Aye, I've seen him before."

"Could Vortigern have been the Iron Hawk?"

Marcus laughed. "Hardly."

"How do you know?"

"Claeri, remember when I spooked Vortigern in the druid's camp? When I told him the Iron Hawk would slit his throat in the night if he didn't leave us alone? He wouldn't react like he did if he was the Iron Hawk. No, *Y Gwalch Haearn* is someone else. And you have seen Vortigern is dead and the Iron Hawk is alive. It could be he was the one who freed me."

"Has he saved your life so that I would follow you? So that he can come again, looking for the treasure, then finally kill both of us?" She still did not mention her speculation that Owein was the Iron Hawk.

Marcus raised Claerwen's face, holding her chin with his big fingers. "Claerwen, don't hold such hatred inside. You've always had such a generous nature, don't lose it to hatred."

"Are you defending him? How can you do that?"

"I'm not defending anybody. I'm only saying that hatred is the kind of thing that will chew you up and spit you out, it can turn a person bitter in a very short time. I don't want that to happen to you, Claeri. I was that way about Drakar for a long time, and it didn't help."

"Even after what they did to you, which was worse than what the Iron Hawk did to my cousin and me, you don't hate them?"

"I hate their cruelty. If the Saxons would settle and live peaceably, I would have few qualms to accept them. But I hate the way they force themselves in, greedy for land, raping and killing our people because of their prejudices against us. I hate the fear our people are put under, never feeling safe in our own land."

Claerwen countered, "The Iron Hawk creates a fear as great as the Saxons. And he is greedy for this treasure, whatever it is. Greedy enough to kill."

Marcus' eyes squinted, his lips in a hard line. "You cannot judge him unless you know why his actions are so unpredictable. In time, I believe it will become more clear. But for now, I think you should forget about the Iron Hawk, he's not worth the anguish he causes you."

Claerwen considered his remarks, but Marcus could see she was not changing her mind. Her face was set in a stony glare.

Marcus changed the direction of his talk. "How did I have the dream, when you had the vision?"

Claerwen rubbed her eyes, then said, "You always had the memories inside you. It took those images from the god to trigger them, to pull them out of you. Like when you remembered singing to keep yourself awake; that happened just after you were singing as we brought the deer in. Or you first remembered being naked after I pulled the soutane from you. In time, maybe you will remember more, maybe not."

Marcus grunted softly. "I think we know enough now to begin planning how to get Dinas Beris back. Perhaps I'll learn who saved my life on the way."

"Are you thinking of fighting for Dinas Beris all alone?"

He grinned at her. "We will have to do a little spying first, to find out what the situation is. Aye, I will fight, but with stealth, not muscle."

Claerwen deeply admired his unwavering spirit. She turned in his arms again to face him directly. Slowly, she smiled and said, "You said you made a vow to me, that you would take me home. I will make a vow to you now, my Marcus, that I will help you fight to take back Dinas Beris."

She hooked her arms around his neck and pulled herself up to kiss him, tentatively gentle at first, then growing in tenacity. His hands caressed her skin, warm and soft as she laid on him, comfortably curved to his body. Together, they rolled over, and her long, tawny hair spread out like a luxurious blanket. He came into her without any more fear and she twined herself around him, enjoying the feel of his skin and his weight on her. They loved each other completely, slowly and carefully to heal the time they had lost.

Afterward, tired and content, they lay with their legs locked together. Marcus slowly stroked one hand along her belly, up between her breasts and back down, over and over.

"I want to apologize, Claerwen," he said, his eyes calmly solemn.

Her eyes came up, full of surprise. "For what?"

"For the way I treated you these last few months. For ignoring you, for my sour temper, for hurting you."

Claerwen opened her mouth to interrupt him, but he pressed a finger to her lips. He continued, "You have saved my life, Claeri, more than once. You followed me across the length of Britain because you still believed in me, when no one else did. What you have been through for me, it still astonishes me. You have killed men to save my life without thinking of your own. You've lost your home, your family, and nearly died trying to bear my child. You've worked day and night to see that I was strong and healthy, warm and safe; you even made me new clothes. You did all that, working all those long days until your legs were tired and shook so much you could hardly stand any longer. And I never had the courtesy to thank you." He looked down and shook his head at himself, then gazed into her eyes again, "You had no right to treat me with such kindness."

She pushed his hair back out of his eyes and smiled up at him. She said, "You are my joy, Marcus, nothing will ever change that. After what you have endured, how could I ever think to blame you for anything?" She felt like an anvil had been lifted from her soul.

"I do cherish you, my Claeri," he whispered.

CHAPTER 27

Mid-Wales
Summer, 469 A.D.

"This is what makes your joints feel so much better." Padrig held up a twig with several leaves on it. "I will grind it up with some other things, a little water, then put it on your joints. It's just like Claerwen's. I taught her a lot, but she started experimenting and discovered a few things herself."

"She was always so kind, so gentle," the miller's grandmother remarked. Padrig spent a lot of time with her now. Since he had arrived nearly a year ago, he had settled in, proffering his healing talents and helping with some simple gardening.

Padrig sighed sadly. The old woman looked at him, empathy in her tired eyes. "I did not mean to remind you of sad times."

"Ah, 'tis no matter. There is an old fool I am, for even hoping." He patted her wrinkled and veiny hands. "I will be back again tomorrow, as usual."

He rose from the bench in front of the miller's house and headed down the path that skirted the village's meadow. Padrig walked more slowly than he used to, a little more tired every day. He enjoyed the company of the miller and his family and decided that this was going to be the place he died, since they had accepted him like family and there was no one else left from his own people.

In the summer, he walked every morning, down to the river and back, to keep his joints loose. The weather was often warm and dry once the sun rose enough to burn off the nightly mist. Bluebells and mallow bloomed, swaying easily in a light breeze, the grass tickling the bright air. Once away from the mill, only the riffling of the trees' leaves and the river water gurgling through its rocky bed could be heard.

He thought about old times and the journey his lifetime had taken. He wondered what had happened to all the years in between. He was lonely, but content enough.

Two men appeared across the meadow, emerging from the forest. Padrig stopped and watched from the trees along the river path. He thought they were hunters because of their bows and simple clothing.

"Oh, Lleu, I hope it's not trouble," he said out loud to himself, seeing how raggedly the men were dressed. Poor people who had been scattered by the Saxons often turned to thievery, and the miller's settlement was not easily defendable. The men walked slowly, then stopped. One pointed toward the settlement and they talked for a few moments. Then they began moving again, heading across the meadow straight in Padrig's direction.

Padrig was surprised that they did not head for the settlement. He stepped back into the heavy brush, watching, trying to decide if he should stay and continue to watch, or go back and warn the villagers of strangers. Then he noticed that these men carried a lot of extra gear packed on their backs, more gear than hunters or thieves would carry. Fascinated, he stayed to observe what they would do.

They continued to approach, heading for the river path. Padrig hid among the trees as they went by. They crossed the path and went straight to the river, stopping to refill a pair of waterskins. He saw the shorter man had straggly dark hair and walked with the grace of a cat, the taller one was grey-haired and grey-bearded, and walked with a slight limp.

Then the shorter man took off his cap.

"It can't be," Padrig said out loud, coming out of the trees. "I can't believe it. It must be a ghost."

He shouted at them, waving, trying to run. His voice could still carry well even if his legs were slow. They turned towards the shout and saw him coming towards them.

"Claerwen! Oh, Claerwen! Is it really you?" He waved madly as he stumbled across the wildflowery turf.

"It's Padrig!" she yelled, running to hug her old friend. Tears ran down his face.

"I never thought to see you again," he wept. "I just can't believe you came back!" He held her at arm's length, looking into her lovely face, then hugged her again. "By the gods, you look fine, so fine! Tell me what happened, where you have been."

Then he took the cap from her hand and saw the dark hair was sewn and glued inside it, her own was braided tightly around her head. He stared at it, astonished at first, then startled to chuckle, knowing how she had learned to make the disguise.

Padrig looked up and opened his mouth to tease Claerwen, and saw the broad grin and mischief in her eyes. Then he realized he had ignored the other stranger.

Padrig turned toward the river, his smile fading. He watched the man as he knelt, bruskly washing his face in the water. The man straightened, drying his beard and the hair around his face, then reached to take off his cap. Padrig stared, unbelieving. He thought he was going to faint as he watched Marcus' black hair shake loose from the cap, his black eyes squinting with mirth in the sunlight.

"Marcus ap Iorwerth..." Padrig whispered. He blinked several times as Marcus approached from the river. "By all the gods my people swear by...look at you, boy!" Padrig was so stunned he went to touch Marcus' shoulder-length hair and heavy beard before he could say more.

"Unbelievable," he finally said, gripping Marcus' shoulders and roughly shaking him. "Look at you, you son of an ugly old goat! Look at all that hair!" Padrig laughed with joy.

Marcus draped an arm around Claerwen's shoulders and grinned, saying, "I told you he'd tease me about my hair. He always does when I come back from somewhere." He reached his other hand out and ruffled the sparse hair on Padrig's head.

"When she left to find you I begged her not to go. I told her you were dead and she would die, too. I was so wrong, so utterly wrong. I should have trusted her judgement; no one knows you better than she does."

They walked slowly to the settlement, Padrig eagerly pumping Marcus and Claerwen on what had happened. That evening, the miller and his family celebrated Claerwen's return with laughter and music and as much mead as they could spare. None of them had ever thought to see her again, certainly never with her husband. This time, tears of joy overflowed instead of tears of sorrow.

Marcus and Claerwen camped in the meadow, not wanting to intrude on the miller's generosity. Rest was welcome after the long trek from the northern highlands.

Claerwen lay on her bedroll, her head resting in Marcus' lap as she watched the night sky. "I still enjoy sleeping in an open summer meadow," she said dreamily.

Marcus stirred their campfire with a long stick, stoking it more for light than heat. He tossed the stick aside and curled over to kiss her, his hands cupped around her face. "You are a woman of the earth," he said. They were quiet for a while, enjoying the peaceful night.

"You're thinking about what we should do next, aren't you?" she asked him. "I always know, when you are so quiet." She sat up to stir the fire again.

"Aye, we have to figure out what this treasure is; that will tell us why all those men want it. We have to know before we can go any further. Besides letting Padrig know we were all right, I wanted to talk to him, to see if somewhere deep in his wisdom he would have an idea what the treasure is, or at least discover a lead."

As Marcus spoke, Padrig came out of the house he shared with the miller and sat on the bench in front. Seeing him, Marcus whistled and waved, inviting him to come talk.

"I thought you'd be asleep by now," Padrig teased as he came out in the meadow.

"No, we were just talking about the treasure that Drakar and Rhun have been searching for all these years."

"You still don't know what it is?"

"No. But once we understand what it is, then we'll know why they want it so badly. I want to go into Conwy next, to learn how our status is."

Padrig nodded. "Cunedda's fort. Official or unofficial?"

"Unofficial."

Padrig snorted. "You've got her spying now, too, I suppose?" Then he frowned at Marcus. "You're going to try to take the fort back aren't you?"

Marcus and Claerwen looked at each other and grinned.

"Just the two of you?"

They grinned again.

"Of all the audacity! You're mad, absolutely mad. You'll be killed. Do you have any idea what is there? How many men?"

"Not yet, but we can find that out soon enough."

Padrig shook his head. "I still say you're mad."

"We have a few ideas." Marcus winked. "But we have to know what they're all looking for. Then we should be able to figure out who is behind all of it."

"So you can go after him. And they still think it's something Claerwen has?"

"Aye."

"Well, what does she have?"

"Nothing!" She held up her hands in exasperation. "All I own, all I have ever owned is right here, except what we left in the fort when we fled."

"And they wouldn't have kept looking for her so long if they had found it," Marcus said.

"You never hid anything, right?" Padrig asked.

"No, I have nothing to hide. See, this is all I have." She indicated the clothing she wore. "And this pouch with food, this pouch with medicines and plants to be made into medicines, this pouch with some extra clothing, and this pouch which is just a spare. There's nothing in it. The only jewelry I have is my wedding ring. I hope they don't want that because they won't get it without a big fight."

Marcus laughed at her. "I thought they wanted my family ring, perhaps to use it against me. But it never could have been on her homestead in Strathclyde. They were already searching there, just when I met her."

"And you were wearing it that night," she said softly, remembering. "I just don't know what it could be." She picked up one of her pouches and looked in it, feeling it was useless to look again. "It's just clothing, not much at that. A comb. The old trinkets and things from my mother she used to wear in her hair."

"May I?" Marcus asked. He was looking at the small pouch with her mother's things in it. She shrugged and gave it to him. He opened it and emptied the contents onto his bedroll.

"What is this?" he asked. He held a thick, round ceramic band to the light of the fire. It looked old and crude, some patterns were etched in the surface.

"I think it's an arm ring. It's so ugly I thought about throwing it away, but it's the only thing I have to remind me of my father, because he gave it to my mother."

Marcus turned the ring over and over, examining it in the firelight. "It almost looks too big for an arm ring. Was your father husky?"

"No, not really. I don't know where he got it from."

"Hmmm," he mused. He tried it on one of own arms. It was not tight enough to stay on above his elbow even though his arms were thick and well-muscled. He held it to the light again and was scratching at a place on the inside.

"There's no inscription, but there's a chip out of it here. See?"

"You couldn't possibly think that ugly old thing is the treasure. It's worthless."

"Look here, under the chipped place. It's shiny."

Padrig and Claerwen leaned forward to watch.

"You're right." Claerwen took it from him. "There's a tiny crack running from it, too."

"I think the ceramic is just a protective coating for something else. Claeri, I know this is sentimental to you, but I think we should break the ceramic."

She handed it back to him and said, "Break it."

He took a flat rock from the edge of the campfire and set it in front of him, then found a small stone with a pointed edge on one end. Gently, he tapped on the ceramic surface along the crack.

"Look...it's gold!" Claerwen exclaimed as a piece fell away. He kept working around the ring, tapping and breaking.

"Can you find a cloth to put under this so I don't scratch the metal? And a bowl of water to wash it off?" Marcus requested. He worked intently, his eyes aching in the dim light.

"Here." Claerwen laid a piece of doeskin on the flat rock. "I'll put more wood on the fire, for light."

Marcus had worked nearly all the way around, and the exposed gold was heavy and rich, crafted in a tightly twisted ridge pattern.

"This part is different. It's heavier."

"I have a tool in the house that would help." Padrig got up to fetch it.

"Padrig," Marcus called quietly, looking up. "Don't tell anyone. If this is what I think it might be, they cannot know. I don't want anyone to be endangered because of us."

Padrig nodded and shuffled off to the house, returning shortly. He handed Marcus a short bone stick he used in his medicine making.

The last section took longer than the rest. Marcus patiently picked and poked until the last ceramic crumbled away. Then he dunked it in the water and washed it gently.

"There's a lot of dusty residue in the grooves. There, that's better." He rubbed the ring dry, then held it out to the light again.

"By the gods..." he began, staring at it.

"It's a torque," Claerwen exclaimed in a hushed voice.

"It's magnificent." Marcus turned it in the light. "It must have thirty jewels in it. Look, rubies, diamonds." He weighed it in his hand. "It's pure gold, not gold plate or gold leaf. This is worth a fortune."

Padrig was staring at the torque, his eyes full of awe, then said, "Not only that. Look on the inside, for the craftsman's mark and tell me what you find."

Marcus found a few obscure marks, like letters, and read them aloud.

Padrig explained, "The last one stands for 'by the hand of.' That's what all craftsmen sign their work with, and their initials before. Those initials are from Brutus' smith. This torque is part of the ancient symbols that Brutus, the first High King of Britain, had made when he established the kingship. Macsen Wledig, the High King at the end of the Roman occupation, hid everything but the crown, for safekeeping, when he saw the turmoil Britain would be in if he lost power. They were considered destroyed after he died, and became known as the 'lost treasure of Macsen Wledig.'"

Marcus and Claerwen stared at Padrig, speechless. Then Marcus looked back at the beautiful thing laying across his big hands, blinking in disbelief. "Macsen's treasure gives the bearer the power of the High Kingship," he mumbled.

Padrig's face showed panic as he stared at Claerwen. "There was a torque, a grail, a spear head, a sword, and a crown. How, in the gods' names, did you get this?"

"It was always there, covered like it was. I don't know how, or when, my father got it."

"Who was your father?" Marcus asked.

"His name was Rhodri ap Gwallter. He was a minor nobleman, but he was like you, never making much of his title.

We lived in the hills along the Afon Dyfrdwy until the Irish raid. He had always said our ancestors had lived in that same valley since the beginning of time." Claerwen stopped. "The Irish...Ifan and Gerallt. They must have been looking for that torque even then. They killed my family, trying to find that, to take the High Kingship."

"I always thought it was an odd place for the Irish to raid, so far inland. They usually stay by the coastline. Your father must have encased it in the ceramic, to protect it. He must have known Macsen."

"And I almost threw it away. I've been carrying this around for years."

She suddenly caught her breath and stared at the torque. "I had a vision of this," she whispered and looked up at Padrig. "When we fled Dinas Beris, I saw a beautiful sword, jeweled the same way. To one side was this torque...and a grail, on the other side, a spearhead, and a crown...the things you said."

"I saw how you stared at that bag of trinkets when we left, Claerwen. Something compelled you to take it with you, didn't it?"

"What does it mean?" Marcus asked, touching her arm when she did not answer Padrig.

Her eyes swept across to him. "It has to do with the succession of High Kings, from Ambrosius to..." She halted, unable to find the name.

"To Myrddin?"

"No." She struggled to remember, but then realized the name had not been revealed yet.

Marcus watched her eyes, darting back and forth under her arched-down brows as if she was searching for the name in the darkness. Drawn by his curiosity, he turned her towards him. "When I was in Ynys Môn, the druids mentioned 'the great bear' would come. I didn't know what they meant, but they said it the same way you once spoke of a great future king."

Claerwen held still for a long time, and Marcus thought she had not heard him. Then slowly, her head raised a little, and she spoke, her voice light and misty, "...to Arthur." Her eyes flickered briefly and she came alert again.

Marcus and Padrig stared at her, knowing they had heard something they could never repeat to anyone else.

Chills ran over Marcus' skin.

Claerwen spoke slowly, "It belongs to Aurelius Ambrosius, now. We must return it to him."

"I wonder where the rest of the treasure is," Marcus thought aloud.

"It must be hidden, somewhere. Do you think it could be in the valley where my family lived?"

"I doubt it," Marcus said. "If it was there, Ifan and Gerallt would have found it after they killed or ran everyone off the land. It seems they've only been searching for one piece, not a whole set. Maybe they don't even know there was more than the torque, or if they do, they believe it is lost. They couldn't have any other treasure; they would have claimed the high kingship a long time ago."

"That makes sense," said Claerwen.

She watched him study the beautiful torque. He ran his fingertips over the ridges and around the gems, his mind lost in thought. She took a breath to speak, but in the same instant he sharply turned his face to her, frowning.

"Don't even say it, Claeri," he chided her.

"You were thinking it," she said very low.

"No." He gazed into the fire.

"Yes, you were." She smiled. "So was I...just for fun."

He looked back at her, his black eyes serious. Then he saw she was teasing him and he relaxed, grinning again, and shaking his head a little.

"Well, it was fun, even if it was just for a moment," he said, and he leaned over to kiss her cheek. "Queen Claerwen."

"High King Marcus ap Iorwerth."

Padrig rolled his eyes.

Marcus became serious again. "We have to hide this again for a while, until there is time to take it to Ambrosius. We cannot take it to Dinas Beris."

Claerwen agreed. "This will be good for Ambrosius. It will stabilize his hold on the throne. Myrddin Emrys will be pleased."

"It will also win us some support for the future," Marcus continued.

"Should we take it to Ambrosius first, and see if he would help us win Dinas Beris?"

"No," Marcus replied.

"No?" Padrig was surprised. "That would be logical to me. Who better to enlist than the High King himself?"

"We cannot be so presumptuous. Ambrosius has more than enough problems with taking over the mess Vortigern made. He doesn't need to be pressured into worrying about a little fort like Dinas Beris. That is my responsibility. I lost it, I will get it back."

"*We* will get it back," Claerwen vowed.

He took her hand in his and squeezed it.

"Where shall we hide this thing?" he asked.

"I have a place," Padrig suggested. "Down by the river, there is a standing stone hidden in deep brush. I found it by accident a while back. We can bury this at the foot of the stone. I walk out there everyday, so I can keep an eye on it until you get back."

Marcus nodded approval. "I will do it now. Can you find the place in the dark?"

"Aye."

"Good. Claeri, stay here and keep watch, in case anyone should still be awake and come outside. We'll be back shortly."

Chapter 28

**Conwy, Gwynedd, North Wales
Summer, 469 A.D.**

"How do we get in?" Claerwen whispered.

She and Marcus watched from a screen of birches. Below them, mud flats fanned out into a delta. Near the end of the delta rose a huge rock, topped by a small fortress. The moon was nearly full and setting; it appeared and disappeared as clouds drifted across it from the sea. Torches lit the fortress' ramparts and the front gates. It looked cold and unfriendly in spite of the summer night's warmth and humidity.

"Cunedda holds a weekly market day that begins at sunrise this morning. There should be a lot of wagons heading into the gates. We can hide in one."

"We can't just walk in, like we're going to market to trade for something?"

Marcus shook his head. "Until we get some gear and horses, and a lot of information, I do not want any chance to be recognized. Not as ourselves, as traders, or any other disguise. I have no sense of how Cunedda is disposed towards me now, whether he thinks I'm dead or not. We have to learn anything we can before we make our next move. Cunedda might even have backed Rhun in taking Dinas Beris."

"Are you thinking that's why he never sent the

mercenaries he promised you against Drakar?"

"Aye, and that he lied to Taran when he sent his apology." Marcus growled softly.

First light glowed in the east through a gap in the clouds.

"It is time." Marcus slipped down between the trees, carefully picking his way so he did not disturb rocks. Claerwen followed, light on her cat-like feet. He still marveled at how quietly she could move. They went down the slope and hid along the road leading into Conwy, Cunedda's fortress.

"Once we get inside, just follow me," Marcus whispered. "I know my way around well enough, I know where we can hide. Just keep that hood pulled down low, so they can't see your face."

"I can't believe we're going to do this."

"Remember, if we get caught, you're supposed to be my little brother getting into mischief and I'm supposed to be chasing after you. Let me do the talking."

They waited a while longer, and the first marketers began to arrive. Most were driving small, lightweight, two-wheeled carts. As it got lighter and lighter, Marcus fidgeted with the waiting.

"Look," he whispered suddenly and pointed up the road away from the fortress. "There's our chance. Do exactly what I do. Come." He took off trotting through the brush that lined the road, crouching low to stay hidden. Claerwen followed.

A hay wagon was stalled in a rut in the road, and the driver was pushing on the stuck wheel and flicking a long rod at his mule to pull while he pushed. The mule strained, braying, then pulled the wagon free. The mule continued forward and the driver leaped back up into his seat. Marcus waited until the man was fully concentrating on his driving, then dashed out behind the wagon, pulling Claerwen with him. They caught up and gingerly climbed into the back, tunneling under the hay.

"Why hay?" Claerwen whispered tightly in Marcus' ear, scratching her nose.

"He has to go off to the side of the market, not into the center. It will be easier to get out unseen. He may also go to the stables instead of the market. That would be even better."

The wagon wrenched harshly along the rutted road and Claerwen wondered if they would get bounced out of the wagon along with the hay. The load shifted constantly and they continuously rearranged it over themselves. They were laying flat on their bellies at first, then Marcus rolled over to hold Claerwen close to him.

"Less to keep covered," he whispered, then grinned at her.

The wagon began to slow as it neared the gates and his expression went serious again.

Then it stopped. A guard asked the driver his name and business and was given a reply. The wagon passed through the gates.

The wagon rattled slowly around the perimeter of the fortress, finally stopping inside a building. The stable. Voices echoed inside, the driver and a stable hand, probably two customers. They walked back and forth by the wagon, talking, negotiating.

Marcus and Claerwen held perfectly still until they were stiff. Finally the voices drifted away. The driver went to get something to eat in the great hall; the other customers got what they came for and left. Only the stable hand remained.

Marcus eased up an inch or two until a gap formed in the hay so he could see. No one was directly behind the wagon. He lifted a little more, turning his head one way, then the other. The corner where the wagon had been left was dark. He could hear the mule rustling; it had been unhitched and was munching from a feed bag.

The stable hand had gone to the front of the building and was driving a bellows for a smith, who was busy pounding on a horseshoe. Marcus pushed up more, enough to see all around and above. There was no way out behind them in the dark corner, only forward past the smithy. Then he looked up into the rafters and saw a window high up for ventilation. It was open.

"Come," he whispered again. Claerwen raised herself up and watched to where he pointed. Her eyes widened when she understood what he wanted her to do. He jumped down from the wagon and pulled her after him, then darted to a row of stalls that ended in the dark corner. He started climbing up the slats, reaching for the edge of a loft that was built across the top of the stalls. He was barely able to reach it, but caught hold and pushed off with his feet hard enough to nearly get his whole chest over the edge of the loft.

He started slipping.

Claerwen scrambled up the slats underneath him, caught hold of one of his boots and pushed, giving him enough leverage to hoist himself on up. He knelt and reached down to Claerwen. She perched on the top slat and locked arms with him, then jumped as he hauled her up to him.

They tiptoed across the loft, trying to keep from squeaking the planks. Hidden by the darkness, Marcus surveyed the rafters above. They led directly to the window, but the lowest beam was too high to reach. He looked around and found nothing helpful, then went back to the edge of the loft. Below, a braided rope hung on a nail between two stalls. He watched the smith and the stable hand; they were still well-engrossed in their work. Silently, he laid down and reached over the edge. He could just reach the rope with his fingertips. Stretching, he got one finger around it and pulled it up.

He went back to the rafters, tying a foot hold in one end of the rope and tossing the other end over the lowest beam. He made a loop and threaded the rope through it, then pulled it up tight to the beam. The foot hold was about waist high, high enough for them to climb up into the rafters.

Claerwen went first, and easily got onto the beam. Marcus put his foot into the sling and had one hand on the beam when voices came drifting closer.

The stable hand was coming back towards the stalls.

Claerwen laid down on the beam, hugging it to her belly. She reached down to Marcus, trying to steady him as he swung on the rope.

The stable boy began to unload the hay from the wagon,

pitching it up to the loft. Marcus and Claerwen were far enough back that they could not be seen, but if the boy came up to arrange the hay, they would be discovered.

The rope's swinging slowed and Marcus watched intently as hay was flung over the edge towards him. He had one arm up over the beam, the other hand gripping the rope. Claerwen was holding his lower hand, when suddenly, she felt it slip. Marcus looked up at her, surprise in his eyes. The foot hold was giving out.

Quickly, he decided he would have to chance a move. He handed his cap to Claerwen so it would not fall. Then he signaled her to move along the beam away from him, and he swung his legs until he caught the beam with them. At least he would not fall down onto the loft, but now he was hanging underneath the beam.

A voice shouted.

Marcus and Claerwen stared at each other, sure they were caught. Then they realized it was the smith, calling the stable hand to help him again. The boy trotted out. Claerwen watched, then signaled Marcus to climb up. She straddled the beam and leaned over to grab his belt, then pulled hard as he wriggled his way around, coming up to sit with his back to her.

"Damn," he whispered, out of breath. He was rubbing his bad knee.

She touched his shoulder and he turned to see worry in her eyes. His mouth curled almost into a smile, then signaled he was all right.

Climbing up the rafters, Marcus quickly reached the window. Cautiously, he looked out, the fresh air feeling good in his face after the dusty hay. The window opened out onto a roof. He heaved himself up and through it, then stuck his head back inside to signal Claerwen to follow.

She came through and stepped down onto a slate roof. Marcus had crept across to a parapet and was scanning the fort below. As she came to him, he said, "We will wait here until dark. This is perfect. There are no other windows that can see this roof. This is the great hall." He pointed straight down. "There is a place we can climb down over there," he pointed again, "and a crawl space under the floor. It's a great listening post."

"You've been there before?"

"Many times. Market day is the best time to be here, it draws just about anybody into the fortress. It's the same in most of the larger fortresses. Let's go back here against the wall where the shade is and so nobody can see us from that window in case they come to close it."

"I had no idea there was so much crawling around in spying. It's just like hunting."

He nearly laughed out loud but caught himself.

"We *are* hunting. Let's get some rest."

The fortress was busy with people. Marcus and Claerwen watched Cunedda go into the hall, probably for a meal, then go out again, returning later after most of the other people had left. Once the marketplace closed, Conwy became very quiet. By nearly midnight, a heavy mist had crept onshore from the sea.

Claerwen was napping when Marcus decided it was time to move. He gently shook her awake and led her to a spot along the far edge of the roof. That side of the hall ended close to the next building, leaving a very narrow space between. A ladder, only wide enough for one foot on each step, ran down the side. Marcus slid over the parapet and went down the ladder, Claerwen following. At the bottom, he knelt and felt around the wall until he found a loose group of stones. He carefully pried them out with his fingertips and set them against the wall, then wriggled on his belly through a gap they had hidden. Claerwen crawled in behind, and they re-set the stones in place.

They worked their way across to a spot near the base of the fire pit. Marcus explained it was the most likely place for someone to be sitting above in the hall, since fire pits were almost always needed, even in summer. Voices echoed above, drifting through cracks in the wood planking that made up the floor.

Cunedda did not take good care of his fortress.

Heavy steps came from the direction of the front door. Two men, talking, greeted a third man. The third man must have been waiting at the fire pit because his feet suddenly scraped and walked towards the first two. All three came back and sat, pulling up benches. Dust fell down on Marcus and Claerwen with each movement from above.

They were talking in heavily accented Welsh. Claerwen listened till she thought her ears would burst, trying to guess where they were from. She was not familiar with many accents or dialects, but once she knew one, she usually could recognize it again. They seemed to mumble a lot, attempting to keep their voices low. Then one spoke a little louder, one who had not spoken yet.

Claerwen gripped Marcus' arm. He twisted until she could whisper in his ear.

"Ifan," she mouthed.

It was nearly pitch black in the crawl space, but she knew he was staring at her to make sure he understood her. She shook his arm affirmatively. They both knew one of the others was probably Gerallt.

The voices raised, making the words nearly distinguishable, but still not enough to clearly understand. The third person appeared to be Welsh, having no accent. The men were beginning to argue.

"Keep your voices down," the third man said, barely audible to Marcus and Claerwen. The other two, ignored him.

"What do you mean you're still looking for the woman? You've had all the time you need!" Ifan's voice snapped.

Gerallt cut in, "You should be looking for the prince. Find him, and you'll find her and the torque."

"The prince is dead. Vortigern saw to that," the Welshman argued.

"Are you so stupid? He escaped, like he always does. No one knows where he is, but he's alive, out there, somewhere. And she's got to be with him. He's probably watching every move you make."

"You're lying. If he was alive, he'd have tried to take the fort back by now."

"After what Vortigern did to him? Don't expect him to be that quick. But expect that one day, he *will* be coming back. And you'll be his supper."

Scuffling shook the planks as the two Irishmen stood, advancing on the third man in anger. Ifan hissed, "You promised us the torque if we helped you sack the fort. Well, we helped you, so where is it? Or are you crossing us, eh?"

He stepped close to the Welshman, knocking him back across the floor as he spat out his angry words, "If you don't get that torque into our hands by another three days, you're dead. You got that?" He shoved the man hard again, knocking him into Gerallt, then punched him in the belly. Gerallt booted him, sending him rolling into a wall.

The old floor supports shook, concrete crumbling from them as the man hit the planks. Marcus instinctively covered Claerwen's head under his arms, dust gritting in their eyes. It sounded as if the whole building would collapse. The Irishmen left, followed a few minutes later by the Welshman.

"Who was the third man?" Claerwen asked after the foundation settled.

Marcus immediately began to wriggle back towards the loose stones. He spoke softly as he worked across, "I don't know, but that man is the one behind all of our betrayals. He's made a deal with Ifan and Gerallt, and he *is* trying to cross them. He didn't talk loud enough for me to recognize his voice. There's something familiar, though, in the pattern of his speech, but I can't place it yet."

"They know we're alive."

"Damn," Marcus swore, interrupting her. "It's blocked. Something shifted when they fought."

Claerwen moved till she could feel with her hands what he meant. "We're trapped?"

He poked at the stones. They were wedged solidly. He

pounded a fist in the dirt. "It will be too late to catch him by the time we get out of here."

"Is there another way out?" she asked.

"I don't know. I've never needed another way out. This floor is in such bad shape, maybe we can break through it somewhere."

"That would make too much noise."

Marcus laid on his back, thinking. In his mind, he reviewed what the room above looked like, every corner, every beam and stone and plank. He speculated there had to be something he could remember that would lead them to a way out of the crawl space. Cunedda must have trap doors and tunnels, ways to escape, just like Dinas Beris.

"Stay here," he said suddenly, and crawled back toward the fire pit.

He laid on his back again, and reached up to the stones that ringed the foundation of the fire pit. Some were loose. He rolled over and backed up as far as he could, still reaching them. He listened a few moments, satisfied that no one was above, then yanked on one stone, rolling away as it fell. Smoke and ash billowed down into the space, followed by sparks and hot coals.

Marcus coughed into his arms as the smoke blanketed him, the ashes stinging his eyes. He rolled again as hot coals bumped him. He was glad he wore a leather tunic, not cloth. He waited, hoping the noise had not alerted anyone.

Scuffling echoed in the smoke and he knew Claerwen was coming towards him. He could her breathing hard as she crawled.

"Claeri, stay where you are," he warned. "I'm all right." The scuffling stopped. No sound came from above.

He used his cap to sweep away the coals as they cooled. Dim light filtered through the smoky gap and he could see that he had made a hole along the edge of the fire pit. The stones were loose, cut to lay together in a pattern with no mortar. They were removed on occasion to clean the pit and sweep the ashes down into its foundation, then replaced in the same pattern.

Gingerly, he pulled and poked, removing more stones. He

had gambled that the fire was nearly out, being late at night. Using smaller rocks, he pushed the coals away across the pit as he opened the hole further.

When the hole was big enough to squeeze through, he called to Claerwen. She crawled to him and he quickly explained what he wanted her to do. "There will be one guard at the front door, and another at the rear. One torch is still burning. Take the torch and put it out in the pit. Then go back there behind that table in the corner and wait for me."

She nodded that she understood and watched as he went up through the hole. He lifted her up after him. She ran noiselessly to the torch and doused it as he instructed. As she turned to go to her hiding place, she saw he had run out the rear door.

A soft grunt and a thud, followed by scraping, came from the doorway. Marcus dragged in the unconscious guard and laid him on the floor, then jumped back to close the door.

"Come here," he called Claerwen. "Take his tunic, the helmet, gloves, the belt with the sword and any weapons you can find on him, and put them on. I'll be right back."

He jumped up and ran again, this time to the front, and dragged in the other guard. He stripped that man of the same items.

As he put on the guard's things, he said, "We are going to march to the stables, looking very official, and commandeer two horses. Follow my lead and let me do the talking." He buckled on the sword. He pulled it out half-way, then slammed it back in its sheath. "Not bad, but I wish I had mine back. Let's go."

They went to the front door and scouted out all directions. It was past midnight and very quiet. No lights were showing in the stable. Marcus strode out, confidence marking his walk. Claerwen imitated him, a pace behind. He went up to the door and pushed it in slowly, gritting his teeth at its creaking. He listened, holding his breath. There was only the rustling of the animals. They slipped inside.

Marcus selected a strong looking mare for Claerwen and

a well-muscled stallion for himself. Cooing softly at them, he unlatched their stall gates and eased the animals out, leading them to the door. He lifted Claerwen onto her animal, then bounded up on the other.

The night was calm and very dark with heavy mist as they crossed the fortress' courtyard. Marcus sat tall and imperious on the stallion as he approached the gates. The guard was leaning casually at his post, but stepped forward, leaning his pike in a salute to the two horsemen. Marcus gave a return salute, as he had seen Cunedda's warriors do many times. Claerwen rode her horse slightly behind and to the side away from the guard and imitated the gesture.

The guard asked what the problem was, why an unscheduled patrol would be going out. Marcus bluffed, saying tersely there was a report of trouble, likely there were thieves up the river and they were going to try to capture them by surprise. The guard nodded and opened the gate.

They moved through, looking straight out, glad for the darkness of the night. The gate creaked as it shut.

Marcus let his breath out long as he turned to look at Claerwen. But in the same instant, a shout rose up behind the gates. The two unconscious guards had been found.

"Ride!" he ordered.

They kicked their horses into a run, following the road along the delta and up the river. There was enough starlight to guide them until the road reached the forest. There it was too dark to negotiate the way at a gallop.

"This way." Marcus slowed and turned off the road into the trees. He dismounted. "We can cut across here to get back into the mountains. Hopefully they will think we went straight on because it's too dark here in the trees, or that we are hidden somewhere to wait for light. I know these woods well enough to get on through, but we will have to cover our tracks."

He broke off a branch and swept leaves and debris over the hoof prints, then tied it to the stallion's tail. He led the horses a few hundred yards, then untied the branch, hiding it in some underbrush.

As Claerwen waited for Marcus, she listened for the soldiers. Hoofbeats neared, but stayed on the road, passing them.

"Claerwen, I'm ready," he called softly.

She turned to move towards him, then halted again. She stared at a large boulder, but the longer she stared at it, the less it looked like a rock. She took a step closer, reaching to touch it.

"Claerwen," Marcus called again, still receiving no answer. He came up behind her and touched her shoulder. In the same instant, she touched the boulder and realized it was not a stone, but the grotesquely slain bodies of Ifan and Gerallt. Claerwen sucked in her breath and pulled her hand back, finding she had touched blood, not moss.

Marcus checked them, and declared them both dead.

"The Welshman killed them," he muttered, "because he knew he would not be able to find us in time." He rose, and washed Claerwen's hand from a waterskin.

Claerwen suddenly exhaled, regaining her senses from the shock, and said, "Then he will go to Dinas Beris. From the clue these two gave him, he will go there to wait for us. Without pressure from them, he has the time to wait."

"The only other rival he has to fear is Rhun, unless he is Rhun himself," Marcus added.

"That man was not Rhun. You spoke of speech patterns, and Rhun's is very different."

"Unless he spoke in a different pattern deliberately when he stayed at the fort. He is a spy, too. Remember how I changed my voice in the convent, when I came as a bard?"

"Aye. But I heard Rhun speak Irish clearly and easily when he took the fort. The Welshman who killed them spoke no Irish. The man we seek is not Rhun."

Marcus' brows jagged down and he took Claerwen's hand. He said, "Aye." He paused a moment longer, peering at her through the darkness. "You're good at this, Claeri. And I still say you have a damn lot of courage. Come. It's time to go."

They slipped away through the forest.

CHAPTER 29

Dinas Beris
Summer 469 A.D.

Marcus and Claerwen approached Dinas Beris from the east, across the river and behind the mountain of the standing stone where they had married. They scouted the area as they closed in, looking for some of the scattered homesteads. Most had been burned, the rest abandoned. Every time they came across one, Marcus grieved silently, wondering if the people had fled or been killed. The closer they came to the fort, the stonier his face became.

"We'll leave the horses here," he said quietly. They had arrived at the eastern base of the mountain behind the fort. He looked up at the rocky face. "It is steeper on this side and there is no terracing, but there is more cover."

They climbed swiftly, flitting from tree to bush, seeing no sentries, no patrols. The grove at the top of the mountain loomed darkly. As they came upon it, they slowed, cautious. But as they peered through the trees, they found it untouched. Not a blade of grass was different than the last time they had been there.

"I hope this is a good sign, but I don't think so," Marcus muttered, mostly to himself. They crossed the grove and threaded through the trees on the opposite side, stopping on a rocky ledge that overlooked the pass and the fort. Marcus inched forward on his belly across the ledge. The sun was high and glaring hard in his eyes until he shaded them with his hand. Claerwen eased down next to him.

"It's still there. At least they haven't burned it," he remarked.

"Can you see anybody?" she asked and wriggled into a better position to see.

"A few men inside the courtyard. The gates are closed. Damn, it's a mess. Look at all the digging they've done. And they've left their trash everywhere. Your gardens will have to be started over."

"I suspected as much. What are they doing?"

"Not much at the moment. Just sitting around."

"All strangers?"

"Aye. We have to find out if Rhun and the man from Conwy are there." He pushed himself back from the edge and sat up, leaning on a tree trunk. He pulled a dagger from a boot and inspected it while he thought. "Tonight, I want to go around to the other side and see if I can get into the tunnels." His eyes brooded heavily.

Claerwen continued to watch. She counted ten men. The hall and the original houses and other buildings were still intact, but there were new ones along the outer wall on each side of the gates.

"They must be housing quite a few more people. They have built barracks along the walls. See, you can just see the edge of the roofs from this side."

Marcus came back beside her to study the fort again. "If I can get in through the tunnels somehow, then I will try to get my supplies out. I just hope they didn't find them when they were digging up the place. If the tunnels are in good enough shape, then we can get in to drug the water supply, too, with that stuff you used on me."

"Belladonna. There should be enough on the high meadow this time of year. I will get it in the morning. When will you go?"

"Around midnight."

"I want to go in with you."

"No, Claeri. It's too dangerous. If something happens to me, then you'll still be all right."

"I don't want to go through that again. I lost you once. I could not bear it again. I would rather die with you."

He looked at her fondly and brushed her cheek with his hand. "Then think of it this way. If I get in trouble, you can pull me out. Truly, I want you to stay at the outside end of the tunnel and wait for me there. If the tunnels are not sound, I may need you to dig me out."

Fear crept into her face. Up to yet, she had been confident, especially since their daring escape from Conwy. But now the reality of the danger began to erode her courage.

Marcus saw her face cloud over, and he pressed his brow to hers. "The gods will be with us. Do not worry."

Midnight came and brought a cold, damp mist with it. After the heat of the day, Marcus was glad of the coolness. They left the horses behind the mountain of the standing stone and hiked around, down to the river. They came along the bank under the hill spur on which the fort perched, then began climbing up to where the tunnel entrance came out. The overgrowth was heavier than ever, but no guard was there.

As Marcus entered the tunnel, he found the candle Claerwen had dropped when she fled the year before. He lit it and took it with him, stepping light and quick up the sloping channel from where he left Claerwen, into the heart of his home. He came to an intersection, one side going straight towards his house, the other to the back wall that sheered up from the spur over the river. He went up the side toward the house, his pace slowing. As the candle was nearly used up, he found an old torch still in a wall bracket and lit it. It festered badly, but burned enough for him to see.

As he approached the end, he saw the tunnel was still blocked, beams twisted grotesquely like broken bones. He searched with his hands over the debris, testing, digging here and there. Much of it was loose. It had served its purpose well in Claerwen's escape, and he thanked the gods for giving his ancestors the idea to make the trap.

Part of the supplies Marcus wanted to steal out of the fort was somewhere in the wall at the fallen spot. He took a broken post and dug a little further along one side. Dust fell occasionally over him and he stopped each time, listening and waiting. He could not afford another cave in. But he had to have the supplies to help himself and Claerwen win back the fort.

"Damn," he muttered as another shower of dirt dropped over him. He shook his long hair, spraying dust from his head. He hoped he was not making enough noise to be heard above. He could not hear any movement or voices; he figured he was almost directly under his house.

Then he suddenly saw what he was looking for. A particular rock, plain, and the same color as the surrounding dirt, but in a definite spot, protruded slightly from the wall. He had gone a pair of steps too far and missed it.

He used his post and dug around the rock, the dirt falling out easily, the rock with it. A cavity opened up and he cleaned it out, then reached far inside. Pulling out a long metal casket, he set it on the floor and opened it carefully. Inside was an oilskin wrapper that was tightly tucked around some gear. He took this out, then replaced the metal casket in the cavity. As he bent to pick up the oilskin package, rocks and dirt shifted from the fallen roof and wall. It rumbled slightly and he froze. Finally, it settled again and he sighed with relief. He took the package and his sputtering torch, and trotted back down the tunnel.

At the intersection, Marcus turned right and went up the other side. This skirted along under the back wall of the fort. He thought he was almost to the door that led into the cellar when he came upon another cave-in. He studied the mess of dirt and rocks, then looked up at the ceiling. This cave-in was not a planned one, like the other tunnel; it was made from digging above. There was a small, jagged hole that led upwards. He could smell and feel fresh air coming through it and when he held the torch away, he thought the could even see a star.

Marcus backed down the tunnel, afraid smoke from his torch would escape through the hole and alert someone. He moved along the wall, searching again for a specific rock. This one he found easily and dug it out. He pulled another metal casket from this cavity. It was smaller and more square. Inside was another oilskin, but made with a leather loop he could sling over a shoulder.

Voices mumbled somewhere above. Hurrying, needing to take the torch away, he thrust the casket back in its hole and heaved the bag onto his shoulder. It was heavy and awkward. Then he gathered the long package under his other arm and started back to the outside.

The torch was used up by the time he was half-way to the outer exit. Finally, he gave up and dropped it. He crept along, feeling his way with the heavy bundles.

"Claeri!" he half-whispered, half-called as he neared the outside. He heard her breathing as she felt her way towards him. "I'm here, be careful, I'm going to drop something."

He grunted as he dropped both bundles. His knee was aching and he leaned over to rub it, panting from carrying the weight.

"Are you all right?" She touched his shoulders and could smell the sweat running from him.

"It's just heavy. Let's get this stuff out of here. It won't be easy on that ledge, so for Lleu's sake, be careful." He gave her one end of the long bundle and took the other end and the smaller bundle.

They moved slowly along the precarious ledge, slower than Marcus was comfortable with. But Claerwen carried her load more easily than he expected, amazing him again with her strength. They emerged from the ledge and circled around to their horses.

"I want to make camp down here," Marcus said, exhausted. They had led their horses down into a secluded hollow behind the mountain. "I came here sometimes when I was younger. We should be safe. There is a spring back there someplace. We can hide these things here, too, until we need them."

Claerwen poked her way through the heavy bracken and found the spring, following the sound of its rushing water. She brought back a full waterskin to Marcus. He was already digging a shallow hole under the shrubbery.

"What is all that?" she asked.

"There are three ingredients here that I will mix together in a certain way. Sulphur, saltpeter, and charcoal. When they are mixed just right and a spark lights it or it's hit hard, it explodes like lightning. This is our war band." He put the oilskins in the hole and started scooping dirt and leaves over them.

She stared at him in the dark. "I've never heard of such a thing. Won't it burn down the fort?"

He finished camouflaging the supplies. "I want to place some all around the fort, outside the walls. We can set it off by shooting arrows into it. And we can shoot some burning arrows inside for effect, just don't hit anything that will burn. But I will blow the gates open with this stuff." He patted the leaves where he buried it.

"It sounds dangerous."

"We have to be extremely careful."

"Do you really think that will fool them into thinking a war band is out here?"

"If we can drug them good enough first, it should work."

Claerwen thought a moment, then asked, "Marcus, where did you learn of these things?"

He turned to her and she sensed he was grinning in the dark. "I stole some from the druids once, a long time ago, then figured out how they made it. They use it in their rituals."

She caught her breath, then exhaled slowly, "I had a feeling it was something like that. These things are sacred! They would kill you if they knew you had it."

He leaned and briefly kissed her cheek and said, "Don't

worry. They don't know who stole it and they'll never know I have it."

"But...how?"

"Don't worry," he reassured her.

Finally, she shrugged and remarked, "You said the tunnels were blocked."

"I have to find another way in while you collect the leaves tomorrow."

"It's almost tomorrow now."

"Aye, let's get some rest."

He laid down on his bedroll, pulled her into his arms, and fell asleep instantly.

They were up again at first light, continuing with their preparations.

Claerwen took off in a slow run, heading for the high meadow, an empty pouch slung on her back. Marcus told her to take the horse and save her strength, but she refused, saying she could reach the meadow just as fast and with much less risk of being seen. He trusted her survival knowledge and watched her jog up the hill, disappearing into the rocky crags. He admitted to himself that many times her instincts in the wild were priceless.

By midday she returned, her pouch full of the leaves and roots that could make a man sleep, relieve pain and indigestion, and ease several other ailments. She set her pouch down and picked up a skin to fetch water when she stopped to watch Marcus.

He had stripped down to his loincloth and was kneeling, bent over a large, spread-out piece of cloth, the powders mixed in a pile in its center. Around him on the ground, he had placed small cups, shaped like half-spheres.

"What are these?" she asked, picking one up.

"They are clay. There's lots of it by the spring. They have to dry completely, then I will fill them with the powders. Then I'll put two together and seal them around the middle, like this." He made a whole sphere out of two halves. "This weather is perfect, warm and dry. None of this can be damp or it won't work." He raised his face to shake his long hair back.

"You shaved your beard!" she exclaimed.

"I do not want anyone to mistake who is breaching the gates." He wiped his hands on a rag. "It's too warm in summer anyway."

"I'm glad you kept the moustache." She knelt and smiled at him, running her finger along it.

He gripped her hand and kissed its palm, wishing he had time to love her right then. He forced himself to look away from her sparkling green-blue eyes and said, trying to distract himself, "You need to cut my hair, it's getting too long again."

"I like it that way." She stroked it. It fell past his shoulders now, thick and shiny blue-black in the bright sun.

He turned again to her, drawn irresistibly by the sweetness in her heart-shaped face. He put his arms around her waist and pulled her down until she was in his lap. "I can't help myself, Claeri. I look at you and I go crazy." He kissed her long and deep, his big hands loosening her shirt, searching underneath, then slipping it from her. He caressed her breasts, each of his hands filled by one, and he watched how they moved as he gently squeezed them.

The sun sparkled in Claerwen's green-blue eyes as she smiled at Marcus, her arms going around his neck. He slipped her breeches off, then picked her up in his arms and carried her down to the spring. He set her among the cool leaves in the shade, tiny rivers of water flowing down through them and over her body. Dropping his loincloth, he came to her, loving her with his whole soul.

"I have an idea," Claerwen said suddenly. It was hours later, the sun having set, and she was looking up from her supper.

Marcus raised his eyebrows in acknowledgment.

"You say these powder balls will explode when they are

hit hard enough?"

He nodded, chewing an oat cake.

"Wouldn't it be easier to throw some of these over the ramparts instead of shooting burning arrows? The impression would be much bigger. In fact, throw some both inside and outside. Once the men are confused, then hit the ones on the gates."

He thought a moment. "That's good. Really good. That would save me a lot of time tonight as well. I was going to place them inside for us to shoot at when we attack. You're right, why didn't I think of that? They will do the same thing if they're dropped hard enough. Then I don't have to carry them with me tonight when I scale the wall."

Claerwen grinned, proud of her idea. Then she frowned, "You figured out how to get in without the tunnels?"

Marcus reached behind him and pulled a metal object out of a pouch. "This is a grappling hook. It was one of the things I needed from inside." He showed her how it opened, like a metal claw. "Tonight I will go around to the other side again and climb up the back wall."

"Over the river?"

"Aye."

"By the gods, that's dangerous."

"I've done it before in worse places." He wiped his mouth on his wrist. "It's getting dark enough now. I should get ready."

He slipped two daggers into his boots and another one into a sheath inside his left sleeve. He strapped one of the swords from Conwy across his back. Then he took the waterskins, filled with the belladonna potion, and the grappling hook attached to a long, coiled rope, and slung them over his shoulders. He tested the weight and balance of all the gear until he was satisfied he could carry it without encumbrance.

"I should be back by midnight," he said and kissed Claerwen lightly. "Don't worry."

It was well after midnight when he returned to the hollow.

She was listening to the night sounds when she heard him coming, the soft rattle of his gear interrupting her thoughts as he moved down the slope to their camp.

He sloughed off the gear, piece by piece, and dropped onto his waiting bedroll next to Claerwen.

"I did it," he said, excitement in his tired voice. He rubbed his bad knee. "It took longer than I thought; I had to wait for some of the men to move away from the well, but I was able to empty all of it in the water. I also found out there are about thirty men. I saw Rhun from a distance."

"And the other man from Conwy?"

"I couldn't tell, not knowing what he looks like yet. But Rhun looked like he's still in charge."

She could tell he was rubbing his knee in the dark, and said, "Let me put some of that painkilling salve on your knee tomorrow before we go in. It might not get sore so easily. Especially, if..." She drifted off.

"If I have to fight hard?" he finished for her.

She nodded. "It's going to happen at last. I'm excited, but I'm scared, too. There was always time in between now and then, but now it's going to happen."

He hugged her, understanding her fear. But he held his jaw tight, determined to keep the fear from creeping into his mind. This was not the time to doubt.

CHAPTER 30

Dinas Beris
Summer, 469 A.D.

Once more, Marcus and Claerwen lay on the ledge overlooking Dinas Beris, watching and waiting. The belladonna was taking effect. They could see men trudging slowly, when they moved at all. Most of them seemed to stay in the great hall or in the barracks. The few that drew guard duty marched dully across the ramparts, not paying much attention to anything.

Night drew in.

It was time.

Marcus and Claerwen rode the horses around to the place where the entry road dipped lowest, where the last ditch crossed it. They tied the horses well, hidden in the edge of the woods.

Marcus ran softly through the darkness next to the road, emerging at the wall a few yards from the gates. He waited, listening. The night was cool and windy, clouds were coming in. They would have to hurry, rain would spoil the powder balls. He could not see any guards, though he could hear them dragging their feet on the wooden rampart flooring. He moved quickly along the wall to the gates. There, he tied several of the powder balls. Seconds later, he slipped back around to the side.

Claerwen was waiting there for him. She had a pouch of powder balls, a quiver of arrows, a bow, and the grappling hook.

This time the hook was attached to a rope ladder.

Marcus whispered urgently, "We have to hurry. If it rains, this won't work. Are you ready?"

"Aye."

He squeezed her shoulders for luck. "Go!"

She took off running along the wall, stopping after a few yards, and threw one of the powder balls as hard as she could. The first one lobbed over the top of the timber fortification and she could hear it smack and crack somewhere, then fall down further. But no explosion came. Her stomach sank. It did not work as expected. She moved on.

Stopping again, she prepared to throw another ball. Then she heard one go off from the other side. One of Marcus' had exploded. Cries went up from inside as smoke puffed up and caught in the wind. She threw her second ball.

This one exploded just above her on the rampart, breaking loose splinters and showering them down on her. She ran further and lobbed another. It exploded inside. More cries rose up.

But she could not hear any more blasts from Marcus' side. She wondered if the powder was damp from the clay, or the clay was too thick and cushioned the blow too much. She kept on along the wall as far as she could before the spur dropped away in its sheerness, using the rest of her clay balls. Some exploded, some did not.

Claerwen drew back a few yards to a spot where the wall was shorter to the ground. She swung the grappling hook and let it fly up. It caught the edge of the timbers and she yanked hard, testing it. It slipped. She dove aside, just avoiding the raking claw as it clanged to the ground. She sprang up and flung it again, harder this time. It went over and stuck firmly between two beams.

Swiftly, she climbed, her gear swinging from her back. As she reached the top, she eased up slowly, peeking through the sharpened tips of the timbers. Men were running across the courtyard, most of them looking dazed from the drug. But some of them ran normally. A guard was trotting along the rampart towards the gate. Another powder ball came from Marcus' side and exploded in the courtyard.

She moved a little higher, then pulled her bow out and slipped an arrow from the quiver. She could see one of the balls laying below, undamaged. She nocked the arrow and drew, clinging precariously with her arm hooked between the pointed timbers, her feet in the rope ladder. The arrow flew straight and hard, shattering the clay casing of the ball. The flint arrowhead sparked and the powder blew, spattering dirt and sparks everywhere.

Elated at her luck, Claerwen edged up higher. She wanted to position herself where she could aim better and set off all the other duds. She also needed to be able to aim accurately when Marcus blew the gates open in order to help him against the men. She worried that so many still were not as dazed as she expected.

She wedged herself between the beams, one leg over the wall to the outside, and tried to find a comfortable enough way to sit there. The wind was blowing harder, and the clouds thickened, threatening rain soon. She shifted her weight again and the gear moved, unbalancing her. It dragged her down the inside of the wall as she tried to cling with her hands to the top, but she could not hang on. She dropped down onto the catwalk, smacking her head on a support beam as she fell.

Lightning flashed in the sky, brighter than daylight, showing a ceiling full of angry, boiling black clouds. Claerwen lay crumpled on the rampart's catwalk, her hair loosened from its tie. She stirred, slowly at first, then came awake. Her head ached, but she struggled to her feet, groggy from the hit she had taken. She stumbled along the ramparts a few steps, forgetting her gear where it had fallen.

Another huge flash of lightning exploded, quickly followed by its thunder. Claerwen stood up straight at this, the wind billowing her long hair out and around her like an aurora. She moved toward the gates, compelled by a force she could not control. The gods were in her again, strong and terrible, the visions in her eyes, fire in her head.

Lightning flashed violently, over and over, striking closely all around the fort. The men scattered around the courtyard, screaming in wonder at the dreadful storm. They had been called to assemble and be prepared to fight as soon as the first explosions came, but most of the men were driven in a daze by the confusing wind and lightning.

Then the thunder quieted a moment, and a gap in the clouds opened. Moonlight streamed through like a beacon and struck the top of the gates. It held their attention long enough to realize a stranger was there. A woman!

Claerwen walked into the light as if drawn by it, her eyes out of focus. Her hair floated in the wind eerily. She lifted her arms gradually to the sky, drawing power from the gods.

"Behold!" she cried, her voice carrying echoey and long on the wind.

The men below her stopped, more emerging from the buildings as the news spread of a woman on the ramparts. Rhun stepped out of the great hall, wearing full battle gear. By his stance, he was angry at his men for their disorganization and superstitious fears. He looked up at the woman and recognized Claerwen. For a moment, his fists were less firmly clenched against his hips, but then he tightened them again, and gripped the hilt of his sword.

"Get that woman up there!" he barked at his men.

Claerwen swayed slightly on her perch above the gates, her arms still raised.

"Behold!" she cried again.

Two men ran for pikes. But before they reached them, another bolt struck, destroying the pikes. The men dashed away, screaming in fear.

"Behold! The one who leads you is false. You will die if you defend him. Flee! Flee while you can!" Another flash, so bright she seemed to disappear for a moment. Then thunder, crashing incredibly loud.

Rhun strode out into the courtyard, howling orders until his throat went raw. The men half-heartedly drew their weapons, but no one stepped forward to climb the steps up to Claerwen. He could see some of them shaking their heads, too afraid to advance.

"Are you going to let one woman scare you?" he screamed at them. "Get up there and bring her to me, you cowards!"

Another flash of light.

Another crashing din of thunder.

"Behold!" she called again. "Go while you can, or suffer the rage of the gods!" More thunder rumbled menacingly, building louder and louder.

An enormous blast shook the earth. Wood splinters, rocks and dirt exploded across the entire fort, shooting brilliantly into the sky. Choking smoke and flames billowed behind the debris, clogging the courtyard. As it cleared, those left alert could see the gates and the platform had been shattered, the woman was gone. Only fire was left clinging along the side beams where the structure had been.

Many of the men were caught in the stinging debris, wounding them badly, some lay dead. Those that could move, ran, walked, dragged, crawled away from the gaping hole.

The thunderstorm began to drift away, growling angrily as it retreated.

Rhun was still berating his men, but none of them would listen. He tried to gather them together, pushing and prodding them with the flat of his sword. He insulted and cajoled them, but their fear was too well imbedded by Claerwen's warning, the violent storm, and the blasting of the gates.

"Look!" someone screamed.

The courtyard was lit against the black night by dozens of small fires started from the splintered debris. Smoke continued to drift across the gateway, brightened eerily by the flames. A lone horseman rode in through the smoke, emerging slowly, each step echoing sharply against the sudden silence of the night.

He was all in black, strong and easy on the horse. He wore a visored black leather helmet.

"The Iron Hawk!" cried one man, blood running down his

face from a lacerated scalp. "*Y Gwalch Haearn!* He's alive!"

The cry was taken up and panic raced through the fort. Those that could move at all, headed for the road. Some dragged injured companions, others were left for dead. They dashed past the Iron Hawk, staring at him, their mouths gaping in fear.

Rhun was left alone, his sword poised.

Claerwen lay unconscious, sprawled over a pile of debris after being thrown by the shattering blast. The gods had left her moments before the final explosion, leaving her with a blinding headache. Slowly, she began to waken, becoming aware of pain. She rolled up onto her knees, trying to rise, but she could not, and held her aching temples with scratched and bleeding hands.

Voices screamed nearby, making her head pound, but they seemed to be going away. Claerwen crawled away from the debris, dragging herself into a shadowy corner of a barrack wall where she was able to sit herself up. Several minutes passed before her eyes would focus, no matter how hard she concentrated. The noise drifted away. She shook her head, trying to clear it. Her body hurt terribly and she wondered if she had broken ribs.

Finally her eyes lost their fogginess and she could distinguish the courtyard. Rhun was still there. She became aware of the fires and lots of smoke. No other soldiers were there, except a dead or injured man laying face down off to her right. But Rhun had his sword out and a metal Saxon-style helmet on his head. He was staring at something. Or someone. Then she saw the flash of another sword directly to her left. She rubbed her eyes, trying to see.

"Oh, no!" she cried in frozen horror.

The Iron Hawk sat on the horse, whirling his big, heavy sword in an arc around him. The horse reared, whinnying loudly, pawing the air, reminding Claerwen of her vision. Although the Iron Hawk had been riding at a gallop in that image, she knew Dinas Beris had been his destination.

She watched as the Iron Hawk leaped off the horse and spanked it away. The animal retreated through the entrance.

The two men circled each other, both concentrating intensely. Rhun moved roughly, side to side, waiting for the challenge to come. The Iron Hawk stalked his prey more directly. They continued several minutes, testing and feinting, not committing to any sudden moves.

Rhun ran out of patience. He circled around, trying to find the best light to fight in, but the fires were not strong enough to glare into the other warrior's eyes.

They continued circling a while longer, then suddenly, the Iron Hawk lashed out, swinging his sword in a strong, even swipe. Rhun blocked it, metal ringing clear and loud in the air. Rhun jumped back, then lunged forward again, hacking down. The Iron Hawk cut off his swing and the swords rang again. They backed off and returned to circling.

Claerwen stayed motionless, mesmerized by the fight.

Again, the warriors swung and crashed sword to sword, sparks flying where they hit. The Iron Hawk became more aggressive, slashing forward at Rhun, forcing him back toward the great hall. Rhun fought strongly, though, not losing control. But he misjudged when he reached the first stone step of the hall and fell. He rolled, panicking as the Iron Hawk's sword arced down. Chips flew from the stone where Rhun had been an instant before.

Rhun ran across to the other side of the courtyard, heading for the gateway. But the Iron Hawk ran faster and tripped him before he could flee the fort. They both went down, the Iron Hawk rolling once and coming back up on wide spread feet. He swung again at Rhun, who rolled the other way. Rhun managed to stand before the Iron Hawk could turn again and tried to cut him in the legs. The Iron Hawk sprawled sideways, grunting as he hit the ground, and the blade passed over him.

The battle took on a more ominous atmosphere as it dragged on. Both men were nearly equal in height and build, but the Iron Hawk's superior concentration gave him the advantage in his blows. He hacked harder and faster, lunging deeper, punching and booting Rhun. Rhun was persistent, showing a lot of stamina, but he was not as good a swordsman. He used panic and fear to spur himself against the legendary avenger. He fought valiantly, taking cuts and slashes when he could not fully counter.

Both men were tiring visibly. The weapons continued to ring harshly, making Claerwen's ears hurt as she watched. She had never seen such a vicious fight and she felt sick with each blow. Still, she could not make herself look away.

Rhun seemed to suddenly resolve to finish the fight and began to rush harder and faster again. He hit at the Iron Hawk with all the strength in his body behind each blow, trying to wear the warrior down. He backed the man against the steps of a house and kicked a foot out from under him, sending him down into the dirt. Then he lunged, trying to ram him through. But again, the Iron Hawk rolled out of reach. Rhun's sword stuck fast in one of the foundation beams. He swore out loud.

Then suddenly, Rhun whirled, a dagger in his hand, and hurled it at the Iron Hawk. It grazed the warrior's arm above the elbow, sending blood streaming down. Involuntarily, he grabbed at it, giving Rhun enough time to retrieve his sword.

The pain transformed the Iron Hawk, and he began flinging the sword in whirling, flashing patterns, meant to confuse his foe. The blade moved so fast, there was no chance to guess how it would fall or lunge when its path changed. Rhun watched, fascinated by the surging blade. Then suddenly his face froze in surprise. The Iron Hawk's fanciful display abruptly ended and he lunged powerfully. This time, steel met flesh.

Rhun had missed the block. The Iron Hawk's blade rammed clear through his foe's chest and into the ground under him where he fell, blood flowing into the soil around him.

The Iron Hawk paused, watching the man slowly lose his life. He pulled off his right gauntlet, and reached to untie Rhun's helmet. As he pulled the helmet off and dropped it, his victim gripped the gloveless hand in a last effort.

"You?" he whispered, staring at the hand, then up into the mask.

The Iron Hawk stood over him, frozen. "Why?" the

warrior asked. "Why?"

"I could...have taken...it," the man answered, the death rattle rasping harshly in his throat already. "I could...have defeated...Vortigern, if I just could have...found the torque. But...you spoiled everything. You spoiled..."

He died, his head drooping over the sword.

The Iron Hawk let go of the hilt, his fingers cramped from holding on so long and tight. He backed away very slowly, breathing roughly.

He stood watching the blood-soaked body for a long time, his head bowed.

Claerwen was stunned at the ferocity of the fight. Though she had seen the Iron Hawk kill before, it was the first time she had seen him in a prolonged duel. She was horrified that she found his swordsmanship almost beautiful.

Silence blanketed the night again. The wind had eased and the smoke from the fires hung with appalling dread over the warrior and his victim.

Then she realized Marcus was not in the fort.

A foreboding seeded panic. Was he hurt or killed in that blast? Or had the Iron Hawk killed him before he fought Rhun? Then she realized the Iron Hawk had to have been the third man in Conwy.

Rage seethed in her as she willed herself up onto her knees. She held her painful body stiffly as she tried to get to her feet. She wanted to look for Marcus, but her long-smoldering rage had become so deep against the Iron Hawk, she craved to kill him with her bare hands. She wished she had her bow and arrows, but she could not evade the warrior from her location in order to retrieve them. She watched the warrior standing motionless over his victim. It struck her then, that a little arrow would not do justice to such a man.

He had to be killed with a sword.

CHAPTER 31

**Dinas Beris
Summer, 469 A.D.**

The Iron Hawk backed away from his victim and took a few steps toward the great hall, holding his bleeding arm with his right hand.

Then something moved in the dark to his right, and he stopped and backed up again.

Claerwen ran out of the shadows, darting for one of the dead soldiers. She yanked a sword from the body and whirled around to face the warrior. She began a long, horrible scream, her face contorted in rage, her long hair flying madly behind her.

The Iron Hawk was clearly stunned at the woman advancing on him. She looked like a berserker, in the throes of a killing madness. He backed up, then, alarmed, pulled his sword out from the body. Blood dripped from it.

"Stop!" he yelled at her. "Stop. Stop, Claerwen! Stop!"

But she kept advancing. She raised her weapon high and slashed across with it. But she was no swordsman, especially against the Iron Hawk. He neatly blocked her stroke, catching the edge of the blade and flung it out of her hands. It fell yards away, harmlessly thumping along the dirt yard. She tried to run for it, but he dashed after her and tripped her. She fell hard, skidded to a halt, screaming again.

"What did you do to Marcus ap Iorwerth?" she screeched, clawing at him as he came down over her and turned her face-up to him. She kicked and smacked with her hands and feet, obsessed with her hatred. "You killed him, didn't you? You killed him!"

The warrior sat on her legs and flung away his bloody sword. He grabbed her flailing arms and pressed them down, disabling her stinging fists.

"Go ahead and kill me, you horrible creature! Kill me now! Without my Marcus, I have nothing!"

"Stop it. Stop fighting, Claerwen. Listen to me," the warrior spoke calmly through her screams. He tried to let go of one of her arms, but her fist rammed up, pounding the side of his helmet. He gripped her hand again, forcing it down.

She twisted and shoved, trying to free herself, grunting and keening her fury. Finally he leaned down and roared in her face, "Listen to me! Stop fighting! Marcus ap Iorwerth is not dead and I'm not going to kill you!"

His words finally broke through her hysteria. For an instant, she calmed, but rage still seethed in her.

"Look at me," he commanded her. "Look in my face." His voice was low and calm again. He carefully clamped one hand around both of her wrists so she could not start hitting him again, and he pulled at a tie under the helmet. He loosened it, slowly, watching her face for signs of panic. Then he reached up to grip the visor and pulled the helmet off.

Marcus' face stared at her.

Her mouth opened and closed, wordless questions coming and going. He waited patiently, watching her face change. She finally realized he was alive. Pain and grief drained from her eyes, joy replacing the ugliness of what she had witnessed. When he released her wrists, she flung her arms up around his neck and hugged him to her.

"It was a disguise! Just a disguise!" she cried softly in his ear, stroking his hair and face. "And you are alive! I thought he killed you. I thought the Iron Hawk killed you! But you were just disguised as that monster. Oh, Marcus, my Marcus..."

He held her, squeezing his eyes closed, trying to hold his own emotions in control.

"Claeri, I—" he began.

"You're hurt!" she realized, and interrupted him.

"'Tis nothing," he said, fatigue sweeping over him. His wound stung badly, but he wanted to talk. He felt dizzy from the pain and tiredness.

"I must bind this right away. You've lost a lot of blood." She gingerly tried to see the wound through the cut in his sleeve.

"It can wait," he said. "I have to tell you something." Another wave of dizziness swayed him.

"Marcus, you're going to pass out. I have to do this now."

He was still sitting on her. She looked into his sweaty, dirty face and pushed the hair out of his eyes. He sighed at last and backed off her legs, rising to his feet. For a moment he stood straight, stretching his back, his head tilted slightly so his face was raised to the sky, his black hair gently blowing in the wind. Claerwen watched her husband, silhouetted against the dwindling fires in the tough leather armor of the Iron Hawk.

Then she saw the crumpled and bloody body of the man he had killed. She could only see the side of his face; from where she sat, it was turned partially away from her. She watched the wind toss the brown hair across the face, then blow it back away again. Then she realized the man was not Rhun.

"It's Taran!" she whispered, feeling her stomach flounce. Even in death, he looked like he was sneering in arrogance. She raised her eyes to Marcus again, finally understanding he had fought the long and gruesome battle. And that he had killed his brother.

"You were the magnificent warrior..." she began, then suddenly felt herself go hot and sick. Before she could say more, she turned onto her knees and retched.

"Ah, Claeri." He kneeled back down to help her. When she was through, he reached to pick her up, but she cried out when he touched her.

"You're hurt." He pulled her hair back to see her brows knotted in pain. "What happened?"

She gasped for breath a few moments until the spasm calmed again. "I fell when the gates blew. I was on the platform."

His mouth opened and he stared at her. "What in the gods' names where you doing up there? You could have been killed. You were supposed to stay on the back wall."

"I could not...help it." She struggled to her feet. "You didn't hear me then." She looked at him solemnly.

His face froze and he looked at her with squinted eyes, "Fire in the head?" he whispered.

She nodded.

He licked his dry lips and exhaled slowly. Then he guided her across to the great hall, up the steps, inside. Kicking benches and tables out of the way as he crossed the room with her, the soldiers had left the place in a shambles. He brought her into the kitchen, hoping there would be some of Padrig's medicines still there. But the kitchen was as neglected as the rest of the fort. He set Claerwen down on a stool and went to search for anything useful.

Marcus rifled all the shelves and bins, finally finding some leftover wine. He sniffed at it, then tried a sip. It was sour, but drinkable. "Here, Claeri, try some of this."

Her face was almost grey. He forced her to drink and she sputtered, but swallowed most of it. Color came back to her cheeks.

"That's awful," she said, wiping her mouth.

"Then it ought to be good for my arm," he replied. He pulled off the other gauntlet, then undid the ties that held the tunic's left sleeve and carefully pulled it off. The wound still bled, but more slowly. His shirt and arm were crusted with drying blood and he winced as the sleeve came off.

Claerwen came to look at the wound, the healer's instinct spurring her into duty. He pulled a small dagger hidden in his left wrist guard and handed it to her. She cut the shirt above the wound and eased it away.

"It's not deep, just messy." She looked for something to clean it with. Everything was filthy. Shaking her head, she pulled out her own shirttail and ripped strips from it.

"Here, drink some first." She handed the wineskin to Marcus. He obeyed. Then she soaked a strip with more wine and poured a little on the wound itself.

"Damn, that stings," he groaned.

"This will at least keep it from getting fevered." Her hands worked quickly in practiced movements and his arm was soon cleaned. She bound it neatly, from just above his elbow, nearly to his shoulder. "I'm sorry it hurts. I will have to start over with my medicines." She paused, looking up into his aching eyes. She began to ask about Taran, but he cut her off.

"We'll talk about him later, Claerwen." His voice was sharp and final; she knew not to pursue her question. He untied his other sleeve and dropped it on the table.

She reached to touch his face, apologizing, "I'm sorry I hit you..." Then her face crumpled in horror. "By the gods, I tried to kill you!"

"Claeri, we have to talk. I have to tell you something."

"I tried to kill you," she repeated, then wrapped her arms around him. "How could I not know that was you?"

"Claerwen," he spoke roughly, trying to stay calm. "Sit down and listen to me." He made her sit on the stool again. He pulled up a bench and straddled it so he could sit with his face close to hers.

She waited for him to speak, but now that he had her attention, he had a hard time to find the words. He studied his hands, dirty and lined with callouses, then looked up into her clear green-blue eyes.

"This was not just another disguise I wore tonight," he began, then paused again, gathering his courage. "I have lied to you, Claerwen. Lied and deceived you. I hate that I had to do it, but it was for your protection." He paused again, raking his fingers through his hair. "I *am* the Iron Hawk," he finally said.

She did not react at first, but frowned a little, as if she had not heard him right.

"Do you understand what I'm saying?" he asked and took hold of her hands. "I am the Iron Hawk. You saw me burn the farmstead in Strathclyde. You saw me, and helped me, in the convent when Drakar's men attacked it."

Her lips parted and she recoiled from him in shock. Her eyes searched his face, darting back and forth, her head shaking slightly side to side. She touched his face, the face she loved so much, then looked at the stained and scuffed leather tunic, the black warrior's tunic she hated so much.

"He... You... But he tried to kill me, three times. And my cousin once. He was there when Alis died. You can't be *Y Gwalch Haearn*, not you!" Her voice drifted up, ending in a high wail.

He sighed tiredly and repeated, "I am the Iron Hawk."

"But he has killed so many men, so cruelly." She looked like she was going to be sick again, but it passed.

"*I* killed so many men. Very cruelly." His lips flinched, but his eyes remained intense, boring into her face.

She thought about the fight she had just watched, then the fight in the convent's courtyard. Her lips moved as if she was reciting the different times she had seen the Iron Hawk and compared him, his movements, to her Marcus.

"I don't believe it," she insisted.

"Do you remember when I came over the wall at the convent, there was a series of flashes? That was some of my powder balls." He watched her eyes harden. "Do you know how I knocked you out?" he asked and reached out to her throat. "Two fingers, pressed here." He touched her under her chin and squeezed lightly.

Her eyes widened as she realized only the Iron Hawk could know that. Then she remembered the northern aurora after the vision in Avebury, and the third image of her vision at the crannog. The gods had given her the clues to the Iron Hawk's identity, but she had not connected them with finding Marcus at the crannog. Slowly, she nodded. Then she pulled away from him and stood up. For a moment she just stood there, shaking, hurting from her injuries, trying to control the hysteria rising in her.

Then she dashed out of the kitchen, keening sobs filling the air as she ran.

"Claerwen!" Marcus jumped up and yelled. "Claerwen, wait!"

She was already out of the hall's front door and running across the courtyard. Her cries rose eerily into the night air.

"Claerwen! Listen to me!" He bounded after her, leaping down the steps. In spite of his pain and weariness, he ran with speed. He caught her, gripping the back of her tunic, and yanked her around. She stumbled, nearly dragging him down with her, but he braced himself and swung her until he could get both arms around her. She struggled hard, wailing, and tried to fight free, but he was too strong and held her fast.

"You tried to kill us!" she screamed in his face. "You poisoned my cousin and me!"

"Listen to me, Claeri. Listen! Stop fighting and listen." She tried to trip him so he would drop her, but he had his legs spread apart and solidly grounded. Then she tried to fall down, using her weight to unbalance him, but he still hung on tight.

"I did not poison you. That was one of Padrig's potions. It only made you sleep. You weren't supposed to see me, so I had to do something quick. I never meant to hurt you. Or Grania."

"Myrddin said it was poison!" She was tiring, her body in agony, but she still struggled.

"He didn't know what it was."

"He's a master healer, he should know!"

"You know as well as I do there's a fine line between healing and poisoning from the same source. Myrddin knows that, too."

She suddenly stretched her face up to his and spat words out, "Then why did you burn my home to the ground? Why?"

"Because I hated Drakar so much by that time, I couldn't bear what he would do to you. His men destroyed that farmstead before I ever got there. Everything was dug up and torn apart. Just like this place is now. He ruined everything he and his people touched. They violated it. I knew they would try to violate you. So I burned it. Then they could never do anything more to it. You couldn't go back there anymore even after I discredited Drakar. Ceredig would not have been able to protect you. So I knocked you out and drugged you to sleep until I could get you away from there safely, without finding out who the Iron Hawk was and so Drakar could not track you. I knew Myrddin Emrys was traveling on that road into Caernarfon and I knew he would help you.

"And for the same reasons, I grabbed you in Caernarfon. I wasn't threatening you with that knife, I only meant to keep you quiet. You don't know it, but you almost walked right into Drakar. He was on the top of that hill and I was following him. If I'd let you make any noise, he would have murdered us both."

Claerwen slowly stopped struggling, but Marcus felt her shaking as he held her tightly, afraid to ease his grip. He was out of breath, and his chest heaved against her. His face was in agony, more from emotion than the pain in his arm. He smoothed her hair, drawing it back from her face, and she looked up at him with deeply solemn eyes.

"Myrddin suggested the reasons for what you do are contradictory to your actions. He insisted you were an avenger," she spoke calmly, but strained.

"Aye, an avenger," he said, irony in his tone. Finally, he let go, then took her hand and led her back inside the hall. He dropped onto a bench, his legs giving out. She eased herself down on the floor, propped up against the fire pit stones, facing him. The harsh ache of bitterness in her eyes disturbed him.

He explained, "I began as the Iron Hawk the day after I first met you, in Strathclyde. I had been planning it for a long time, as another way to spy. I even spread rumors before the first time I actually put this thing on." He pounded a fist on his chest. "I never intended to kill, only scare. But I found out that creating fear has a terribly high price. The more I frightened those superstitious fools, the harder they tried to kill me. And I let my anger take control of me. Afterward, I thought, perhaps it would serve as a better warning to Drakar and others like him."

"Then it truly was an accident, when Alis was killed? Drakar hit her when he...he was fighting you?"

"Aye. I held back, because I did not want to do just that, to her or Grania. That's how he beat me."

"He beat you? But, you said you took Grania out of the building. I don't know what to believe now."

"Drakar knocked me against a beam and I was stunned. He thought the fire would take care of all of us. An oil lamp was spilled. Alis was dead when I came to. All I could do was save Grania and run."

"All those fights you were in. Always alone. That's what Myrddin said. The Iron Hawk always fights alone. That he can fight like ten men together. That he never speaks. No one else ever knew either, did they? Not even Owein?"

"No. Nor Padrig, nor my father. And you never saw it in a vision."

"No. The god only gave vague clues. Myrddin didn't know either. I once thought it was Owein." She suddenly remembered the third image of her vision and blurted, "Is that why you said it could be the Iron Hawk who freed you from Vortigern? You found a way to free yourself?"

He reflected a few moments then started to smile, then laughed. "Aye, it is true. They used the villa where I was kept prisoner as a barn. There was a mule tied there and I tickled him with a piece of straw to make him kick. He broke the iron rings the shackles were chained to. Vortigern was already gone, headed for his death at Doward, though I didn't know that then. They had left my clothes piled in a corner and didn't search them. The two daggers were still in my boots. I was able to break the lock on the door, and slip out. Vortigern must have taken all of his Saxons with him. I took the mule. But I still don't remember how I got on that boat..." He grinned a while longer at the memory, then let his smile slowly fade.

He looked Claerwen square in the eyes and said, "The Iron Hawk must stay just between the two of us."

Her expression had remained steadfastly solemn during his entire explanation. Now anger stirred behind it and she accused him, "You plan to continue using that identity, don't you? Until you're killed, like the others."

"I want to leave a door open in case I need it again. But I am not planning on using it."

She didn't believe him. "It is like a dark side. A side of you I don't know. A side I'm not sure I want to know."

Her cold gravity hurt him, and it showed in his eyes. He was terrified she would turn against him, letting her hatred for the Iron Hawk kill her love for him.

His voice went low and hoarse. "It is like when I see the fire in your eyes. Nothing scares me more than that. I would rather face an entire war band alone." He tried to make the comparison, but it did not make sense to him after he said it.

"That's not the same!" she retorted. "I have no control over the gods. They use me at will, you know that. I trusted you, Marcus. I even asked you if you knew who the Iron Hawk was and you said 'no', right to my face, several times. Your dark side is part of you; you are the one who controls it."

He was quiet a moment. He felt defeated. After all they had been through, all they had won, he felt utterly defeated.

After several minutes of staring at the floor, he finally said, "It is true. Whenever I would put this on," he indicated the black tunic, "it was like another part of me would take over. I could fight harder and longer, it gave me a power I could never wield as Marcus ap Iorwerth. Maybe it was the fear it created. Not only does fear make men fight harder, but it makes them make mistakes as well. Mistakes I could take advantage of.

"But if I told anyone, some of that power would diminish. And I was in a position where I could not afford that. Even if I told you, then I would worry. That distraction could have meant my life. When I held the sword against you in the convent, that was a warning to leave the Iron Hawk alone, to stay out of the trouble. Claeri, I'm sorry. I never meant to hurt you."

"When did you decide to do this tonight? And why

without telling me? How did you think you were going to transform back into yourself without my finding out?"

"I thought that bringing the Iron Hawk back from the dead would frighten them more than if I showed up as myself. Between that and the fire, it worked well. But it wasn't planned. It was a last-minute idea. I took the gear out when I got the powder out, partly so they wouldn't find it accidentally, and partly because I needed the sword. I honestly don't know what I was going to do; escape and come back undisguised, I suppose."

Claerwen's face reflected her disappointment. "I think you wanted me to find out. I think it has been too lonely, too hard to bear alone. By the gods, Marcus, you could have told me. And now I wonder what else there is I don't know."

She was shaking again. She slowly rose, struggling to her feet, still watching Marcus' face with her haunted eyes. Exhaling stiffly, Claerwen tried to relieve the pain in her body, then sniffed back as a sharp pang caught her.

"I will see if I can find any food," she said quietly through gritted teeth.

He watched her walk slowly away toward the kitchen, debating if he should let her go to think alone while she worked, or if he should try again to explain his actions. Finally, he rested his face in his hands and asked himself, "What have I done?"

Chapter 32

Dinas Beris
Summer, 469 A.D.

"By the gods my people swear by," Marcus muttered as he came down the steps of the great hall and surveyed the fort's courtyard.

It was morning again. He and Claerwen had spent the rest of the night camped on the hall's floor, too exhausted and hurt to check on the condition of their house.

Claerwen followed him out and stopped, the smell of the dead bodies rising powerfully. A heavy drizzle muddied the courtyard.

"I will make a pyre for them," he said, his deep voice going deeper. "I do not want them buried in our land. Not even this one."

Claerwen saw he was staring coldly at Taran's crumpled body, his eyebrows so low she could hardly see his eyes.

He spoke again, low and evenly, "I took his helmet off as he was dying. And he recognized this."

Marcus held up his right hand, his family ring on the third finger.

"I had hidden my rings and other valuables in the tunnels with the powder before I left last year. I wore it last night for the same reason I shaved the beard; I wanted no one to mistake it was me. When I decided to use the Iron Hawk identity, it was too late to take the ring off and hide it. When Taran saw it, he knew I was behind the mask."

Marcus continued, "Taran was the third man in Conwy. He slew Ifan and Gerallt. He hid behind Drakar and Rhun and a whole network of bribed loyalties in order to have us killed. All so he could steal that damn torque."

Claerwen studied the body and asked, "Why was he wearing Rhun's clothes? I don't understand."

"He was trying to throw the blame onto Rhun, like he tried to cast blame on Owein before. If he had found the torque, he would have declared Rhun's death and emerged as a claimant for the high kingship."

Claerwen was shocked. "He had no backing! How could he possibly take the high kingship, even with the torque?"

"Taran had enough vanity and false pride to believe the torque and Celtic animosity toward the Saxons would be enough to sweep himself into power. He had the same ideals I do, Claerwen, but he was greedy for the power, seeing only the glory of it. He never understood that the reality of freedom is not won by glory, but by hard, day-to-day, filthy, sweating work. He said I spoiled it, then he died."

Marcus spat on the ground, disgusted by Taran's empty-headed ambition. He clamped his mouth in a stern, flat line and went to inspect the fort, assess the damage, count the bodies, and make sure no one else was hiding, shaking his head at the mess.

Claerwen toured her ruined gardens while he was gone. When he returned to the courtyard, she mentioned her observations, saying, "This will take the rest of the summer and fall to clean up and repair. I will have to plant as much as I can right now to have enough to harvest for winter. I may have to take anything left growing wild on the abandoned farmsteads."

Claerwen lugged aside a fallen tree bough from one of the garden beds. Underneath was another dead body, and she squeezed her eyes shut and held her hand over her mouth, feeling sick when she discovered it. She stepped back a few paces and turned around. When she opened them again, the sword and the helmet Marcus had used the night before were on the ground in front of her. One of the powder balls laid a few feet away.

"There is far more damage than I expected from the powder charges." Marcus had come up behind her, but he stopped when he saw what she was staring at, her face greyish again.

"Except for the gates, the damage was not from these." She toed the clay ball.

He watched her turn around and come to him, her eyes still holding the same grim look from the night before.

"Tell me what happened," he asked warily.

She frowned when he placed his hands on her arms. He was only being affectionate, but she stepped back out of his reach and paced a few yards towards the great hall as she spoke, not wanting to look at the black tunic he still wore. She explained what had happened, through her fall onto the rampart. She soothed the bump on her head. "I don't know how long I was out."

Marcus came forward and touched her hand where she rubbed her head. "I was afraid you were in trouble. When I didn't hear you, I got worried, so I went to blow the gates. It took too long; I had to strike one of the Conwy swords into the powder. Then the storm came in, and there was no more time to find you."

He looked at the gaping hole where the gates had been. His face turned stony when he thought about how close she came to being killed.

She continued in a low voice, "When I woke up, the god was in me. I went to the platform; I don't know what I said. I think I raised my arms and the lightning kept hitting, over and over, rumbling, burning. It scared them all away. Except him. Then I fell again, I guess when you blew the gates underneath me. I woke up over there." She pointed towards the barracks.

He looked her up and down, then said, "You must still be in a lot of pain." She moved very stiffly, and could not bend over from her waist. She waved her hand, indicating it was not so bad.

"But you could have been killed! Ah, Claeri, the risk I put

you in... Maybe we should have stayed up north, like you wanted." He reached to her, but she would not come to him.

Anger grew in his face as he gazed past her at the helmet and sword on the ground behind her. He picked them up, scowling heavily. "Damn," he muttered at the blade, then he turned back to her.

Claerwen took the helmet from him. She turned it around until the front looked back at her. "This is different from the one I found," she mumbled, lost in thought.

He saw her eyes had grown even sadder than they were the night before. Claerwen stroked the mask of the helmet, wiping some of the mud and drizzle from it. She had not listened to what he had said. She was deep in grief when she thought about how many times he could have been killed in the years since she had known him.

"Claeri? Talk to me. Please." He reached again to her.

But she sniffed back the tears before they started and raised her head proudly. She took a deep breath and said, "I will clean this for you and put it away. It's time to get to work." She hugged the helmet and started back to the hall.

Marcus watched her, stunned that she would not even let him touch her. She clearly was not ready to talk, needing to work out her fears and the shock of his lies.

It began to rain.

Marcus went to one end of the barracks and began ripping off the wood, slamming it into a pile on the ground. He tore leather curtains down from doorways and windows, tossing them to the wood. The more he worked, the angrier he grew, giving him strength against the aches and pains his body still carried from the night before.

By mid-morning, Marcus had tied together a crude sledge framework from the wood and covered it over with the leather curtains. Then he went out to find the horses. The stallion was gone, probably grazing in the hills after Marcus released him the night before. The mare was still tied by the road. Marcus strung together a simple sling around the mare, then slipped two protruding poles from the frame into the sling. The horse would carry one end of the sledge, dragging the other end. He tested the frame with his weight and deemed it satisfactory. Then he turned to look at the dead men around him.

Marcus stripped off his boots, tunic and breeches, not wanting to further ruin them. The cut up and bloody shirt, he tore into rags. The other garments could still be mended, but he did not want the smell of dead men on them. He would let the rain wash that from him as he worked.

He led the horse around to the first body, coughing at the smell. He searched it for any weapons, piling what he found near the hall steps. Then steeling himself, he hauled the dead man onto the sledge. He pulled the horse to the next body, and the next, repeating the tasks as he circuited the yard.

Claerwen came out of the hall, wiping her hands on a rag. She cringed when she saw what Marcus was doing. He was leading the horse to Taran's body, the last to go.

She eased herself down the steps to him and asked, urgency in her voice, "Can you come, please? I was cleaning the kitchen and I kept hearing something under the floor. Then I thought I heard a voice."

"Where?" he asked, alarmed.

"Along the side, over here." She pointed.

He picked a large dagger from the pile of weapons, then stopped, listening.

"Help me!" a soft cry came, like the wind. Claerwen looked at Marcus and he nodded; he had heard it, too. The call came twice more, faint and muffled.

"Who are you?" Marcus shouted loud and far. His voice echoed against the stone and timber walls.

"Down here! Owein!" came the reply.

"Owein! He's alive!" Marcus exclaimed. He ran along the side of the kitchen house, calling. Finally he spotted a hole and knelt down to look in it. "Damn, watch out," he called into it. He dug with the knife, scratching furiously at the dirt wall that hid the building's foundation.

"Here, use this." Claerwen dragged a piece of beam from the barracks he had been dismantling. It was sharp on the end where it had been broken off and he used it like a lever to dislodge a bigger chunk from the wall. When the hole was big enough, he tossed the beam aside and laid down to reach inside. He locked arms with his cousin and pulled him out.

"By the gods, are you hurt?" Marcus asked Owein, propping him up against the wall. They saw he had lost weight and was heavily bearded and unkempt.

"No, not bad. They kept me prisoner under there. I need water."

"There's a waterskin on the horse," Marcus told Claerwen and she went to get it.

Owein drank long and gratefully from the skin. He surveyed the pile of bodies on the sledge and exclaimed, "Damn, cousin. I heard the noise last night, but I wouldn't guess you'd had such a fight."

"We thought you'd been killed. Claerwen found your dagger in a battlefield near Ynys Witrin."

"Claerwen?" Owein asked, surprised. "Then she followed you, too. I escaped, when they attacked the fort. I went south, trying to find you. Rhun and some of his men followed me. He had a helmet like the Iron Hawk's, but he was no warrior, not like the Iron Hawk. I don't know where he got it. I killed him and five of his men. The others captured me and brought me back here. They only kept me alive, thinking I could tell them where Claerwen was, but I didn't know. They said Vortigern had you. I guessed you were dead."

Claerwen exhaled, "Rhun was the false Iron Hawk."

"Aye," Owein rested his head back on the wall.

Claerwen knelt, testing his brow for fever. She looked up at Marcus and told him, "He will be all right, but we should find a place for him to rest. I will see if his house is suitable."

She rose stiffly and Marcus watched her move away, wincing for her pain. When he looked back at Owein, his cousin was staring at Taran's body.

Owein leaned over and spat on the ground. "He is the cause of all this. The filthy, jealous maggot!" He spat again. "None of us saw it and we all should have seen it so bloody easily. You were right to kill him."

Marcus stared at his brother's body. "I didn't. The Iron Hawk killed him," he half-lied.

Owein's eyes narrowed into a hard frown, moving from the body to Marcus. After digesting the idea, he said, "No matter, he had been trying to have you killed for a long time. When he negotiated the alliances with Cunedda and in the south, it was for himself, not you. He even faked his affair with Grania, just so she would turn to Rhun. He made Rhun his puppet, planted to pump information out of Grania, and then thrown away when he was no longer useful."

"I figured as much. But he didn't sack the fort just to take it from me. He was looking for a special torque that would have given him a far greater power."

Owein looked up to see Claerwen walking back, then saw Marcus' eyes fill with sorrow as they followed her. Owein raised an eyebrow, sensing something was wrong. As she came up, she told them Owein's house had been ransacked, but she had straightened it enough for him to rest there. She and Marcus helped Owein to walk around the hall and into the house, easing him carefully into his bed. Claerwen left to scrounge food for him and fuel for the fire pit.

Owein frowned at Marcus and asked, "What's wrong, cousin?" He tipped his head towards the door Claerwen had left through.

Marcus sighed tiredly and shook his head. "I hurt her, Owein. I can't talk about it."

Owein grunted, then asked Marcus to continue about Taran, wanting to know the rest before he drifted to sleep.

Marcus told him, "Ifan and Gerallt have been searching for an extremely valuable torque for many years. Taran made a deal with them and was going to cross them, but he killed them before they fully realized what he was going to do. What I don't understand is how Taran found out about the torque."

"What did Ifan and Gerallt look like?" Owein asked.

"I only saw them after they'd been killed. Both were dark haired, greying at the temples, one was greyishly bearded, with light eyes and a hawk-like nose, the other had dark eyes and a chin that protruded like a rounded knob with a cleft in it. I couldn't tell height or weight from how they were lying."

Owein closed his eyes a moment, thinking, then said, "When the three of us were in fosterage at Dun Breatann, Taran would go off alone sometimes. Once I saw him get into trouble; he was listening to two men without them knowing. I think he was about ten years old. They discovered him and somehow he talked himself out of trouble. Your description vaguely fits those two men."

Claerwen returned with food, water, and dried peat. She listened, then helped Owein drink again. She said, "That would have been about the time my mother, Grania and I fled to Strathclyde. Taran was two years younger than I am. If those men were Ifan and Gerallt, that means they followed us to Strathclyde. But why didn't they attack us again? Why wait four years?"

"They wouldn't dare do it under Ceredig's nose," Marcus stated. "That would have openly branded them as traitors. They waited until they were certain the torque was not in the old homestead in Gwynedd before they tried in the north, and then they had to find a good way to disguise their theft. That's when they recruited Drakar. And Taran would have been fourteen and still have another three years in Dun Breatann; he probably re-established his alliance with them. I had finished my fosterage the year before and was gone from Dun Breatann, already into my third year working as a spy."

Marcus suddenly stopped, an idea striking him, "He was still in fosterage in Dun Breatann! He could have seen us the night we met, Claerwen. He would have known from then on there was tie between us. And he could have followed me, or had me followed, every time I went to see you, after I pulled you out of Caernarfon. He was there in the convent when you and I pledged marriage, confirming you were the same woman he'd seen me with before and that's how Drakar found you. He told Drakar. Damn! I trusted Taran. He was my brother."

Claerwen shivered, wet from the rain, and added peat to the fire pit. She said, "A bond of blood does not guarantee a bond of trust. As when I trusted my mother, who bound me to Drakar." Her eyes flashed hard, and the men went silent as she left the house.

Owein stared after her, then at Marcus. "You've broken her trust?" he guessed.

"Aye," Marcus growled.

"You'll get it back. She loves you too much."

Marcus rose, scowling at the fire pit.

"What does the torque mean?" Owein asked, suddenly changing the subject.

"It's the torque of Macsen Wledig. I have it hidden."

"Part of Macsen's treasure? It exists? You found it?" Owein's eyes opened wide.

"Only that one piece. By accident," Marcus replied.

"Then you could claim the high kingship."

Marcus shook his head. "Aurelius Ambrosius has taken the throne from Vortigern. It belongs to him. We will return it to him as soon as we can leave here. I do not want to be high king."

He stared out the window toward the hall. The only thing he wanted was Claerwen's forgiveness.

Chapter 33

Dinas Beris
Summer, 469 A.D.

After Owein had gone to sleep, Marcus finished disposing of the dead men, leaving them piled on the sledge in a rocky field east of the fort. He built a pyre around them and lit it when the rain stopped, late in the afternoon. Dressed again in the black leather breeches, tunic and boots, he watched with his face set like starkly chiseled stone as the pyre burned down, then rode the mare back to the fort.

Marcus strode into the great hall, going directly to the fire to warm himself. His hair was still damp, hanging down in his face in disarray, and he raked it back. He held his bandaged arm, trying to find a comfortable way to hold it and stop its aching. The bandaging was wet and stained with blood; the difficult work had re-opened the wound. Too tired to care, he stared dully into the fire.

Claerwen came in, carrying an awkward bundle of rags and wool blankets. She padded silently on bare feet across to a table and dropped her load on it, then saw Marcus in the black leather, his back towards her. He had not heard her come in.

For a few minutes she silently studied his figure, and the sight of the Iron Hawk's leather prompted a long string of images to flow through her mind, partially recalled from old visions, some from new ones. All of them showed her Marcus, in disguises, as the Iron Hawk, as himself, all of them showing the enormous struggle of his quest for freedom. But what stayed in Claerwen's heart was far more clear than the exhaustion, the starvation, the horrible beating by Vortigern's Saxons. In every image, his eyes reflected deep pain, far down in his soul, an ache that transcended time and distance, that he would never be free from in his lifetime.

As the final image faded, Claerwen realized that, as the Iron Hawk, Marcus had never killed for the sake of cruelty, only for the sake of his people's freedom and his love for her. He had never wavered in his beliefs, his courage, or his honor. He was as incorruptible as Myrddin had described, and he was as courageous and tough as she had felt in her first impression of him, all those years ago.

Having lived with her hatred of the Iron Hawk for nearly six years, it had become a habit. But as she watched Marcus' wide shoulders hunched with the pain in his arm, Claerwen also sensed the pain of his fear, his distress that he had lost her love. With new understanding, she felt her own heart wrench free of the bitterness, dropping the hatred like cut chains.

"How you have suffered..." she suddenly spoke very quietly, her voice filled with emotion.

Marcus turned his head, startled that she was there. When his eyes met hers, he felt her compassion wash over him, her spirit a tangible force. He turned around and took a step towards her, searching her beautiful green-blue eyes. A tear fell down one cheek and he reached to brush it away.

He whispered, "I would suffer it all again, a thousand times, if only to keep from losing you, my Claeri."

She reached to gently lay her hand against his face, her fingers in his hair. Her eyes locked endlessly with his and she returned, "And I would suffer it all for you a thousand times more, if I could just ease the pain in your heart."

Marcus swept his arms around her as she rushed into them, and they held each other, clasped tightly together.

"You already have," he murmured. "You already have..." He held her face in his rough hands and kissed her lips tenderly.

Claerwen hooked her slender fingers around his big hands and kissed each palm. "You are still cold from the rain," she said, and she picked up one of the blankets, wrapping it around him.

His eyes ran over her, noting she had changed her clothes, to an old-fashioned tunic and undershift that were too big for her. His mouth almost flinched into a smile as she moved, the tunic's shoulder falling down her arm on one side. She pulled it up, and saw his eyes watching.

"I hope you don't mind. I found them in your father's house. Were they your mother's?"

"Aye...aye, they were. My father kept everything of hers, all these years, since she died. I was four years old then. No, I don't mind." He paused, then asked, "They destroyed everything in our house, didn't they?"

Claerwen nodded. "They even chipped the walls open, looking for that torque. We can save a few things, perhaps, but we will have to start over."

"Ah, Claeri," he breathed in his deep voice, his eyes going sad again. He sat on the table and pulled her so she stood between his knees, his hands on her hips, fingers gently squeezing. "We're supposed to be celebrating, singing, dancing, drinking. We should make love day and night, to celebrate our victory. We did what we set out to do, in spite of the odds, in spite of all the things that went wrong.

"But there's no glory in the taking of lives. That's not honor, not heroism. I've killed my own brother. The people of my clan are gone and I don't know if those who survived will or are even able to return. Sometimes, I think you were right, that we should have stayed in the north, alone and forgotten by all this." He sighed, long and tired.

Claerwen tossed her long hair over her shoulders and ran a finger down his moustache, letting it hang where it reached his chin. "But 'all this' would have chased us down eventually. Taran would never have let you live. He knew you were too clever and too smart, that you would have figured out he was behind it all. And the gods would never have let him go on to destroy Ambrosius. They sent you to stop him. We have won back our home, and we have won a piece of freedom for Britain, even if no one else ever knows about it or how it was done. For that, I have no regrets."

He smiled finally as he watched her unwind his soiled and soaking bandage. "You've such a generous spirit, Claeri. You've found a way to forgive me, but I don't deserve it because of my lies. How do you always make the pieces of our lives fit together into a whole? Where did you learn so much wisdom?"

She laughed at his question as she checked and cleaned his wounded arm. "Padrig has wisdom." She looked up into his black eyes and her face went wistful. "Taran's lies came from his greed, and his greed destroyed him. Your lies hid a cruel side of you that is hard to accept. But in doing so, you have also saved many innocent lives, including Ambrosius', not just mine."

She tied clean bandages around his arm and asked if he was warm enough.

He draped his arms over her shoulders, pulling the blanket around both of them and pressing his brow against hers. "Your love is like a warm blanket. I carry it with me everywhere." He kissed her again.

She smiled at him, her eyes light and sparkling. She said, "I do so treasure you, Marcus. I could never stay angry with you. Just as I could never live without you."

He grinned back, his eyes glittering as he caught her optimism, and he rubbed his face against hers. He whispered in her ear, "Welcome home."

EPILOGUE

**Winchester
Autumn, 469 A.D.**

Aurelius Ambrosius, the High King, sat in his finely carved chair, his feet stretched out before him to warm at a brazier. It was late and he was tired. He sipped idly at a cup of wine.

A knock came at the doorframe of the small garrison room.

"Come," he called.

"They are here, Father."

"Send them in. And stay here Myrddin; you are the one who arranged this meeting."

Myrddin went out the door and returned a moment later, followed by another man and a woman, whom he introduced as the Prince and Princess of Dinas Beris.

Ambrosius stood. He was tall and broad-framed, impressive in his Romanized attire in spite of the deep circles under his eyes. He poured another cup of wine for himself, then gave the ewer to his son to pour for their guests.

With the practiced eye of a natural leader, Ambrosius carefully studied the man as he came forward, noting he was not tall, and had a certain wildness about him, enhanced by a magnificent mantle of wolfskin. He walked with a slight limp, but carried himself as regally as any prince. Then he turned to the woman, and as she emerged into the lamp light, he saw she had an ethereal beauty such as he had never seen before. She held out something wrapped in a delicately embroidered cloth.

"This belongs to you, my Lord," she spoke softly.

The High King raised an eyebrow and flipped back the edges of the cloth.

His eyes widened as he gazed on the object in her hands. His son came forward, smiling broadly.

"Where did you find it?" Ambrosius asked, a hint of suspicion in his voice.

"It was more as if it found them," Myrddin interjected.

The High King stared at his son's odd observance, then pulled a wry face, suddenly losing the irritation his tiredness had brought on. "Aye, aye, so you have told me."

He took the object and its cloth. He watched the gold glitter, then looked up at Marcus ap Iorwerth, respect marking his words. "It truly is magnificent. And I am grateful, indeed. My son has called you the most selfless, incorruptible man in Britain, as well as her best spy. You could have kept this and used it against me. But instead, you have brought me strength, more than I could ever wield on the battlefield. I am in agreement with my son, and in your debt."

Marcus ap Iorwerth's intense black eyes held Ambrosius' gaze. Calmly, he replied, "We ask nothing of you, my Lord. To keep our freedom is all we have ever sought for ourselves. And while this has been a very long and difficult journey, we also know it is one that will continue for a long time yet to come."

Ambrosius considered Marcus' words, nodding to himself that this rough-looking man was no uneducated brute, but a man of sincere vision who understood the realities of life. He said, "Aye, the journey is not done yet, is it? It is only beginning. This torque is only a symbol, a fancy piece of metal and stone. Cold, hard, unfeeling. But sometimes a symbol, such as this, is enough for nations of people to rally around, to give them the coherence they need to face, and defeat, adversity. Let us hope that this symbol will be enough, at least for a good beginning."

They raised their goblets, clinking them together, and acknowledged their hopes, their fears, and their continuing quest for freedom.

ACKNOWLEDGMENTS

Without a doubt, I would most like to thank my husband Peter for his long-suffering patience, and occasional impatience, during the research and writing of this book. *Diolch calon, cariad.*

Among many others, I would also like to express my gratitude to the following wonderful people:

To Robin Weaver, my editor, who deftly sifted through my work and helped make it the best it could be.

To Kathy Keel, who guided me with profound ease through my hordes of questions.

To Geoffrey Ashe, whose dedication to seeking the historical side of the Age of Arthur has provided the wealth of knowledge that has greatly enhanced the background of this book. I was lucky enough to have had the chance to meet and study Arthurian history with Geoffrey during one of the tours he hosted in England and Wales.

To the friends and associates who have suggested, criticized, encouraged, listened and wished luck.

And to the many, many writers, researchers, archaeologists, librarians, and historians, both in Britain and the U.S., who have courageously kept after the quest to discover Dark Age Britain.

To all of you, *diolch yn fawr*.

AUTHOR'S NOTE

Dark Age Britain is one the most difficult periods of history to interpret due to the lack of recorded documentation. Society was oral, not literate. Given that druids were the keepers of history, genealogy, science, and the gods know what else, much was lost when they were driven underground or annihilated during the Roman invasion. Even with a strong Celtic cultural revival after the occupation ended in the early fifth century, little was recovered, and society continued to be oral. It is presumable that without druidic discipline, the stories were carried from generation to generation with haphazard embellishments instead of accuracy; the ordinary man was not trained to remember great scads of knowledge in precise detail and preferred to add his own touches.

And this is our legacy from our Celtic ancestors: We have many versions of the Arthurian Cycle and its related tales. We have the diligent work of archaeologists and historians who strive to piece together the obscure, the rare existing documents, the wild tales handed down to us, and the physical archaeology, most of which has not yet been fully explored.

The *Macsen's Treasure* series chronicles the years leading up to Arthur's reign. *Into the Path of Gods* begins the series; the subsequent volumes will carry the same foremost characters throughout. Each installment can easily be read alone, but they are well tied to each other and follow chronologically.

Several characters are historical: Ambrosius, Vortigern, Ceredig of Strathclyde, Cunedda. There has been enormous speculation over Myrddin's (Merlin's) reality; however, most feel there had to have been a real Myrddin on which to base the legendary magician. Arthur himself has been treated much the same way. (For fascinating reading on Arthur, see Geoffrey Ashe's *The Discovery of King Arthur*.)

AUTHOR'S NOTE

The other characters are fictional, although I have spent so much time with them, Marcus ap Iorwerth's face haunts my dreams at night. It has been suggested that this comes from a former life, and these are memories pushing their way out of my subconsciousness. Hmmm...

Into the Path of Gods is fiction and should be taken as such. But the further I delved into the historical side of the Age of Arthur, the broader the scope of this project became. Over time, I learned to recognize patterns in the Celtic culture of Dark Age Britain, enough to start asking questions that no one else had answered. I began posing my own theories, attempting to answer my own questions, possibly even to prove them.

One of the most gnawing questions grew out of the conflict resulting from the waning Old Religions and the spread of Christianity. It is known that Christianity converted the pagan holidays to their own use in order to achieve ease of continuity into the new belief system. Many other symbols, customs, and traditions were adapted as well. Could it be that symbols of Britain's ancient High Kings had been adapted along with the holidays, items that became well-known, such as Excalibur and the Holy Grail?

It is highly conceivable that important symbols of the ancient kingship were manufactured and carried down through the centuries, as the current monarchies of the world still do, i.e. crowns, sceptres, ceremonial swords and such. Grails were important items in the Old Religion rituals, very likely used in kingship ceremonies as well. If Midwinter became Christmas, likewise it is possible the kingship grail became the Holy Grail, the quest for truth and holiness in druidry transformed into the quest for truth and holiness in Christianity.

Macsen's Treasure is not specifically named in any of the old legends; I have collectively gathered the symbols and dubbed them for the last true leader Britain had as the Roman occupation crumbled, Magnus Maximus, or in Welsh, Macsen Wledig. If he truly had such treasure to hide for its safekeeping, it could easily have been lost in the burgeoning turmoil after his death in 388.

AUTHOR'S NOTE

Each volume in this series highlights one of the pieces of the treasure and ponders the possible fate of each piece historically, attempting to strip away myth. Symbolically in connection with the ancient culture, I have tied each with one of the four natural elements as is basic to the Old Religions. The poem fictionally attributed to Myrddin explains the connections.

A few other notes:

Most of the place names are attempts at their old Celtic versions, considering the Celtic characters would tend to use old Celtic names, not Romanized, definitely not Anglicized. Winchester and Avebury are exceptions; their familiarity and closer proximity to the Saxon Shore made it more logical to use their Anglicized modern names. Dinas Beris is derived from Llanberis, the modern name of the pass near Mt. Snowdon. Since Christianity was still very new and not so prevalent in the remote mountains of north Wales, it is doubtful the prefix "Llan," which means church, would be used in those times. I borrowed the name "Dinas," or fort, and attached it to Beris, hence making "Fort of Beris" instead of "Church of Beris." We can now make a wild assumption that Beris was one of Marcus ap Iorwerth's ancestors.

A note about the name "Wales": this is derived from an Anglo-Saxon word, *wallia*, meaning foreigners, and was not used until probably the sixth century. Likewise, the word the Welsh popularly use to call their country, Cymru, was not used until approximately the same era. Obscurity of time has lost the correct earlier name; in fact, each area was called after its ruling tribe and there may have been no cumulative name for the Welsh tribes. To avoid confusion, I have stuck to modern names again, such as Gwynedd and Strathclyde.

One last, quick note: To those who say King Arthur was king of England, remember, historically, England did not yet exist, not until the Saxons, Angles, and other invaders permanently established themselves *after* Arthur's demise. Many Medieval legends do call it England, but those who wrote them were not historians. Arthur was High King of Britain.

—K.C.G., September 1997